We gratefully acknowledge the support of the Canada Council for the Arts and the Ontario Arts Council for our publishing program. We also acknowledge the financial support of the Department of Canadian Heritage through the Canada Book Fund.

A Hero is a work of fiction. All the characters and situations portrayed in this book are fictitious and any resemblance to persons living or dead is purely coincidental.

Cover design: Val Fullard

Library and Archives Canada Cataloguing in Publication

Mendel, Charlotte R., author
    A hero : a novel / by Charlotte R. Mendel.

(Inanna poetry and fiction series)
Issued in print and electronic formats.
ISBN 978-1-77133-193-7 (pbk.). — ISBN 978-1-77133-194-4 (epub). — ISBN 978-1-77133-196-8 (pdf)

    I. Title. II. Series: Inanna poetry and fiction series

PS8626.E537H47 2015   C813'.6   C2015-902264-9
                                                    C2015-902265-7

Printed and bound in Canada

Inanna Publications and Education Inc.
210 Founders College, York University
4700 Keele Street, Toronto, Ontario, Canada M3J 1P3
Telephone: (416) 736-5356 Fax: (416) 736-5765
Email: inanna.publications@inanna.ca Website: www.inanna.ca

MIX
Paper from
responsible sources
FSC® C004071

a hero

CHARLOTTE R. MENDEL

inanna poetry & fiction series

INANNA PUBLICATIONS AND EDUCATION INC.
TORONTO, CANADA

To my sister Tessa,
for her loving support throughout my entire life.

PROLOGUE **RANA**

RANA SAT ON THE CHAIR Mohammed had made for her, which was propped under the shade of the house. Even so, she could feel sweat dampening her armpits. The heat was unbearable for longer every year now, and if the scientists were right about global warming, it would be impossible to live in the Middle East in a few years. *Stop it*, Rana told herself sternly. *You're supposed to be meditating. Focus on your breath and stop thinking.* Rana counted to ten, slowly, as she breathed in. She relaxed the muscles in her neck as she breathed out, feeling the tension release with her breath.

A painful peck on her big toe ruined her concentration.

"Go away, Henny Penny," Rana snapped. The hen looked longingly at her big toe, poking enticingly out of her sandal. "You'll be soup," Rana warned. "You know you're past your prime." She shoved Henny Penny away with her foot and sighed in annoyance. Inside it was the kids, outside the chickens. No quiet place just for her. *I'm supposed to be thinking of positive things*, Rana chided herself, *not grumbling about the heat and the chickens.* She closed her eyes again. *Thank you*, she thought. *I love my son so much; I love my husband, I love my sister-in-law Fatima, who is more like my sister, and her children. I love my chickens and my garden. I am so lucky to have all these things. I am so grateful.* And Rana felt a genuine rush of gratitude in her heart. Really, she was so lucky.

Rana opened her eyes and gave a small start; Fatima was

smiling down at her, twisting a strand of worry beads in both hands. "Don't get up. I just came to see where you were."

Rana jumped to her feet and searched Fatima's face anxiously. She had lost weight; her eyes, huge and brown, gazed softly and sadly out of her diminished face. "Sit down. You look tired."

Fatima bent to stroke the chair before she sat. "It's beautifully made," she said. "Mohammed made it for you, didn't he?"

"Yes." Rana gave a short laugh. "I remember exactly what he said when he gave it to me: 'Since you spend so many hours out there anyway.'"

Henny Penny circled nearer, convinced that Fatima's worry beads were a delectable treat.

"It was such a lovely thing to do," murmured Fatima.

"Mm-hmm," Rana replied. Fatima's need for everyone to sing Mohammed's praises all the time was getting on her nerves.

Henny Penny took a flying leap at the worry beads and Fatima shrank back as Rana grabbed the bird. "That's it!" she shouted. "Into the pot with you!" She threw the bird with such strength, Henny Penny was propelled to the other end of the courtyard, squawking with offence.

Rana turned back to Fatima with a grin of triumph, but Fatima was not watching Henny Penny's undignified rout. "Was he a hero?" she asked tentatively.

Rana took her hand. "Yes," she said with emphasis. "He was."

CHAPTER 1 **AHMED**

AHMED CLUTCHED HIS SIGN and hoisted it higher, striving to lift it over the heads of the crowd, so the soldiers surrounding the massive rectangular mass of humanity like spectators around a boxing ring could see it. So the snipers skulking on the rooftops above couldn't fail to read it: OUR COUNTRY WANTS FREEDOM. A surge of fierce joy gripped his heart as he felt himself jostled from all sides, his voice rising in unison with his fellow protesters: "Bye Qaddafi, Kassam next! Bye Qaddafi, Kassam next!" He could smell the rank sweat emanating from the armpits of the man next to him, his arm also raised above his head, stabbing the air in time with the chant: "Bye Qaddafi, Kassam next!" Or perhaps the smell came from the man in front, whose main breakfast ingredient had obviously been garlic. There were so many, pressing and squeezing, trying to move forward, striving to get to nowhere in particular.

Ahmed turned his head from side to side, smiling as he chanted. He had read about the special bonds soldiers form for each other in war. This must be what it was like. He felt a strong sense of love for Smelly Armpits and Garlic Breath. He probably didn't have a thing in common with either of them; they were no doubt ignorant, uneducated men. Yet here they all were — class, money, education thrown aside as they joined forces to fight for something they all believed in.

How incredible.

A hand, holding an open pack of cigarettes, snaked around in front of his face. Ahmed turned his head and grinned at his friend Moussa.

"I thought I'd lost you. How's it going?" he shouted, shoving a little harder to his right in order to open up a space for his friend.

"Humanity stinks," Moussa shouted at him.

"What?"

"It reeks! Take a whiff. Like animals."

Ahmed grinned. "That's exactly what I was thinking!" He took a drag of his cigarette, blew the smoke up into the air to mingle with the other scents. "But animals don't do this. They don't fight for freedom and democracy. They don't battle to improve their world. We're making history, my friend. History!"

"I know. Great, isn't it?" Moussa said in a happy tone that reflected the feeling bursting out of Ahmed's breast. And he grabbed the other end of Ahmed's sign and they lifted it together, shouting, "Bye Qaddafi, Kassam next!"

A wave of protesters suddenly caved in towards them on the right. A woman's scream quavered in the air, followed by a stream of expletives. Ahmed caught the words, "tear gas." He turned to his right and looked over the heads of the people now pushing towards him: there was smoke billowing up several metres away, creating a radius of empty pavement as the crowd melted around it in all directions. He felt himself stumbling backwards, pressed by the wall of people flowing in his direction. He turned quickly before he fell and began to move in the opposite direction, mindful of controlling the panic, not shoving or using his superior weight or height to hack his way out over the bodies of others. These were his fellow protesters, his brothers. He would not act like a beast, devaluing human life, like *they* did. The inhuman other side.

"Faster, brothers, faster!" he called out, catching the arm of a younger boy who was about to fall in the crush, pulling him upright. Another canister landed in front of him, belching out its poisonous smoke. Moussa grabbed Ahmed by the arm and pulled him to the left, as a new crescendo of screams slashed through the air.

"What are you waiting for?" Moussa shouted in his ear.

Ahmed glanced at the cloth swaddling Moussa's face and nodded, reaching into his bulging back pocket even as he continued to thrust his way forward. He dug out the plastic bag he had placed there earlier and opened the knot with trembling fingers, extracting the vinegar-soaked bandana and wrapping it around as much of his face as he could while he stumbled along.

It was too late. He could feel an itch in his eye, and knew within seconds it would become a horrible burning sensation. This had happened before. Too many times to count. Why the hell hadn't he covered his face earlier?

Ahmed fought to keep his eyes open, resisting the urge to shut them and rub. *You're okay*, he told himself. *Just keep breathing.* He could feel his skin burning now; tears and mucus seeped from their respective orifices and rolled down his face. It felt like he couldn't breathe. Panic surged through him and he began to push harder, thrusting people to the side in his effort to get away.

"Relax. Just breathe," Moussa's voice came in his ear.

Ahmed tried to take a deep breath. "This is not going to kill me," he spoke to himself. "Do not panic. Even if I feel that I cannot breathe, I can. I am." He tried to focus his mind on the facts he knew about tear gas. To panic was the worst thing you could do. He tried to look up through his streaming eyes, resisting the urge to close them and rub them vigorously. That also was the worst thing to do.

He saw they were headed towards a dark alleyway between two buildings. Shots ruptured the air behind them; were they using live ammunition now? *Those bastards, picking off unarmed men one by one. Fucking barbarians.*

Moussa and Ahmed stumbled into the alleyway and leaned against the wall, fighting for breath. People pushed past them down the alley, and they flattened themselves against the wall to let them pass. Some of the protestors grinned at them and held up two fingers in the sign of peace. Through the streaming slits of his eyes, Ahmed peered back at the square. The united mass of chanting brothers had dispersed within minutes. Only a few continued to sprint through the clouds of smoke. There were two bodies on the ground.

For a second he thought he was suffocating again, that he could not breathe. He focused on his breath. *In, out, in, out. Calm down. Look at the ground. Spit out the saliva. Help get rid of the poison. Let it flow from my eyes and nose and mouth.*

There was a packet of cigarettes under his nose again. He squinted upwards. Moussa was grinning at him.

"Lost your cigarette in the hustle, my friend."

"Not right now. Still not breathing right." Ahmed pressed his hand against his stomach and began to rub rhythmically in an effort to calm himself down.

"Not surprised. It took you about an hour to get your bandana out. What were you doing, admiring the smoky patterns created by the tear gas canisters?"

Ahmed tried to grin. *In, out, in, out. Rub, rub.*

"Or were you too wrapped up in the thought of making history?" Moussa snorted out smoke.

"If it were easy, it wouldn't be history," Ahmed wheezed.

"Sure it would. We'd still be grabbing our right to freedom with both hands, even if Mr. Kassam pissed off without a fight. Freedom for our country — that's history no matter how it happens."

"It would be harder to be a hero," Ahmed croaked.

"If you keep inhaling tear gas as though you've never seen it before you might be history yourself. Make any difference to you whether you're a dead hero or a live one?"

"I didn't mean that I personally want to be a hero," said Ahmed, slightly embarrassed. "But I do feel heroic when I'm in the midst of a demonstration. I feel like we could change the world. We're all heroes! I look around at my fellow protestors and I feel ... it sounds strange, but I feel ... love. We are all in this together. It's amazing, isn't it? The feeling of unity, of belonging. I've never felt it before."

"I bet you haven't. Spent most of your life raging at the ignorance of the masses, pompous moron that you are." Moussa held up two fingers in the peace sign and shouted, "Bye Qaddafi, Kassam next!" at a couple sprinting past. "Screw heroism! I'm just having fun!"

"I'm not trying to be a hero," Ahmed repeated.

"I think it's over for today," said Moussa. "Let's go home."

Ahmed pushed open the door of his brother-in-law's house and let himself in quietly. He wanted to get up to his room and clean his face with vinegar before anyone saw him, but as soon as he clicked the door gently shut, his sister, Fatima, rushed out of the kitchen.

"Oh my God, what happened?"

"Relax, it was just a bit of tear gas," Ahmed soothed, glancing in the hallway mirror as he spoke to see what his face looked like. His eyes and nostrils were red-rimmed, and there was dirt on his face.

"Come in and have a cup of tea and let me clean you up," Fatima insisted, sweeping him before her with her hands on his shoulders.

His nostrils were assailed by a medley of aromas as soon as he entered the kitchen. He ignored the chair Fatima proffered and started to lift lids off pots, inhaling the tomatoey, garlicky fragrance. One pot was filled with a variety of vegetables, simmering in a tomato sauce. Rice steamed leisurely beside it, emitting scents of cumin and chilies. On the table lay a number of small dishes, brimming with olives, hummus, baba ghanouj, stuffed grape leaves, and tabouleh salad.

His arms were tugged from both sides, and he smiled down at the upturned faces of his twin nephews.

"Tell us about today! What happened, Khalo Ahmed?" they begged, and he turned around to look at the circle of expectant faces before him. The twins Abdul and Ali, his twelve-year-old niece Zaynah, Fatima's sister-in-law Rana, and her son Mazin all gazed at him, eager for news. Even little Na'aman stared at him from the floor.

"It was very similar to yesterday, and the day before, and all the days before that," Ahmed said. "There was a huge crowd of people, all shouting and waving their fists."

"What were they shouting?" interrupted Abdul, unable to contain himself.

"They were chanting, 'Bye Qaddafi, Kassam next!' over and over again. It was like a huge wave of voices, beating against the rock of soldiers."

"But water cannot beat rock," chimed in Ali.

"Yes it can. Slowly, with time, water beats rock into sand," said Ahmed, lowering himself into the chair that Fatima had placed near him.

"I hope it won't take as long as that," Rana quipped.

"Of course not," Ahmed said. "How long did it take with Qaddafi? Mere months. Anyway, the soldiers started throwing tear gas at us and we had to run. Ouch." He jerked his head sideways as Fatima gently wiped his face. Zaynah was crouching by him, placing the slippers that he wore in the house by his feet.

"Thank you, Zaynah," Ahmed said. "You are always so thoughtful."

The girl smiled to herself and returned to her seat at the kitchen table.

"Why can't we go tomorrow as well, O'mmy?" begged Abdul.

Fatima laughed indulgently. "I know you think you are adults at the age of nine," she said. "But it is very dangerous. Besides, you know your father would never permit it."

"Tell us more," chorused the twins. "Did anybody fight back? Did you throw rocks?"

"It's time for you to get back to your homework," Rana said. She pointed towards the chairs and the twins slumped towards them. Rana perched on the edge of a chair, leaning towards Ahmed. "I wish I could go to the demonstrations. It's terrible to believe in something so much and not be able to participate." Her intense face peered into his. He could see the restlessness in the black depths of her eyes. She needed something to focus her enormous energy on. It was a pity she and Hamid could not have any more children. He glanced at Mazin, her eleven-year-old son. He was sitting with his head bent, studiously doing his homework.

"Women don't go to demonstrations."

Rana shot to her feet. "That is not true! I know they do!"

Fatima put her soft hand on her sister-in-law's arm. "Calm down, Rana."

Ahmed felt irritated. "Very few go. Sometimes women have their own demonstrations, just the women, but there wasn't a single woman there today. It was all men." He didn't mention the woman's scream he had heard when the first tear gas canister fell; what was the use? Rana couldn't go anywhere, even if they organized a demonstration just for women. Her brother Mohammed wouldn't permit it, and that was that. It wasn't any use arguing or begging; that would only infuriate Mohammed. His anger stopped just short of forbidding Ahmed himself from going, so he wasn't about to do battle for anybody else.

Rana paced back and forth in the kitchen. "Imagine how powerful our demonstrations would be if all the women joined too. It would double our forces!"

Ahmed skidded his chair over to the table. "Anybody need help with their homework? Zaynah, have you finished already?"

"Yes," his niece said shyly, self-consciously touching a flower that she had tucked behind her ear.

"You are so clever. How come she finishes her homework before you two?"

"She hardly has any homework," Abdul replied in an outraged voice. "She is only a girl. We have much more homework than she does, much more difficult."

Ahmed laughed and scooped Na'aman off the floor, cuddling his pudgy body and kissing him. Na'aman crowed with delight and touched Ahmed's face.

"I have new shoes," Zaynah whispered in his ear.

"Really? Let me see."

She held her foot up to display a solid, leather, walking shoe.

"What are you doing wearing shoes inside the house?" snapped her mother.

"They are new, O'mmy. They are not dirty."

"We have new shoes too!" screeched the twins, propping their feet on the table.

"Ya rabbi, take off your shoes at once. All of you!" ordered Fatima. She leaned towards Rana and Ahmed. "Two thousand liras each. A great deal!"

"I have finished, O'mmy," Mazin piped up, and Rana leaned over him to check his homework, her face softening.

Ahmed closed his sore eyes for a moment, revelling in the soft fingers that immediately began to explore his closed lids. How nice it was to be in the midst of his family, cuddling soft babies and smelling the aromas of a delicious meal.

The door banged and Mohammed entered the kitchen. "Something smells good," he said, going straight to the pots and lifting the lids to breathe in the spices. "Abi!" cried Zaynah, and wrapped herself around her father's free arm.

There was a sudden flurry of activity. Fatima quickly began to carry the food to the table, gesturing to the children to tidy their homework away. Mohammed sat at the head of the table and a glass of tea was placed before him. Dishes of food fanned out in front of him and he began to eat, even before the rest of the family had found their seats. Ahmed saw his sister bend her head and mouth the words "Bismi'Allah" before raising the first morsel to her lips; they had been brought up in a more traditional household, and Fatima still prayed religiously five times a day, even though Mohammed was staunchly secular.

"So, who wants to tell me about their day?" Mohammed asked his children.

"I got very good marks in my math test, Abi," said Zaynah.

"Good. Sit up straight when you eat. Abdul, are you a pig, that you need to shovel the food in that way?"

"I am very hungry, Abi."

"Starving, obviously." Mohammed glanced at his brother-in-law. "I assume you've spent your day as profitably as usual, in one of those useless demonstrations?"

"Yes," said Ahmed peaceably. "And you? How was your day?"

"I treated a German Shepherd that belongs to one of the more eminent citizens of this city, Saleh ibn Rahman. Unfortunately, the dog has cancer and there is nothing I can do, but these rich people, do they listen? If they want to throw their money at me, let them. They all know I'm the best veterinarian in the whole city, probably the whole country. Where did those shoes in the corner come from?"

There was a pause. "The children needed new shoes," murmured Fatima.

"How much did they cost?"

"Only one thousand liras. Down from five. Such a deal."

Mohammed looked at her. "One thousand liras each? For three pairs of shoes? Do you think I am made of money?"

"The old ones had holes," explained Fatima. "I know you wouldn't want our children to look like beggars."

"Beggars," snapped Mohammed, his voice rising. "What exactly do you mean by that? My children are as well-dressed as they need to be. They look perfectly fine to me. Don't they look fine to you, Rana?"

Rana coughed up a piece of rice in surprise.

"Forget I asked," Mohammed continued after a second's pause. "How can I expect any support from you?" He turned back to Fatima and looked at her for a second. "Perhaps our ideas of what the children need don't tally. When you think you need to buy shoes, or clothes, or anything else for that matter, you should ask me first. I'll inspect the articles you want to replace and make a decision. You just buy, buy, buy, without any thought of how hard I have to work...."

"I understand that you work hard," said Fatima.

"You know nothing about it. Once I have ensured that a purchase is really necessary, I will give you a budget."

"God forbid that Fatima should control any facet of her own life," interposed Rana, ignoring Fatima's pleading look.

"Who asked you for your opinion?" shouted Mohammed. "Just because your husband is a weak fool and allows you to do as you want, you think I should follow his example? Then my wife would be scattering her unwanted opinions about just like my sister. God forbid. When is Hamid getting back, anyway?"

"He won't be back till late. And if you're an example of strong intellect I'm very glad I married a 'weak fool.'"

"Silence woman!" bellowed Mohammed.

"Have some more hummus with your pita, dear," said Fatima.

But Mohammed's blood was up. He eyed his sister balefully for a few minutes, then snapped his head towards Ahmed. "Here's another one who is bringing ruination to this family. Those demonstrations will lead to nothing but trouble."

Ahmed carefully spooned more tabouleh into the mouth of his pita. "What trouble? Do you think they're going to invade the house of every protestor? Can they take on every single citizen?"

"Every single citizen? You're talking rubbish. The vast

majority of people support Kassam. If you weren't so young and stupid, rushing off with your little placard to march for freedom — as though you had any concept of what the word meant — you'd know that. Read the news. Educate yourself. Kassam is a good man."

"I don't care whether he's a good man or not. I want the right to vote for my leaders. Every Arab nation is rising up and demanding that right, one after the other. Regime after regime is falling, the heads of their dictators rolling.... I will fight for democracy against whoever tries to stop it." Ahmed stopped abruptly, surprised at himself. Usually, he tried to avoid confrontation with his dominating brother-in-law.

"You're a fool, and fools like you are dying every day. If you listened to what Kassam is saying, you'd realize he's implementing reforms in response to the protests."

"Reforms with one hand, death and destruction with the other," Ahmed shot back bravely. "Who believes in his reforms? Not me. I'm in the middle of the action every day. I see people being beaten, dragged off to prison to be tortured, killed. You know the army randomly picks houses to raid, raping and killing..."

Fatima rose from the table. "Children, it's time to go upstairs."

The twins' voices rose in a cry of protest. Mohammed's gaze, which had been riveted on his brother-in-law, jerked to his sons. "Obey your mother at once," he ordered.

All the children stood immediately. Mazin glanced at his mother, who made a gesture with her head toward the door. They trooped by Mohammed, stooping to kiss his cheek as they passed. Fatima held little Na'aman up to his father's face. He grabbed Mohammed's moustache and delivered a delightful baby chuckle, shouting out "Abi!" in excited adoration. The father's face loosened and he gave his son an Eskimo kiss.

Ahmed waited, straight-backed in his seat, his hand surreptitiously reaching to press against his stomach, until the children had disappeared.

"The soldiers themselves are so sick of the violence they are being forced to perpetrate that they are defecting by the thousands and joining our side."

Mohammed turned from watching the exit of the children. "You forget what you are fighting for. You want the right to vote? Kassam has implemented new election laws; the government is revising the constitution to allow other parties to run. Essentially, you've got what you were protesting about, but you continue to congregate because your young blood thrills to do this dangerous, useless work. And then you bleat about the violence — the violence you have caused by your demonstrations, where you protest a situation that is already in the process of being changed anyway."

Ahmed took a long drink of water as his hand chafed his stomach beneath the table, calming himself so that he could speak gently. "When? When are these excellent changes going to happen? Kassam has been making promises like that ever since he came to power. All lies. We want to vote now. We don't want that bloodthirsty tyrant in power for one more day."

"You fool, do you think entire constitutions are changed in a day? That's what I can't stand about young people. You all have this ridiculous notion that change should be instantaneous. Instant gratification, just like the Americans. And look how happy they are."

"At least the women are free," interjected Rana, unable to contain herself any longer.

Mohammed smiled contemptuously. "And how well they deal with freedom, jumping from marriage to marriage, immersed in their careers as their families fall apart."

Rana looked at him rebelliously. "I want to go to the demonstrations as well. The only reason Kassam is promising these reforms is because of the protestors. We are trying to make the world better, while you? What are you doing? Criticizing. Undermining."

Mohammed waved his fork in her face. "As long as you are

living under my roof, you will not go near any demonstration. I admit that the protesters helped change come about, but now that change is underway their continued demonstrations are the cause of the violence." He glanced at Ahmed and pushed his chair back from the table. "You are the problem, now. Not the solution. This discussion is at an end. I have some work to do."

Ahmed bent his head to hide his anger and waited tensely until Mohammed had left, then he slumped back in his chair, fuming. He wanted to shout that the conversation was not finished. He had a million facts to fling into that ignorant old fool's face. It hadn't been the call for democracy that had sparked the ire of the people. It had been the brutal torture of the schoolchildren in Maraa, the death of thirteen-year-old Husni Al Husnein. It had been their unbelievable violence and brutality that had caused this. They would be brought down, those bastards. One by one. He looked up to see Rana's brooding eyes on him. He felt a rush of irritation — if she hadn't joined the conversation he might have had another chance to speak. She only infuriated her brother every time she opened her mouth — why could she not shut up? He pushed his chair back from the table and went up to his room, shutting the door firmly behind him.

CHAPTER 2 **FATIMA**

"CAN WE WATCH TELEVISION?" pleaded Abdul and Ali. "Our favourite show is on."

Fatima eyed them wearily. By the time the evening rolled around, she always felt exhausted. "You can watch one show, but only if you put yourselves to bed afterwards. I'll give you a good-night kiss now, shall I?"

Their grins plummeted and they eyed each other out of the corners of their eyes, without saying anything. Fatima bent down to kiss each cheek, and turned to go.

"But O'mmy," began Abdul, still eyeballing his twin furiously.

Fatima turned. "Yes?"

Abdul gave a great nudge that sent Ali toppling over on his side. "Go on, you tell her."

Ali sat up straight. "Let's say it together."

"Could you come back after the show?" they whispered in unison.

Fatima folded her arms and looked at them, then crossed over to a chair and sat down. She really couldn't stand up a minute longer. Not a single minute.

"What for?" she asked, though she knew the answer. She also knew she should be pleased that her almost-grown sons still wanted their mother to come and kiss them good night. But she felt like she was in a sea of arms, all reaching out to her. All wanting kisses and hugs, endlessly. It was really because of Na'aman, bless his loving soul. She had thought her childbearing years were finished. After the twins, there were three miscarriages, one after the other. Year after year. Then, when she was thirty-six, she had carried a baby to term and delivered a stillborn baby girl after an excruciating labour. She had been convinced that her insides were damaged and had begged Mohammed to let the doctors remove her ability to have children. He had refused on the grounds that she was mistaken, and there was nothing wrong with her. In the end, he had proved right; two years later, she had given birth to a healthy little boy. But in the innermost recesses of the guiltiest section of her heart, she wished that he had allowed the operation. She felt utterly exhausted all the time.

"If you don't come to wish us good night before we go to sleep, bad dreams come," said Abdul.

"How could that be?"

"It just is," insisted Ali. "You make the bad dreams go away."

"Well then, I'd better come back, hadn't I? Can't let those bad dreams get the better of us," she joked, quelling a momentary urge to mock their desire to join the protests and fight tear gas and bullets when they were still spooked by bad dreams.

She walked heavily to Zaynah's room; it was Na'aman's room too, but he spent the majority of his restless nights squashed beside his mother, on her side of the bed. Mohammed wasn't amenable to little feet kicking him awake in the middle of the night. "Are you ready for bed?"

"Yes, O'mmy." Zaynah, bless her heart, was already tucked underneath her covers, writing in her diary.

"What are you writing?" she leaned against the door post. You didn't have to expend energy with Zaynah. Not like the others, whose need for attention was a bottomless pit. Conversely, she felt a sudden desire to get into bed with this child who made so few demands, and stroke her hair. Pluck out the flower that still dangled behind her ear.

"I am writing about my day at school."

"Was it a good day?"

"Yes."

"What did you do?" Sometimes extracting information from the quiet children stole as much energy as fending off affection from the demanders. On the other hand, she could just leave, abandoning all efforts to probe into her daughter's day and instead stumble downstairs to help Rana clean up, and put Na'aman to bed. Then, finally, she could go to her own bed. If she was really lucky, perhaps Mohammed would be asleep, and she could snuggle beneath the covers and allow her body to relax into nothingness.

"Played. Studied. Nothing interesting happened," said the child, forestalling the anticipated next question.

Fatima crossed the room and bent down to give her daughter a kiss. "Lights out in half an hour, okay habibti?"

"Okay, O'mmy. Good night."

When Fatima got downstairs, Rana was washing the dishes. Na'aman held out his arms to his mother, and she lifted him onto the counter, settling him with a piece of pita.

"Thank you for keeping an eye on him," she said to Rana, picking up a tea towel and starting to dry.

The water sloshed in the sink as Rana scrubbed a plate with unnecessary rigour. "I am so angry. *So* angry."

Fatima looked at her out of the corner of her eye and sighed inwardly. More energy was required. She wished it was something that could be divided into dollops each morning, so much for each person. "It is bad for your health, this frequent anger," remonstrated Fatima. "I know you want to help me and protect me, but do you really think it bothers me when he threatens budgets? So let him put me on a budget, if it makes him feel better. It's not like anything will change, I am so frugal anyway. He doesn't like me spending money, I know that. I live with that. We are so lucky, compared to so many. Most of our neighbours share their beds with family members. Our children each have their own bed. What do I have to complain about?"

"Your husband," retorted Rana. "And don't start telling me how so-and-so's husband beats her on a regular basis. Mohammed beats you verbally every time he opens his mouth."

"That's not true," Fatima said softly. "I spend hours with him when you're not even there. Usually, he is gentle with me."

"What, in bed?" snorted Rana.

"And during our Friday evening strolls. You know how I love those walks. Why would I love them if he was, as you say, beating me verbally?"

Rana placed a dish on top of the pile, which trembled dangerously. Fatima picked it up and rubbed it with her tea towel resolutely. Rana needed to talk. Just for a few minutes. She could spare a few minutes for Rana, who did so much for her.

"You might enjoy your strolls, but I bet he talks all the time and you just listen. Am I right?"

Fatima dried another dish slowly, reflecting. Rana was right, but that wasn't the point. "He's a very complicated person."

"Well sure, all human beings are complicated. But what comes across is a bully, and even though you don't like me saying that, you can't think of a single fact to refute it."

"Yes I can," protested Fatima. "For years during our Friday strolls we used to pass this little old woman walking her dog. We'd nod to her as we passed, but we never spoke. The dog grew older, the woman grew positively ancient, but still they'd go walking together every Friday. Then, one day, the woman passed us in the same place, but she was alone."

Fatima dried another dish. She could almost feel the waves of impatience undulating through the flesh beside her. "I felt Mohammed's arm jerk when she had passed, and I looked up into his face. He had tears in his eyes."

"Whatever for?"

"That's what I asked him. He just said it was tragic. He didn't elaborate, but he meant that it was tragic that the dog had died after so many years together, leaving the old woman alone."

There was a short silence. "So, the fact that he feels a rush of misplaced compassion for a complete stranger means he doesn't bully his whole family? What's your point?"

Fatima wasn't sure what her point had been, but she had done her best and she could do no more. Not tonight, at any rate. With great care, she spread the damp tea towel over the counter so it would dry overnight.

"Somebody has got to stand up to him."

"Why?" Fatima turned away tiredly. "It doesn't do any good. It makes him worse."

"I completely disagree. You think the solution is to creep around him like a little mouse, but that's not going to change him. Besides, you're frightened of him — admit it. But with me, it's different. He's my little brother. I remember changing his nappies. He was lovely then. When did he get to be such a bully? Ranting and raving all the time, throwing his weight and opinions about." Rana threw her sponge into the sink and gripped its edges. Fatima saw she had tears in her eyes. "There are women organizing women-only protests. Some of them even protest alongside with the men. And here I am, with all my energy and beliefs and passionate support for the changes in store for my country, and instead of helping bring about those changes, participating in this crucial period in our history, I am washing dishes."

Fatima winced at Rana's rising tone and glanced at the door.

"What is it?" Rana asked. "Are you worried about Mohammed hearing, or the kids? They're not asleep yet, are they?"

"That's the problem," Fatima replied. She went quietly to the door and opened it suddenly. There was nobody on the other side. Na'aman held out her tea towel helpfully when she returned.

"Zaynah," she whispered.

"Is she still listening at doors?" Rana asked. "She's an anxious little thing, isn't she?"

This was a subject that Fatima could identify with. "It's strange behaviour, but I've twice found her listening at the door when Mohammed and I are having an argument. It's as if she hears raised voices and wants to know what's going on. I'm not sure it's healthy for a twelve-year-old to creep along hallways and listen at doors."

"Maybe she's getting fodder for her stories, since she's such a little writer," Rana said fondly. "There's certainly enough fodder in this household, with all the fights and misery that man creates. What am I going to do? Should I allow myself to be cowed into submission by one bully when my fellow women are defying a whole government of bullies?" Rana stooped suddenly, and planted a loud kiss on Na'aman's cheek. He giggled happily and held out his pudgy little arms. "I could just go. He's out at work all day, how would he know?"

Fatima placed a restraining hand on her arm, as though Rana were heading out the door that very instant. "God forbid. Don't even talk like that. Somebody who knew you would see you and report back. He'd find out."

Rana shook off her arm irritably. "So he finds out. What's the worst he could do? Throw me out of the house? That would go against the patriarchal, generous image he has of himself."

Na'aman threw his soggy piece of pita on the stack of cleaned, dry plates. "Down, O'mmy. Na'aman wants to go down."

Fatima lowered her son to the ground and straightened up slowly. "I must take him to bed."

Rana turned to her sister-in-law and placed both hands on her shoulders. "You look so exhausted. I'm sorry for burdening you with my problems. I know I go on a lot. I hadn't even started on how sick I am of his snide jibes at Hamid. What right does he have to criticize my husband? Hamid is a million times more developed as a human being than he is. Mohammed hasn't got a shred of self-understanding...."

And she was off again, her voice ratcheting up the scale and her eyes fixed on Fatima's face, commanding her wavering attention even as Na'aman pulled determinedly at her skirt from below. Fatima's gaze slipped to the left of Rana's face to glance at the clock on the wall. Almost nine p.m. Time to put Na'aman to bed. His long afternoon naps, anticipated with longing throughout the interminable mornings, enabled her to put him to sleep fairly late. Only an hour to go before she could lay her own head on the pillow.

"I'm sorry, so sorry," Rana exclaimed. "Here I go again. You must go to bed. Shoo, shoo."

Fatima hugged her sister gratefully and scooped Na'aman onto her back, where he giggled in delight.

"But Fatima," Rana said just as she reached the door. "Don't you think I'm right about my husband? It's disgusting, the way Mohammed criticizes him, isn't it?"

Fatima sighed. "It's not very sensitive, no."

"It's absolutely unacceptable. You can be sure that I will stand up to him…"

Fatima slipped out the door, quelling a momentary desire to modify her sister-in-law's perspective. She had spent long years trying to reconcile the two vigorous siblings, and still felt at times that she could tweak this judgment, nudge this black-and-white opinion just a little. But not now. Not at nine in the evening.

She crooned to her youngest as she washed his tender limbs and dressed him in a long, cotton shirt for the night. Then she lay on his mattress with him, stroking his head and singing softly in his ear. She lay with him long after his quiet breathing told her he was asleep. It was lovely to snuggle close to his warm, beloved body, inhaling his sweet breath and consciously relaxing all the muscles of her body. Her favourite time of day was this quiet interlude with her son, as she examined the familiar contours of his face with unperturbed love, a simple act that was impossible as he raced around throughout the day. Her children were the source of such joy. The only touch of sadness was Mohammed's prohibition on religion: he had forbidden her to teach them anything. She had prayed to Allah for guidance in this matter and in the end, Fatima believed, Allah had chosen to speak to her through the most unlikely source: her secular husband. "All children are open vessels into which a loving parent can pour their values and beliefs," Mohammed had told her, perceiving her sorrow at his prohibition on religious education. "The real motive behind religion isn't the necessity of praying in a certain way five times a day, but rather the encouragement to act in a reasonable way. Since you are the best of women, and possess many excellent virtues like compassion, kindness, generosity, and love, you should focus on passing those onto your children. In that way, they will end up better human beings than most of those children who are praying five times a day. Do you understand, habibti?" And she had tried to understand. She visualized her children as open vessels, and tried to guide them towards the essence of goodness. She felt sure that Allah would approve of both her efforts and her children, and that one day, they would pray too.

Sometimes Fatima would stretch out on Na'aman's bed and lose herself in daydreams. These were precious minutes, stolen from the time between the needs of her son and the needs of her husband.

Finally, guilt drove her to her feet. Mohammed would be angry if she tarried too long. Sometimes, he would be writing intently in his journal and she could recite her evening prayers peacefully. Very occasionally she would creep upstairs and find him sleeping. Oh joyous nights, when she could lie in bed and savour the feeling of privacy that the night afforded. But Mohammed was usually waiting for her. Nine times out of ten.

Zaynah's light was already out. She popped into the twins' room for the requisite kiss-to-dispel-bad-dreams, and then tiptoed to her own room, praying that tonight he would be sleeping.

He was not. He was sitting up in bed, perusing an animal clinical reference book. Did he really read those things?

"Where have you been?" he asked.

"Cleaning the kitchen. Putting the children to bed."

"Why does it take you so long? The children are old enough to put themselves to bed now."

"I don't know," she answered wearily.

"I have gone through all our receipts to see when you last bought shoes for the children. Six months ago. You simply cannot buy shoes every few months. They are too expensive. Why did you buy shoes today?"

"I told you. They are all growing so quickly...."

"Then buy bigger shoes, so they will last longer. It is stupid to buy shoes that are exactly the right size when the children are growing so fast. What is the point in buying shoes that won't fit in two months' time?"

"There is no point. But the shoes wear out quickly too, especially the twins'."

"What are they doing to them? Playing sports? Scuffing them along the roads? Give them one pair of shoes for school and make them wear the holey pairs when they go out to play. Inspect the school shoes every day and give out punishments if they have been ill-used."

Fatima stood beside the bed, hesitating. Mohammed patted the covers. "Come to bed already."

"Isha," Fatima whispered.

"Oh yes, you mustn't forget the evening prayers," Mohammed retorted sarcastically. "We'll certainly need Allah on our side if your fool brother continues to risk all our lives by attending those protests."

Fatima self-consciously kneeled in the corner of the room that she judged to face Mecca and began to murmur her evening prayers. Both Isha and Fajr, the early morning prayer, were five-minute embarrassing affairs as she faced the corner of the room, conscious of the contemptuous eyes of her husband boring into her back. But the other three prayers throughout the day were times of quiet contemplation and joy, as Fatima focused her whole mind on her prayer to Allah.

Rana was wrong. She did not fear her husband; she pitied him. He was so unhappy. What was life worth if you did not believe in Allah?

As soon as she had finished, Mohammed jumped out of bed and began to pace the length of the room. Fatima lay down and watched him through half-closed eyes.

"Rana is getting out of hand. Did you hear how rude she was to me during dinner?"

Fatima mentally probed her mind, where she imagined that stores of energy were kept, stacked like precious blocks of dwindling gold. Was there enough left for this? It was important not to say the wrong thing. To soften his anger without igniting his paranoia was like stepping delicately on a road covered with potholes. She thought of Rana, gripping the edges of the sink with white knuckles, and how horrified she would be if she knew how much she resembled her brother. Except that she was a woman. Except that she had been forced from an early age to comply with the restrictions and limitations of her sex. Her strong nature had been constrained within a role; unlike her brother, she had been silenced from childhood on when her views were expressed too strongly. Perhaps it was because of this that Rana had begun to explore herself, trying to understand the world and her place in it. Perhaps because she was told so often that she was not modest enough, not quiet enough, not gentle enough, that she had begun to ask, in her struggle to be the best person she could: *Is this true? What is my character? What truly are my faults and strengths?* Perhaps it was because of this that she developed an awareness of her own self that Mohammed lacked. Or perhaps, it was simply that she was different from her brother, born with a greater ability to view herself as she truly was, and with the desire for self-improvement.

"I think Rana was just trying to protect me. She sees how careful I am with money, and perhaps she felt a budget was unnecessary."

"She should keep her opinions to herself!" Mohammed snapped. "Pay some attention to her own family instead of sticking her nose where it's not wanted. Budgets? If her husband was ever present, he might see fit to put her on a budget. Or no, what am I saying?" Mohammed hit his forehead dramatically with the book that was still in his hand. "*She's* the husband in that family. Her weak and pathetic fool of a husband gives man a bad name. He has no control over her whatsoever. He lets her make every decision. That's probably why she thinks she can make decisions in my family!"

"They just have a different way of interacting with each other," Fatima interjected smoothly. "Neither way is wrong, they're just different."

"Different?" shouted Mohammed. "What is the purpose of getting married, in your enlightened opinion?"

"Well," hesitated Fatima. "To procreate?"

"To contribute healthy, balanced, well-educated individuals to the next generation. Anyone can procreate, the challenge lies in the final result. Will one's creation contribute to society in a positive way? That is the basic question every parent must ask. In our case, of course," he added pompously, "the children are exceptionally bright. We have an added responsibility to groom them for leading positions in society."

Fatima wondered silently in what way Rana's son Mazin could be considered as lacking in his ability to contribute to society in a positive way.

"If a father absents himself from family life, and exhibits weakness of character when he is present, what will happen to his offspring?"

Fatima wracked her brain briefly, before Mohammed answered himself. "He will also be weak! That poor child Mazin hasn't got a chance. Compare him to our sons!" Mohammed waited a moment, then asked impatiently, "Well?"

"He's ... gentler than our sons," Fatima ventured. She was determined to say nothing negative about Mazin, whom she loved dearly. He was a wonderful little boy. Perhaps he wasn't quite as robust as her own strapping twins, but so sweet and sensitive.

"Gentler? Lacking a father figure, pampered ridiculously by his mother, he has become a woman. He shows no manly characteristics whatsoever. His eyes fill up when I raise my voice, for God's sake. He prefers Zaynah's company to the twins. I would be ashamed of such a son! I am ashamed of such a nephew. I must take things in my own hands. It is my duty, since his father is so sinfully absent."

Fatima roused herself. This must not be the conclusion to their conversation. Mohammed could rant and rave as negatively as he wanted within the confines of their room (though the chances of Rana overhearing were considerable), but he must not take action. That would guarantee everlasting hostilities in their home. "Hamid spends a lot of time with his son, in their own room at night. You know he takes him out for long walks and special times during his day off. He does work long hours, but he loves his son and would be very offended if you tried to intervene in any way."

"I am the head of the family. If I see something wrong, I have a duty to correct it."

"That's true," replied Fatima. "And I agree that Mazin doesn't have the same … masculine energy as our boys have. But he's young yet; it will come. He's doing so well at school, and he's a very nice boy. Kind and considerate. I don't think there's anything to worry about at all, certainly not now. Time will tell."

"He's a namby-pamby mother's boy."

"He'll grow out of it," Fatima insisted.

Mohammed shrugged his shoulders. "Maybe I will leave it for a while. But not too long. It's for his own good."

Fatima smiled at him. She contemplated saying something about his wisdom, but didn't want to risk him thinking she was being sarcastic, which would lead to a paranoid leap of logic that would undermine everything she had just accomplished.

Instead, she patted the covers invitingly. "Come to bed. You must be exhausted."

Mohammed lay silent for a few moments, then rolled over to her, slipping his hand under her cotton robe and stroking upwards until he reached her breasts. This too, was expected. A nightly ritual. She closed her eyes and felt his hands squeezing their fullness, and his fingers circling her nipples. The hand slipped down and Fatima opened her legs as his finger touched her most private place, exploring, opening, and then he was on top of her and inside her and she looked up into his handsome face, his eyes tight shut, his breath coming fast. She loved his face; she thought him beautiful with his strong, aquiline nose, his high cheekbones. His full, sensuous lips. She wished he had touched her longer down there; she waited for his brief touch with longing. Once, she had dreaded these nightly mountings. They were an inevitable, painful part of marriage that had to be borne each night. But since she had had the children, it had ceased to hurt. And lately, lately, she had wanted his hand to stay between her legs, stroking. She liked his movement within her, and repressed the urge to lift her buttocks towards him, to meet him halfway, to forcefully, aggressively, thrust her body against his, to rub and grind. Of course, she would never do such a thing. In eighteen years of marriage, she had never exhibited such behaviour. Mohammed would be shocked, maybe even repelled. She repressed a smile at the thought of his reaction as his head dipped lower, his breathing more ragged. She lifted her own head and breathed in his breath, just like she had done with Na'aman. His face contorted as he groaned and fell forwards, burying his face in her long, black hair. She wrapped her arms around him, holding him tightly. It always amazed her that her body could produce such a reaction in this man. So strong, so in control, yet her body reduced him to a spasm within minutes. What a wonderful gift she gave him each night — a moment of pleasure so intense that he was momentarily lost inside it.

CHAPTER 3 **MAZIN**

THERE WAS SO LITTLE TIME during the day when he could be by himself. From the time his mother roused him for breakfast, through the long school day and the evenings with his cousins, there was only this pre-bedtime sliver of time where he could count on privacy. While his father still worked, and his mother cleaned up downstairs, the room was his. Mazin would stand in the middle of the room, assume a fighting stance, and instantly transform into the hero of his current book. The stick he had broken from off their neighbour's lemon tree on the way to school was his wand, and he jabbed and waved it in circles as he shouted curses and counter-curses, battling unspeakable enemies. The broom in the corner served as a restive mount, bearing him at a gallop toward the terrifying monster who apparently didn't know the inevitable conclusion to these battles and was keen to engage, writhing and slashing with its spiked tail, even knocking the brave soldier from his mount and forcing him to fight momentarily from a supine position, his plastic sword plunging and destroying everything in sight.

Despite his muttered oaths and cries, Mazin heard Fatima's soft footfalls pass on her way to the kitchen, and he was immediately flattened against the door, transformed into a magically two-dimensional stealthy spy. He slid the door open a crack to ensure there was nobody lurking; then, he slipped out and tiptoed down the corridor like a professional sleuth.

He bypassed the twins' bedroom with special caution and bent to scratch at the bottom of Zaynah's door.

"Come in," she whispered.

Mazin bounded over to her bed, grinning, and snatched back the covers. "What are you reading? *Fairy Tales from Around the World*? Is it good?"

Zaynah sat up in bed. "S'okay. Have you been studying for your tests next week?"

"Yes. You?"

"I want to do well in secondary school. I want to do better than you and the twins, when they get there," Zaynah said with sudden heat.

"Flowers in hair look pretty," Mazin mused. "I wonder how it would look on me. Do you have another?"

"You'd look weird," replied Zaynah. "You're a boy."

"I just want to look at myself. See if it's really weird."

"Kids at school are already teasing you for being a wimp. You'd better be careful. At least try and act normal, okay?"

"You think I don't know that?" Mazin retorted bitterly. "They act like fighting is a sport. I'm rotten at it because of my size. If I were big, I'd trounce them till they begged for mercy. Girls don't throw their weight around like animals. I wish I were…"

"No you don't," Zaynah said savagely. "You don't know anything about it. It's awful being a girl. I wish I were a boy. I'd put up with a few fist fights no problem just so I could be … free."

"You're free. What can I do that you can't?" Mazin sauntered over to peer at the photos stuck to Zaynah's wall, picking up a pen from her bookshelf on the way. "I love the one of Abdul laughing — or is it Ali? It's like his entire face is one huge mouth with a border of chin and eyes. It's like he's laughing with his whole being." Mazin began throwing the pen in the air and catching it again.

"You know perfectly well that I'm not free. When you're an adult, you can do any job you want. Even now you can walk around the town more freely than I can. If you said to your mother, 'I'm going to see my friends,' she'd say, 'okay.' I have to say who I'm going with and where. And I have more household chores to do too."

"Nobody can walk around the town anymore. Not with this war going on." The pen dropped onto the floor.

"Be quiet," hissed Zaynah. "They'll kill you if they find you here. You'd better go. I don't want to talk about the war anyway. I'm sick to death of the subject."

Mazin eyed her in surprise. It was a subject they talked about endlessly, at every opportunity. He hadn't thought it was possible to get sick of it. "All right, I won't. Which photo do you like best?"

Zaynah glanced at the photos in a bored way. Every time Mazin came into her room, he gawked at her photos, and she always acted bored. In reality, she examined them in detail for hours every day, as she lay in her bed. She had memorized every nuance of every expression. She regularly rifled through the stacks of photos that her mother kept in her bedroom drawer in search of new ones. But they had to be exactly right. "I like the one of me as a baby sitting on Khalé Nadia's knee," she said off-handedly.

"I know why," Mazin said triumphantly, "because it's so funny. Khalé Nadia is so fat that you're sitting on the very edge of her knees and she can barely reach her arms around you to prevent you from falling off." Mazin giggled, switching his attention to an old family photo taken when his Khalé Fatima was young. "Even when they were children Khalé Nadia was fat and Khalé Fatima wasn't. You'd think sisters would both eat the same stuff."

"Good night, Mazin," Zaynah said, picking up her book again and wiggling back into the cave of her covers.

Mazin picked up the pen and put it carefully back on the shelf. "Walk home with me tomorrow?"

"Of course."

Mazin slipped out the door and crept along the corridor to his own room. It was almost time for his father to come home. Although Hamid came home late and was often tired, he always brought his dinner upstairs so he could talk to his son while he ate. Afterwards, they often played a game. There were phases where they played the same game every night with apparently obsessive competition (although Mazin always won at least half the time): chess, bridge, Scrabble, and a brief period with crossword puzzles until Mazin, who could never think of the word, became too frustrated to continue. Their current pastime was Sudoku; initially, Hamid would bring a copy of the same Sudoku puzzle for each of them, to see who could finish first, but Mazin claimed he enjoyed it more without pressure.

"But then what's the point of doing it together?" Hamid had asked. "You might as well be alone."

"We could do the same one together," Mazin had suggested, but Hamid hadn't liked that idea, so they did them separately, with frequent comparisons and suggestions.

Mazin had just taken up his stance, sword in hand, when his father came through the door, bearing a dish of steaming dinner in one hand and a napkin with some sweet cakes for Mazin in the other.

"Baba!" Mazin grinned in delight, and launched himself at his father as soon as he had put the food down on the nighttime table.

Hamid hugged him with the mixture of affection and anxiety he always displayed towards his only child. He began to eat while Mazin told him about his day, a normal day filled with successful math results and a funny story the teacher had told, carefully censored to exclude the boys looking for him all over the playground but never finding him because Mazin was a soldier whose life depended on the success of his hiding place. After Hamid had eaten, he pulled the Sudoku puzzles out of his pocket and smoothed them out on either side of the nighttime table. Mazin attacked Sudoku methodically, filling the obvious squares first, then filling all the remaining squares with minute, potential numbers. Every so often, his father glanced over at his son's absorbed face. "You've got that whole row already?" he would ask.

Thus Rana found them, bursting into the room on a wave of energy that dispersed the silent bubble of the Sudoku-solvers. "Bedtime!"

"I only have a few more to do!" begged Mazin. "Baba, I'm stuck." Hamid pored over his son's puzzle, trying to decipher the tiny numbers crowded into the squares. "I know the next step is in here, and I've tried to see where I can eliminate numbers, but I can't find the next step."

"Bedtime," said Rana again, plucking both Sudoku puzzles off the table and turning down Mazin's bed covers with the other hand.

"O'mmy!" protested Mazin, but found himself bundled out the door in the direction of the bathroom. Rana would have come in to brush his teeth for him, if he hadn't firmly shut the door in her face. "Don't forget the back teeth," she called through the door. "Inside and out, three brushes each."

When he had finished he kissed his parents and pulled his covers over his head. He always slept with his head under the covers; partly to create the illusion of privacy and partly so his parents couldn't see anything if they glanced in his direction. If he didn't move, they would think he was asleep, and they would talk about all sorts of interesting things, like the war or Mohammed. Sometimes even him, although he suspected that there was another place and time they reserved for talks about him (even though he had no idea where that might be); or perhaps they saved the subject till last, when he was most likely to be asleep. It was true they talked for hours, every night, and he always fell asleep.

"Are you exhausted?" he heard Rana whisper as she switched on the small lamp by their bed.

"Yes, these long days are hard."

"Isn't it possible to come back a little earlier?"

"You know me, Mr. Nice Guy, conflict avoider." Mazin could hear a smile in his father's voice. "Dealing with Mohammed would exhaust me much more than working in my nice, quiet office."

"I wish I could avoid him," Rana said. "He makes me so angry. It's not just that he's trying to control my life in ways that are insupportable, but he's so *paranoid* and, and ... *negative*. Every conversation is unpredictable. One never knows in which direction his twisted mind will veer."

Mazin heard a rustling sound. He knew Hamid was stroking Rana's hair. "I suppose there is no point asking you to detach?"

"I try, but I'm not like you. You remember that period when I used to focus on my breathing as soon as he started to shout, as per your advice? Trying to block him out and relax my body. He almost assaulted me in his furious assumption that I was ignoring him." Rana sighed and hunkered further down in the bed, so her husband could massage the top of her scalp. "Do you remember the time I tried to shower him with love? Your advice again. And that didn't work out too well."

"I didn't tell you to shower him with love," Hamid denied, enjoying the feel of his wife's long, silky hair travelling through his hands. He noticed that some of the strands of grey were multiplying into patches. "I said that you needed to understand that he is a person who is desperate for love. Unbelievably insecure and, as you say, paranoid, he brags frequently and cannot handle the idea that he's wrong about anything. If he's always right, then it must be that everything you do — unless he has officially sanctioned it — is wrong. Since it's impossible to win an argument with him, you are in the unpleasant situation of always being in the wrong in his eyes. I thought it might help if you realize that the basis of his unbearable behaviour was a need for love. I read that much negative human behaviour stems from basic emotions like fear or a desire for love."

Mazin didn't think this conversation was very interesting.

He closed his eyes, and immediately was transported to his school. He was staggering into his classroom, dragging behind him a bloodied Kassam with his hands tied behind his back. All the students gazed at him in open-mouthed admiration, but he focused on the teacher only: "I've caught him. Now there shall be peace."

"But if his basic problem is a need to be loved, then why did my efforts to be loving backfire so disastrously?" asked Rana, shifting up in the bed so she could take a turn scratching Hamid's head. "Do you remember? He had been complaining about how he was always excluded from the children's birthday celebrations, which in itself was ridiculous, since we only bake a little cake to mark the day. So what did he think he was missing? Perhaps he imagined we were conducting clandestine parties that cost hundreds of lira...."

Hamid chuckled and bent his head to the left to give her hand better access. "So you made a point of inviting him to Mazin's cake-eating ritual...."

"And he said he couldn't possibly take time off work for such a trivial purpose. So I pretended to be sad and said how much Mazin revered him, purely to make him feel loved because of course I was relieved the bastard wasn't coming."

Kassam, who was looking at Mazin in feared awe, faded as Mazin heard his own name. He always enjoyed his birthday cake, especially as so many kids in school didn't celebrate their birthdays at all. His mother usually slipped him a few coins on his birthday too. Why did O'mmy say such a bad word? He didn't like it when she did that. Other mothers never said bad words, he was sure. And what did "revere" mean? He suddenly wanted to know desperately, but if he asked he would only be shushed angrily. Did it mean "fear"? That was certainly the main feeling he had towards his Khalo Mohammed.

"He said that I was destroying his relationship with Mazin. Pressuring him in an unacceptable way and creating unrealistic expectations in the boy that could only lead to disappointment.

Do you remember? He said he had four children of his own and it was absurd to imagine he would come to Mazin's birthday when he couldn't make it for his own children. Then he started his standard never-ending rant about how I spoil my child and what disasters would befall Mazin if he continued to think that he's the centre of the world. In short, what a bad mother I am," Rana rolled over and buried her head in the pillows. "It makes me so angry. I could kill him."

Suddenly, Kassam leapt towards the classroom door in a bid to escape. Everyone else was frozen with terror, but Mazin pursued Kassam relentlessly down the hallway. He had listened to his mother ranting about his uncle for years; he had heard enough to spill the gist into Zaynah's avaricious ears the next day. It was sufficient.

"It's like he sees everything through a distorted mirror," Hamid said, reaching over to touch his wife's shoulder. "I wish I could wave a magic wand and tell you how to deal with him, but it's not like I've found the perfect way either. I just avoid him."

"I wish I could be detached like you. Let his comments bounce off me like bubbles."

"How can you? You are his sister. It would probably be worse if you tried. One of the reasons why Mohammed feels so negatively about me is because he knows I avoid him. The less he sees me, the angrier he feels. Since he has no awareness of himself and what motivates his feelings, he thinks he's really angry about my manifold faults, but the fact is whenever I spend time with him his criticisms stop for a while. Have you noticed? After I've spent an evening listening to him respectfully and showing him affection he remembers that I'm quite a good guy."

"I don't even know how you do that."

Hamid laughed. "Don't exaggerate. Mohammed is great to have a yak with once in a while. He's knowledgeable and intelligent, and his perspective on things is often bang on. I just wish I didn't have to live with him."

For a few moments, Mazin's mind wandered between two scenes as he tried to jerk back to wakefulness: the pursuit down the hallway intensified as both the rabbit and the hare acquired supernatural powers, but a weird conversation with a masked policemen kept intruding. Within minutes, he slept.

There were hiding places all over the schoolyard; it amazed Mazin that the other boys didn't seem to know about them. He was lucky because they never found him. So long as he catapulted out of the classroom fast enough to enter the parking lot before they got to the doors, he was sure to be safe. Often, he could peek out from his hiding place and watch them lumber out of the school building in pursuit, calling his name, breaking up to search in several different directions at once. Oafs. Bullies. He had never done anything to them. When they were really young he had just ignored them, tripping around the schoolyard during breaks in his own little world. Once, Rana had seen him, hands in pockets, doing what appeared to be a dance in the corner. She had called him over. "What are you doing?"

He had been delighted to see her, rushing over and wrapping himself around her lower torso. But she had glanced at the watching students and held him at arm's length, repeating her question. He had been puzzled. What had he been doing? Playing, of course.

"But why aren't you playing with the other boys?"

"I don't want to."

"You must," she had insisted. "Nobody else is playing by themselves. You see? Everybody is playing with somebody else. That's what you're supposed to do at school. Let's call one of your friends over and start a game. Which one is your friend?"

And he had looked blankly at the various groups of boys, and could not say.

Rana had given him a little shake in frustration. "You look strange dancing around with your hands in your pockets. I don't want you to do that anymore. I'm coming by next week again and I want you to be playing with someone."

So he had approached a group of boys and asked to join their game. "Sure," they had replied, but it was a silly game, something with marbles, and he couldn't seem to get his marble to hit the other marble. Then the boys laughed at him, and he sat back on his haunches and felt puzzled again. Why did he have to play with them when he didn't enjoy it?

The next day, he was twirling around in his corner, around and around until he felt sick with dizziness, when he suddenly remembered. He looked around for the other boys; perhaps they were doing something more interesting today. There they were, all in a bunch by the fence that encircled the school-yard, and they looked excited. Mazin walked over to them, determined to make a friend in time for his mother's visit next week. He elbowed through the crowd, and saw the cornered rat they were throwing rocks at. It was a large rat, and it ran back and forth in the small space its tormenters allowed it as they took careful aim. It was dragging one of its legs, and it left a trail of blood as it ran. As Mazin drew near, the rat sat up on its haunches, like a little old man. It seemed to Mazin that the rat looked directly at him, before a stone hit it right in the face and toppled it against the wall. The boys cheered, and slapped each other on the back. The rat, miraculously, pushed backwards from the rock and started to weave its way along the wall in a disoriented manner. Another rock crashed in front of it and it sat up again on its hind legs, cowering. It was horrible. Mazin felt sick. He stepped in front of the rat and faced the boys. "Stop it."

They looked at him incredulously for a moment, then started to shout, "Get out of the way!" "Move!" "Idiot!"

The only thing Mazin felt was anger. He was not frightened. "You go away. You are the idiots."

And then a rock had sailed out of the air and hit him in the chest. At the same time, another boy launched himself at

Mazin, and he disappeared under a pile of flailing arms and legs until a teacher intervened.

Mazin rose from the fray bloody but triumphant. There was no sign of the rat, which had been forgotten when the larger battle started, and that meant it had got away.

When his father got home that night, he told him about the rat, and what he had done. His father could not understand. "How can you feel sorry for a rat? It's a rat. They're disgusting, disease-ridden creatures. It's natural for little boys to kill rats. You must be tougher, Mazin."

But when the twins told the story gleefully at the dinner table the next evening, laughing over the ludicrousness of their cousin's behaviour, Mazin received support from an unexpected party.

"I spend my life with animals, and most of them have more sense than human beings," Mohammed reprimanded his spluttering sons. "Whether it matters or not if a bunch of boys torture a rat is a philosophical question above your heads, but it is a fact that the act itself derives from cruelty. Not bravery, not sport. Just stupid malice. That's what it is every time that a group gangs up against one, or someone stronger hurts a weaker person. Stupid malice, every time. But," Mohammed piled some tabouleh and hummus on a corner of his pita, "it is a brave act to speak out against cruelty, especially when a group of people are engaged in it."

Mazin gave his uncle a tremulous smile, even though Mohammed did not look at him.

Mazin then tried to look at his plate, but he couldn't resist shooting a quick glance in the direction of his mother. She had told him to be brave before, often, as though she doubted his capacity for bravery. As though she somehow rated bravery in little boys by their roughness in the schoolyard, whether they managed to push others aside to get to the swing first, and certainly by whether they could destroy pests such as rats without compunction. But Khalo Mohammed had said it was not brave to do that when you were in a group of boys. It was brave to stop them. Could he explain to his mother that his bravery in this matter hindered his ability to play with them normally as she requested?

Because although they say little girls hold grudges more than little boys, the option of joining in was denied to Mazin after the incident of the rat. The other boys thought he was weird, and did not want to play with him.

So, for the first time in his life, he had dreaded seeing his mother. He wondered if she would be fooled if he hovered on the periphery of a group, but it was impossible to enjoy his own form of imaginative play when he was near others. In any case, he didn't know when she was coming, so inevitably she found him crouched on the ground, completely alone. "What are you doing?" she asked, and there was a trace of weariness in her voice.

Mazin jumped up as if he had been scalded. "O'mmy-I-cannot-play-with-them-they-don't-want-me-to-because-I-was-brave," he gabbled his rehearsed line, then pointed to the ground. "But look, O'mmy, there is a trail of ants going towards the grass, and each one is carrying something. Look!" and he bent towards his mother confidentially. "I bet if I follow them I'll find their nest, but I'll have to keep it a secret so the other boys won't find it. They'd just try and destroy it, because of stupid malice, and then I'd have to be brave again...." He looked at his mother out of the corner of his eye. She was smiling at him, tiredly, so he knew it was all right.

Years had gone by since then, and it was doubtful whether any of the other boys even remembered the incident of the rat. Still, Mazin was designated scapegoat for the rest of his life, and was forced to rush out of the school as soon as the bell rang and cower in some hiding place until the coast was clear. He didn't mind. He knew they wouldn't find him, just like he knew Zaynah would wait for him.

When the boys had slunk off in defeat, she called him and he skipped over to her, satchel swinging in his hand.

"You shouldn't skip," she said, but not in an unkind way. "It looks weird."

"You skip."

"I'm a girl. How many times do I have to tell you?"

"It's just strange that a particular gait should be limited to one sex only," said Mazin.

"Do you want me to give you a list to memorize or something? I'll call it, 'How to behave in order not to be beaten up for the rest of one's life?' Honestly Mazin, it's like talking to a two-year-old. You don't seem to get the simplest things."

"Well, people are strange. How come you understand them so easily? There's nothing logical about the way we're supposed to behave, it's just a learning process."

"Everybody in the whole world gets it without learning it like math. There's something wrong with you." Zaynah reached over and pinched his cheek affectionately.

They both turned right at the next intersection without even asking a question, even though left took them directly home. Right led past the square where the protesters often gathered, and a mixture of triggers including anxiety, fear, curiosity, and an intense feeling of excitement overrode the knowledge that their mothers would not like them taking this route home. They heard the chanting before they saw them: "Freedom! Freedom! One, one, one! We the People are one, one, one!" They slowed as they reached the square, keeping to the edges of the crowd. There were only a couple of hundred people there today, and they strained their eyes for Ahmed as they walked slowly to the other side of the square. Suddenly, Zaynah grabbed Mazin's arm and pointed. He squinted in the direction of her finger, looking from face to face, all of them intense and focused. Then his eyes slid over two familiar countenances and he jerked in shock.

"Do you see them?"

"I can't believe it."

"Those stupid twins. I've seen them whispering and nudging each other at the breakfast table and I knew they were planning some mischief, but I never thought they'd do anything this bad." Zaynah pushed a few strands of hair off her face and took a deep breath. "We'll have to go and get them."

Mazin looked doubtfully in the direction of the twins again. They were in the middle of the crowd, their joined hands raised high above their heads as they stabbed the air in time to their chant. "Freedom! Freedom! One, one, one! We the People are one, one, one!"

"But Zaynah, I don't see any other women here."

"I'm not joining the protest," she answered fiercely. "I'm protecting my little brothers." And she started to push her way through the people. "Excuse me, sorry!"

Mazin followed close behind, and as the crowd parted politely to let them through, his fear abated and he felt jubilant. President Kassam referred to the protesters as terrorists, and even Khalo Mohammed dubbed them as foolish idealistic young men infected with a mob mentality that made them dangerous. In all their after-school detours, as they slipped along the edges of the crowds with hammering hearts, they had never seen anything awful, but the fear that they might was always present, and they had never actually pushed through the crowd before. As they got further in, they lost sight of the twins and Mazin grasped a fold of Zaynah's sleeve between his fingers. "There they are," she said suddenly, veering off to the left, and then they were right in front of the twins. Mazin laughed to see the comical looks on their faces as they spied their sister mid-chant and stared at her, mouths still open.

"You're coming home with me right now," Zaynah said.

"No we're not," Abdul and Ali said simultaneously. Mazin had always envied their ability to speak as one.

"Yes you are," snapped Zaynah. "You have no choice in the matter."

"What are you going to do, drag us off physically?" Abdul asked, and the twins looked at each other and sniggered, then up went their grasped hands into the air and they shouted right into their sister's face, "Freedom! Freedom! One, one, one! We the People are one, one, one!"

Zaynah raised her voice to be heard. "No problem, don't come. I will tell Abi what you have been doing and then you won't be able to move for a week, though of course you can shout anti-government slogans from your beds. You come with me right now, or I'm telling on you." Zaynah turned on her heel and maneuvered her way back to the edge of the crowd without even looking behind her. Mazin looked at the twins for a moment before turning to follow her. They looked back in dismay, all traces of cocky defiance gone.

He risked a glance back as they broke free from the stragglers on the perimeters of the throng. Sure enough, the twins were right behind.

Abdul caught up to Zaynah as she marched to the end of the square. "We're doing something we believe in, Zaynah. Our country needs as many voices as it can get. We know Abi is against it, but it's only because he's old and fearful and wants everything to be peaceful and safe. If you told him, he'd beat us."

She rounded on him angrily. "Have you any idea what *they* would do to you if they caught you?"

The twins laughed uneasily. "We always stay in the middle of the crowd, see. They cannot catch us, among so many."

Zaynah grabbed them both by a hand and pulled them into an alleyway. She rounded on them. "You are stupid. They don't have to catch you. They just have to mow you down with machine-gun fire. Then they pick you up, bleeding, and drag you down to the police station."

The twins stood with their backs against the wall of the building, facing Zaynah. The expression on their faces reminded Mazin of the cornered rat, except that this time, in order to save them, they must not be spared. "They throw you into a dungeon." Mazin pushed his face a little closer to the twins. "The walls are dark and slimy. Other people crouch in the shadows, or lie if they have no strength. Their faces are hopeless. Their bodies are broken."

"Then the questions start," interrupted Zaynah. "Who are you, what illegal activities have you been involved in, what names can you give us? And it doesn't matter what you say, if you spill your guts or if you try to be brave and keep it in, they beat you, with fists, sticks, whips, cables, metal rods. They'll force you into a tire so your arms are pinned to your sides. They'll hang you by your wrists from the ceiling. You will be electrocuted, burned with cigarettes."

"They don't do that to children," Abdul said.

Mazin looked at him. His face looked shocked. Mazin felt a little sick too. Of all the things he had heard about the war, this disturbed him most. In their daily conversations about the situation, he would always focus on the future: what democracy would mean to them, the next generation. How it would impact their lives. How nothing could stop the Arab Spring, a huge wave of humanity struggling for the right to freedom. It did not matter what Kassam did, he was convinced. You could not stop a tidal wave. Mazin felt privileged to be alive at such a time, to be young, to be a witness.

Zaynah was different. She was fascinated by the terrible things, and raked over the details of atrocities until Mazin felt ill. She would say, "It said on the Internet that there were thirty-one methods of torture." She would wait expectantly for his question, which never came. "Don't you want to know what they are?" she would ask, and then she would begin to reel off the ones that had been mentioned in the article she had read, and Mazin would struggle not to imagine the cigarette butt burning into his own skin. That was the problem; his imagination took over whatever she described and began to busily apply it to his own body. He couldn't stand it.

He would put his hands over his ears and shout, "Stop!

Stop!" Zaynah would smile in satisfaction, and desist. But he couldn't imagine the type of person that could hurt another person like that. He knew that the desire to hurt could overcome you when you were very angry, like he had wanted to hurt the boy who threw the rock at the rat. But how could anyone hurt someone who was tied up? Who was screaming in pain? He did not want to live in a world where people could do that to each other. It was like living among monsters.

"Don't you read anything? Haven't you heard?" Zaynah shouted at Abdul. "Sure they do it to children. This whole thing started because of what they did to a child. Even before the protesters rose up in the thousands to bring down the government, even before the government was really scared. They tortured and killed children because of a bit of pro-democracy graffiti. And you think they wouldn't torture you?" Zaynah turned her head and spat in contempt. Both the twins gazed at her with round eyes.

"Do you still think it's all fun and games, shouting your silly chants among the big men?"

They shook their heads.

"You must promise me never to attend the protests again." They still gazed at her owlishly. "Promise me!" she yelled.

"We won't, Zaynah," said Ali.

"You too," she said, jabbing Abdul in the chest with her finger.

"I don't want to die," Abdul answered, and only then did Zaynah allow them to emerge from the dark alley and resume their walk home.

"But I want to do something," he added.

"There must be lots of things that you can do that are more useful than shouting in a crowd, lost to view because you're half the size of everybody else so you're completely useless anyway."

"So they wouldn't shoot at us," Abdul began again, but Zaynah rounded on him immediately. "The midst of the crowd is their target, not individual people, idiot. They just shoot.

You're not helping anything by being there, and you're risking your life. If you want to be involved, why can't you pass out pamphlets or something? Do odd jobs for families whose menfolk are in prison? I'm sure Khalo Ahmed would have a long list of things that need to be done." A sudden worry rose in Zaynah. "Khalo Ahmed didn't put you up to this, did he?"

"Of course not," the twins chorused. "He knows nothing about it."

"He never saw you? How long have you been going to the protests anyway?"

"We've only been twice," Abdul said sullenly. "We were going to tell Khalo Ahmed, but you got to us first. How come you walked home past the square anyway? O'mmy has forbidden it."

Zaynah frowned in contempt. "Who are you to talk?"

"You see?" said Abdul. "It is impossible to ignore what's going on. It is part of our lives. Even for you, a girl…"

"Don't start that," warned Zaynah.

"…feel the urge to see what's happening. We must contribute in some way."

"There must be dozens of ways that won't put you directly in the line of fire. Talk to Khalo Ahmed. But remember your promise to me. If I ever see you here again, I will tell Abi."

"We will keep our promise. But we must do something."

Mazin knew just what they meant.

CHAPTER 4 **RANA**

BREAKFAST WAS ALWAYS a lovely time. Mohammed never ate much for breakfast because his stomach bothered him, even though Fatima constantly told him it was the most important meal of the day. Once he had grabbed some coffee and a piece of flatbread and left for work, Rana took over the kitchen. Every day, she managed to concoct something different, despite the war. Food shortages had impacted them in many different ways; it was nearly impossible to get fruit, and sometimes it was even hard to find vegetables in the local market, the souq. But even before the war Rana had been resourceful. In one corner of their small, square courtyard, with the help of the boys, she had erected a small, square box. It stood about three feet high, four feet wide, and four feet long. One side of the box opened, releasing a powerful smell of chicken droppings. Inside, there was a battered pan containing water, and a stick traversing the length of the box, about a foot from the ceiling. Here the hens roosted, and in the corner they had created a nest of straw from the imprint of their laying bodies. Rana collected the eggs every morning before the others were up, dividing them into four piles for the four families who shared the courtyard, selecting the biggest for her own family and the next biggest for the two spinster sisters who lived next door. Hessa and Hazar were two gentle, timid souls who apparently suffered (or were blessed, depending on your point of view) with mild intellectual disability. They were too shy to speak beyond a whispered salutation, but they lived in perfect harmony together. Rana felt protective of them, as she felt protective of all gentle creatures, and more so since she had witnessed Hessa slip out the door as Mazin and Zaynah passed on their way to school and press a sweet into their hands. Watching from the window as the children trotted off to school day after day, she observed with interest that Hessa never gave anything to the twins, but always to Mazin and Zaynah. She liked them twice as much, after that. It had been hard to extract information from the other neighbours about where the sisters received the means to support themselves. She learned that they had been born in that house and had stayed there as the other occupants had died or left, never marrying. "Perhaps they killed everybody," she joked to Fatima. They never asked for anything, but Rana would often make a little extra — not hard to do when you were cooking for ten — leaving it on the doorstep so they would be spared the embarrassment of one-sided thanks. She knew other neighbours did the same thing, even as to leaving it on the doorstep, as the sisters were so painfully shy. Every day, she left them presents of the second biggest eggs and greens from the garden.

Rana clucked to her ten hens, and scattered feed for them to eat. There was no rooster. Rana had a friend just outside of the city who had a rooster and whenever the hens became broody, she would exchange a dozen of her own hens' unfertilized eggs for her friend's fertilized ones, and slip them under the unsuspecting hens. Male offspring and aging hens were transformed into soup. On bitter days when she raged against her gender, the hens' rooster-less existence consoled her: a male's role could be reduced to the one act of procreation, and you did not even need to have them around for that.

More miraculous than the miniature henhouse that made Rana inordinately proud, was the crude fenced-in corner of their courtyard (that a cat might topple with its paw) in which she had constructed a rectangle from large stones, filled it with earth and chicken droppings, and planted a vegetable garden. Tomatoes, cucumbers, lettuce, onions, coriander, and a variety of other herbs painted the corner green and provided all the families sharing the courtyard with fresh salad every day. Of course, Mohammed had pointed out that there was nothing left of the courtyard but a skinny path snaking between ugly enclosures, but he'd clapped Rana on the back as he said it. They all knew there were people suffering from food shortages. They all knew how lucky they were, and how this little bit of enterprise made one less thing to fear during the war.

While other children complained about the sameness of their everyday food during the shortages, little miracles of ingenuity awaited Rana's household when they sat down to breakfast: sometimes there would be a series of small bowls containing olives, tomatoes, boiled eggs, fried eggplant, hummus, and labneh, to be scooped up with flatbread or pita. Or she would produce an omelette, laden with herbs from the garden. On Fridays, their day of rest, she would get up even earlier to make ful medames, a warm broad bean salad with tahini or hummus, lemon, and olive oil, and a thick layer of diced onions over top. It was very rich and filling, with the unfortunate side effect of increasing Fatima's longing for bed.

Fussing over the large pot of tea simmering on the stove, Rana would watch the children straggle in out of the corner of her eye, followed soon after by Hamid and Ahmed. The twins, invariably jostling each other, always sat down and started to shovel food in automatically. At least they weren't picky, and they certainly enjoyed eating. Zaynah and Mazin always smiled up at Rana and thanked her, having imbibed her instructions regarding politeness. But Ahmed and Hamid both understood how much Rana wanted them to enjoy their breakfasts, and would always provide a smile and compliment. For half an hour, Rana presided over a large family, sitting at the head of the table and watching them all with love. It made her feel like she had a whole brood of kids. She had never mourned her inability to have more children, though she kept up a constant lament in the company of other women, who viewed her almost-barrenness as a tragedy. "You have not been blessed by Allah," they would say, "though you are a good woman." Fatima would mirror their words, and Rana reacted appropriately, pulling sad, pious faces. But Hamid never blamed her for their lack of children, and she didn't fret over it. There used to be a vague sting of disappointment every month when her period rolled around, but that had quite faded. She thought perhaps that Allah had other plans for her. Maybe she was destined to do something else with her life. She didn't delude herself with ideas of grandeur, like she felt young Ahmed probably did. She just wanted to keep herself open, in case another purpose was her destiny.

Fatima always tried to make a brief appearance while Mohammed inhaled his modest meal — though he never acknowledged her presence — but then she would disappear again, returning with a gleeful, squirming Na'aman in her arms some time later. Rana was pleased to have given her an extra hour in bed, and Fatima never failed to praise the food with genuine wonder.

Then the men and the older kids bustled out the door, and the house seemed miraculously quiet. The women settled comfortably into their routine: cleaning, going to the souq to shop and gossip with their neighbours, and preparing the next meal. Fatima read and played with Na'aman while Rana tended her garden. Throughout the day, no matter what they were doing, Rana kept slipping her hand in Fatima's pocket to retrieve her cell phone, checking to see if anyone had tried to contact them. Despite her best cajoling, Ahmed refused to communicate with anyone other than his sister throughout the day. In reality, he was texting his sister-in-law, whose avid questions about where he was and what was happening differed from Fatima's simple desire to know whether he was all right. There was an unspoken rule that he would reassure them at least twice during the day, which resulted in Rana's frequent exploration of Fatima's pocket, as though it were possible to miss him.

The instant Ahmed texted them, they would whip out the cell and hover over it together, until Fatima was assured he was still alive and whole and returned to the amusement of her son, whereupon Rana would continue to pelt Ahmed with questions for as long as he would let her.

R U safe?

Fatima always asked first.

Yes. Tho live bullets today.

No! Come home.

Crowd gone. All over.

Fatima smiled in relief, and handed the cell to Rana, who had been hanging over her shoulder.

Where R U?

City Centre.

What happened?

Thousands people. Big demo. Tanks and guns. Shelling. Many dead. Awful.

How started?

Man climbed gov building to put opposition flag, shot down.

Rana's heart beat with the pain of the violence, with her intense desire to be part of it.

U OK?

Yes. Moussa bullet arm. Hospital no take. Bring there?

Rana called Fatima over and showed her the message.

"Text Ahmed that he can't possibly bring his friend here. Mohammed would have a fit. Why can't he go to his own home?"

"Fatima!" cried Rana in anguish. "This could be our contribution to this valiant struggle. We can hide him. It's just his arm; we could probably patch him up before Mohammed gets home."

Fatima looked anxious. *Bring,* Rana texted, and switched off the phone quickly.

She ran to prepare, ignoring Fatima's fluttering, useless hands and ejaculations of fear. *Boil water, find clean cloths, bandages ... is that all we have? Allah help me... iodine to kill germs, what else?*

"Should I boil the cloths?" she asked Fatima, strewing newspaper around an isolated chair where the injured man would sit.

"How can we take care of an injured man?" cried Fatima. "What do you know about gunshot injuries?"

"Nothing!" snapped Rana. "And we can't even research what to do on the Internet because it has been disconnected. This bloody government. That murderous Kassam." She felt a sudden desire to weep, and held it back, rushing to the window to look out for the umpteenth time. "I wish I'd asked Ahmed how long it would take to get here. Do we have any painkillers?"

"Aspirin."

"That's not enough. Let's phone Dr. Sharabi, he'll help us. He has to; we've been going to him for years. Do you know what his political affiliations are?" Rana glanced out the window again. "They're coming! Allah help me. Phone the doctor, quick!"

Rana rushed to fling open the door. Ahmed was supporting Moussa with one arm; his other hand was pressed against a balled-up cloth that he held to Moussa's upper arm. It had obviously been ripped from Ahmed's shirt sleeve.

"Come in, come in." Rana scanned Moussa's pale face anxiously, but he looked up and gave her a shadow of his cocky smile. "Bastards," he said.

"Make sure nobody sees you entering," whispered Fatima.

They got Moussa onto the chair. Rana gave orders to hold his arm above his head in order to minimize the bleeding, and she began to swab at the wound with iodine. Moussa cried out in pain, and Fatima fed him as many aspirin as she dared, then rolled up a clean cloth and put it in his mouth, so he would have something to bite on.

"Lucky for you your arm caught it," said Rana, grimly. "I can see an entry and an exit hole, so there's no bullet in your arm. Again, lucky for you. I wouldn't have known how to extract a bullet."

"Of course not, you're not a doctor," said Fatima. "Why didn't you go to a real doctor? Why did you come here?"

Ahmed looked at his sister, his eyes wild and fearful. "You have no idea what it's like. You're just marching along, holding your sign, believing in what you're doing, and suddenly bullets are raining down from the sky, and the thundering of machine guns deafens your ears and the air is filled with smoke and people ... people falling...." Ahmed stopped for a second, and took one of his hands away from Moussa's arm to wipe his eyes vigorously. Moussa jerked his arm downwards away from the source of the awful pain.

"Hold his arm tight!" barked Rana.

Ahmed snapped back to attention, holding his friend's arm elevated with both hands.

Moussa reared back in his chair, his face sweating.

"Poor boy. This is awful," murmured Fatima. "But why did you come here, why? We aren't qualified to help him."

"Where should I take him?" cried Ahmed. "Do you know what's happening at the public hospitals? They've been under the control of Kassam's intelligence agency for months! Military staff wait at the doors to cart any protesters off to prison cells for interrogation and torture. Any medical staff that tries to help the protestors are themselves carted off for similar treatment. Doctors are terrified to help the wounded. Many of them abuse us, verbally and sometimes even physically. Taking him to the hospital would be like taking him to prison."

"But what about private clinics? I've heard those are sprouting up all over the city."

"They are not *sprouting* up," replied Ahmed. "Each one is a target for the government's violence. They are frequently raided, their contents destroyed, their doctors rounded up. If we were desperate, I know someone who knows someone. I could find one with his help. But it was easier to bring Moussa here." Ahmed looked at Rana with admiration. "I knew you would look after him."

Rana smiled in pleasure at this unexpected praise from her brother-in-law. "It's almost over," she said to the groaning Moussa. "The bleeding has almost stopped and I am going to wrap this bandage around your arm and then hold it in place with a tourniquet. You mustn't move it until it heals."

"Don't worry," groaned Moussa.

"I think the only thing that could happen to it is infection, so we will keep swabbing it with iodine every day or so."

Moussa whimpered.

"What do you mean 'we'll' keep swabbing it? How will we do that? Moussa has to go home now, before Mohammed gets here," said Fatima. "I don't know why you couldn't have taken him to his own home in the first place. Surely his family could have taken care of him?"

"He lives with his mother, and she is ailing herself. He didn't want to worry her," said Ahmed coldly to his sister.

Rana glanced at Fatima's face. She knew that Fatima was rigid with worry. Gentle Fatima hated the fighting, the violence. She couldn't care less whether she lived in a democracy or not, and deep down she was angry for the desperate anxiety her brother created. She listened to her husband when he prophesied that Ahmed would bring destruction upon the family, and Rana could not soothe away Fatima's worries by pretending there was no risk of soldiers smashing down their door one day in a raid. Fatima couldn't understand why Ahmed would endanger them in that way. What cause was worth that?

"Moussa," Rana said gently. "I'm finished. The wound is as clean as I can get it and I've wrapped a snug bandage around your arm, which should stop the bleeding completely. Do you feel able to go home now? Ahmed can help you."

Moussa nodded weakly. "My mother will be upset."

"But she'll look after you well. I will write a note telling her what needs to be done. Do you think she has iodine in the house? Fresh bandages? I can make her a little parcel of the things she needs. And if something happens, if it gets infected, you must find a field hospital."

Rana was pleased, for Fatima's sake, that they managed to get Moussa out the door before the children got home from school. They might have had to ask the kids to keep what they had seen a secret, and she hated doing that. The day settled back into its regular routine, as though there had been no interruption. The children had a snack, and then they did allocated household chores and their homework, stopping to play with an insistent Na'aman along the way.

When Ahmed came home, the twins rushed towards him as usual. "What happened today, Khalo Ahmed? What did you do today to secure our democratic future?"

Ahmed looked down at them wearily. "Not today, little ones. I have to wash up."

They chorused their disappointment, but Ahmed walked determinedly to the bathroom and shut the door. Rana noticed Zaynah looking after him with a strange expression in her eyes. Surely the girl wasn't foolish enough to have a crush on her own uncle? Zaynah caught her aunt's sharp look, blushed and looked down at the rice she was stirring. Rana's eyes slipped over the rest of the children. Where was Mazin? He was probably in their shared room, resting or reading. She noticed that he seemed to need more time to himself lately, although he had always been an introspective child. Rana knew that she should try to give him as much space as possible, especially in this chock-full house where he shared a room with his parents. But she loved him so much, she thought she would just take a peek to see what he was doing.

Rana went quietly up the stairs to the landing. She would only glance in if the door to their bedroom was ajar, of course; she wouldn't bother him if it was closed. When she approached, she saw that the latch hadn't been closed, so it was possible to push gently without turning the handle. The door slid open an inch or two, and she applied her eye to the crack.

Mazin stood before the mirror, his profile to the door. He had taken one of Rana's shawls from the cupboard and draped it over his shoulders. There was a rose behind his ear.

"Really? Do you really think so?" he simpered in a strange voice.

Then crossly: "What on earth do you mean? I've never heard so much rubbish in my entire life." He inclined his head closer to the mirror and made a little pout of distaste. "Do yourself a favour, take a bath. You reek. Perhaps a little perfume?"

"Outrageous!" he snapped at his own reflection, pirouetting to the left. He regarded himself from that angle, his back to the door. "You should be punished. Naughty boy!" Mazin flipped the cloak over his shoulder.

Rana backed away from the door slowly, her hand pressed to her mouth. She had to be alone for a few minutes, but her bedroom was taken. Where could she go? The bathroom? That would grant her five minutes maximum, before someone pounded on the door to get in. Anyway, Ahmed was probably still in there. Too many people shared the same bathroom. It was … outrageous that there wasn't a single place she could go in the world to be alone for a few minutes. She needed to *think*.

The courtyard. Now that she had taken up the majority of the space with her garden and chickens, nobody used it much. The women hung their laundry to dry, but they would have done that in the morning. The courtyard was the only place.

Rana stemmed her desire to run and walked sedately to the back door, past the children sitting at the table doing their homework. She felt her face must look ravaged, different somehow, but nobody paid her the slightest heed.

She wrested off the cover of the metal tub that stood outside the chicken coop and grabbed a handful of grain. Then she squatted down and opened the door. There was one hen lying in its customary corner, presumably laying an egg, but the rest rushed at her with frantic clucking noises, and began to peck the grain from her hand. Rana had often wondered if they looked at her and thought only "food," or whether she represented something a little more, something akin to "protection" or "mother."

But she was not thinking of the hens right now, although her eyes were fixed on them. What had she seen? What did this mean? Nothing. Her son was destined to be an actor. But why was he dressed up in a woman's clothes? And what was the meaning behind that curiously feminine flick of his wrist? Rana didn't know much about homosexuality, but she had seen several American shows with homosexual people in them. "Gay," they were called, but Rana could never understand this. She knew gay meant "happy," as she had looked it up to make sure. Pretending you were happy because you were a homosexual seemed ridiculous and pathetic to her. On this issue, she shared her brother's view that it was another American vice, bred on the beds of bored wealth and decadence.

"Rana, are you coming in to serve out dinner?" called Fatima. "Mohammed is coming."

She went inside and mechanically began to put the food on the table, her face rigid. It was all too much. The horror and fear of the war, and now this … this sin. This repulsive, disgusting possibility. No, it could not be. Her little boy, her beloved Mazin. What did she know about it? Rumours about other people, snippets from the Internet, unrealistic American movies that had as much truth to them as all their happy endings. She sighed. If only the Internet was available now, she could check whether this was fairly common behaviour for young boys of a sensitive nature. Perhaps Mazin was destined to be a great actor and was merely acting out a role? *Please, Allah, please make it something banal like that. Only acting.*

Allah?

Why would Allah listen to her? She hadn't prayed in years. It was a sin. Life was too hard. She foresaw a life of ostracism, labels, and misery for her son.

"Is there no meat in the soup?" asked Mohammed.

"It's vegetable soup. Meat is very expensive right now," replied Fatima. "How was your day, habibi?"

Mohammed sucked in air through his teeth. "There must have been a bomb downtown today. I heard a huge blast just after lunch and I rushed downstairs to the basement. The floor actually shook; I was terrified my clinic would be blasted apart."

"It would be a shame if the animals lost their medical supplies," said Ahmed sarcastically.

"Especially since there is such a shortage of medical supplies in the city," replied Mohammed. "You look remarkably healthy, Ahmed, so I'm assuming you had the sense to stay out of the thick of things today?"

Ahmed turned red, and looked down at his plate.

Mohammed looked at him. "No? Well, you'll be glad to know that my animals' medical supplies aren't obtained at the cost of brave people like you. You've got your own sources, no? Activists who smuggle supplies for makeshift hospitals across the borders of neighbouring countries?"

Ahmed attacked his food silently, spooning soup into his mouth in a steady motion.

"Maybe that's a job for you, Ahmed," Mohammed continued with a trace of amusement. "I expect there's a lot of danger involved, which would suit your yearning to be a hero."

"They are heroes," Ahmed said quietly.

Mohammed snorted. "Perhaps we have a different definition of 'hero'. My definition is someone who protects his family."

Ahmed finished his soup and laid his spoon down carefully. He took a deep breath, gathering the energy to enter the fray. "There are different ways to be a hero. Since I don't have my own family yet, and by that I mean children," he amended with an affectionate smile to Fatima, "I can't protect them heroically. This leaves me free to pursue a younger man's idea of … doing the right thing. I believe in every man's right to vote for his leaders. I think it is worth fighting for."

Mohammed waved his fork at Ahmed in a passive-aggressive fashion masked as amused affection. "The problem with you is that you've got too much time on your hands; time and young men are a combustive combination. Nobody is a hero in this war. Heroism isn't just about bravery — a hero implies someone with noble qualities. Nobody has noble qualities in this war." Mohammed stopped to take a drink of water, eyeing Ahmed over the rim of his glass. "Your side are ranting and raving because you can't think of anything else to do. Instead of waiting to see what results your initial ranting and raving may have had, you forge ahead blindly, minimizing the impact of your initial rebellion. You're acting like sheep, doing the same thing day after day without thinking. There are no leaders; no level head is emerging to take the field. Nobody is saying: wait, look what's happening in Libya and Tunisia and Egypt and all the other countries whose peoples were so happy to throw over the governments so they could vote. What's happening with them?" Mohammed paused for a moment, waving his fork like a baton. Ahmed did not answer. He knew what was happening with them, but if he tried to enter a fact-for-fact competition with Mohammed he didn't have a chance. Mohammed could pull facts out of his head like a magic hat.

"Former protesters like you find themselves forced to impose a new order on the mayhem once they've managed to oust the old regime," Mohammed continued after a moment. "Have peaceful, prosperous democracies taken over the field? No, everything is bloody chaos." Mohammed paused to wipe up some hummus with his pita.

"So what are you saying, that we shouldn't fight for democracy because it's going to be really hard once we get it? What kind of argument is that? We've never governed ourselves, so of course there will be some growing pains. Just like there was in Europe when they overthrew their kings and queens."

Rana couldn't help herself. She lifted her head and listened for Mohammed's reply.

"With the exception of England, the Europeans bumped off their royalty. What's to stop you heroes from slashing at your symbols of repression? Down with the Alawites, in with the Sunnis, oh and let's kill off those Christian bastards as well, since they didn't support us in our *heroic* bid for democracy. If you guys get into power, there will be just another set of tyrants. No heroes."

Ahmed picked up his glass and swallowed some water. He couldn't think what to say. Mohammed always confused him like this — he knew that was just one side of things, he knew what he was doing was vitally important — but Mohammed's grain of truth always planted itself in one's brain and grew like a weed. It was probably true. There would be chaos and murder after the regime fell, and a different group of people would be waiting to be tortured in the prison cells.

"You may be right," Rana interjected suddenly when she saw Ahmed didn't know how to respond. "I hope you are, because it means that one day, after we've taken the inevitable and necessary step of overthrowing the tyrants ruling us today, we'll have stable democracies like the Europeans. But first, we have to murder our nobility."

"And call ourselves heroes while we're doing it," sneered Mohammed.

"Everything is comparative," replied Rana. "Those who are doing something are heroes compared to those who are too frightened to do anything."

Mohammed leaned towards her, a tic beating in his forehead. Rana saw Mazin stiffen out of the corner of her eye. He hated it when people shouted, and suppertime seemed to morph into a battlefield rather frequently of late. The twins had stopped eating, and were swivelling their heads from speaker to speaker, mouths agape. "Are you suggesting that

I am too frightened to do anything?" Mohammed hissed at her. "Are you calling me a coward in front of my own children? How dare you?"

"I wasn't calling you a coward," Rana tried to say, but Mohammed's voice rose to a shout as he leapt to his feet.

"And you are calling your own husband a coward too, I suppose, in front of his own son? You are a stupid, narrow-minded, ignorant fool...."

Rana was shouting now too, as both tried to outdo the other in order to be heard. "It came out wrong! I was thinking of the doctors who have no political affiliations but nevertheless put their lives at risk...."

Fatima leapt to her feet too, grabbing Na'aman in her arms. "Children, upstairs," she commanded.

"Your husband should beat you, instead of giving you free rein to voice your uninformed opinions and rear a weak, spoiled, effeminate son."

"I meant that the doctors are the heroes," screamed Rana. "I wasn't insulting you at all! And look at you, spitting out insults as though it were your right! Of course, you'll go over it again and again in your own head and figure that you behaved well while I was insufferable. Well, *you* were the one who said disgusting things, and I said nothing! You twist everything!"

Mohammed strode over to her chair and tried to jerk it backwards. For a second, she thought she was in a movie, as it was all so bizarre. Then she felt his heavy hands on her shoulders as he heaved her up and propelled her towards the door leading from the kitchen to the hallway. "I won't have anyone calling me a coward at my own table. Get out of my sight," and he slammed the door after her.

Rana stood outside the door, her breath coming in short gasps. In a few minutes Mazin came out and took his mother by the hand. She led him upstairs.

Once the bedroom door was firmly shut behind them, Mazin collapsed against his mother and began to cry. "I thought he was going to hit you," he said.

"He was close to it." Rana looked down at Mazin's averted face, realizing that she was still panting. She forced herself to take several deep, long breaths, trying to relax. She smiled at her son. "The problem with Mohammed is that he never listens, and therefore he rarely understands what one is trying to say. I do think he should get involved in the protests, but of course I didn't mean to imply that he was a coward." She glimpsed Mazin's tear-stained face and a converse irritation overwhelmed her. "You're much too old to cry. Men don't cry."

"Tell me what men do," Mazin whispered. "Do they protect their mothers against their uncles?"

"What do you mean?" Rana asked him sharply.

"Should I stand up to him, in the event that he hits you, and hit him back?"

"Of course not."

"So I'm not to cry, and I'm not to be violent. I'm just to be, I guess. Is that the right and heroic thing to do at my age?"

"At your age, options are limited. But at least you're a man, and you will outgrow the limitations set upon you." Rana gave his arm a little shake. "But I'm serious about not crying. It's time for you to toughen up a little bit."

Mazin went over to his single bed in the farthest corner away from his parent's bed, which took up the entire centre of the room. He sat and rested his forehead on his hands. "Do you say that because Khalo Mohammed said I was effeminate?"

"Of course not," snapped Rana. "Do you think I let that man influence anything I do? You know perfectly well I've been nagging you about toughness ever since you were born. When someone pushed you in the playground, didn't I exhort you to push them back? Even the twins, two years younger, used to push you around."

"It's because I didn't care who went first on the slide," Mazin replied vehemently. "I know strength is admired and people think I'm weak. I go to school, you think I haven't learned that?

I can't be what I'm not. I don't like to hit and I can't believe that I have to force myself to be violent so I can be a big man."

Rana walked over to him and ruffled his hair. "What credentials do you think society should have to define big men?"

"I don't know. Intelligence? The ability to work hard? Have you ever noticed that I get all A's, and the twins don't?" He lifted his head and his dark eyes bored into his mothers'. "I'm going to be more than them when I'm grown up, O'mmy. I'm going to have a better job, and I will be respected, without ever raising a hand to anybody. Isn't that enough for you?"

"Yes." Rana tried not to frighten her son with the intensity of her gaze. "What do you imagine yourself doing? Work-wise, I mean. When you've become a grown-up."

"I don't know. There are so many things I'd like to do."

A great weariness swept over Rana. She felt disappointed, even though she didn't know what she expected her son to say. If he had answered "actor," would she feel relieved or annoyed? Had she wanted to hear him say he wanted to be a computer programmer, something safe and ordinary like that? This day had been too much for her. One thing after another. She lay on her own bed with her back to her son and closed her eyes. Moussa's arm, the worries about her son, the argument with Mohammed. She knew that his fury would go on and on unless she apologized. What had she said? She could barely remember. Obviously, she hadn't meant he was a coward; it had come out wrong. A minor insensitivity compared to his grotesque behaviour, shrieking insults about herself and her son. There was no comparison between them.

Rana turned over on her other side with her eyes still closed. She did not want to talk to Mazin anymore. He was the real source of her worry, and she could not be assuaged. If he turned out to be homosexual, the whole family would be humiliated. They would have to throw him out. *No. Not Mazin. He is a good boy.* He would just have to keep it to himself and marry a nice girl like everyone else; he could marry someone like

Fatima, who would be glad if her husband left her alone most of the time. Anyway, he probably wasn't homosexual. It was absurd to jump to these conclusions just because she saw him strutting in front of the mirror once.

Rana rolled over again and opened her eyes to look at the door. She felt thirsty, but didn't dare to creep out and get a glass of water. She had two choices: she could hide in her room for days or write an apology that stated she had uttered words that he had misunderstood. And then, instead of getting an apology back, she would have to endure a further lecture in which he justified everything he had said and berated her for her perceived wrongs. And it would not matter if she tried to reason with him gently, pointing out quietly what she had meant, and what he had said. He would never, ever think for a single second that he had done anything wrong, or that she wasn't entirely to blame. It was so frustrating.

There was a gentle knock at the door. If Rana hadn't wanted water so badly, she would have ignored it. In a house where bedrooms were shared, the desire for privacy was respected. But she felt she would die of thirst. "Who is it?" she asked, though she knew.

"It's me," said Fatima. "I just wanted to know if you're all right, if I could get you anything."

"I'm fine. A glass of water, maybe."

When the knock came a few minutes later, it was Zaynah who pushed open the door. Rana could hear the sounds of loud voices from the kitchen. "Thank you, Zaynah. Who is your father shouting at now?"

Zaynah looked down in embarrassment. Rana listened for a moment. "Ahh, Hamid has come home. Leave the door ajar, please. Just a bit. Good girl."

Rana maneuvered herself as close to the edge of the bed as she could, despite her son's warning: "Don't, O'mmy."

"You should teach your wife to mind her step," she could hear Mohammed shouting. This was followed by Hamid's soft tones. Rana raised her head so both ears were free to listen.

"It's a terrible thing to call someone a coward. I can't believe Rana…"

"You can't believe! Ask her! Go straight up there and ask her!" Mohammed bellowed.

A few minutes later, Hamid appeared in the doorway. He carried a plate of food in one hand, and a glass of water in the other. He looked tired, but he smiled down at her.

"Thought I'd eat up here and get a bit of peace," he said, going to the small corner table by the window that often did double duty as a dining table. Hamid sat down and began to eat. He did not even ask her what had happened.

"Hello Baba," Mazin beamed, and came over to give his father a hug.

Rana remained stretched out on the bed, without talking, while Hamid checked Mazin's homework and parried some questions his son had saved for him. They played a game of cards, and then Hamid took out two photocopied Sudoku puzzles from his pocket and laid them out on either side of the bedtime table. Father and son picked up pencils and went to work.

Rana, lying on her bed, probed her insides cautiously for damage, for the familiar tendrils of depression that so often coiled around her heart after an argument with her brother. But there was nothing. She felt detached.

Soon she grew restless, wishing Mazin would go to sleep already so she could talk to Hamid privately. She was used to rushing around in the evenings, washing dishes, cleaning up, managing the settling of the household into night. She liked to pop her head into the bedroom and see the two most beloved people in the world engaged in their friendly competitions. Sometimes, she would look over their shoulders and exclaim over their prowess, since she couldn't do Sudoku at all. But she didn't want to watch it all evening, especially when she was bursting with the need to talk to her husband herself.

Finally, they both got up to wash their teeth and prepare for bed, slipping under the covers at the same time. Rana lay rigidly on her side with her back to them both, listening for the change in breathing that indicated sleep and readying to kick if Hamid's breathing changed before Mazin's.

As soon as she was sure Mazin was asleep, she rolled over towards her husband. He was wide awake and opened his arms to receive her, nestling her like a fragile bird under his arm. "Rough day?" he murmured into her hair.

"Parts," Rana said. And she told him in detail about the argument with Mohammed, and how she had fixed Moussa's arm.

"My goodness," Hamid laughed. "Your days are so much more interesting than mine!"

Rana lifted her head to listen to her son's breathing again.

"Oof," snorted her son in protest, and then she knew he was asleep and dreaming. Still, she debated about sharing her worries with Hamid. She loved him; he was her best friend and loyal supporter. But men were funny about things like homosexuality. She was almost sure that his reaction would be instant denial, which would not assuage her worries at all. Would there be a chance that he would look at his own son differently? Might he not start to probe, ask questions, or change how he interacted with his son? That would be terrible; there was something so beautiful about their relationship, just as it was. She decided not to mention it. She would wait a while, and see what happened. Probably she was being ridiculous, and Mazin was too young to even think in terms of what direction he was going in. He was different from other boys, he had always been. Even at six years old he hadn't had any friends. And that had nothing to do with his sexuality. The thought was preposterous. He was sensitive, with a vivid imagination; he saw a rose and he stuck it in his hair in order to copy his beloved cousin. He looked in the mirror and was transformed into something else, just like when he used to dance in the corner of the school in that odd way that used to annoy her so much. How could she have thought that any of this was connected to his sexuality? He was only a child; she was being ridiculous.

Rana snuggled deeper into her husband's warm armpit. "There are only two choices open to me. Either I must apologize, or spend weeks in a cold silence, escaping to my room as soon as dinner is finished."

"Why don't you say that you are sorry for having sparked such an unpleasant and upsetting conversation?" suggested Hamid. "That way you would be telling the truth, and appeasing him at the same time."

Rana lifted her head and caught some of his armpit hairs in her teeth. Hamid laughed and jerked away from her. "Who made you so wise?" she asked. "How come I had the luck to marry someone who could help me grow as a human being and become ... better? Wiser."

Hamid beamed down at her. "I didn't do so badly myself. You're rather clever too when you put your mind to it."

Rana reached over him to turn out the light, pinching him on the way. The room was plunged into darkness. "It's a shame Fatima is unable to influence Mohammed's character in any way. She's a darling, and I couldn't ask for a better sister-in-law, but she is incapable of saying a word against him."

Hamid heard the soft rustle that meant his wife was discarding her clothes. He reached over to turn the light back on so he could watch his wife undress. "If you were a fly on the wall of their bedroom, I think you'd be surprised. I bet Fatima exerts her influence in more ways than you think. I bet she's up there now, letting the waves of his anger bounce off her, waiting for an opportune moment to say, 'I didn't hear Rana call you a coward.'"

"Do you think so? Perhaps you are right, but she still won't influence him."

"Mohammed listens, even though he doesn't seem to. There have been several occasions when I've made a suggestion to him, which he's rejected vehemently, and later adopted. I think his automatic reaction is to rebuff, but then when he's on his own he mulls it over."

Rana slipped on top of her husband and sat up, straddling him. "So according to you, poor Fatima will whisper something in my defense and suffer ten minutes of shouted abuse and ridicule, but then sometime in the night he'll reflect on her words?" Rana lifted her hands above her head to stretch, so Hamid could admire her breasts. She was proud of her husband's love of her body.

He reached up and cupped them. "Something like that. If he's really angry the transformation might take a little longer, but I've often heard him adopt one of my opinions as though it was his own, even though he had argued against the exact same opinion." Hamid reached up to kiss the hard softness of her nipple. "I love you."

Rana pulled away from him. "Doesn't it embarrass him to do that?"

"I'm not sure he's even aware of it. He has a selective memory about these things. Bend down so I can kiss you."

Rana reared back in the opposite direction, and leant against his bent knees. "If what you say is true, then there's hope he'll let me contribute in some way to the efforts of the brave protesters. He might even begin to support the protest movement himself! It's important to present our side logically, without emotion...."

"Your husband forbids you to have anything to do with the protests," Hamid interrupted sternly.

Rana smiled. She let her own knees fall slightly apart, so that he could glimpse her sex. "You, I can manage." She watched him looking at her. When his hand began to creep towards her, she arrested its movement.

"Rana..." he sighed. She could feel him pressing against her back. She lifted herself over his penis and hesitated for a moment before she pushed herself against him.

He groaned, but she did not let him in. "Rana."

"Yes, dear Hamid? You were saying that you understand how frustrating it must be to believe so passionately in a cause and yet be prevented from supporting it. A woman of my strength and energy..."

"Rana!" Hamid cried more urgently.

She glanced at her son's back, although he rarely woke up once he was sleeping. She began to rub along his penis, back and forth, slowly. Images came into her mind as she closed her eyes. She was wearing a beautiful dress and her hair was spilling down her back. The man was a king, with an air of authority, but his face transformed each time: he could be a famous movie star, a man she had glimpsed on the street, or Kassam himself with his extraordinary blue eyes. She was there against her will, and she was outraged. He offered her food and drink, but she stood aloof, her long black tresses a veil. He would come and part the tresses, but if she tried to push him away it only inflamed him more. He laughed, his hands travelled along her body, pulling her against him. Sometimes she ran, but he ran faster. He bent dark eyes of lust upon her, and despite herself, some inner flame burned in response.

Hamid gripped her thighs, and Rana opened her eyes and gazed down at him as she rubbed back and forth. This part took time. The man had to overwhelm her protests with fiery kisses, his passion trailing a red-hot path to her nipples. She beat futilely against his back, biting her lips at the same time so her yearning could not escape, so he would not know. It was vitally important that he should not know. Only when this imaginary man thrust inside her could she climax, pressing against Hamid with a whimper. He whispered again, "Rana," but waited still, as she positioned herself on top of him and slid slowly down, enveloping him like a sheath. Then she allowed him to move, and they rocked together until his face contracted as if in pain and he shuddered. Rana lowered herself leisurely until she lay on top of him, careful to keep them still joined, savouring a sudden feeling of joy. Surely, this profound union was unique to them. The rest of the world could not experience it this way. Look at the West, and how women leapt from lover to lover, husband to husband. How could they be experiencing this intense connectedness that forged an unbreakable bond between two people? They were joined. Two human beings, literally joined. Fatima could never experience such a thing with Mohammed. It seemed ludicrous to even imagine them together. Rana often attempted to exhort bits of information from the bashful Fatima, but she still could not visualize them together in a way that seemed realistic.

Rana rolled off her husband and picked up his underwear to wipe first him, then herself. She lay back with a sigh. Hamid turned onto his side and placed his arm across her; she knew it was only minutes before he would be fast asleep. Only then would she extricate herself gently and creep to the bathroom in the hopes that the rest of the household slept and she could bathe in peace. Rana turned her head and looked at her husband's face. She knew every line, every crease. Every hair in his nose. She felt one with him.

It had not always been so.

She had known nothing about sex at first; there had been no Internet in Rana's youth and nobody had explained anything. The first night of marriage had been a cruel destruction of expectations. For years, she had been masturbating, surreptitiously rubbing a roll of sheet between her legs while powerful men chased her through the mazes of her mind, disrobing and mastering her, while a warm heaviness permeated her lower body. From the moment she was betrothed to Hamid, his face had dominated her imagination: his face looked down on her with a sardonic sneer as he clasped her to his breast and the sheet moved rhythmically between her legs, achieving warmth but never climax because who knew there was such a thing? The hand had stayed slow and cautious and never forgot the siblings who shared her room, was never allowed to speed up or become unruly.

Before their marriage, Rana's imagination had raged. Hamid's fingers wrapped around his teacup were stroking down her skin. Staring at his hands, nobody could accuse her of immodesty — the Koran itself told Muslims to "lower their gaze and guard their modesty." She had never been left alone with him, but twice she pretended to stumble as they walked together with their chaperones so she could feel his body against hers. She had felt like a wound-up spring of frustration.

How could the reality fail to disappoint? Hamid had not been the experienced, bold lover of her imagination. His hands had been irritatingly clumsy, he was in an agony of embarrassment, and he kept deferring to her wishes by repeating, "Do you mind if I do this?" or "I'm so sorry, could you move a little to the right?" until she wanted to scream. Her dreams of futile resistance had ill-prepared her for taking charge herself, so she lay woodenly, contaminated by his confusion. Then, after agonizing minutes of fumbling down below, he had tried to maneuver his way in, apologizing as he went. The pain had been a shock, and she cried out as he contritely continued to push. She had to restrain herself from shoving him away.

It had not gotten better all at once, though Rana did like other aspects of her new husband. He was a good man, and she soon grew to love him as a partner and a confidante, if not as a lover. Then, one day, they had been left miraculously alone in the house and he had come into the bathroom while she was in the shower. Laughing, he had taken off his clothes and stepped into the shower with her. He had captured the showerhead and teasingly sprayed it between her legs. She had giggled and fended him off, but he held her and continued to spray while she struggled. This was more like it! This was fun! Then he had not been able to control himself anymore and he was inside her, but not before the stream of water had evoked a curious sensation.

The next time she was in the shower, she had immediately directed the stream between her legs again and instantly the same sensation returned and intensified, like pressure building in a volcano. Her eyes had widened with shock at the spiralling pleasure, and her mouth had dropped open in utter amazement as her body responded to the stream of water. A secret nodule that had magically — unbelievably — burst into flame when stimulated in just the right way. Rana had cried out in sheer incredulity, and crouched over the showerhead, drawing that little nodule up the spiral staircase of sensation to crescendo again and again, laughing and gasping because it was like magic. How incredible that the human body contained this hidden, magic spot, created for no earthly reason except pleasure. Thank you, Allah.

But the bathroom had its limits, so the desire to exploit this newly discovered miracle led to surreptitious explorations in bed.

"What are you doing?" Hamid had asked. "Have you got a pain?"

There had been a strange reluctance to tell him. Even though Allah had included astounding surprises in His design of the human body, human beings had tainted this miracle with shame. "Nothing," she had replied, desisting.

But night after night, her fingers had crept along to rediscover the phenomena, to see if fingers could achieve the marvels of showerheads, until one day, when Hamid had jerked the covers back abruptly and got slowly to his knees. He had stared so fixedly that Rana froze in fear, until she saw his penis jutting against the cloth of his boxers. His intense excitement had transmitted itself to her, and her hand began to move again, until he pushed it away and put his own finger there and massaged with gusto in entirely the wrong place, and she had giggled and shyly moved his finger a smidgen to the right, and when the miracle started to happen she closed her eyes to shut out his sweating face, and heard his delighted chuckle when she gasped, and then he was sliding inside her and there was no pain at all, and she had wrapped her legs around him to push him deeper.

"Our marriage is perfect," she had whispered to Hamid. "Too perfect. I am almost frightened."

He had stroked her hair. "Frightened?"

"I don't deserve so much happiness."

"Of course you deserve it. You are a wonderful woman."

She had shaken off his hand impatiently. "I don't deserve more happiness than anyone else."

"We all have our fair share of trials and tribulations. If you are especially lucky in your marriage, then perhaps there will be other areas of suffering."

"How can you say that? Everybody is rich and safe in America, while half the population starves or dies of AIDS in Africa. It's not equal!"

"If it's not equal, then you don't need to be frightened by your joy, do you?"

And she had smiled, revelling in their intellectual equality, his ability to guide her to new understanding while soothing her, and to the growing intimacy within every facet of their relationship.

Fifteen years later, the promise of those early times had been fulfilled. He was her confidante, her advisor, her lover. She no longer worried about the unfairness of this gift. Without Hamid, her life would be nothing. She could not survive in Mohammed's household without him. She would take his advice and apologize for having sparked such an unpleasant and upsetting conversation. Perhaps she would write it, in case bile rose in her throat and choked her when she faced him. The outrageousness of being forced to apologize when his own behaviour was so diabolical. Why did she have to? He would not really kick her out of the home, not for something like this. She could stay out of his way, disappearing into her room as soon as he came home. That would not be a hardship; it would be a relief!

Not to Mazin. Not to Fatima. She must appease the lion in his den, for the sake of others. She took pen and paper and scribbled the necessary words to create peace and harmony in the home. Then she crept downstairs and left it beside the coffee pot in the kitchen, where he would be sure to see it in the morning. She continued onto the bathroom to wash away the residue of her husband's love.

CHAPTER 5 **ZAYNAH**

ZAYNAH CROUCHED UNDER HER COVERS, scribbling furiously, searching her memory for every word uttered between Ahmed and Mohammed at the dinner table. Argument and counter-argument. As though somehow, through the writing, truth would come. At almost thirteen, she believed in absolute truth. Every opinion was either right or wrong. Her instincts prompted her to side with Ahmed — her brave, selfless uncle. Her handsome, brilliant, wonderful uncle whose sensitive lips trembled at the corners when her father yelled at him. Those same sensitive lips that she sometimes imagined, in wicked moments, pressing against hers in an unbrotherly fashion. At such times she hated her father, but her respect for him was too great to dismiss what he said. He must be right because he was older and smarter than anyone. And sometimes, when a frozen silence reigned around the dinner table after a dispute, she could feel the tinge of condemnation. Furtive glances around the table showed faces stiff with varying emotions, all negative. Her mother avoided Mohammed's eye, treating him like a difficult child that should be appeased. *Acting like a long-suffering martyr*, Zaynah sometimes thought. The children trembled before him in trepidation. Rana's face reflected fury and hate. And her father's face looked weary and old. *It must be very hard*, Zaynah thought, *to behave well when everybody thinks you are unreasonable.*

These thoughts she scribbled in her diary, as well as a minute depiction of her day, ranging from school gossip to the particulars of each meal. She wrote and wrote in a frenzy, determined to inscribe every detail and still have time to read before her mother came to put her light out. Then Mazin would visit, and after that, if there was opportunity, a clandestine sojourn outside the doors of various occupants in the household, once the family had retired. She did not know why she felt compelled to do this; somehow, it felt like if she knew what was going on, then she could help. If Fatima cried because Mohammed criticized her expenditure, Zaynah could refrain from asking for anything, and prevent the twins from asking too, even if they needed it. Sometimes she had discovered through the door that her father was furious about something, and the next day had managed to pacify his anger by innocently painting the incident in a different light. She was sure that keeping her finger on the pulse of her family enabled her to promote peace and harmony. And when she overheard things that were not meant for her ears, she never, ever passed them on. It was an unspoken pact with the unaware informants — their secrets were safe with her. For example, her father would never know that his sister and wife were patching up protesters. Zaynah wouldn't even spill that particular tidbit of information to Mazin, having learned from experience how uncontrollable secrets became once they got away from you.

She scribbled frantically, racing against time.

O'mmy entered the room, smiling at her daughter and asking her usual tired questions before turning the lamp off. As soon as she had gone, Zaynah switched it back on again — just a few more sentences would complete this vital exposé of her day.

Five minutes later there was a light knock at the door and Mazin slipped in, giggling like a schoolgirl. "Khalé Fatima almost caught me," he panted, throwing himself over the foot of her bed. "What are you writing?"

Zaynah's first instinct was to snap the diary shut, but then

she remembered there was something she wanted to show
Mazin. Thumbing through the diary, she found the page and
held it out to him. At the top it was written: *What is a Hero?*

"Are you still writing about that? Don't you know that
my mother apologized to Khalo Mohammed days ago? Even
though she didn't even call him a coward in the first place."

"I know it happened days ago, but she's still showing her
hate all the time and he feels it. It's no wonder he gets so angry
with her, having this person hating you in your own home."

"Of course she hates him, she gets the brunt of his anger
every time. Everybody hates him."

"No they don't," Zaynah snapped. "He supports the whole
family. We couldn't even live in a house like this without him,
and eat better than anybody else at school. Your mother should
think about that sometimes."

Mazin leapt to his feet in anger. "My mother's the one that
keeps the house together, and makes sure we have good food.
All he's doing is making the money! That doesn't give him
the right to act like a king and boss everybody around and hit
them when they disagree with him! My poor mother has been
depressed ever since that fight, even though she apologized."

"All right, keep your voice down! It doesn't matter. They're
both hotheaded siblings and they're both stupid. You haven't
even read my diary yet. Isn't it an interesting question? What is
a hero? What exactly does it take to be a hero, do you think?"

Mazin looked down at the diary. Below the title there was
a list:

1. *Someone who fights for what he believes in.*
2. *Someone who protects his family from harm.*
3. *Someone who is noble.*
4. *Someone who helps others even when it puts them in*
danger. Like the doctors who help the protesters even
when they don't believe in what they're doing. They are
showing compassion.

Mazin looked up. "Ammo Ahmed is a hero, why don't you list his traits? He's modest, kind, gentle, full of love for his family. He's fighting for what he thinks is right."

Zaynah looked at him with shining eyes. "Yes, he is a hero, isn't he?"

Mazin nodded solemnly. "The twins spoke to Ammo Ahmed today and asked him how they might contribute to the fight for democracy."

"How do you know that?" Zaynah demanded, jealous of his information.

"I went with them," Mazin retorted simply. "Ammo Ahmed more or less said they were too young to do anything and it is too dangerous. Then the twins, you know the twins, they jumped about begging for something to do, and Ammo Ahmed said that the biggest issue was the people who have been hurt but cannot go to the hospital because they would be dragged off to prison along with anybody who dared to help them, but what could children do for them?" Mazin's brow furrowed in concentration. He had listened avidly to the conversation in order to repeat every detail to Zaynah. "Then the twins said they could help those heroes who had set up makeshift clinics for the protesters who couldn't go to hospital. They said they could wipe foreheads and bring water, that sort of thing. Ammo Ahmed said he would think about it and let them know."

"He shouldn't have said that. He can't ask the twins to do anything if their father forbids it."

"That's exactly what I thought!" Mazin yelped in delight. He sidled over to the wall and began to scrutinize the photos that covered it. "I almost told him he was totally out of line, and that Khalo Mohammed would kick him out of the house quicker than..."

"He's not out of line! He sees all those poor people suffering and his compassion and heroic instincts compel him to accept any help he can get," interrupted an inconsistent but loving Zaynah.

Mazin grinned at a photo of himself as a baby sitting in the dust with a chicken perched on his fat, baby knee, obviously debating whether it was worth pecking. Mazin's face, as he stared at the chicken in helpless disbelief, was just beginning that crunching-up process that a baby's face undergoes before it starts to cry.

"Excuse me," barked Zaynah. "I don't want to disturb you or anything. Would you like me to exit my room so you can look at my photos more conveniently?"

Mazin turned. "You're very argumentative tonight. I'm going."

Zaynah almost snapped back "No I'm not," but cut it off just in time. It was true that Mazin depended on her to be his sounding board. He poured every emotion into her ear, and she listened. She was a great listener. But everything annoyed her today, and she wasn't sure why. Perhaps there had been too many late-night sojourns recently, hovering outside doors to gather information instead of sleeping. But her father was so angry lately, she had to trace the nuances of his changing moods, so she could act appropriately the following day. If she discovered that he was still angry because Rana thought he was a coward, then she would find an opportunity to call him brave. That, coupled with Fatima's gentle insistence that he had completely misunderstood what Rana had meant, that she had not been thinking of him at all, might move him out of the angry and resentful bed that Rana had made for him. It was already working; the last two nights he hadn't mentioned Rana at all.

She would not listen tonight. She was too tired.

The following day was Friday, and as usual the family sat down to a late breakfast together. Rana's food offerings had been a little less varied lately — Zaynah noticed that she often seemed tired — but there was still ful medames on Friday mornings to warm the belly and the soul. Zaynah dispensed cheerfulness, watching her father out of the corner of her eye as she urged him to take a little more, serving Ahmed with a hand that trembled slightly, in its effort to curl around the ladle attractively. Rana stood by the stove, removed, stirring the ful medames while the rest of the family ate.

"You're not going to work today, Abi? It's a rest day," Zaynah chided him, noticing his work clothes.

"Sick animals still need to be fed, even on rest days," Mohammed answered, smiling. The twins noticed his composure and dared to commence an under-the-table tug of war with a pen.

"What are you doing?" Mohammed asked, not ungently.

"Ali thinks he is stronger than me. Hah!" exclaimed Abdul, pausing for a second to gauge the effect this was having on Mohammed. Reassured by the smile tugging at Mohammed's lips, they both stood up at exactly the same moment and pulled up their shirts, exposing skinny little chests. "Who is stronger, Abi? Who is stronger?"

Mohammed laughed and beckoned them over. "I have to look closer," he said, poking and prodding each of their chests in turn. They dissolved into giggles as his fingers dug into the crevices between their ribs. Zaynah's antenna waved around the table: Ahmed was grinning and Fatima was smiling in delight. Even Rana had turned from her incessant activity at the sink.

Zaynah tried to catch Mazin's eye to exchange a look of contempt, but he was smiling so hard she could see the food in his mouth. What was the matter with them all? Why on earth did her mother look so proud? Because she had spawned silly twins? If Zaynah bared her chest, they would beat her senseless. Proud? It was ridiculous.

Zaynah glowered down at her plate and watched the twins surreptitiously for the rest of the meal. They were so full of themselves today.

Mohammed got up to go, hesitated for a moment, and then bent over to kiss his wife on the cheek. "Goodbye, Fatima."

"Goodbye." Fatima shot an anxious look at Rana as her

husband closed the door behind him. "Have you noticed that Mohammed has suddenly started to say goodbye when he leaves for work?"

Rana, now that he was gone, took her place at the table and ladled some ful medames into her bowl. "So?"

"He didn't used to," said Fatima feebly.

"Perhaps he's learning the basics of politeness. It is fairly normal to bid people farewell when you leave them for the day."

"He's working more, too. Have you noticed? He comes home later and later. And he never worked more than an hour or two on the weekends but now the weekends are like regular days."

"Good." Rana slammed her spoon on the table and got up.

Zaynah watched them with interest as she began to clear the table, but lost interest in Ammé Rana's rigid back after a few moments and returned her attention to the twins. It seemed to her that there was a naughty expression on their faces. Definitely a mischievous glint. Perhaps their squirming self-satisfaction wasn't only due to their father's indulgent attention. And they were whispering again; it got on her nerves sometimes, their incessant whispering. It couldn't be anything to do with Khalo Ahmed; they had only talked with him last night. She began to rush through the dishes.

The twins left the table and went up to their room. As soon as Zaynah had finished cleaning the kitchen, she rushed upstairs, stilling her footsteps at the summit so she could creep along to the twins' room and listen at the keyhole.

"Zaynah!" Rana's voice floated up from below. "Can you feed the chickens for me?"

A wave of frustration engulfed her, but she dashed downstairs obediently. She would feed the chickens so fast they would think a hurricane was spewing corn on them.

Normally, it was her favourite chore. The chickens were so funny, with their hierarchies of dominance. She especially liked the chicks scuttling around with their incessant peeping, all fluffy and vulnerable. A new batch of chicks had just hatched, and as Zaynah opened the door to their coop, anticipation overcame irritated resignation. She bent forward, clucking at them affectionately, holding the grain in her hand so they would have to come close to peck. The dominant hens marched forward to demand their share first. Three of the hens had gone broody, and the fertilized eggs had been distributed indiscriminately under them. The resulting chicks viewed all three as Mother, while the Mothers supervised and protected them all, thereby demonstrating the benefits of community childrearing in their own quiet way. The maternal hens dropped bits of choice grain on the floor for their adopted progeny, clucking with a distinct warble that clearly said: Come and get it. The chicks zipped around, cheeping maniacally, while Zaynah smiled and chucked some grain further out so that the gentle could also eat. The chicks were the lowest in the hierarchy, but their mothers would bristle and peck at any hen that bullied them, except for Henny Penny. In the absence of a rooster, Henny Penny was Queen of the harem, and pecked aggressively at all and sundry. Henny Penny taught the chicks that strayed too close that not all hens were Mothers, as her vicious beak flung yellow, peeping blobs hither and thither through the air. "Naughty Henny Penny!" Zaynah scolded, waving her away as she eyed a chick malevolently. She scooped the chick up and nestled its softness against her lips. It was important to view them as collectively adorable, rather than forming favourites, in case they turned out to be roosters. Eating one's favourite ruined the flavour of the soup. She hoped they would all be hens.

Zaynah stiffened suddenly. She distinctly heard the sound of a door closing and feet clattering down the stairs. Certain now that the twins were focused on nefarious plans, Zaynah scattered the rest of the grain willy-nilly and hastened to her own room. She stopped only long enough to grab a scarf, which she wrapped around her head to hide her hair and partially obscure her face as she slipped out the front door. The twins were just turning the corner at the end of the street, marching defiantly in the direction of the square. Zaynah's heart started to beat faster. She felt like a sleuth, but she also felt frightened. These were dangerous times, and the twins did not seem to understand that. She was their older sister, and it was her job to protect them. It was too bad she hadn't had time to recruit Mazin's aid; she would have felt safer with him by her side.

Zaynah rounded the corner and stopped dead, fading sideways into the shadows of a convenient alley. The twins had also halted and were looking around furtively. They were still several blocks from the main square. What were they doing? Zaynah hardly dared to breathe as she peeked around the brick corner of the alley. The twins were gazing up at an enormous billboard featuring the benign face of their murderous dictator. They looked around again, then Abdul bent down and Ali removed his shoes and shimmied up his back until he was resting with his knees on his brother's shoulders. Abdul slowly stood up, leaning heavily against the bottom of the billboard. Was this why they had been comparing strength at the breakfast table? To see who would carry whom? But what were they doing?

Once Abdul was standing, Ali looked around once again at the deserted streets. They had picked a time when most people would be at prayer. Ali crooked one knee and placed his foot on his brother's shoulder, then the other foot, and as Abdul had done he slowly uncurled his body to its full height, leaning heavily against the billboard. His head now hid the dictator's chin. He reached up, his hand gripping a marker, and finally Zaynah understood what they were doing. She watched, mesmerized, as scars dripping blood materialized over the face of the dictator; fangs protruded from his thin lips and snot dripped from his nose. A gaggle of young people approached from the other end of the street. Both Zaynah and the twins froze; the young people drew nearer, shading their eyes against the sun as they peered at the human ladder. Zaynah's heart hammered painfully against her ribs. What would she do if fingers pointed in denunciation? She would rush forward, grab the twins by the hand and run. Not home, not directly leading Death to her family, but plunging down circuitous routes in an attempt to shake off their enemies. She would risk her life to save her brothers. She knew that quite simply.

The gaggle of students pointed at the poster. For a second, the blood roaring through her ears prevented her from hearing what they said. But then she saw they were laughing, slapping each other on the back and then slapping Abdul, who teetered dangerously.

"Good for you!" she finally heard. "Together we'll succeed!" As soon as they moved on, Zaynah leapt out of her hiding place like an avenging angel, pelted across the street and delivered a maiming blow to the formerly vaunted skinny chest. Ali skidded down his brother's back as Abdul folded gracefully to the floor, in the very act of inserting a snake in the dictator's ear. The twins sat on the pavement and looked meekly up at their enraged sister.

"Are you mad?" she hissed. "Have you not understood anything I've said to you?"

A family appeared on the other side of the road, strolling in their direction. "Get up and start walking," growled Zaynah. The family stopped before the desecrated poster, looking up at it. As one, their heads turned to scan the retreating backs of the three children. Zaynah walked with a straight back and her head held high, her fingers gripping her brothers' hands like steel traps. All senses were trained on the street behind her, but there was nothing, no sound of pursuing footsteps fuelled by righteousness. As soon as they stood in front of their own door she stopped abruptly and wrenched the twins around to face her. "What do you think you were doing?"

They shrugged, irritatingly in unison, and watched her.

"Did someone put you up to this?"

Two heads shook vehemently.

"And how do you think graffiti, vandalism, is going to help our cause?"

Owlish looks.

"Answer me!" she screamed suddenly into their faces, dispassionately observing her spittle land on Abdul's cheek.

"Just a bit of fun, Zaynah."

"Don't take it so hard, Zaynah."

She burst into tears, and at the same time leaned forward and vomited into the shrubbery lining the walkway leading to their house. The twins looked on in silence, exchanging anxious looks.

"Are you all right, Zaynah?"

"Do you feel sick, Zaynah?"

"I'm not sick," she intoned dully, wiping her mouth with the edge of her scarf. "I am frightened. Unlike you imbeciles, I understand what might have happened to you, to our family, if someone who happens to support the government walked by while you were ... having your fun!"

There was a note of bitterness in her voice. The twins strived to erase it, interchanging sentences. "It's not like you think."

"We'd thought it all out really carefully."

"On Fridays at prayer time the streets are practically empty."

"We calculated exactly how long it would take us."

"We watched the street during the same period of time for several Fridays running..."

"...so we knew it was unlikely anyone would see us."

"There wasn't much danger." They both stopped, gazing into their sister's ashen face.

Zaynah took several deep breaths, trying to draw pure air past the acridness in her throat. "Ten people saw you today," she said. "Ten people. That's the possibility of death to every member of our family, multiplied by ten. And for what? To add some snot to the nose of Kassam, as though that helps the cause in any way!" She leaned forward and grasped their shoulders; she wanted to shake them until it hurt. "You fools. How could you? After all I've told you?"

The twins shook their heads, staring in disbelief at the tears coursing down their sister's face.

"This must never happen again. You aren't just risking your own lives, but the rest of the family too."

They nodded eagerly; no, it would never happen again.

Zaynah laughed harshly. "Do you think I'll ever trust you again? You've already broken promises to me, remember?"

"You can trust us, Zaynah,"

"We didn't know it would upset you so."

"It's nothing to do with how upset I am!" Her voice soared again, and the twins involuntarily glanced towards the house.

"Shhh, Zaynah. It's all right. We promise never to do it again."

"We really promise now. Double promise. We can exchange blood if you'd like to bind us to our promise."

"But quiet down some, Zaynah. O'mmy will hear."

Zaynah looked at them. "That's what I want," she said quietly. "For her to hear."

Both twins grabbed one of her hands. "No, Zaynah! She will tell our father."

"Yes," Zaynah replied quietly. "That is the only way."

Now it was the twins turn to cry. They seized both her hands, covered them with kisses, dropped to their knees and begged. "We will never do it again, we promise! Give us one more chance, one more!"

Then the door opened and Rana walked out, closely followed by Fatima, blinking in the sunshine. "What's going on?"

"The twins have desecrated a poster of Kassam."

The harmony of their expressions ebbed away. "Be quiet! Come inside, quickly!" Their strange furtive glances down the street mirrored those of the twins earlier. It was impossible to know whom one could trust, so it was safer to trust nobody. They were ushered into the kitchen, that warm family haven of delectable cuisine smells where less than an hour ago anxiety was focused on Mohammed's mood. Now, perhaps, it was focused on life and death.

Rana sat the children in a row and stood before them, arms crossed. "Now, what has happened?"

Zaynah sat silent, knowing she had said enough. The twins burst into speech, but Rana held up a peremptory hand: "One at a time! Ali, you first."

As they spoke, Rana's face grew darker and Fatima clutched the fabric of her dress convulsively. When the twins had finished, Rana ordered the children up to their rooms.

"What, me too?" asked Zaynah. "What have I done, apart from saving the family, probably?" Fatima made a movement as if to order her to get along too, but Rana forestalled her. "Perhaps Zaynah has earned the right to stay."

Zaynah felt speechless with gratitude and hunkered down at the table in an unconscious desire to observe without being observed, as was her wont.

The two women looked at each other. Fatima's eyes questioned mutely.

"You'll have to tell Mohammed."

"But he'll be so angry!"

"Nevertheless," Rana's dark eyes flickered towards her niece. Fatima understood; it was not a secret.

"He will punish them," she whispered.

"Perhaps he will restrict their freedom. That would be a good thing."

"Perhaps he will…." Fatima grabbed her sister's hands, tears running down her cheeks. Zaynah's eyes immediately filled and she was around the table and on her knees before her mother in seconds, burying her face in her mother's knees and sobbing.

"I'm so sorry, O'mmy! It's all my fault."

"What have you to be sorry for, child?"

"I meant for you to hear. I could have kept it to myself, but I wanted them to be punished."

Fatima's slim brown fingers grasped her daughter's chin and

raised her face. She gazed into her luminous, tear-filled eyes. "Of course you had to tell me, Zaynah. You did exactly the right thing. Your father must punish them so they never do such a thing again, and that is the right thing too." Fatima's voice caught a little on the last words, and mother and daughter hugged and wept together.

Zaynah lay on her bed most of the afternoon, filled with an indescribable dread. Mazin crept in and lay down beside her at one point, and she whispered into his ears the whole story.

"I wish I'd been with you," he said.

"I wished that too, but it wouldn't have made any difference. Would you have done the same thing?"

"Yes!" he answered stoutly, but something in his voice drew her to her knees, the better to gaze into his face.

"You wouldn't have told on them, would you?"

"Yes I would. I would, Zaynah! They are jeopardizing all our lives. We've already told them, you and I. We tried to do it by ourselves, but they wouldn't listen."

"They'll listen now."

"What will he do?" Mazin asked.

"What will he do?" Zaynah repeated dully.

They waited, hand in hand. There was no sound in the house. Even little Na'aman was silent, oppressed by the pervading atmosphere of trepidation. Fatima brought him in for his nap, starting when she perceived Mazin on the bed. "You shouldn't be in here," she said severely.

"Please, O'mmy, he brings me comfort," pleaded Zaynah. "It's only Mazin."

Fatima looked at him for a moment, smiling uncertainly, beseechingly at her. Then she nodded and left the room.

They lay there, the two of them, hour after hour. "He should be home soon," said Mazin.

"He often gets home really late these days," Zaynah replied. "He might not be here until bedtime."

"Let's go and see the twins."

"What?"

"Let's offer them ... comfort. However bad we feel, imagine what they must be going through."

"How can we offer them comfort?"

"I don't know, you'll think of something. You always give comfort to me when I'm in trouble."

Zaynah ruffled his hair in a burst of affection. Then her eyes filled with tears. "I can't," she said. "I can only give comfort when the pain is caused by others. This time I have caused the pain."

"No, Zaynah!" Mazin protested. "You mustn't feel guilty. You had to tell someone, of course you did." But he did not suggest going to visit the twins again.

In the early evening, the front door banged and the household tensed as one. Zaynah and Mazin sat up in bed, holding hands tightly, listening. There was nothing to be heard, so imagination took over. Fatima was placing food in front of her husband. Probably they were alone in the kitchen; Rana would have tactfully disappeared. She would sit with him, watch him eat. He would smile and joke with her, pleased at this rare opportunity to be alone with his wife, his good mood of the morning carrying him through.

Then she would tell him. Zaynah could picture the changing expression on his face exactly. His face was always so expressive. One could tell whether he was angry by looking at one feature only — his brow, his mouth, his eyes, all bespoke anger, or amusement, or sadness. But what would he do? The waiting was unbearable.

Their tense ears heard his steps mounting the stairs, slowly and heavily. "He's sad," Zaynah whispered. "He will talk to them, and they will see his sadness, and be ashamed."

They heard him go into the twins' room. Zaynah's ears strained, but she could not hear her father's voice. "He is speaking quietly," she said. "Let's go and listen at the door."

"You can't do that," protested Mazin, shocked.

"Why not? I do it all the time. How do you think I know everything that's going on in this family?"

"It's not right," Mazin said. "This is a private discussion between father and sons."

"What do you think I'm listening to when I creep down the hallways at night? Public conversations?" Zaynah put one foot out of bed; it had just touched the floor when it froze.

The silence of the house erupted in a cacophony of screams. The twins. Zaynah's foot remained riveted to the floor. She focused on the texture of the cold, smooth tile under her toes. One twin was screaming, the other was crying for mercy. "Please no, please no, please no," he wailed.

Then another sound entered the mix. Fatima's voice, beseeching and entreating outside the door, intermittently supplicating her husband and praying to Allah for mercy.

"It's enough, it's enough!" the poor woman cried, her voice breaking. "Please, Mohammed, merciful husband, it's enough."

Zaynah glanced at Mazin. His teeth had clamped down on his lips and a drop of blood stained the pallor of his face. Still, the screams went on. The second voice had changed from cries to whimpers, like a dog in pain. The horror of it! Her soul revulsed as images entered her mind unbidden, exacerbating the reality being endured on the other side of that door. Zaynah closed her eyes, her foot still glued to the floor. She could almost feel the ... what? The hand? The belt ... striking into her own flesh. How long could he go on, inflicting pain on his helpless sons while his wife sobbed on the other side of the door? And it was her fault. All her fault.

As abruptly as they had begun, the screams stopped. Fatima's voice also cut off mid-invocation. Zaynah heard the door open and close, and her father's heavy tread retreating down the hallway to his own room. Instantly, she was up and out the door.

"Where are you going?" Mazin called. "Hey, wait!"

Zaynah slipped into the twins' room on the heels of her

mother, trepidation beating against her ribcage. The twins were lying face down on their beds, their shirts crumpled on the floor. Welts criss-crossed their backs, red and sore-looking. Fatima wove from one to the other, stroking their hair back from their sweat-covered foreheads, her tears mingling with theirs. Zaynah crossed the room and took Abdul by the hand, bending to whisper in his ear, "It is over now. The worst is over." She whispered the same message in Ali's ear, the only message of comfort she could think of. It must be a relief to them that it was over, even as it was to her.

The door opened again and Rana came in, bearing a bowl of warm water and some clean rags, antiseptic cream, and bandages. She motioned to Zaynah with her head. "Bring some more water."

Zaynah rushed downstairs, eager to do her bidding, eager to help to bring relief to her wounded brothers. She hovered beside Rana as she worked, taking the sullied rags and cleaning them, grinding her teeth when the twins whimpered. They all jumped when Mohammed appeared in the doorway. Zaynah looked him full in the face as he gazed impassively on the ravage of his sons' backs. "Give them some aspirin to help with the pain," he said.

The backs, cleaned, daubed with antiseptic cream, and swathed in clean bandages, finally looked tolerable. The twins, fortified with aspirin, agreed to eat something. Zaynah could have broken into hysterical laughter; she had been so certain that recovery would take weeks. She and Fatima sat on the floor, one beside the head of each twin, and spooned a little broth into their mouths as they lay on their stomachs. Abdul looked fixedly at Zaynah's hands as they traversed the space between bowl and mouth. She did not know what he was thinking; she did not know if he had any energy left to think at all. "I didn't know," she whispered at last. "I didn't think it would be like that."

"I'll never forgive him," Abdul whispered.

Zaynah felt relief. I'll never forgive *him*, he had said. Not her.

Later, she crouched by Ali, smoothing his hair away from his eyes. "I didn't know that would happen," she whispered again.

"Neither did I," he responded, and a tear seeped out of the corner of his eye. Zaynah wiped it tenderly away.

All evening, she read to her brothers. Usually, family members had to eat at the table unless they were sick, but nobody summoned her today. Regular rules were suspended for the moment. Fatima also could not keep away. She listened to her daughter read, stroking first one hand, then another. Zaynah wished she would go away; she could look after all the twins' needs herself. She could read and stroke heads at the same time. But when Fatima pulled a mattress into the room, squeezing it between the two beds, Zaynah protested. "I can do that! You don't need to sleep here with them. You won't sleep well on that tiny mattress. Let me!"

"They might have a bad night," Fatima reasoned. "You need your sleep, Zaynah. Go to bed now. You have been wonderful." She hugged her daughter briefly. "No guilt now. Make sure."

Zaynah slumped against her mother, her momentary jealousy dissipating like the wind.

At the door, she turned around and said clearly to her comatose brothers, "I will look after you every second of every day until you are well. I will clean your injuries, feed you, help you to go to the bathroom. And you will get well as though this had never been. You are already over the worst of it! Good night, my beloved brothers."

CHAPTER 6 **Fatima**

D URING THAT FIRST, TERRIBLE NIGHT the twins woke
up frequently, moaning in pain. Each time, they encountered a soft hand, soothing them back to sleep.
Fatima felt she had been transported into the state of new
motherhood, when each bleat from her newborn's mouth had
galvanized her entire body into wakefulness. Each time the
boys shifted their heads from side to side, unable to roll over
on their backs, her eyes jolted open, listening. They would
settle into slumber again, and she would close her eyes and
stifle her weeping against the pillow.

The next night was better, and on the third night they did
not wake once. Fatima staggered downstairs to feed Na'aman
as soon as Rana and Zaynah entered to give the twins bowls
of hot porridge and milk.

"I'll take Na'aman to the souq by myself today," Rana
instructed, noting the ravaged face of her sister-in-law. "You
need to sleep."

But when she got downstairs to shoo her sister-in-law to
bed, the gentle Fatima was adamant. "I feel like I should be
with my little Na'aman today. I've hardly seen him these past
few days."

Na'aman stared up at her in adoration. "I love O'mmy,"
he said, planting himself firmly between her knees. "O'mmy
come to souq."

"He might be a bit clingy for a day or two," said Rana. "He'll be happy to see your face bending over him if he wakes in the middle of the night."

"Not yet," cried Fatima. "I have to sleep with the twins until they are completely better."

Rana caressed Fatima's hair. "You don't want to go back to your own bed, do you?"

"The twins need me still," Fatima repeated stubbornly.

Shouts drifted down the stairwell, and Zaynah burst into the room, holding her schoolbooks. "Mazin and I are off to school now. See you later."

"What's all the shouting about?" asked Rana.

"Abdul wanted to watch television and Ali wanted me to read. I told him I didn't have time anyway. Stupid twins. I should think they're about ready to go back to school now. How long is this holiday going to continue, anyway?"

Fatima laughed into her daughter's face. Children, how they bounced back so easily! It was different with adults.

"See? They don't need you, and you're obviously exhausted. You'll make yourself sick." Rana placed a steaming cup of mint tea in front of Fatima, and scooped Na'aman up with one hand to settle him on the floor with a puzzle. He started to writhe and cry, shouting "O'mmy! O'mmy!" Fatima quickly stood up and took him in her arms. "What is it darling? Look at this nice puzzle."

"I want to sit with O'mmy!"

"Well then, you mustn't touch hot tea. Ouchy."

Fatima scooped up the puzzle pieces from the floor and dribbled them over the table, settling back in her chair with Na'aman on her knees. "The twins have only slept through the night once. I'll stay with them two more nights, just to make sure that it's a pattern."

"Tell me the real reason," Rana said quietly.

"All right." Fatima looked her square in the eyes. "I can't abide the thought of him touching me with the same hands … that hurt my children."

"The twins are a bit wild, Fatima, and they needed to be taught a lesson."

"Such a lesson?"

"I know he's a brute and I cannot believe I'm taking his side, but it's true you are ignorant about what's going on. It would be terrible if something happened to them. Much better they receive 'such a lesson.'" Rana suddenly bent over her mint tea, convulsed in laughter.

"What?" asked Fatima, beginning to smile.

"Our positions are reversed from last week. Now you're the one full of hatred and I'm the one protecting his actions!" Her face sobered. "Mind you, I'm still full of hatred."

"What strong language you use," protested Fatima. "I don't hate him at all. I'm just not ready to sleep with him yet."

Rana instantly became alert for a possible tidbit of information about Fatima's secretive love life. "I expect he'll leave you alone, in that respect, for a few days."

Fatima laughed harshly. "He never leaves me alone."

"Really?"

"Every night, without fail, except for the rare occasions he happens to fall asleep before I come up."

"We only do it once or twice a week," murmured Rana encouragingly.

"Mohammed is very ... energetic."

"Every night?" whispered Rana in awe. "Do you ... enjoy it?"

Fatima took a sip of her tea, flushing slightly. "I enjoy his pleasure." She was not about to admit to Rana her recent instincts to thrust against her husband, pulling him further into herself.

"But do you ... reach orgasm?"

"Really, Rana," Fatima put down her tea and cuddled Na'aman. Usually, he would protest against interruptions when he was engrossed in a puzzle, but today he gave himself up to the cuddle with pleasure.

Rana changed track immediately, realizing she wouldn't get

anywhere along those lines. "But even if you're angry with him, which you must often be, since he's so endlessly critical, you never refuse him?"

"'If a man invites his wife to sleep with him and she refuses to come to him, then the angels send their curses on her until morning'," Fatima quoted the prophet.

It was Rana's turn to say, "Really, Fatima."

"And he's not endlessly critical," continued Fatima. "There are a handful of things he worries about, like money, and the children of course. In most things, he is supportive."

Rana snorted. "He even looks at you critically. I've seen him, watching you through half-closed, condemning eyes while you stir the soup. I often wonder what he finds to fault in the act of stirring: are you wielding the spoon with too much strength? Too little?"

"You're completely wrong, Rana. He looks at me with love." Fatima bent her head to hide another blush. "He looks at me because he thinks I'm beautiful."

The twins bellowed for their mother, and Fatima stood up quickly, Na'aman clutching painfully at her tresses. She shifted him further up her hip and took the stairs two at a time.

The twins were engaged in a cautious wrestling match, and one had inadvertently wrapped his arms too tightly about the sore back of the other.

"That's enough," Fatima said sharply. "I can see it's time for you to return to school. Get back into bed."

With the spectre of school looming, the twins skidded face-first into their beds. "No, O'mmy. We can't go to school with backs like these."

"They should come to the souq with us," said Rana from the doorway. "Get rid of some of their animal energy."

The twins waxed enthusiastic about the prospect of an outing, and Fatima went upstairs to put her burqa on in preparation for their outing. Na'aman lifted an edge of the veil and giggled at his mother's form of peekaboo.

Na'aman pushed his own stroller all the way to the market while the twins raced on ahead, taking turns to jostle each other into the road in a frenzy of energy after their three-day incarceration. The pace slowed once they got to the souq, with its narrow, sheltered avenues lined with sellers hawking their wares. The distinct smell of the souq permeated the air: jasmine flowers, herbs, spices, bread, fish, meat, sweat, and garlic. The women walked slowly down the length of the main aisle of the souq. Rana, who had thrown a loose scarf over her hair, twisted her head this way and that, looking for the best fish, the freshest vegetables, the cheapest everything. Some shop owners knew them and greeted them by name. Every so often, Rana would stop and pore over a potential purchase; if it was one of her regulars she did not haggle, but if not she could bargain for ages, pursing her lips as though it wasn't quite up to standard, something she didn't really want anyway. Fatima stood a little behind during these lengthy interactions, relieved she wasn't involved, keeping a sharp eye on her children.

There were shops Fatima especially loved, like the spice shop with its towering pyramids of cumin and paprika, and the sweet shop with its lines of colourful temptations nestled in the shade under the awning. If she was alone, she enjoyed inspecting the baubles on display in the window of the jewellery shop, where the offerings were encased in glass rather than laid out in long rows on tables in the open air. But Rana was always in a hurry, checking off the items of her mental list as she strode purposefully from vendor to vendor. The children also enjoyed the myriad sounds and smells of the souq. When it was crowded and the people shuffled along shoulder to shoulder, Na'aman would shout with glee and excitement.

After endless minutes of bartering, Rana rejected a perfect fish on the grounds of its smell. Fatima sighed a little, trailing in Rana's wake, wondering if it had been a mistake to come here when she was exhausted. Just negotiating a pathway through the vendors and shoppers was tiring. She noticed that the vendors, intent on looking into the eyes of potential shoppers as they bellowed out their prices so their voices might be heard over the competition, slid over her cloth mask and lingered on eyes they could see, even though she was there to buy as much as anyone else. Rana fell into step beside her, finally satisfied with her choice of fish. Fatima mentioned the vendors' eyes, knowing it was the type of detail Rana found interesting.

"It's no wonder they skip your face — you have no face. It can be disconcerting, you know."

"I'm surprised you're not used to it," Fatima responded drily, "since so many women choose to wear the niqab or the burqa."

"There aren't many women who wear them through personal choice. Either they were brought up that way and can't conceive of doing anything differently, or their husbands require it. Mohammed couldn't care less whether you wear it or not and yet you still choose to. It's incomprehensible to me."

"I feel safe," Fatima said simply. "I can see the world, but they can't see me. No more worrying about whether a man is looking at me too long, or whether my expression is appropriate. How many times have I unwittingly heard passionate political arguments in this very souq, at the back of an empty store, and when the disputers turn anxiously to see if I've overheard, I can see their faces relax through the mesh. It's only a religious woman, nothing to worry about."

"I'm sure they'd relax anyway, with your pretty, gentle face. But I do understand what you mean about the attraction of invisibility."

"Na'aman!" Fatima called sharply. The twins had stopped to look at an array of cheap, plastic cars, and their little brother had toddled up behind them. He was in the act of reaching out a pudgy hand to grasp one of the alluring dinky cars when his mother's voice arrested his hand.

"O'mmy," he said, a world of longing in his voice. Both twins gazed at her too, unsure if they were still in too much disgrace to beg for a dinky car.

Fatima walked over, examined one of the cars.

"You know Mohammed will berate you for buying something cheap and worthless. You know it will break in two days," admonished Rana over her shoulder.

A spark of defiance ignited in Fatima's breast. She fumbled under her burqa to open the money pouch that hung around her neck. "It's only a few coins."

The children were speechless with grateful amazement. They held their new cars in their hands as they walked, inspecting them, memorizing every detail.

Rana stopped at the bakery to buy some pita. There was a lineup, as was so often the case during these hard times. Fatima would have preferred to stand to one side and wait, observing in her invisibility, but she knew Rana would be bored by herself. She stood next to her, holding Na'aman by the hand. "Why don't you like burqas? They're common enough."

Rana laughed. "You probably think I'm becoming a modern feminist through too much exposure to the West. Believe me, I'd rather wear the burqa than flaunt my body the way Western women do. They pity us, assuming we're downtrodden and ignorant, second-class citizens in our own land, under the thumbs of our husbands, because they mistakenly equate equality with freedom, and freedom with happiness."

Fatima glanced at her sister-in-law. She wondered whether Rana embarked on these familiar rants in public because she wanted people to hear her.

"It is true that our roles are dictated to us, and sometimes our husbands are chosen for us as well," continued Rana, "but there is no inequality in that. A man can no more choose to stay at home and look after the children than a wife can decide to work. We rule over our domains just as much as the men rule over theirs. We reign within the house. And as for happiness, really!" Rana's lips formed a moue of disgust. "You think they are happier? I pity them. First, because they rate happiness so highly, and connect it with material possessions instead of realizing it can only come from within. Second, because Western women have not escaped our 'drudgery,' as they see it. In fact, they are worse off, trekking out to work every day and then looking after the house during their second, endless shift. What would you prefer, working like a crazy person all day or sipping mint tea and strolling around a souq?"

Rana paused for breath, and Fatima looked at her out of the corner of her eye. She knew just how much Rana resented her inability to contribute to the political struggle going on in her beloved country, her railings against the limitations unfairly levied at her sex. She knew that Rana endorsed all of these opinions, and yet her opinions did not contradict one another. "All their freedom has increased their misery tenfold. There is so much violence in the West, I have heard people are afraid to go out at night."

Fatima couldn't repress a giggle. Rana shot a quick glance at her. "Yes, I know there happens to be a war here right now, but before the war we weren't frightened of anything, were we?"

They had finally reached the baker, and Rana made her purchases.

"So why don't you try wearing the burqa just once to see how nice it is to be safe from prying eyes," suggested Fatima as they wended their way home, clutching their packages. The twins had tried to use their sore backs as reasons not to carry, but Rana would have none of it. Under Fatima's anxious eyes, she had given them two bags each, one for each hand, "to balance it out," she said. Fatima watched them saunter down the street, worrying that the weight would pull at their healing welts, but they were soon jostling one another into the road again, and she relaxed. Little Na'aman did more than his fair share, struggling with a stroller heaped with provisions.

"No thanks," Rana replied. "The burqa is hot and uncomfortable, limits your vision, and muffles your breathing. Why do we have to wear masks because of men's lust? Surely it is for them to cover their eyes? It's not our fault they have lustful feelings, is it?" Fatima gazed at Rana with a feeling of incredulity. Such outrageous ideas her sister had! She could hardly follow her sometimes.

The sudden *rat-a-tat-tat* of a machine gun blasted through the hazy heat. Both women joined hands instinctively. "Abdul! Ali! Come here close to us," Fatima called. A group of men rushed past them, almost knocking them over in their haste. There was another eruption of gunfire and then a more ominous explosion, deafening them. Instinctively, the women bent double and began to run towards home. More people rushed past.

"What's happening?" Rana shouted at them.

"The army is attacking the protesters. We are unarmed, and they are mowing us down like animals!"

Fatima touched the cell phone in her pocket, suddenly aware that it hadn't vibrated all day. Her mind had been so taken up with the plight of her twins over the past few days that she hadn't been thinking about Ahmed at all. She was suddenly convulsed with worry.

Within minutes they were inside their own front door, panting and looking at each other with a mixture of horror and relief. "Ahmed," Fatima mouthed wordlessly, holding the cell phone towards Rana.

U OK? Pls answer – U OK?

They hovered over the phone for agonizing minutes.

"Bad men shooting," Na'aman whimpered, his face crumpling. Fatima looked up, suddenly aware of the proximity of the twins, also hanging over the tiny phone. "Go up to your room," she ordered.

"Please, O'mmy," said Abdul with sudden maturity. "We are worried about Khalo Ahmed too."

"He's texted back!" cried Rana, and Fatima drew Na'aman close to her as Rana read: *Am OK. Home in 2 mins.*

"Alhamdulillah," murmured Fatima. "Praise God." She turned to the twins. "Upstairs, quick, and take Na'aman with you. I'll bring up some food soon."

The needs of the children anchored them. In the midst of chaos, they still needed to be fed. The women bustled around the kitchen, with Fatima preparing a simple meal for lunch while Rana launched into a flurry of activity around supper, simultaneously chopping vegetables for salad, marinating the fish, and preparing the rice. Their ears were attuned to the sounds penetrating from outside the door: shouts, gunfire, tanks.... Was that a bomb? Hearts beating, ears straining, they focused on the food between their hands.

Fatima took a tray upstairs. Rana sprinted over to the window and opened the shutters a crack. People were rushing hither and thither on the street, like chickens with their heads cut off. Several soldiers appeared at one end, firing down the length of the street. They turned to the door of one of the houses and blasted it open, marching inside as if they owned the place.

"What's going on?" asked Fatima.

"Pandemonium. Don't look, Fatima. They have gone into our neighbour's house."

They returned to the table, chopping, chopping. Dear God, where was Ahmed? Neither woman feared for Mohammed; what harm could come to him, ensconced in his little veterinary clinic in the poshest part of town?

Each second stretched impossibly. They chopped, straining to hear a quiet knock that would signify the end of their fear, or the peremptory *thump* that meant invasion, humiliation, possibly death. Fatima suddenly ran upstairs to don her burqa again. If soldiers were to bang at the door any moment, at least they should not see her. There had been rumours of atrocities against women, rape used as an instrument of terror in regions with strong rebel bases. She wondered if their region had a strong rebel base or only an ordinary one? Surely, the whole country was in revolt by now.

Finally, a soft tap at the back door. Ahmed must have climbed over the wall of the courtyard, no doubt to avoid leading the soldiers to his home.

He sat in the kitchen, ashen-faced, rubbing his chest.

"Are you hurt?" Fatima cried, but he shook his head no and put his hand down deliberately on the table. Rana placed a glass of mint tea before him. Fatima stroked his hair. Ahmed began to chafe his stomach, gazing at the window anxiously, drinking his tea in burning gulps.

Silently, Rana refilled his glass. "Can you tell us what's happening?"

He looked at her as though he had forgotten she was there. Then at the face of his sister, suffused with consternation. "I've heard of this happening in other towns, but I didn't expect it to come to us. We are too small, too insignificant. They've launched a major military operation against us. I don't understand." Ahmed bowed his head, sloshed more tea into his mouth. "Hundreds, maybe thousands of soldiers have been deployed. They were firing live ammunition at us and they've surrounded the town with tanks. There are snipers on the rooftops. They've targeted the mosques because they say they're being used as headquarters. They're doing house-to-house raids. I've brought destruction to the family, exactly as Mohammed predicted. I have to leave."

"You're in no condition to go anywhere," protested Fatima, even while her heart palpitated, and she glanced at Rana for support.

"Do you think someone saw you, and can identify you as one of the protesters?" asked Rana.

Ahmed shook his head. "I don't think so. But who knows? Maybe they've planted spies among the protesters. I will not endanger your lives."

"Are they going to kill all the young men in the town, as well as their families? So they come to the door and they find you. You're a young student, living with his nice, middle-class family. If they know you're a protester they'll also know the head of the household is staunchly pro-government," Rana's voice contained a trace of bitterness. "If they know so much."

In truth, it did not seem like Ahmed was capable of making any decision. His hand chafed his stomach and his eyes cast about aimlessly. "Is Moussa okay?" Fatima asked softly.

"He stayed at home today. He won't go out again until his arm is completely healed." Ahmed shot a wan smile in Rana's direction. "It's healing very nicely, Rana. You should have been a nurse." His eyes shifted away and back again. His hand chafed. Rana did not want the children to see him like that, and managed to persuade him to lie down until dinner. Then laughingly, she tugged at the end of Fatima's burqa, "I'm going out to escort the children home from school. If you don't accuse me of gross hypocrisy, I'd love to borrow a burqa."

"You can't go out!' cried Fatima in a panic.

"I must. Do you want the children to be alone on the streets right now?" Rana gazed into her sister's eyes until she shook her head, mutely. "It will be all right, Fatima," and she sailed out the door.

The ordeal of dinner was almost over; the first dinner in which the twins had participated. Fatima wanted them to stay safe in their beds for another day, but Rana had insisted on it. "If they are well enough to drive us crazy all day, they can sit at the table. It's back to school for them tomorrow. If there is school."

I'm still sleeping with them, Fatima thought mutinously to herself, and made a point of discussing the terrible nightmares that had been assailing the twins for the past few nights, for Mohammed's benefit. He had made a special effort to come home in time to eat with his family, even though he often seemed to come home long after their regular dinner hour lately. Fatima meant to make her husband feel guilty and also obtain the right to sleep between her boys for another night or two. The twins gazed at her in fascination; they didn't recall any nightmares but any detail about themselves was so fascinating that they could almost remember waking up in the middle of the night.

At some point, the conversation rolled inexorably towards the subject of war, as it seemed to do every night now.

"Were you at the protests today?" Mohammed asked Ahmed without preamble.

Ahmed nodded, bent like an old man over his soup, which he wasn't eating.

"It seems the government thinks we are important enough to crush, and we have to prepare for the worst," Mohammed continued. "They will probably disable mobile phones, landlines, electricity, and the Internet. Security forces might shut off water and power. Flour and food could be confiscated. So Fatima and Rana, you must stock up on water and flour and other necessities tomorrow. Ahmed, you will accompany them for protection and I think the boys should stay home from school to help. Zaynah, you must stay home as well to look after Na'aman and to cook. Many people will be trying to stock up, so you'll probably have to go further afield than your usual haunts. Is everyone clear?"

"I'm sorry." An anguished whisper from the other end of the table.

"It's too late for that now."

"I have brought danger to this family, exactly like you said I would. I am ashamed."

"I don't think your participation in the protests is what will make or break our safety, Ahmed. Our country is spiralling towards chaos, and atrocities are being perpetrated on both sides, but especially on the side of the government forces."

As soon as the meal was over, Mohammed got up from the table. On his way out, he paused behind Ahmed and laid a hand on his shoulder. "It must have been terrible," he said.

Ahmed sat on at the table, rigid with shock.

Fatima sang softly to Na'aman, enjoying the warmth of his body against hers. He clung to her, nestled his nose in her neck, whispered, "I love you, O'mmy," again and again with intense passion. Quiet joy enveloped her, as this soft body burrowed against her like a little animal, and the twins waited for her next door, secure in the knowledge that they were loved and cherished. She felt, rather than saw, the presence in the door-way. She opened her eyes. Mohammed stood there, watching her. "You will return to our room tonight," he said, turning on his heel before she had a chance to implore.

Fatima rose from the bed slowly, her joy shattered. With a heavy tread she drew near the twins' room and opened the door. The twins needed her. If she were a true mother, she would not risk their physical and emotional recovery because of an arbitrary command. Ali was already asleep after the excitement of the day, so she sat down on Abdul's bed and caressed his hair.

"Ali's going to have bad dreams because you didn't kiss him," said Abdul. He had been struggling against the weight on his eyelids in his determination to stay awake until his mother came.

"I will kiss him now."

"Too late," announced Abdul with satisfaction. "If you are not awake for the kiss, it doesn't work."

Fatima laughed, bestowing kisses anyway, and then stood indecisively in the middle of the room. What would Mo-hammed do if she merely stretched herself out between her wounded twins and fell asleep? He would certainly storm down the stairs in search of her, incensed at his long wait, finally convinced, and astounded, that she was not coming. Her lips twitched. Seeing her asleep, he would immediately assume that she had simply succumbed to her habitual fatigue. Would never think that her insubordination was a deliberate act. Would he sling her over his shoulder, even so, and cart her away?

"Lie down," said Abdul. His eyelids drooped, soothing the ache in his eyes, then jolted open again as his legs spazzed in an involuntary twitch.

"Do you think you are well enough to sleep alone now?"

"Mmmm," came the indecipherable reply. Fatima set her lips; both twins were sprawled over their beds in poses of exhausted relaxation and it was futile to pretend that they needed her presence.

A faint creak as she passed Zaynah's door made Fatima pounce uncharacteristically on the handle and wrench it open, catching Zaynah in mid-air as she launched herself towards her bed.

"What are you doing?" snapped Fatima.

Zaynah looked at her in surprise. "Nothing, O'mmy. I needed to go to the washroom."

"Not true!" Her own anger shocked her, and then clogged her throat like tears. "You are always listening, listening. Creeping around in the middle of the night. It's not natural!"

Zaynah set her jaw stubbornly. "If I know what's going on I can help the family."

"That's not your job. You are too young to feel such responsibility." Fatima gathered her daughter in her arms and held her tight. "You mustn't worry about things so much. People love, and fight, and love again. That's what people do."

Zaynah wrapped her arms around her mother's back. "So you aren't mad at Abi for forcing you to abandon the twins?"

The use of the word "abandon" irritated Fatima. "What do you mean by that? What have you heard?"

"I did hear Abi..."

"You were listening!"

"He was speaking quite loudly...."

"You must stop listening to conversations you aren't meant to hear! Do you want us all to feel uncomfortable in our own home?" Fatima cast about in her mind for the types of noises her innocent daughter might hear if she listened at her parent's keyhole. Shouting, certainly, but nothing worse. Rana and Hamid, however, could be a different story. She had heard them herself, sometimes, hurrying towards the washroom with averted eyes. Nothing much, perhaps a muted groan. What would a young girl think if she heard a muted groan?

"I'll try to stop, O'mmy."

"Do you promise?"

"I promise to try."

"Good," said Fatima, too tired to dig deeper even though she felt she ought to. Perhaps tomorrow morning, when fatigue wasn't darkening the edges of her vision. She could talk to Rana, get her advice about how to phrase the necessary message. Rana was good at things like that.

Fatima went straight to her corner and began her evening prayers without looking at Mohammed. She prolonged her prayers as long as she could — it was so restful — until Mohammed began to pace back and forth behind her, thumping his feet on the ground to express his impatience. For a second, exhausted despair bent her head. Then it occurred to her — a message straight from Allah — that she need not relinquish any more energy that night. She could close her eyes and rest, regardless of what Mohammed said or did. There was no need for her to solve his battles this night, soothe his feelings, stroke his hair.

She lay like a rag doll under him, closing her eyes against his absorbed face. She did not open them as he slipped his hand here, and there. She did not breathe his aroma as he poised over her, and penetrated.

Afterwards he sighed, lying beside her. "You don't know what could happen to them."

Fatima lay, motionless as a corpse.

"Terrible things happen to people, children, who show support for the rebels. It wouldn't have been enough to ask the twins politely to desist. Strong measures will save their lives. You cannot understand, sheltered as you are within the walls of this house."

And you, Fatima thought, *what do you understand, sheltered within the walls of your veterinary clinic?*

Her silence irritated him. "Do you want me to describe what

has been done to boys like Abdul and Ali in graphic detail?"

And she thought again: *How do you know? You know nothing.*

They lay in silence; Mohammed's arm rested on Fatima's stomach. She thought how it had wielded the belt against the soft, bleeding skin of her children, again and again. She knew all about the horrors of war: she did not need convincing that strong measures were needed. What Mohammed failed to understand was their differing definitions of "strong measures" for children.

Her skin itched to purge his hand.

As though he felt her antipathy, Mohammed rolled over onto his back, taking his hand with him. "I remember once my mother gave me a beating, when I was very young. I don't remember what I did to deserve it. Probably I criticized her somehow, told her I didn't love her in the childish way of young children. I remember running around the room trying to get away from her as she beat me and beat me, screaming at me to apologize. I wouldn't."

Fatima turned her head slightly and looked at her husband out of the corner of her eyes. She could well believe the story — her mother-in-law had been a tyrant and she was shamefully glad when she died suddenly of a heart attack soon after the birth of the twins.

"But you know the strangest thing? The next day I hugged her and apologized a hundred times. 'I'm sorry, O'mmy, I'm sorry, O'mmy.' Later, some of her friends came to visit, and my mother pulled up my shirt and showed them the bruises. My whole body was black and blue. 'In the end he capitulated,' she told them proudly."

Fatima tentatively reached up her hand and touched the side of Mohammed's face. She wasn't sure why her husband was telling her this, but her sympathetic response was automatic. Perhaps that was why.

"Fatima, my love, we must not be at loggerheads. Anything might happen, these days."

Fatima smiled. "To a vet?"

Mohammed looked at her unsmilingly. "We are all in danger now."

Usually, Mohammed's energetic exit from bed in the morning roused Fatima sufficiently to begin her own reluctant leave-taking. Rana had once told her how silly it was to drag herself out of bed in order to provide an unrequired presence during her husband's two-minute breakfast. When Fatima explained that it was the dawn prayer to Allah that spurred her from her bed, Rana had laughed. "What do you pray? Please, Allah, do I have to get up?"

The kitchen radiated coffee and fresh bread smells. Rana was cutting up tomatoes and cucumbers while Mohammed threw the last dregs of his coffee down his throat.

"Goodbye, Rana." He put his hand briefly to his wife's cheek. "Goodbye, Fatima."

There was silence for a few moments after the door banged shut. Rana looked up in surprise. "Aren't you going back to bed until Na'aman gets up?"

Fatima regarded her in consternation. "Have you noticed that Mohammed has started saying 'goodbye' every morning?"

Rana shrugged indifferently. "You've mentioned it. So what?"

"It's strange. He never used to. And he is working much longer hours too, not only on the weekends but during the week as well. I asked him if it was very busy at work, and he said he was looking after many animals of families who have left the country and abandoned their animals because of the war."

"I've noticed he scratches his nose more often too."

"Really?"

"Don't be ridiculous. I never look at him. Why you see the need to obsess over trivialities when life is so complicated right now I'll never understand. Do you count the pitas he eats at dinner? Do you agonize over his bowel movements?"

Fatima rose to escape back to her favourite place: bed.

"Where do you think you are going?" Rana's voice was oddly querulous. Fatima looked at her in surprise.

"You just assume that you can totter off to bed and I'll feed the rest of the household — mostly your kids — day in, day out, don't you? How dare you take this for granted?"

Fatima stared at her incredulously. Rana claimed to hate Mohammed so much, and yet they were *exactly* alike. Both were unpredictable, capable of creating unpleasantness for no reason.

"It's incredible to me ... it's incredible to me...." Rana sat down suddenly.

Fatima was shocked to see her chin quivering. "What is it, Rana?"

"That you worry whether your bullying bastard of a husband says goodbye or not in the morning and you don't even notice how depressed I am, how exhausted...."

Distress clutched Fatima's heart. Not Rana, not now. Her sister had to be the strong one, holding the family together. "Have you been depressed?"

"I've felt awful since that huge fight with Mohammed, and I haven't been able to shake it off."

"But you are getting along together fine now!"

Rana snorted, brushing away her tears contemptuously. "Have you seen us talking? It's a cold war. It's almost worse than the shouting."

"I'm sure Mohammed has forgiven you completely. He never talks about it, and I know he would if it still bothered him. It's been a long time since that fight, Rana. Are you sure that's all that's bothering you?"

Rana looked at her with irritation. She was not prepared to chat about her obsession with Mazin's sexual direction with Fatima, who could not even disclose whether normal sex was enjoyable for her. "After all these years together, you still think I need a reason to be depressed? It just happens, sometimes. I used to try and find reasons for it. Oh yes, that old weight-on-the-heart feeling again. It must be because I'm barren or my nose is too big. Now I realize that there is no rhyme or reason, and nothing to do but get through it. Of course, contention exacerbates the problem, and whatever you say there hasn't been a healing process since that fight with Mohammed. Not from my perspective, anyway. Over the years, I have tried everything with him: deflecting his anger, standing up to him, avoiding him, ignoring him. Nothing has worked. So now there's nothing new left for me to try, other than accept the fact that we have an unhealthy relationship. No matter how good at communication I am, how intelligently I examine each issue and search for solutions, I can never improve my relationship with my brother. I am defeated. "

Fatima rubbed her sister-in-law's shoulders. "I'm so sorry you are depressed Rana, and that I didn't notice. How can I help you to get through it?"

Rana's eyes filled with tears again at this sympathy. "I don't have the energy to do everything that is expected of me. Haven't you noticed that my meals have become much less varied lately?"

Mutely, Fatima shook her head, her hands rubbing at the stiff flesh.

"I don't know what the point is. The effort I put into those meals and nobody even notices...."

"They do, Rana! Of course they do. The children love your food, and often boast about how much better it is than their friends', especially since this dreadful war started." Fatima observed a ghost of a smile. "Why, just the other day Abdul was saying that his friend ate the same thing every night, while his Ammé Rana dished up diversity like no war existed. Well, not in those exact words," Fatima added, seeing skepticism flit over the expectant enjoyment on Rana's face. "But something very similar. And Mazin is so proud of the way you feed and care for us all." Fatima was surprised to see Rana's forehead furrow in a frown and deftly changed tack, reflecting again on the similarities between the two siblings. Keeping the peace with them both was like juggling eggs. "And you know exactly how much Hamid needs you. And I, well, I just don't know what would happen to this household if you weren't here to run it." Fatima released her sister's shoulders and sat down suddenly, her energies momentarily drained.

Rana patted her hand. "You're a good person, Fatima."

Fatima felt a rush of pleasure. "Am I?"

"Yes. You are a lovely sister. Compensation for my SHIT brother."

Fatima's look of shock changed to mirth as Rana started to giggle. Fatima hid her face in her hands and laughed.

CHAPTER 7 **MAZIN**

MAZIN LIKED MATH. He liked the fact that there was a logical solution to every problem. It was just a question of working it out, following the steps. Only one answer was right. Not like in Arabic, where the teacher would give the students a specific subject to write about. You could memorize the grammar, you could learn how to write a technically perfect sentence, how to write a beginning, middle, and end for your essay, but the quality of writing and expression could not be learned like that. Mazin smiled down at his math book. He was good at Arabic, too. He was good in all his subjects — not only good, but the best in the class. The other students knew it too and sometimes solicited his help. Today, one of the bullies had actually asked him to explain something. Could you ask someone for help and then beat them up after school? Surely not. Mazin felt sure things were changing. He would study hard, understand everything, keep his position at the top of the class, and gradually he would carve out a place for himself. He might not be surrounded by friends, but he would be respected as a genius. Mazin immobilized his face mid-grin. Zaynah had told him to stop dreaming all the time because his expressions were imbecilic. She told him to focus, all the time, and not to forget for an instant.

"Watch what other people do and imitate them," she had said. "If they're not making stupid faces to themselves, then you shouldn't be. That's how you focus on normalcy. Got it?"

Yeah, sure he got it. But it was so boring and relentless to be aware all the time. Especially when 99.9 percent of the time nobody was looking at him. He had finished his math sheet before anybody else. Did he really have to sit here controlling his thoughts just on the off chance someone would look at his face? It was boring.

But it was worth it, if only they would leave him alone. If only he didn't have to hide from the bullies all the time. How blissful that would be. It had been so great during those two weeks when his mother had escorted them back and forth from school, after that awful day when it had rained bullets and the soldiers smashed down doors and carted people away. Naif's father had been taken away, along with his two older brothers. Naif was a bully and Mazin hated him, even though Zaynah had said he should pity him.

"Why should I? The way he swaggers around the school it looks like he's glad they got taken. Transformed the stupid lout into a hero."

"Don't be stupid. Of course he's sad but he's not going to show it every minute of the day, is he? Wouldn't you be sad, imagining the terrible things they were doing to your family?"

"He hasn't got an imagination," Mazin had said stubbornly.

Khalo Mohammed had ordered the family to stay home from school that first day and stock up, so his mother had taken him and the twins for miles, going from shop to shop to find all the purchases on the list. His arms had been sore for days afterwards, from dragging all that stuff. When they had returned to school, his mother had escorted them to and fro every day for two weeks, waiting for them in the schoolyard. How Mazin had loved to saunter out with the other, normal children after school, safe in the presence of his mother, instead of hightailing it for safety like some runaway racehorse.

After that awful rainy-bullet day people were on edge, waiting for the next episode in the ongoing saga of hostilities. But nothing else had happened. It was like the soldiers had disappeared. As week followed peaceful week and became peaceful months, life returned to normal.

And normal for Mazin meant hurtling out the front door as soon as the bell rang.

"Focus!" Zaynah's voice screeched in his head and he froze, mentally examining the expression on his face. *Definitely scrunched up. Not normal. Relax.*

The teacher began to gather up the math sheets. Mazin put his homework in his backpack and slung it over his back in preparation for a quick getaway. He leaned forward, ready to spring, and then self-scrutinized again. *No good. No good at all.* He looked like he was about to start a race while everybody else was still shuffling their books. Mazin glanced around and slipped his backpack off, dropping it between his knees where it was hidden by the desk but could be snatched up at any moment. He fumbled with his books, like everyone else. He threw a smile to the left so his right neighbour would think he was exchanging pleasantries with the student to his left, then a smile to the right to fool his left neighbour, then a quick glance around the room to see if anybody was noticing these antics and chalking him up as one pathetic fool.

Before the bell had completed its first peal he was out the door and running. As soon as he was secure in his hiding place, Mazin morphed into a policeman, finger-gun cocked, ready to mow down the dangerous criminals that would appear unsuspecting any minute now. He squinted down the length of his gun, and then felt a moment of utter panic at the abnormal contortions of his face before he remembered he was alone. How wonderful the sense of relief felt! He smiled to himself, made his smile huge, even wagged his tongue about. He could do what he liked, look how he liked! Seventeen hours of freedom. He squinted down his gun again. There — the criminals had emerged and were looking around the schoolyard. How could he have thought they would leave him alone because he helped them in math? *Bang bang, you're dead.*

And there was Zaynah, waiting for him as usual. Waiting until the bullies gave up and went away. *Bless Zaynah.*

But what was Zaynah doing? She wasn't stopping … surely she wouldn't leave him to walk home alone. No, she was approaching his enemies. Mazin wanted to shout, "Stop, Zaynah!" but he knew that his hiding place would be discovered and then the game would be up. He would sport new injuries every day and his mother would ask: "Why can't you fight back? What's wrong with you?" He must stay quiet and not move. What did Zaynah think she was doing?

He watched in agony as she marched up to Naif and Sami and cleared her throat loudly.

"What?" Naif asked.

"I was just wondering what you were doing."

Mazin recognized her tone of voice. It was the condescending older-sister voice Zaynah frequently used on the twins when she thought they were being particularly stupid.

"Nothing," said Naif, and turned his back on her.

Zaynah tapped him on the shoulder. Naif swung back around, Sami imitating his every move.

"What?"

"I asked you a question."

"None of your business."

"Actually it is. I think you're looking for my cousin Mazin and that is very much my business."

Naif grinned at Sami, whose head swung back and forth to follow whoever was speaking.

How stupid they look, thought Mazin.

"What if we are?"

"Why do you want to beat him up?" Zaynah asked conversationally.

"He's a wimp."

"True. You're much stronger than him, but he's much smarter than you."

"Is not," Naif growled.

"Sure he is. And you know it too. If you left him alone, I bet he'd help you with school work."

There was a short silence. "He's weird," interjected Sami.

"Bright people are often a bit weird," confided Zaynah, "but he's a lot less weird than he used to be, haven't you noticed? I'm coaching him on how to be normal; I expect he'll be just as normal as you soon." Zaynah beamed at them.

They didn't quite know how to answer this older girl talking in a weird way about their weird classmate. Sami gaped at her open-mouthed, while Naif tried to think of something clever to say.

Zaynah waited a moment. "So, do you agree to leave him alone from now on? In return, Mazin will help you with your homework and stuff. Okay?"

"I don't want that weird wimp to help me with my homework."

"Okay, so he won't help you, but you still have to leave him alone because you're making his life miserable and we have to stick together when there's a war on."

Mazin marvelled at her confidence.

"We like beating him up," Sami objected stubbornly.

"You can't even find him, let alone beat him up. I'd think you'd be glad to give it up, considering how stupid you look hunting through the schoolyard every day without finding him."

"We'll root him out eventually."

"Yeah? When? What do you think, he stays in the same place?" Zaynah suddenly pushed her face close to Naif. "You'd better stop. Nasty things happen to bullies. Things have already happened to you, haven't they? Ever think that maybe you're being punished?"

A look of dull rage spread over Naif's face. "You just shut up!" he screamed into her face.

Mazin trembled behind the safety of his gun. If Naif did something to Zaynah, he would have to jump out to protect her. He could not let anything nasty happen to his cousin after she had tried to help him. Anxiety and fear pulsed through him. Who asked her? He didn't need some avenging angel fixing his problems for him. If he had to go out there, his problems would get a lot worse.

Zaynah was backing away, one slow step at a time with each word. "I'll shut up if you leave Mazin alone, but if you don't, I'll say worse things every day. Worse, and worse, and worse."

"I'll beat you up too," Naif bawled after her.

"Yeah," Sami parroted, dancing on the balls of his feet as though dying to attack. Mazin hoped he wouldn't make a fool of himself. If he launched himself at them with all his strength, he might get in a punch or two.

Who was he kidding? They would slaughter him. He took a deep breath, trying to control the tremble in his hands. The anticipation was worse than the reality. Always. The dentist alone had proved that many times.

Zaynah had stopped, mouth ajar. "You'd threaten a girl with *physical violence?*" she asked with such shock that the boys looked almost abashed.

"If you say things like that..." Naif sputtered.

"Well I won't, if you stop tormenting Mazin." She walked forward, closing the distance between them, and put her hand on Naif's arm. "I don't want to say anything to upset you, but I'm really sorry about your father. If there's anything I can do...."

She was incredible. This cousin of his was the most amazing person he had ever known. He loved, loved, loved her.

Mazin could see Naif had no idea what to do. He looked sheepish and sad and stupid all at the same time.

Zaynah turned around and tripped away to her usual waiting place by the school gates. They watched her for a moment, huddling together in order to pretend they were talking, and then they sort of sauntered off, casually, taking their time, as though it was their idea entirely.

As soon as he was sure they were gone, Mazin threw himself on Zaynah in an agony of admiration and love.

"Stop it! Someone will see!"

He released her and grabbed her hand, covering it with kisses. "You are the best cousin, you are the bravest … you know what you are? You're a hero!"

"A hero?" Zaynah asked softly.

"Totally a hero. Even if they don't stop, you're still a hero. Let's look up what you wrote in your diary about heroes — I bet you fit the bill."

"Someone who fights for what she believes in," Zaynah whispered. "Someone who protects her family from harm."

"You see?" interrupted Mazin.

"Someone who is noble and helps others even when it puts them in danger."

"Exactly!" crowed Mazin.

Zaynah frowned. "I don't think it counts if you aren't frightened. They just looked like silly boys to me; I knew they wouldn't hit me and I wasn't frightened for one second."

"Your definition doesn't mention fear."

"Well, maybe I'll add it," Zaynah tossed her long hair over her shoulder. "Race you home."

During dinner, Mazin wanted to tell everybody how Zaynah had stood up for him. He knew she would be really pleased, especially for Ahmed to hear it, but it was hard to know how to phrase it so that he himself didn't look like a total loser. He worked out speech after speech in his head as he scooped pita and hummus and salad into his mouth. *How to phrase it: "Do you know what Zaynah did at school today? She faced down two bullies all by herself!"* Consciousness made him glance up at some point, aware that expressions were flitting across his face. His mother was looking at him, but she smiled at him and winked. He grinned back. His mother had been watching him a lot lately. Maybe it was her way of helping him remember about keeping his face normal. *How comfortable one could be with family! How nice to be surrounded with people who love me and want to help me.* Perhaps he didn't even have to mention that he was being bullied. No, the protection of family was the heroic element, according to Zaynah's diary. It seemed impossible to make her look good without looking like an idiot himself.

His Khalé Fatima's voice sliced through his thoughts. "What on earth happened to your arm Zaynah?"

Zaynah held out her arm and pulled her sleeve back slightly so they could see the jagged red scratch gouged out of her forearm. "I was feeding the chickens when the black rooster attacked me. He was only a chick like, yesterday, and I used to hold him in my hand. I can't understand it."

"Roosters are unpredictable that way. Sometimes they turn out gentle and sometimes nasty," Rana said.

Mazin, ever attuned to the nuances of his mother's face, knew exactly what her glance towards her brother meant.

"What are you keeping roosters for?" Mohammed barked at Rana.

"I am not keeping roosters," Rana replied with dignity. "It only became apparent which chicks were roosters a few weeks ago, and I haven't had a chance to eliminate them yet. You and I will do it tomorrow, Mazin."

All thoughts of crediting Zaynah for her brave act flew from his head. "O'mmy, no!"

"It's about time you learned to do it yourself. Tomorrow I'll hold the roosters and you can chop their heads off."

"I can't even watch you doing it, O'mmy! I can't possibly do it myself."

"A few years from now and you'll be a soldier, killing men," Mohammed spoke grimly from the head of the table. "Of course you can kill a rooster."

Again Mazin read his mother's glance: mind your own business for once. His hopes rose. Maybe if Khalo Mohammed pushed too hard, his mother would do an about-turn and change her mind. It had happened before.

"We'll do it for you, Ammé Rana," the twins chorused.

"That black rooster is mean and I'd love to kill it," Abdul added.

Rana looked sternly over the table at Mazin, daring him to say anything else. "Mazin will do it."

Mazin shot a desperate look around the table, but only Ahmed was looking at him. His uncle delivered a sympathetic wink, lifting the weight of Mazin's worry momentarily.

As soon as supper was over, the children filed up to their bedrooms as usual, but Mazin was so anxious to talk to his mother that he was unable to use this precious time of aloneness to play. He struck a stance in front of his mother's mirror, but headless chickens scuttled across his vision. He lay across his bed and picked up his book, as that always did the trick. In a moment, he was immersed in a fantasy world of someone else's imagination, and only the sound of his mother's clucking ousted him from the pleasant world inside the book. His mother was feeding the chickens, which meant that she would be alone in the courtyard for a few minutes. This was his chance.

Mazin slipped down the stairs, a prisoner escaping from a den of evil thieves. He hesitated before the kitchen, ears wide for approaching footsteps even while his brain concocted plausible excuses in case of capture. But the kitchen was empty, and within seconds he was standing beside his mother, who started violently when she saw him.

Mazin broke into giggles. "Didn't hear a thing, did you? I can be quiet when I want to be. Sometimes, I even think I have the power to be invisible." And he thought of the bullies searching fruitlessly for him for years.

"What are you doing Mazin? You're supposed to be in our room."

"May I?" Mazin took a little chicken feed from his mother's hand and squatted to offer it to the chickens. He liked the feel of their wattles bumping against his hand as they pecked.

The dominant ones pecked the others out the way. The black rooster was the most dominant of all. He shouldered his way to the front and pecked frantically and rather unpleasantly in the centre of Mazin's palm.

"I wanted to talk to you," Mazin told his mother without looking up. "You know I can't kill this fine fellow."

"You don't have a problem eating him, do you?"

"Oh no, he'll be very tasty. But I don't like killing them, O'mmy, and you know it."

"I know it. Once I heard a soldier explaining what it was like to kill a person. He said the first time was terrible, but then each time it became easier."

"Ouch!" The black rooster had swept some of the feed off Mazin's hand to see if more delectable offerings were hiding underneath.

Rana laughed. "What?"

"The scrape of his beak is painful."

"You see? He causes pain and needs to die. Tomorrow it will be hard for you, and after that, easier."

"But O'mmy, your story doesn't make it better for me. It just means that people can get used to anything, even if it's terrible."

Rana rattled the feed container. "Killing an aggressive rooster isn't terrible. It's unpleasant, but something you must get used to. Especially since you like to eat roosters so much!"

"But you don't mind killing them, and nor do the twins. Why do I have to be forced to do something I hate? Is it again to make me a man? Does a man really have to be aggressive in order to be a good man? I think there are different types of people, and I am one type, and if everybody were like me then this horrible war wouldn't be happening. I think I am better than people who have no problem killing chickens, O'mmy."

"To have morals that dictate right and wrong is not the same as pandering to weakness. When good men rule a country there is no war, but the ruler cannot be weak. I do not want a weak son."

Mazin looked at his mother in surprise. "I am not weak."

"In some ways you are," Rana snapped. "You will kill this rooster tomorrow and all the other roosters besides, and I don't want to hear anything more about it!"

Mazin kept his head down as he let the rest of the feed trickle through his fingers. His mother sounded angry with him. Why was she so angry?

He got up without a word and went directly to his room, lying with his face to the wall until his father came in, carrying his supper on a tray. "Am I weak?" he asked him.

Hamid put the tray down carefully on the side table. "Good day to you too." He bent down to kiss his son. "I've never seen you fight," he said. "For all we know, you could be the strongest of us all."

Mazin sat up in bed and drummed his heels against the side. "That's not what I mean. Is it weak to dislike killing chickens?"

"No, I would think it was natural to dislike it. Nasty job."

"My mother is making me kill the black rooster tomorrow. She said I was weak."

Hamid scooped some rice into his mouth with a spoon and considered carefully. "Maybe she was angry about something else. Your mother never criticizes you pointlessly."

"She thinks I'm weak! And she's right. Today, at school, Zaynah stopped the bullies from hurting me. A girl stepped in and spoke up when I was too frightened. Why am I so scared about everything, Abi? I don't want to be. How can I change myself?"

Hamid got up and bent over his son, hugging his stiff body. "You are wonderful just the way you are," he said gently. "But sometimes we have to do things in life that we dislike doing. If you are scared to do it, you are twice as strong and brave as those who don't care about it. When you succeed in killing that rooster tomorrow, it will mean you are stronger than the twins or Zaynah. Do you understand?"

Mazin nodded uncertainly. "But why was my mother so cross?"

Hamid shook his head and sat down again to his meal.

"She watches me a lot lately, Abi. What is she thinking?"

Again Hamid shrugged, watching his son out of the corner of his eye as he scooped rice into his mouth.

"She wishes she had a better son," Mazin said bitterly.

Hamid guffawed and pulled two Sudoku puzzles out of his pocket. "She loves you more than life itself, silly boy. You are the best son we could have."

Mazin smiled tremulously at his father, and stretched out his hand for the Sudoku puzzle.

The next day, the whole family gathered for the rooster-killing after school, with the thankful exception of the men, who had not come home yet. Mazin had spent the day preparing himself for it, as best he could. Although he had been present on other chicken-culling occasions, he had refused to watch, staring at the horizon through blurred eyes, trying to blot out the squawks of the horrified spectators, the mother and siblings of the victim. *It is so quick*, he reminded himself. *The rooster feels nothing, knows nothing.*

"Why did you hide?" Zaynah had demanded after school, angry with him for shooting out the door to his hiding place as usual instead of walking out like a normal person. Naif and Sami had lounged around for a while, leaning against the school wall, smiling in Zaynah's direction. She had been furious.

As soon as the coast was clear, Mazin had come creeping out.

"What's wrong with you? I've sorted it all out," Zaynah had said.

"Maybe you have, maybe you haven't. My way, I'm certain of safety."

Zaynah had blustered in contempt, and had marched in front of him for a while, until he reminded her that this was an auspicious rooster-killing day.

"Are you scared?"

"No." Mazin had spent the entire day imagining the moment of murder. His dreams had been filled with inept axe strokes, while the rooster erupted in humanlike screams of pain. "Have you watched it?"

"Often. So have you." Zaynah began to zigzag drunkenly along the sidewalk in front of him. "It's hysterical when they run around after their heads have been cut off."

"Hysterical," muttered Mazin, hoping she wouldn't indulge in her tendency to paint gruesome pictures in order to scare him.

"Come on, let's run. Ammé Rana said she wanted to do it right after school."

Mazin slowed his pace, and Zaynah skipped back to him. "Come on!" She started to skip around him as he dragged his heels.

"Zaynah, what do you think my mother thinks of me?"

"What?"

"Do you think she feels contempt because I'm weak?"

Zaynah reached over and tousled his hair. "Nah. You're all right. We all love you."

"It's just recently, I feel … she watches me a lot. I thought it was a look of love, but now I'm not so sure. When I really think about it, and I've been thinking about it ever since she called me 'weak' yesterday, there's more worry than love in her look."

"There's a touch of worry in your head. Your mother loves you. Mothers always love their children, no matter their faults. Now come on!"

Mazin resisted as she grabbed his arm and pulled. Zaynah pushed him in aggravation. "It's always about you and your little problems. Don't you know I have a list of problems I need to solve? There's a war going on and men are being butchered daily, so excuse me if I don't weep with pity because you're reluctant to humanely kill the stupidest animal in the world!"

"And you're helping to solve the problem of the war, I suppose?" Mazin replied, striving for a tone of deep sarcasm.

"No, I have enough to do with my own family."

"Nothing is going on right now," Mazin replied. "No fights, nothing."

"That's where you know nothing and I know everything. Here you are mewling about whether Ammé Rana is worried about you when I know she is depressed!" Zaynah cried triumphantly.

Mazin felt a rush of guilt. "Why is she?"

"She just gets that way sometimes. She broods, just like Abi. She's sad about her relationship with him."

Mazin pursed his lips. "That's nothing for you to solve."

"I'm aware, and I help, unlike *some* I can mention. Knowing this, I'm kinder to Ammé Rana and help her more, rather than obsessing about how she's looking at me."

"How would we survive without you?"

"And that's just the tip of the iceberg. My father has started saying 'goodbye' to my mother when he leaves for work in the morning."

"So?"

"So, why has he started doing that? Does he think he's going to die? Does he think we are? Does he know something we don't?"

"How would he die, working in the richest and safest part of town?"

"Maybe he's fighting secretly. Maybe ... maybe he's a *secret hero*."

Whether it was a release for the fear and anxiety building up in him all day or the idea of his terrifying uncle fighting heroically, Mazin began to giggle uncontrollably. At first, Zaynah was inclined to be annoyed, but as Mazin dissolved into hysterics and had to halt his progress, bending over and leaning against the wall for support, she began to laugh too.

Rana, peering out of the window to watch for her son's approach, was grimly relieved to perceive Mazin's hilarity as he stumbled up to the door of the house, clutching his cousin for support. "I've been worried about you all day," she said, ushering him in the front and out the back door directly. "Obviously a complete waste of time, as worry always is."

A block of wood sat squarely in the middle of the courtyard, with a gleaming axe alongside. All mirth departed as Mazin looked at it with nausea. The cousins were hopping around in glee at the prospect of a show. Even Na'aman laughed lustily and stretched his hands out to the scattering chickens. There were also neighbours from the four houses that shared the courtyard, joking and laughing and looking forward to getting a chicken from the massacre of males in their prime and females in their decrepitude. Mazin was reassured to see Hessa and Hazar standing timidly to one side, grasping one another's hands. He had always liked these two, simple neighbours, and he knew they liked him. Sometimes, as he walked by their house on the way to school, the door would open and Hessa would appear, gliding up to him with eyes lowered and a shy smile on her lips as she slipped a sweet inside his palm. Good sweets they were, although somewhat past their shelf life, perhaps. These simple sisters were anticipating the joy of meaty meals for several days to come, and he would be the one to provide it. If there was no hint of disgust in their gentle faces at the method of acquisition, then how could he be squeamish?

Mazin grasped the axe firmly with one hand, eyeing his opponent in what he hoped was a ruthless manner. This was war. This enemy had brought down family members and it was up to him, Warrior Mazin, to wreak revenge. Mazin was the captain of an army, all standing behind him agape at his bravery. This foe — Black Spur (so called for the deadly spurs that had ripped off many a man's face) — was feared by all. Only he, Warrior Mazin, could defeat him. He had to move carefully, watching his wily opponent's every move.

"Get on with it," chorused the twins.

The base rabble that always trailed in the wake of his great army were getting restless, clamouring for the meat and gold that this conquest would yield. Warrior Mazin drew up his mighty chest and advanced. Black Spur bristled evilly, timing his attack to coincide with the descent of Mazin's hand. He shot straight up in the air and slashed at Mazin's chest. Mazin leapt back in surprise, a thin line of blood etched against his shirt. *Wounded*!

"I'll hold him for you, Mazin," Abdul offered.

"Stand back," Mazin hissed.

Rana stooped a little to look in the face of her son. "Are you sure, Mazin? It's hard to hold the chicken and chop at the same time. I can hold him for you, if you like."

"No," Mazin said again. How this rabble clamoured. Perhaps some of them were spies for Black Spur, hired to distract him. Wickedness. And he wounded, too.

But not helpless. He drew himself up to his full height.

"At least put the axe down by the wood until you've got him," a fellow soldier whispered. Mazin laid the axe down, then turned swiftly and sprinted towards the enemy in order to surprise him. Black Spur was ready for him, leaping up in a flurry of squawks and feathers to slash again, but Warrior Mazin got one hand around the enemy's legs and the other around his neck, bearing him triumphantly to the chopping block as Black Spur writhed and shrieked. Before the spies could rise up against him, Warrior Mazin laid his enemy's head on the block, released his neck to grab the axe and chopped off his head in one, clean movement.

"To Warrior Mazin the victory!" screamed his army.

"Well done," said a soldier softly. "I was frightened that it would take more than one blow and the blood would freak you out."

Warrior Mazin did not deign to reprimand the soldier for his foolishness. He stood up, chicken head raised high in hand, as though it were a trophy and a thousand cameras were on him.

Then Black Spur gave a little flip, landed on his feet and began to hop around the courtyard, wings flapping uselessly. He careened towards the chicken coop, then turned and headed headlessly for Mazin, whose warrior-status had disintegrated in one fell swoop as his mouth fell open in horrified disgust. He leapt to one side as the rooster lurched towards him, but as though tied by some invisible sense (obviously not located in the head) to his killer, Black Spur executed several gigantic leaps in the air that carried him unerringly in Mazin's direction.

"O'mmy!' he cried in horror. "O'mmy!"

"It's all right, my little one. Come here," Rana enfolded the mighty warrior in the warm circle of her arms that protected against all things, even headless chickens.

"Well done," she whispered into his hair.

Mazin peeked over her shoulder at Hessa and Hazar. They looked at him, smiling and nodding. They would have meat for their supper.

Black Spur finally collapsed on his side and lay still; Warrior Mazin returned at once, puffing out his chest with pride as a soldier examined his wounds.

"Do you want to do another one?" the soldier asked.

"I have killed the worst," he said. "You lot can manage the rest." And he strode into the house with his head held high.

CHAPTER 8 **RANA**

WHEN RANA WOKE UP in the morning it took a few seconds to remember why her heart felt constricted. Usually, she leapt out of bed before anyone else in the house was awake, efficiently preparing house and food to bolster the spirits of each member of the household before they departed to meet their various challenges. But her constricted heart weighed on her very lungs, sucking energy just to breathe. It had been weeks, and still Mohammed's fury permeated every aspect of her waking life. "But you said you felt fairly detached," Hamid had protested when she had woken the first time, her hand over her heart and tears streaming down her face. He had looked at her bewildered, his strong wife reduced to jelly. How could the rest of them survive if she succumbed? "Cheer up," he had urged. "You mustn't take it personally. Remember, these are his issues, not yours."

Such advice had not helped; nonetheless, duty had now kicked in.

Rana rose from her bed and donned her clothes slowly, wondering if this was how Fatima felt all the time, this relentless lack of energy. Probably not, because her own fatigue was inextricably linked with melancholy. It was a wretched feeling that she could not shake off, stemming not only from her brother's determination to wrench a direct apology from her, but from worries about Mazin. Mazin. Her beloved son.

She could feel herself watching him surreptitiously, even when she tried not to. Wondering what he was and how he would end up. When her thoughts became unbearable, she felt he could feel her burning eyes and sense her love had changed. Become more guarded, so as to protect, in case … in case it had to be withdrawn. In case … he had to go away and she could never see him again. She could not think about that. It would not happen; she would not let it happen. Why should something as minor as sex ruin one's entire life? He was not gay, and if he was, then he would just have to hide it. There was no other alternative.

But he cannot be gay. He's just a child, and it's stupid to think and worry senselessly about things that will probably never come to pass. Stop staring at the poor child. Put it out of your mind, stupid woman.

But with Mohammed, she was surely blameless. She had apologized for sparking such a terrible fight, but that was not enough. He wanted her to admit that every protester was a fool, to concede that he was right to avoid the senseless brutality on both sides, and this she simply would not, could not, do. Since their fight, he had heaped so much abuse on her head that any apology for her original comment — she couldn't even remember what she had said — would be ludicrous. She only recalled that she had not been thinking of Mohammed at all when she had made the forgotten comment, had certainly not called him a coward, nor consciously implied that he was one. She clung to that certainty in the face of his continuing rage at what he called her inadequate apology. His determination to force her to her knees and acknowledge before all that he was right and she was wrong … gall rose in her throat. She felt rage, hatred, fury at a life that forced her to live in such close quarters with someone she hated. "You should protect me," she hissed at Hamid through clenched teeth. "It is the same as if he were physically abusing me. Why don't you say something to him?"

"You really think I could improve the situation? I told you it all stems from insecurity. He will only feel that we're ganging up on him if I say anything."

Rana peered at him dimly through wet eyes. *I called the wrong man coward*, she thought, and then felt ashamed that she was letting the malevolence of her brother seep into her purer relationships.

Hamid paused beside her on his way to the bathroom and pushed a strand of hair out of her tired eyes. "Try agreeing with everything he says. Try surrounding him with a halo of love in your mind. Yes!" Hamid placed his fingers over her mouth to prevent her talking. "I know you've tried it all before. One more time. He can't berate and ridicule if you're smiling at him with love and agreeing with everything he says. Right? Promise you'll try?"

Rana nodded her head listlessly and meandered downstairs to gather eggs for breakfast. As she passed the kitchen door, she glimpsed Mohammed leaning against the counter, wolfing down some pita bread. "Sabah el Kheer," she muttered in passing. She thanked Allah that he would be gone by the time she got back, and that there would be a whole, blessed day before she had to see him again. Frequently, he got home so late that she did not see him at all. Those were the best days. But it was impossible to know the time of his arrival, since it was as unpredictable as his mood. Accordingly, tension would start to build in her stomach as the afternoon wore on, tightening the stranglehold around her heart. Mentally, she would prepare for an evening of invisibility, snide comments or criticisms, and sometimes, a direct attack. The events of the evening were as unpredictable as the hour of his return.

She watched the children, then Hamid and Ahmed, transferring food from hand to mouth. Every day, she waited for one of them to say, "Boiled eggs again?" or even, "Where is the salad?" But the twins plonked down and ate so single-mindedly she wondered if they even noticed what they ate. Zaynah and

Mazin were too polite to comment; the adults continued to mouth their usual polite platitudes.

"Boiled eggs again," Rana snapped at Fatima when the others had left. They were idling over their coffee while Na'aman investigated the crumbs on the floor beneath the table.

"They were delicious," murmured Fatima, stirring more sugar into her tea.

"Aren't you tired of eating the same thing every day?"

Fatima's soft fingers caressed the back of Rana's hand. "I know you've been feeling a bit low lately. Yet you get up every day and make breakfast for the whole family while I loll on the bed with Na'aman. Do you think I'm complaining?"

"It wouldn't be complaining to suggest a fried egg now and then."

Fatima giggled.

"It doesn't take any longer. I just have to crack the eggs in the frying pan. Otherwise, it's hard to believe anyone cares what I put in front of their noses, the way they wolf it down. What are you laughing at? You're no better. It doesn't matter what's put in front of you, I get the exact same compliments. Would it hurt to suggest a fried egg? An occasional omelette?"

Fatima snorted into her coffee and that set Rana off. Both women laughed and laughed till tears streamed down their faces. Na'aman gazed from face to face, chuckling delightedly.

"That was therapeutic," said Rana, wiping her eyes. "Now I have to go to the souq."

"I'll come with you. It's good for Na'aman to get some fresh air."

The women scurried upstairs and into their separate bedrooms to prepare. On a sudden impulse, Rana carried her pencil case of makeup and a hairbrush into Fatima's room. "Let's put on some lipstick, make ourselves look good." Rana began to brush Fatima's long, rich hair. "It's so beautiful, it's almost a crime to cover it up when you go out."

Fatima laughed. "That's the whole point. You cover it up

because it's beautiful. All this beauty is for my husband alone! Ouch! Careful with the knots!"

"Sorry. All my beauty is for Hamid too, but it makes him proud when other men think I'm beautiful."

"Oh hush," said Fatima, shocked.

"What, you think I'm spouting Western ideas again?"

"No," Fatima protested, but Rana was off.

"You think I long for the freedom that Western women have? You think I feel unfulfilled because I can't participate in my country's struggle for freedom?"

"No," murmured Fatima again, knowing that there was no stopping her now.

"You're wrong. Western women wrongly equate equality with freedom and freedom with happiness."

"You've said this before, Rana."

Rana lifted up the thick strands of black hair and let it trickle through her fingers. "I have more to say."

Fatima sighed and bent her head, focusing on the gentle hands caressing her hair.

"Has their freedom made them safer? Why do you think the levels of violence are so much higher in the West than here, in peaceful times? Because of the women. They have battled for equality and now they can make all these choices, so many choices. I would feel quite oppressed with such limitless choices. How glad they are to be free to choose their own men! They choose, but whoops! They got it wrong. Never mind, they can just choose another one, like a new dinky car at the store." Rana began to braid the long, thick tresses, without interrupting the flow of her speech. "Poor little one-year-old Johnny will just have to spend his life shuttling back and forth between different mothers and fathers and new mothers and fathers, but at least they're *free*. Then Johnny becomes a screwed-up teenager without familial values and gets involved in drugs, then crime to pay for them, and his mother ends up scared to go out walking on her own at night. But she still considers herself free! So lucky to make her own choices!"

Fatima listened with a faint smile. "Perhaps our husbands are selected for us, but most of us manage to carve out successful marriages, unless our husbands are brutes."

"Exactly! And we raise children who mirror values that are important to us: the value of family, integrity, obedience. Yes, even if we have to beat them sometimes."

Rana buried her nose in Fatima's hair. Fatima reached up a hand to caress her cheek.

"And do you know the reason most of us end up happy in our marriages?" continued the indomitable Rana. "Because we aren't indoctrinated with the belief that we have a right to be happy. So if our marriage is hard, we work on it, instead of giving up because 'working on it' is hard work, and hard work doesn't constitute happiness. Even you, married to an impossible man, have found ways to cohabit with him relatively peaceably." Rana sat down on the edge of the bed, suddenly exhausted mid-braid. "My energy is low."

"I understand exactly how that feels."

"He sucks the energy from all of us."

Fatima turned around and took her sister's hands in hers. "You know he always gets over it."

"Onto the next battle." Rana deftly removed a powder brush from Na'aman's hands, zipped up the makeup case and placed it on her own lap. Na'aman started to cry, reaching desperately towards the stolen treasure. "How do you stand it?"

Fatima laughed at her, slipping the hairbrush into Na'aman's hands. He stared at it, not wholly mollified. "You were the one who told me that the twins needed that lesson, harsh though it seemed."

"I don't mean that," Rana replied impatiently. "I mean all of it."

"That's the only thing he's done in the past few months that really upset me."

"How can you say that? It's like living with a ticking bomb.

He's violent and unpredictable. I just want to stay away from him as much as I can. But you have to share your room, your bed. There's not a single corner in this house you can call your own. Pucker." Rana began to apply lipstick to Fatima's cupid-bow mouth. Na'aman stretched out chubby hands, coveting the lipstick.

Fatima, lips incapacitated momentarily, pointed towards the corner where she prayed.

"Oh, that's why you pray. I always wondered. Right, eyeliner next."

Na'aman, breathing stertorously, inched his way over to the discarded lipstick.

"He's a very good husband in many ways. I'm lucky, really, compared to so many women."

Rana retrieved the lipstick from Na'aman just as he discovered the miracle of the removable top. He began to howl again, refusing to desist at the reappearance of the hairbrush. Fatima took him on her knee and began to tickle his feet, lifting her face to the side so Rana could continue her work. Sad howls morphed into happy ones. "He's a good husband. Ouch!"

"You moved your eye," snapped Rana unrepentantly. "There's nobody here but us — for whose benefit are you mouthing platitudes about good husbands? He's violent and totally incapable of understanding anybody's perspective but his own. He lives in a black-and-white world of his own perception, which might have been bearable if his perception wasn't so unremittingly negative all the time. I hate him." Two tears seeped from under Rana's lids and she shook her head vehemently, pushing Fatima away when she tried to return the favour by brushing Rana's hair.

They started for the souq. Na'aman pushed the stroller as though he was king of the world while Fatima, happily invisible under the niqab, took her sister's arm. "What a lovely day. One could almost imagine we were at peace."

"Nevertheless we are at war, inside the house and out."

Fatima gave her arm a little shake. "It's not that bad, Rana. You just feel that way because you are down."

"And why is it only me who gets down? Not you, who must suffer so much more than me, in silence."

Fatima, unobservable, observed Rana's face. "I don't think I get depressed the way you do. Perhaps it is my nature, and perhaps it is because of Allah. Have you tried to pray?"

Rana twitched her shoulders. "I try to calm my mind. I try to think positive thoughts. That works much better."

"Apparently not," whispered Fatima.

"You're not me!" cried Rana. "Don't judge me."

Na'aman teetered perilously close to the edge of the sidewalk and Fatima leapt forward to grab him. "Walk here, Na'aman. Cars are dangerous. Streets are dangerous."

"Maybe you are impervious," Rana resumed when she took her arm again. "If he looked at me with that intense, brooding look of criticism all the time the way he looks at you, I'd spill the pot of soup on the floor in nervousness. That would give him something to criticize."

"I've told you before, he looks at me in love." Fatima blushed.

"And rides you every night to prove it."

"Rana!"

"And you don't even reach orgasm."

"Stop it this instant. I will go home and leave you."

"How do you do it? Do you love him?"

Fatima had been looking in fear at her son in case he was listening to the filth coming out of the mouth of his aunt. She relaxed, knowing Rana was done. "Yes."

"Why? Tell me why you love him. Maybe it'll help me see him in a positive way."

"There are many reasons. Apart from the things that don't touch you, like his absolute love and loyalty for me, and the fact that we have four children together, he supports us all without complaint. I have no anxiety about whether we'll have enough money when we're older."

"Isn't that a man's job? So does Hamid, so what, it's to be expected, not lauded. And even though it's their job, Mohammed does it as unpleasantly as he can. He controls everything. He resents giving you money and makes you feel guilty every time you spend any."

Fatima was silent.

"Is that all?" Rana cried, a note of desperation in her voice. "Give me something more, Fatima! Convince me. Give my mind something positive to fix on."

Fatima grabbed her sister's shoulders and whirled her around. "You want more? My husband is good, and kind, and true, and honest, and noble. He has integrity. Do you want more? He has strong, moral values, and he sticks by his values consistently. Look around you, at all the stupid men killing each other. Most of them are like chickens, following one another with no real understanding of what they are doing or what the consequences will be. Mohammed is an intelligent, thinking human being, so superior to these beasts...."

Rana was surprised when Fatima's voice started to choke, because she could not observe her rising emotion under the niqab.

"Okay," she said, patting Fatima's arm. "You are right, he is all those things. Plus he is paranoid, violent, insecure, deeply unstable...."

"He lives his life according to Allah's doctrines, even if he doesn't realize it and doesn't pray. I know in my heart that he is beloved by Allah, and that is how I cope with his current attitude to religion. He says religion only causes problems and hatred. When I try and tell him of all the good men and deeds that religion has created, and how the best in every man is that bit that believes in Allah, and the more a man believes in Allah the more he will lead a righteous life, he begins to spout facts about terrorists and what they do in the name of Allah. He says the majority of men are stupid, and religion in their hands is dangerous. But he can talk as much as he likes.

His wife knows that Allah loves him because he lives his life as a righteous man."

"In what way?"

"He strives always to do what is right. He does no harm to his fellow man."

"Except in his own family. He's totally screwed up when it comes to them. But yes, he is also intelligent, honest, and chockablock full of integrity. Point scored, Fatima. Thank you, I will try and focus on those qualities when I clear my mind to calm myself. Maybe it will help."

They entered the souq and were immediately engulfed in the smells and sounds of a busy human thoroughfare. Rana perked up immediately, forging ahead, her head swivelling from right to left as she took in all the wares. Na'aman giggled delightedly as he was swept into the throng.

Rana bargained for that, fingered this, examined the other. She purchased a bit of nougat for Na'aman and popped it in his mouth, as he smiled beatifically up at her. She haggled fiercely for some oranges, smelling them and poking her nails into their skin to check their freshness.

When she had finally made a purchase, she rounded on Fatima. "I don't care if he's honest and noble and integral, he makes me miserable. Criticizing every move I make, everything I do. Misinterpreting everything I say. He makes me utterly and completely miserable, and there is no way I can get away from that, not if I clear my mind and think of him positively until my son is grown. And you can't help me."

She looked at the material that was Fatima's face. "Can you?" she asked in a small voice.

"Would it help if you thought of him as sick?" Fatima asked gently. "When he criticizes you, can't you think, poor Mohammed, he is insane. He can't help it. He is to be pitied."

A sputter of laughter gurgled from Rana's lips. "That's a switch, Fatima. From noble to insane. Which is it, then?"

From the tone in Fatima's voice, Rana knew she was smiling.

"A bit of both," she said.

That night, once she was sure by his twitches and sighs that Mazin was asleep, Rana poured into her husband's ear the entire conversation. "I really think it might help, thinking of him as insane. Imagine such good advice coming from Fatima."

Hamid recoiled a little from his wife's hot breath in his ear. "Why not? Who knows him better than Fatima?"

"I've known him all his life," protested Rana. "And anyway, I didn't think she was analyzing him like that. She's lovely and I adore her, but she floats through life without thinking too much about her direction. Not like me, agonizing over every step." Rana sighed and pushed her mouth against her husband's ear.

"That tickles," Hamid said, withdrawing again. "Do you think it will help you feel better, thinking of him like a sick person?"

"Absolutely. From now on, my energies will be devoted to working out how I can introduce him to a therapist without him knowing." Rana slid on top of her husband so she could look him full in the face. "How come you've never told me to think of him as sick, with all your good advice?"

"I'm sure I have," said Hamid. "One way or the other. I've certainly preached the solution — loving detachment. That's the only way to handle crazy people. Love them as much as you can, but detach from what they say and do. After all, you can't take a loony seriously, can you?"

Rana giggled. "I shall hang a 'Mad Dog' sign on his back. Mentally, of course."

Hamid ran his fingers through her hair. "It is pretty astute of Fatima. What is the definition of 'insanity'? There's that famous quote that says insanity is 'doing the same thing over and over and expecting different results.' That's Mohammed to the letter. Or it means perceiving the world a certain way and making everything that happens, or is said, fit into that perception. So when he labels you as 'a bad mother,' it doesn't actually make a difference what you do or what the reasons are. He will see it through his perception of you as a bad mother."

Rana reared up to look in her husband's face, pulling her hair out of his hands. "Give me an example."

"Well, when you invited him to participate in Mazin's birthday cake event. You did it so he wouldn't feel left out of things, but he, as an insane person, has to make everything fit his perception, so your invitation is seen as another example of your bad mothering and he begins to attack you for making Mazin think he's the centre of the world. That's why you must — *must* — detach yourself from what he says about you because it has nothing to do with reality."

"I'm nothing like him, am I?"

"Well, you share some traits ... ouch!" Hamid cried out as Rana dug her nails into his hand. He was surprised to see tears in her eyes.

"You must never say that. You can't imagine how insulting it is. Take it back."

Hamid raised his hands and caressed his wife's cheeks. "You're nothing like him here, these beautiful, smooth cheeks. Or here," he said, his hand stroking through her hair. "And I don't think Mohammed has anything quite like this," he crooned, lifting his head to circle her nipples lightly with his tongue. Rana smiled, pressing herself into her husband, feeling him rise against her with pleasure. His hands stroked down her back and cupped her buttocks. "You definitely beat him there. Oh my love, I want you so much it almost hurts. Please let me."

Rana glanced over at Mazin's open mouth before positioning herself to slide up and down along her husband's shaft. "Do you know Fatima and Mohammed make love every night?"

"I think this is a detail I shouldn't know," Hamid said.

"Every night," Rana whispered, guiding him in. "Imagine the energy he must have, after working all day."

"Such energy," Hamid murmured, without knowing what he said.

Rana was bending over the stove stirring the large pot of vegetable soup when Mohammed entered the room. She sensed his presence without even turning around. A palpable tension descended, emanating from the suddenly repressed children around the table, and the fluttery movements of Fatima as she scurried to serve her husband. *He's a bully*, Rana fumed, and then curbed the thought instantly. Thoughts like that had a way of imprinting themselves on expressions. *He's insane, poor man. Mad Dog on the loose.*

Rana ladled the soup into bowls and helped Zaynah carry them to the table, keeping her head down in a suitably modest way.

"Abi," Abdul was saying. "Do you remember telling us that it's bad when a group gangs up against one person? But if someone sticks up for that person then that's brave, right?"

No, please. Not the subject of bravery versus its wicked counterpart. Why did the twins have to forgive their father as though their beating had never happened?

Mohammed nodded his head, spooning broth into his mouth. *Like a pig*, Rana thought, again curbing the thought. Everyone was spooning food into their mouths. *How strange it is, that when you feel negatively towards someone then everything they do is repulsive.* She risked a glance towards her brother, now pontificating some pompous response. *Repulsive. No, sorry, not repulsive. Insane. Mad. Crazy. Loony. Poor man, insanity is a bit repulsive.*

"It is a brave act to speak out against cruelty, especially when a group of people are engaged in it. Going against a swarm of kids takes brains as well as guts. Has something happened of that nature?"

"Yes, Abi," chorused the twins excitedly. We beat off Mazin's attackers. There are these kids that wait for him every day after school to beat him up, but we showed them!"

Rana saw a glance slither between Mazin and Zaynah.

"But Mazin is twelve, and you are only nine," said Mohammed. "Why can't he beat off his own attackers?"

Ahmed slammed down his water glass in excitement. "That's exactly what the protesters are doing!" he cried. "They are speaking out against cruelty, bravely risking slaughter at the hand of the army that oppresses them."

Bless you, thought Rana.

Mohammed speared a piece of zucchini with his spoon. "No, the protesters are trying to topple a government and seize power. The situations would only be analogous if the twins were likely to start torturing others as soon as they had vanquished the current powers that be." He turned to the twins with an amused air. "Are you?"

"No, Abi!" the twins insisted.

"We're not *likely* to start torturing others...." Ahmed sputtered.

"It's happened everywhere else; do you think you're different from the rest of humankind? Are you saints, to forgive the wrongs that have been done you? You will massacre every Alawite you can find. It will be genocide. Now my boys," Mohammed turned firmly towards the twins. "Tell me what happened."

"Well, Zaynah told us that these big guys looked for Mazin every day after school to beat him up...."

"...So, today, we each got a big stick and as soon as they came out the door, we ambushed them and they were so surprised that they took off," Ali finished Abdul's sentence.

"And where was Mazin?" Mohammed asked quietly.

"He was hiding."

His gaze swivelled over to his nephew. "You were *hiding*?"

Contempt dripped from his voice. *Not my son*, thought Rana. *I can't keep my promise to agree with everything he says if he attacks my son.*

"Yes," answered Mazin, lifting his head bravely. "There's

this group of three or four that try to catch me every day. It's been going on for years, and for years I've been hiding and they never manage to catch me." Mazin shot an angry glance at the twins. "Zaynah already spoke to those boys last week and dealt with the problem. They probably weren't even looking for me today, and I didn't need your stupid help. I bet they'll step up their efforts to find me and beat me up again now. Thanks a lot. All you've done is create more problems!"

Mohammed looked at his nephew incredulously. "Am I to understand that all of my children — even my daughter — have been trying to protect you while you've been *hiding*?"

There was a pause. Nobody spoke. "Hiding doesn't solve anything. Since you've apparently been hiding for years, it must be obvious to you that it's not helping. The only way to stop bullies is to stand up to them."

Mazin looked at his mother. Rana took a deep breath, re-membering her internal promise to treat her brother with loving detachment as you would an insane person, trying to blot out the fact that the word "hiding" sounded worse than "fucking" on Mohammed's tongue. "Your uncle is right, habibi. Bullies don't stop unless you make them."

"I can't make them. I'm not good at fighting."

"You must learn to fight," Mohammed interjected. "I can teach you a few moves if you like. Let's do it right now, after dinner. You just need to be exposed to it, in order to lose your fear of being punched. When you're in the middle of a fight, you can't feel pain because your adrenalin kicks in. There's nothing to be frightened of. I'll show you."

Mazin looked at his mother again with a stricken face. She nodded encouragingly, "It'll be fine," she whispered.

"What's your mother saying?" barked Mohammed. "Don't whisper at my table. That boy is a weakling, and it's completely your fault. I've told you a thousand times to toughen him up, but you prefer him to be bullied at school for years on end?"

This is not about me, this is about him, Rana thought to

herself. *I am a wonderful mother.* She cleared her throat. "It's a great idea to teach Mazin some fighting moves, thank you."

Mohammed looked at her narrowly, leaning back in his chair and poking a toothpick between his lips. "I just hope it's not too late, and that you haven't turned him into an irrevocable coward."

Rana smiled tremulously at Mazin, trying to communicate telepathically how brave she thought he was.

"Did you see your nine-year-old rescuers from your hid-ey-hole, Mazin?"

"Yes," Mazin answered.

"So why didn't you come out and help them?"

"I didn't want to reveal my hiding place. It has protected me for years, and I need it. I thank you for offering to teach me how to fight, Khalo Mohammed, but I don't think I'm going to be good at it and I doubt whether I'll be able to fight off my tormentors tomorrow because of your lessons. Unless Abdul and Ali happen to be around again, my hiding place will be pretty important."

Was that a note of sarcasm in her brave son's voice?

Two points of red appeared on Mohammed's cheeks. "You will not hide again. I forbid a nephew of mine to behave like a coward."

Rana leapt to her feet like a mother tigress. She could not stand by and watch her brother abuse her son docilely; the desire to strangle him would overwhelm her and something terrible would happen. "Come Mazin," she said quietly. "Let us finish our dinner in our room."

"Sit down!" Mohammed shouted. The children jumped at the sudden bellow. Fatima stood up and started to wave them towards the door. "Sit down!" Mohammed yelled again.

Everybody hunkered down in their seats. Mohammed leaned towards Rana. "Listen carefully. I am going to teach your son to fight because you have raised him to be a coward, and that is no way for a man to live."

Rana looked into Mazin's eyes. "He is not a coward. He is the bravest boy I know. He is different, but he does not struggle to conform to others. He is proud of the way he is. He knows he is more intelligent than anyone else in his class, and he will have a great job while they will shovel shit. He knows...."

Mohammed's fist slammed onto the table as he emitted a great, fake guffaw of mirth. "Mazin the genius — of course! Does it give you solace to pretend he's a genius on the inside when it's so obvious he's lacking in every area on the outside? He's effeminate, weak, spoiled...."

Rana placed her hands over her son's ears and began to steer him towards the door.

"You will sit down and listen to me. Mazin and I have put up with your destructive mothering long enough!"

She felt her shoulder jerk back and she was spinning around to once again face the room. The children sat stone cold around the table, gaping foolishly or looking down. Mohammed's furious eyes were inches from her own and his words bounced off her numbness: "My children are at the top of their class and normal, praise Allah. Do you think you're protecting Mazin from his abnormalities by pretending it doesn't matter because he's a genius? He will be made to be normal. *I will make him.*"

"Over my dead body," Rana answered quietly, inching again towards the door. If only she could get to the door.

"I told you to sit down!" Mohammed screamed, but she continued her slow retreat, and still he advanced, his face contorted, his hands reaching out for her. She grabbed for the door handle and wrenched it as he wrenched her arm, and there was an insane moment when he was dragging her back into the room and she was flailing ineffectually at his yanking arm, while someone started to cry and someone started to scream. Mohammed kept baying in fury, until she managed to thrust her arm out of his grasp and stagger to the table where she picked up a knife and held it before her. "I'll kill you if you come near me."

Then came a savage blow to her right cheek, which sent her spiralling to the floor, and another to her chest area, and she realized that Mohammed was quite right. There was no pain at all. And through weeping eyes she saw Mazin pummelling his uncle from the side, not a coward now, and his uncle shake him off like a fly and Mazin tumble to the floor in slow motion. That sight propelled her to her feet, and she grasped her son with one hand and again aimed for that elusive door, but again the insane fiend came after her, fists swinging, shouting that he wanted her out of his house forever, until somehow Fatima's soft body materialized between them.

And mother and son escaped.

CHAPTER 9 **AHMED**

AHMED SLUMPED OVER MOUSSA'S BED and took another drag of his cigarette. "You don't want to come back now, Moussa. The soldiers have returned, pointing death at our heads. I expect to be killed every time I go out there. Our side has got arms now, and we have rebel snipers on the rooftops, picking off soldiers even while they aim at us. They, in turn, are killed by the army's snipers on other roofs. It's a nightmare, Moussa, and it's getting worse. Much worse."

Moussa bounced up and down on the bed. "Arms? About time. Where do we go to get arms? I'm ready, my friend, I'm ready. Peaceful protests while they take potshots at us are in the past. It's revenge time. Where, my friend? Just tell me where."

Ahmed lay back on Moussa's stained pillows and aimed his ash in the direction of the pickle can on the floor that served as an ashtray. He put his other arm over his eyes to hide their expression.

"Hey Ahmed, lighten up. It's got to get worse in order to get better, don't you see?"

"In a way I see. It's just that everything is shit right now."

"So you know people who have been killed? That's tough, my friend. I'm sorry."

"I know people, but nobody I'm close to. It's not just that. Home is ... really tense right now. Half of my family isn't talking to the other half, and the stuff that comes out of Mohammed's mouth sometimes ... it makes you shudder. He's so full of rage and hate and the way he describes that fight between him and Rana is totally wacko. Does he think I wasn't there? Describing how Rana defied him and was rude to him and how it's his duty to help Mazin. Poor kid. He takes him out back every night and pounds away at him."

"Surely he's not really hurting him?"

"There are no broken bones or anything, but he's teaching him how to fight. Mazin is fighting tears every time he comes in. Poor kid."

There was a knock on the door and Moussa's mother came in, bearing a tray with olives, labane, and pita. There were also little cups of sweet tea.

Ahmed sat up abruptly, holding his hands out for the tray, not knowing what to do with his cigarette. "Thank you, that's so kind."

As soon as she had gone, he put the tray on the floor and slumped back on the bed again. Moussa started to eat with relish. "So what does Rana think about it all? She doesn't look like the type of woman who would put up with too much shit."

"She never comes out of her room when Mohammed is in the house. At least he hasn't kicked her out, although he threatened to. You might see Rana as strong, but all that strength does is cause trouble. Fatima is the one who persuaded Mohammed not to chuck his sister out on the street, I'm sure of it. She's the one with the real power to sway him."

"What about Hamid?"

"Hamid stays out of the way. I wonder if they talk about leaving, between themselves. It's not like they'd have a problem finding another place to live, what with everybody leaving their homes and flying to other countries to become refugees."

Moussa popped an olive in his mouth and chewed with relish. "That Mohammed sounds like a bully. He needs to be taught a lesson. He's against the protests, isn't he? Cowardly bastard."

"Actually, he's become a little less extreme than he used to be. Doesn't rant against my stupidity so much."

"Miracle. Finally sees we're right." Moussa held out the remains of the labane. "You sure you don't want a bite, before I finish it off?"

Ahmed held his stomach as though it hurt. "Go ahead."

"Sure?" Moussa asked again. "You need to fortify yourself for tonight."

"I'm not sure I'm going tonight."

Moussa leapt to his feet. "Not going? Are you joking? There's a huge demonstration planned. We are part of this. You can't back out now."

"I'm telling you, Moussa, things have changed. It's not a demonstration anymore. It's a fight. You won't even recognize the way they're doing things now. We have been organized into fighting groups under different leaders."

"Who's our leader? Anyone I know?"

"I don't know him personally. His name is Muhammed Deeb. Most of the leaders have received weapons training, and that's what gets them leader status. Deeb gave us a few lessons, but I still don't feel ready."

Moussa laughed gleefully and did a little gig about the room. "We have arms, arms, arms! Now they'll see what we're made of. What are we using?"

"AK-47s."

"This is great. Will the leader have time to give me a lesson tonight?"

"Technically, learning to shoot a gun isn't that complicated. You pull back the charging handle, aim and fire. They gave us some tips as well, like keep your rifle at head level always, even when you're running, so you're ready to shoot if an enemy pops out of nowhere. Always keep an eye on your ammo so you don't run out unexpectedly. Some of us have received army vests too, with pockets to carry magazines and water. Do you have something with lots of pockets in case you don't get one?"

Moussa hopped from foot to foot. His excitement was palpable. "I have pants with big pockets going down the sides. An AK-47. I can't believe it."

"I have a bad feeling about this. I think the army is going to come at us full force tonight. Mow us down."

Moussa laughed again. "We'll be doing some mowing of our own, my friend. Just let me have at a nice gun."

"A gun doesn't help if they send in their warplanes."

"They're not going to bomb a little town like ours, Ahmed," Moussa said in a thrilled tone, as though Ahmed had suggested they might be passing out medals. "And if they do, then we're in just as much danger staying at home. So how does it work? Do I join your group? Come on!"

"Your arm is barely healed...."

"It's fine."

"Do you even know how to wield a gun?"

"You just said it wasn't hard. Point and pull the trigger."

"And shoot off the head of the man in front of you."

Moussa cupped his friend's face between his hands. "We have to do this, Ahmed. This is the way we achieve democracy for our country. Peaceful demonstrations were fine, but they still came with their guns and blew us up. We can't just let them blow us up as though we were animals going to the slaughter, can we?"

"Will killing and being killed really achieve democracy?"

"Are you kidding me? If we fight back long and hard enough, we'll win. We can't chicken out, or worry about our little lives. We are giving our lives for the future of our country, and proud to do it!" Moussa raised his fist in the air and shook it.

"I'm not a hero," Ahmed said in a small voice.

"If you go to fight because you know it is the right thing to do for your country, even though you are frightened, then you are a hero, my friend. That is what a hero is."

The gun felt heavy in Ahmed's hands, making it twice as hard to raise his arm and jab it in the air, again and again.

"Victory or Martyrdom For Us All," the crowd screamed with every thrust. "Victory or Martyrdom For Us All."

Ahmed felt exposed, as though hundreds of guns were pointing right at him. He tried to focus on the crowd, what that used to mean to him. How wonderful it had felt to be a part of this huge movement, at one with his fellow man where he had never felt at one before. He glanced at Moussa, standing next to him, shouting till his voice became hoarse. His face was alight with joy, or passion, or anger, it was hard to tell which. Why couldn't he drum up that passion anymore? Was it fear? Was he a coward?

"Victory or Martyrdom For Us All! Victory or Martyrdom For Us All!"

His arm ached. He was here, and therefore he was not a coward. Moussa was right; this was the only way forward. Terrible. Frightening. But the only way. It was useless to hold non-violent protests when the other side was using guns. They had to fight.

"Victory or Martyrdom For Us All! Victory or Martyrdom For…" the chant splintered and rose again in a mighty shout as gunfire broke out on two fronts at once. "We're sitting ducks," yelled Moussa.

Ahmed gestured towards an alleyway as he began to run. "There are sandbag walls in every alleyway and street. Do you think we've been resting since your arm was hurt?"

The friends dived behind a sandbag wall, along with several other rebels.

"So how do I shoot this thing again?"

"I guess this is what they mean by training on the job," Ahmed laughed at his friend, and showed him what to do, trying to remember his own brief training session. He had hoped the leader of their faction, Muhammed Deeb, would have time to explain the rudiments of gun-use to Moussa. But when he had walked up to Deeb minutes before the scheduled start of the protest and introduced Moussa to him, Deeb had clapped Moussa on the back without a word and commanded someone to take him to their warehouse to get "kitted out." No training, no nothing. No time.

"Make sure you don't kill one of our own," Ahmed told Moussa.

"Didn't we practice with slingshots and homemade bows and arrows when we were kids? I was a good shot, remember?" Moussa laughed at Ahmed's anxious face. "I'll only shoot when it's a clear shot, okay? I know this is life and death; I'm not stupid."

The sound of gunshots ricocheted over their heads, and Ahmed peered over the top of the sandbag. Two soldiers were sprinting towards the building opposite their position. He took careful aim and fired. The soldiers ducked and weaved their way into one of the buildings. More soldiers came behind them, running directly towards their sandbag wall. Ahmed shot again, then leapt away as bullets exploded against the sandbags. One of their comrades yelled and clapped his hand over his eye, then keeled slowly over. More soldiers came, a whole army it seemed, all shooting at their sandbag.

"Come on Moussa," Ahmed yelled. He bent over and pelted into the open doorway of the building alongside. Wary of possible snipers, he flattened himself against the wall and inched into the next room, staying close to the shadows. There was a table in the middle of the room and a few chairs. Was he inside someone's house? Why hadn't they locked the door? Had the door been blown off? He tried to remember seeing a door, as he inched towards the first window. When he got there he crouched to the floor, then cautiously raised one eye above the sill. The glass had been blown out and he could see men and soldiers running like ants in every direction. He raised his AK-47 slowly and took aim at a soldier, peering with one eye through his sights, taking the time to position his target directly in the crosshairs. Fire. The soldier fell. Ahmed lowered his rifle slightly and blinked, staring at the mound on the ground. Two other soldiers grabbed their fallen comrade under the armpits and dragged him into a building, just like he would have done, had Moussa fallen.

A volley of rounds blasted out from Moussa's gun. "Allahu Akbar," Moussa was screaming as he shot. "Allahu Akbar!"

"Be careful not to shoot any of our own," Ahmed repeated anxiously, peering through his sights again just as the windowsill in front of his face exploded, dust and smithereens blinding him for a second. He had the presence of mind to duck quickly, pulling Moussa down with him. Bullets continued to rain in the window above them.

"We've got to get out of here," Ahmed hissed.

Moussa turned to him and pointed to his forehead. A line of blood disappeared into his hair. "A bullet grazed my head," he said in wonder, touching the blood and looking at it with reverence. "Is that a sign that Allah is with us, or is that a sign?"

Pounding steps could be heard at the entrance of the house. Ahmed leapt away from the window and ran towards the door at the opposite end. Behind it, there were stairs. Ahmed took them three at a time, trying to keep his gun at eye-level in case a sniper materialized. They gained the upper floor and catapulted into one of the rooms. There was a single bed in the corner and a woman and child cowered next to it. Ahmed stopped dead, unsure what to do. There was going to be a shooting match in a moment, and they would probably be killed, and it was all his fault for choosing this room. He motioned frantically to them to get under the bed, not wanting to talk. The child was clutching a well-worn teddy bear, and he bent his head as though to consult with it. Footsteps were pounding up the stairs. Ahmed and Moussa positioned themselves on either side of the door and waited for the footsteps to find them. Ahmed did not even have time to look to see whether the mother and child had followed his instructions. Not that it would protect them, if the battle raged within the room. *That won't happen if we are killed quickly*, Ahmed thought to himself. *Why is my life worth more than theirs?*

Then the soldiers came through the door, shooting, and there was no more time to think. For a minute — or maybe it was only a few seconds — the sound of gunshots filled the room and Ahmed's finger clamped down on his own trigger with surreal abandon, wondering how it was that he was standing. Then a massive explosion rocked the floor and suddenly he was not standing anymore. His eyes were blinded by dust and his trembling, frozen finger finally released the trigger.

Surely he was dead? There had been four or five soldiers at least, and only him and Moussa against them. He must be dead. But his eyes itched and he could feel a vibration against his pant leg. His cell phone. Fatima must be worried.

Relieved not to be dead, Ahmed tried to open his eyes. They were filled with dust. He patted the pockets of his vest gingerly until he located his water. It slid out and he splashed some water into his eyes and throat. Now he could see, dimly. There were bodies on the floor. Moussa's? He sat up, slowly, focusing on his body to see if he was hurt. Everything ached, but there was no sharp pain. Surely there would be a sharp pain if he had been shot? How could he have escaped being shot, in such close quarters with a bunch of soldiers? He turned his head slowly, carefully, and saw that the entire wall of the room he was sitting in had disappeared. It was like he was sitting in a backless dollhouse, exposed for play. "Allahu Akbar," he murmured, confused for a moment. That would explain his miraculous survival; none of this was real. It was a play, and he was merely a doll, manipulated at the whim of others. *What a relief.*

Then he saw that the bed had gone. The woman and child. The teddy bear was still there, lying on the floor in the middle of the room as though it had been thrown there by the hand that still gripped it. Ahmed blinked his eyes to see more clearly, and then his mouth opened and a strange, keening cry pulsated from his lips. The cry went on and on, as though his mouth and throat were independent from him. As though some great puppeteer were pulling the strings and he could not stop it. Nor could he remove his stare from the teddy bear, and the little hand clutching it.

Ahmed crawled on his hands and knees to the bear, drawn by repulsion, drawn by the strings in the hands of his relentless puppeteer. His mouth continued to wail of its own accord until it began to retch. Only when his stomach was finally empty did he manage to turn his head away. He was not a doll manipulated by some greater hand. No, it had been his own choice, this death and destruction.

Ahmed crawled over to the other bodies, looking into faces as he retched. Some of them lay face down. He tried to flip them over, but he did not have the strength, so he gazed at their profiles. No Moussa. Where the hell had Moussa got to?

One of the soldiers was conscious, and he asked for some water.

Still weeping and gagging, Ahmed supported the soldier's head with one hand and poked the tip of his water bottle between his teeth.

"Thank you," the soldier said.

There was a whine of aircraft overhead and then another huge blast. Pieces of plaster still clinging to the remaining walls fell with a crash and another cloud of dust billowed up.

Ahmed coughed and stumbled to the gaping wall to look skywards. Two warplanes were flying overhead, leisurely choosing the ultimate location for their weapons of mass murder, while the rebels shot fruitlessly into the air. Behind the first aircraft, two more warplanes were approaching. Ahmed looked down at the piles of rubble littering the street below, the carefully constructed sandbag walls, strewn willy-nilly. Shutters waved drunkenly on their hinges and gaping, mouthlike holes in the buildings opposite made it look like they were shouting at one another.

Ahmed turned around and started to stumble towards the door. He had to get out of here.

"Water," groaned the soldier on the floor again.

"They are bombing the city," Ahmed said, as he knelt down and held his water bottle to the other man's lips. Then he remembered that the other man was fighting for the side that was bombing the city.

His hand shook. "Can you hold the water yourself?" he asked.

The soldier just looked at him.

What did it matter? He could just as easily be killed here as there. It was like a nightmare, except one could not force oneself to wake up during the worst bits; one could not suddenly fly away when they were just about to get you. His cell phone vibrated again. He propped the soldier's head on his knees so he could continue to hold the bottle with one hand while he maneuvered his cell phone out of his pocket with the other.

R U OK?

Bombs here.

Here too.

R U OK?

Yes. Come home.

Try.

The soldier moved his head to one side, to indicate he had had enough. Ahmed placed his head carefully back on the floor and tried to push the door open to get out. It was blocked. He pushed harder, putting whatever strength he had left into it, but there was something big on the other side and he could not budge it. Finally, he went back to the hole in the wall and looked down at the street. There were windows and holes in the floor below him as well; it would be easy to climb down to the street. Only the fear of seeing the woman and the child again made him hesitate, as he peered down in the grips of terrified indecision. Then another plane whirred overhead, so he slung his gun over his back and began to climb.

Holding his AK-47 in front of his face as though it were a

shield, he ran in a crouch along the road. Several people were scrabbling in a mound of rubble, chucking the debris behind them as they dug. "My child, my child," a woman wept. Others scanned the skies, ready to shout at everyone to take cover if another warplane appeared. *I am becoming indifferent to all this*, Ahmed thought as he passed the wailing woman. *One becomes indifferent to pain and horror.* Then he bent his head and felt the hot pulse of tears behind his eyelids.

A flurry of shots rang over his head and he bolted into the nearest alleyway. *Am I incredibly lucky or are the army soldiers' rotten shots?* he thought. A desperate desire to get home overtook him, even though it was no safer there. He remembered dimly a time when there seemed to be a purpose to what he was doing, but the world had gone crazy. There was no longer right or wrong or reason. It was all mad chaos.

Home. He picked up his AK-47 and fired it indiscriminately at the opposite building as he pelted to the next alleyway. That was what Deeb had told him to do if he needed to get somewhere and they were firing at him. "Just shoot in the general direction of the enemy and run as fast as you can, in order to make it as difficult as possible for them to kill you," Deeb had instructed. Ahmed prayed that he wouldn't hit any innocent civilians, although the lines between guilt and innocence were fast blurring for him. The woman and child in that house had been innocent. Was he guilty? He must be guilty.

His shooting sprint had paid off and he was safely in the next alleyway; safe so long as there were no snipers on the roofs or soldiers hidden in any of the buildings or warplanes overhead.

"Here, over here," came a disembodied voice and Ahmed turned and stumbled towards an overturned, smoking car in the middle of the alleyway. Two comrades squatted behind it, sharing a cigarette. "Victory or Martyrdom For Us All!" one of them said.

"What's happening?" asked Ahmed. "Are we supposed to keep fighting?"

The comrade shrugged. "How are you supposed to fight bombs dropping out of the sky? Our leader told us, if the warplanes came, to hole up and live."

"So are you on your way home?"

"We were on our way home with five, now we are two," the comrade said, holding out the cigarette to Ahmed. "There are snipers and soldiers everywhere. It's safer to find a place with your back against a wall and a pile of sandbags or a burnt-out car in front of you." The comrade patted the heap of metal in front of them. "That way you are protected, plus you can shoot at anything coming towards you. The only thing we have to worry about now is the warplanes."

Even as he said it, a military helicopter sprang over the top of the adjacent building like the triumphant winner of a hide-and-seek game. Ahmed leapt over the burning car and raced down the alleyway and a huge blast filled his brain and then he was flying through the air. A searing pain slashed through his body and detonated in his head and he knew no more.

It was hard to return from such a pleasant dream. Fatima had been there, picking flowers in a field that stretched like a green velvet carpet dotted with crimson flowers as far as the eye could see in every direction. Fatima would know the name of the flowers, but he was too exhausted to open his mouth to ask her. And little Mazin was there, rolling about and laughing with Zaynah. Such sweet children. Perhaps he was in heaven? But the chirping birds and tinkling river were interrupted by a rasping cough, seemingly right inside his ear. He strained to listen, to hear whether his ear would cough again, and caught murmured voices, a clank of metal against metal. He was so hot. Then Mazin and he were running towards the river in order to leap into the black waters and shriek as the icy water dispelled the horrid heat, and then he wasn't thinking anything and he slept.

A scream reverberated through his head and he jerked and

froze, immobilized by the pain coursing through his legs. If he were dead, he would not feel pain. But how could he be alive? Ahmed tried to marshal his meandering thoughts, which used all their force to entice him back into unconsciousness. His mind dipped and weaved between the painless black pit where velvet fields lay and the hazy desire to know the truth. He would be perfectly happy to be dead, but the odours assailing his nostrils were not heavenly smells. They were heavy, pungent, acrid. His ear coughed again. He wanted to cough himself, banish this thick stench from his nostrils, but he was frightened of waking the horrendous pain again. With enormous effort, he opened one eye, trying to focus on the ceiling above his head. It was dark. The stench was sickening.

Ahmed watched the light for a few minutes, while his mind prodded him back to the velvet field, which would take away the thirst and the stench.

"You awake?" his right ear said.

"No," said Ahmed.

"About time. Would you like a cigarette?"

His ear could not be so stupid as to propose a smoke when he could barely breathe. With great trepidation in case that debilitating pain returned, Ahmed tensed the muscles in his neck in preparation for inching his head in the direction of his right ear. Tensing his neck muscles did not hurt. Next step. He moved his head one millimetre to the right and froze. Nothing.

A pack of cigarettes appeared over his face. "My name is Jamal. Want one?"

Ahmed gathered his courage and turned his face to the side. No pain. Maybe it had gone away. A man lay on a cot that was jammed next to his. He was propped up on one arm looking at Ahmed, two laugh-creased black eyes twinkling out of a swathe of bandages. Cautiously, Ahmed raised his head higher and looked beyond the man. A line of cots extended to the wall on either side of Ahmed's bed, and there was another line opposite him in the same pattern, with enough space between every two beds for a person to squeeze through. A long table supporting an assortment of buckets, sponges, bandages, and medical implements squatted in the corridor between the lines of beds. Light bulbs had been rigged to the ceiling, casting a circular muted glow that failed to reach the next light's orb, so some men lay in almost darkness. The cots opposite were wreathed in gloom, but Ahmed saw that most of the men there had bandages over their eyes. Next to this group, several one-armed men were huddling under a light bulb playing a game of cards. Ahmed's eyes flickered back to his companion, whose eyes nodded and smiled as he held his cigarette pack out patiently. Ahmed looked from his swaddled face down his body, and saw that one of his legs was missing. *Oh how terrible. Poor guy.* He smiled at him, and then raised his eyes beyond him. A group of men were chatting and smoking. Ahmed squinted at them, but he couldn't see any bandages.

"We are in a field hospital," he stated to his companion, letting his head fall back on the mattress.

"That's right," the man said encouragingly, holding out his cigarettes.

Ahmed grinned suddenly. "I am not dead."

"Well, you were almost dead when they brought you here. We laid bets on you. Rashad, you owe me a chunk of cash."

The man called Rashad stumbled over and peered into Ahmed's face. "You sure you're not dead?"

"I don't think so."

"Shit."

"Sorry." Ahmed was glad to see someone who could walk. "Would it be possible to get a glass of water?"

Rashad limped to the long table between the lines of beds and dipped a cup into one of the buckets. He carried it back carefully, so as not to drop the precious liquid.

"Thanks," Ahmed said, raising his head as high as he could and drinking awkwardly. As he collapsed back on the bed, exhausted by this small effort, another crippling agony shot through his legs. He cried out in anguish, and tried to reach downwards so he could hold his limbs, console them for whatever hurt had been done. But the movement brought a wave of pain so awful his vision blacked at the edges and he prayed for the release of unconsciousness.

"Try not to move too much," Jamal said. "You've been badly hurt, and I could still lose the bet with Rashad."

Please, lose your bet with Rashad, Ahmed thought, scrunching his face up against the pain. *Better dead than this.* But after a few minutes the pain abated somewhat and was replaced by an ache that allowed Ahmed to open his eyes. The dark, twinkling gaze viewed him with concern. Ahmed was moved by the man's compassion for him, in the midst of his own terrible loss, in the midst of all this death and destruction.

"I am so sorry about your leg," Ahmed said.

"I am sorry about yours too," Jamal replied.

Ahmed tried to smile. "They certainly hurt. Dear God, I've never felt such pain. Do you know what's wrong with them?"

"They were blown off by a bomb," Jamal said quietly.

Ahmed lifted his head right up so he could look at the absence of his legs and a wave of pain smashed into his skull and his eyesight dimmed, and was extinguished.

When consciousness came to reclaim him, he resisted. The black pit held no horrors or revelations. But thirst again raged in his throat and awareness plucked his mind back from the abyss of the black pit even as he yearned for it. Smell came first, the same acrid, putrid smell he now knew was wounded men and blood. Sound came next: a blend of Jamal's cough and murmuring voices, punctuated by an occasional groan. Feeling came last: his back flat against this hard mattress, ending where his legs were supposed to begin, except there were no legs. And the fact that there were no legs and never would be anymore was impossible to realize. What was the point of living as a young man without legs? What work could he do?

What wife would have him? And there was no direction to turn in to hide his tears.

A rough hand encased his for a moment and he screwed his eyes tighter, willing the unwanted spectator to go away. "I reacted just the same," Jamal whispered. "It's awful to lose our legs. But hey, look on the bright side. We've given as much as a man can give for any cause — more than those who have died even because our suffering will continue for years. But at least we don't have to fight anymore! Rashad, bring this man some water."

"Ahmed. My name is Ahmed."

"You should be able to move your head, Ahmed, and your arms, but be careful with everything else. Move with caution, until you figure out what brings on the pain. I have to tell you that sometimes it just attacks, like a tiger, right in the middle of the missing legs. Go figure."

Ahmed lifted his head for the water and looked at his surroundings again. For a minute, he thought they must have moved him while he was unconscious, because the current room was suffused with light. Then he saw the sun streaming through the holes in the walls and realized that they were lying in a bombed-out building. "Where are we?"

"We're in the nice, safe rich part of town. Safer, I should say, but not immune," Jamal gestured to the bombed-out walls.

"What is the date?"

"March 6th, 2013."

"You done?" Rashad asked irritably. "My foot hurts if I stand up for too long."

Ahmed took another sip and nodded. Rashad sat on the edge of his bed and took a sip of water from the same glass. "Why do you have to give me water?" Ahmed whispered, wondering if they were left to fend for themselves in this rich, safer part of town.

"See any nurses?" Rashad snapped, rubbing his leg gingerly.

Jamal leaned forwards. "Don't worry, we are being looked

after. Our blessed doctor is often here, and several times a day volunteers come in and give us food. Help us to do our business, you know."

"Who looks after us medically? Who cut, who did..." Ahmed gestured towards his legs, unable to finish.

"We are in the best hands in the world. Our doctor is a wali — a saint."

"A saint," Rashad echoed and bowed his head in respect.

The sightless men in the row of cots opposite raised their voices, "May Allah bless him and grant him peace. The best man in the world. A hero!"

"His hand is gentle and sure. He helps always and heals where possible," another man called.

Suddenly, it seemed like Ahmed's bed was surrounded by maimed men, calling upon Allah to praise the doctor who had healed and protected them. As Ahmed looked at them, his weak eyes again filled with tears. He felt that this devotion was a sign to him directly from Allah: "There is greatness in the world. Do not give up. Maybe you too, can contribute to the good, now that you are freed from dispensing death." Ahmed lifted up his head again, surveying the men who vied with each other to provide stories that exemplified the doctor's unselfishness, kindness, bravery. He measured the space between the beds with his eyes, to see if a wheelchair could squeeze between them. If so, he could help others, even legless, even deformed as he was. Cut down in his youth, he could still bring comfort to others who were less well off. He would get better, and then there would be many worse off than him. That thought comforted Ahmed inexpressibly. He would fix his mind on that future day, focus on healing, and perhaps, through that focus, keep the hopeless, helpless misery at bay.

Jamal leaned towards him. "Do you know what happens to doctors who help the rebels? They are taken into custody and tortured. Our doctor is a brave man, truly a hero. And so skilled! He worked hours on you. All during the night of the warplanes there was a stream of wounded pouring in here. I myself have been here for weeks, ever since a soldier lobbed a hand grenade right at my leg. Two comrades brought you in. The doctor told them that they had to find a cot somewhere because every cot was taken. They laid you on the floor in another room of this building..."

"We'll call it the reception area," sniggered Rashad, who had moved closer to hear above the hubbub.

"...with a number of others. Comrades kept coming all night, carrying the wounded, and after they'd laid them down in the reception area they ventured out into the murderous night again to raid bombed-out houses or break into abandoned apartments. They brought back anything they could get their hands on: cots, blankets, pillows, food. That night, the doctor must have operated for twenty-four hours straight. He was staggering and covered with blood by the time he'd finished. Some of the rebels helped him in what used to be the kitchen of this house. Now it's an operating room." Jamal stopped for breath and lit himself a cigarette. "Want one?" he asked Ahmed.

Ahmed shook his head.

"Apparently, there's a working stove in the kitchen so we can boil water to sterilize the doctor's tools and stuff," Jamal continued. "There's never any shortage of volunteers, so we're well looked after, nothing to worry about."

Rashad snorted. "They know it might be them, next time around, dependent on someone else to pee."

"Relatives come too," said Jamal. "The comrades do the best they can, but there's nothing quite like the touch of a woman's hand on your forehead to bring comfort."

An intense desire to see Fatima or Zaynah seized Ahmed. Just thinking of them made the penetrating ache in his legs subside. "Have my family been to visit?"

"They have to know you are here. I don't think the comrades that brought you in knew you well. They brought you a cot, but I haven't seen them since."

Fatima's fearful face flashed across his vision. "I have to get them word! They'll be dying of worry. What day is it? How long have I been here? "

"It's Wednesday. You've been here a week. One of the comrades will get word to them, don't you worry."

The ache pulsed. Ahmed cursed his weakness as tears threatened again. "Does it stop hurting so much, after a few weeks?"

"Eventually, it will stop. The doctor will give you something for the pain. He's due to come soon."

A wave of relief engulfed him. Pain medication. He was worried there wouldn't be any.

Cries of Jazak Allah Khairan — may Allah bless and reward you — swept across the room and the lines of men tried to sit up in bed to reach their hands towards the doctor who was now entering the room. A gaggle of men around him bore pails of water and food. The doctor stopped at bed after bed, exchanging a few words with each patient. Occasionally, he would give a command over his shoulder and one of the men would approach with fresh bandages and soapy water. For a moment, Ahmed strained to see through the bodies of the men in-between, but the pain in his legs drained his curiosity and he fell back on his mattress. Jamal looked over at him. "We're all learning to extract bullets and sew up wounds these days, although the patients prefer dentists, medical students, and nurses, with tailors coming in a close second. Not that they have much choice in the matter, poor devils."

Ahmed closed his eyes. He did not want to talk. He wanted the blessed release of pain medication; the ache was making him nauseous. Then perhaps he could eat something. The doctor would tell him what he should do. He waited in breathless anticipation.

"Jazak Allah Khairan," the men shouted with love in their voices. "Jazak Allah Khairan."

Now Ahmed could hear the doctor's voice replying, "Wa 'iyyakum."

Then the faintest of breezes and a different smell — clean and antiseptic — wafted up Ahmed's nostrils and a voice beside him asked, "Has this man woken up yet?"

He frowned, his eyes still closed. He must be sleeping, dreaming again about his family. How strange that it was so hard to differentiate between the states of waking and sleeping. And the never-ending, debilitating ache was still there, even in his dream. Could Allah not have taken it away, in all His mercy?

"Yes," Jamal answered. "He was awake just now. He's in a lot of pain."

Ahmed felt the faint prick of a needle in his arm.

"Who here can ensure he eats something next time he wakes up?" the doctor asked. "He must eat."

It was surreal, hearing Mohammed's familiar voice parrot the doctor's speech. *I am not asleep*, thought Ahmed, and opened his eyes.

And looked straight into the face of his brother-in-law.

CHAPTER 10 **MOHAMMED**

MOHAMMED PACED BACK AND FORTH in his room, waiting impatiently for Fatima to come upstairs. Thoughts whirled around his head incessantly: even though Ahmed had promised not to say anything, he knew that a secret discovered ceases to be a secret. This was the beginning of the end of his clandestine life. Should he tell Fatima himself before she found out? She would find it hard to reconcile his attitude towards the war with his current occupation. Sometimes he found it hard to understand himself. How could he explain it to her?

Mohammed pulled open the drawer in his bedside table. He only wrote in his journal intermittently, but perhaps it held some kind of explanation about how it had all started. Some insight into his head space at the time.

Settling himself on the bed, Mohammed cocked his head to listen for Fatima's footsteps outside the door. Quiet. He flipped the pages in his journal and began to read.

6/1/12

I am always exhausted after a day of work at the veterinary clinic. I know that I need time to myself, that it is essential to my peace of mind and happiness, yet there is really no place or time to be alone. The relentless need for a few moments by myself sometimes drives me out of the clinic and into the streets, where I join with the mass of humanity hustling along the sidewalks. I am as alone as I can be.

My brain atrophies in this job. The same work, day after day. I haven't done a new procedure or encountered a problem I need to research in order to solve, for months. Years, perhaps. Are intelligent people always, ultimately, bored at their jobs?

What advantage, then, in intelligence?

Another round of injections. A spaying. A clipping of toenails. Hardly interesting work, yet I can't turn it down, as the money is essential. The future is completely uncertain and anxiety gnaws my stomach at night. My main clientele — the well-off middle classes — are leaving the country in droves, fleeing the war. I have been forced to lay off all my staff, saving one intern who wants to gain experience. Hope springs eternal in the youthful breast; the interns are always sure they will have a fulfilling and lucrative future in this country. So many optimistic assumptions. I see the reality and wonder how much longer I'll have the means to feed my family. No point talking about it with Fatima, as she would only worry ineffectively and why should we both be condemned to that? My own worries disturb my nights and plague the days, but it changes nothing, impacts less. What will be, will be. I can repeat that to myself as often as I like — it doesn't soothe me. It is necessary to my peace of mind to feel in control of my destiny, and this war makes a mockery of control. We are all guinea pigs running around in chaos.

Still, I am alive. My family is healthy. I will do everything in my power to support my family, to keep them healthy, even if it means slaving away at something I am utterly sick of. Sometimes, I feel resentment about this, but it always dissolves when I observe Fatima's gentle face. She is the most beautiful woman I have ever met. Going home is a pleasure, when you have a woman like that waiting at the end of your journey.

I try to give the most boring jobs to my current intern, Wadi. That's what he's here for, after all, to learn by doing. I constantly debate the pros and cons of accepting interns; they take on a modicum of tedious tasks, but I have to suffer their presence all day. Wadi talks non-stop about the war. Of course, he is all for it, as most young people are, but it was funny to see how he skirted the issue when he first came to me, before he knew how the land lay. I told him outright that I supported Kassam because I believe that he is fundamentally a decent, reasonable human being forced to do inhuman things by the current situation. If the war hadn't spiralled out of control, Kassam would have instituted reforms gradually.

"But ideally," Wadi insisted, "you must believe in democracy."

These young people are so ... young. And yet they think they know everything.

"Tell me why you believe in democracy," I said, knowing his answer would take me through the pile of dreary bills I wade in once a week.

And when he had done spouting about the fundamental right to vote, to free speech, and to equality, I asked him if he were religious.

"No."

"So, if we get a democracy and it turns out that the majority of people are religious and they pass a law that all women have to cover their faces when they go out, whether they want to or not, is that the type of equality you are looking for?"

"That won't happen," he said with the complete confidence of the young. "Once we get democracy, religion will start to disappear, just like in America."

"Ahh, America. Is that your ideal? Because you obviously know nothing about the country if you think religion has disappeared there. Would you like us to be like Americans?"

"Yes," he said simply. "I love their culture. They've got it good over there, with their money and freedom."

"And happier," I said, sealing the last envelope. "Would you say they were happier?"

"They must be."

"Let me enlighten you. The Americans think that if they

buy one more of this or that happiness will be theirs, and they buy and buy and buy without stopping to wonder how come they're not deliriously happy. Why the transient pleasure they feel during the purchase disappears as soon as they see that the neighbour bought a better this or that. Even when they own three houses and five cars and have outdone all the neighbours, they still aren't happy."

"At least they can choose the best leader for their country," Wadi muttered.

"The majority of people are stupid, Wadi," I said, standing up and brushing off my trousers. "So the majority of the votes will not go to the best leader, just the best liar. You've seen the types of leaders America produces. They meddle when we don't want them and disappear when we do, rather like policemen. And the worst of them are sure to be elected twice, like George Bush with his war on terror."

I walked in to check on the spaniel bitch recovering from her spaying surgery, leaving Wadi gaping behind me. Of course, when I say most people are stupid he negates everything I've said because he thinks that's crazy. But I always speak the truth as I see it (that's why I can't stand politicians) and the vast majority of people I've met are incapable of thinking for themselves. Where is the advantage of turning the choice of leader over to the people, most of whom neither consider nor care about the greater good?

I always arrive home tired. I have limitless energy, and if it were a job I loved I could do it for 16 hours straight, but I am bored and I am an introvert, and the relentless society of other people wears down my capacity for control.

Everyone scurries around, as soon as I come in, and plates of food mushroom over the table in front of me. The children beam in my direction. Zaynah, so bright it's a pity she wasn't born a boy. A worrier like her father, watching everyone covertly, always trying to keep the peace. My rambunctious twins, bubbling with energy and mischief. They need a strong hand to keep them in line. Respect is vital, and so far I feel successful in this aspect of fatherhood: all my children are respectful to their elders. Little Na'aman is still just a baby of course; I hope he keeps his loving nature.

It is strange, the way the food appears by magic on the table as soon as I sit down. It wasn't like that before Rana came. I distinctly remember watching Fatima bustle around, cooking and preparing. How I loved to see her round arms cutting up my salad; it was all I could do not to grab them and cover them with kisses. Even when she washed the dishes with her back to me, I could see the outline of her back, and below, and I could hardly wait until the night came and I could plunge into her softness and feel calm for a moment. My soft and yielding lover.

Lately though, the gentle contours of her face are marred by worry. It is not the war; she isn't interested in politics and so long as her family is safe I don't think she really follows what's going on. Perhaps she worries about Ahmed, but not enough to dissuade him against participating in those demonstrations, the young fool. It is only a matter of time before the government sends the big artillery in to smash our little town to smithereens, and then there will be reason enough for the lines of worry etched around Fatima's eyes.

But now I believe it is Rana. Waves of hostility radiate from that viper in my nest. No doubt she spends her days pouring poison into Fatima's innocent ears, hence her constant look of anxiety. Rana is disrespectful to my face. How can I teach my own children the importance of respect if she flouts my authority and spews contempt at my dinner table? The twins watch her, and it is only a matter of time before they begin to copy her. It is only possible to instill a value such as respect by example. Will I have to beat my own children in the future because she is teaching them disrespect? I wish I could extract this poison from my home, but it is hard enough to make ends meet, even when we share housing. I'm not sure Hamid would be able to afford a house of his own, though at this time houses are probably going cheap with everyone fleeing from the war.

Rana watches me out of the corner of her eye, as though I am some unpredictable monster. It makes me angry. Home is supposed to be my sanctuary from the trials and boredom at work. Instead, I feel that everyone is waiting for me to behave badly. There is no doubt in my mind that my behaviour has worsened since Rana took up residence with us. I have always been a quick-tempered man, but it is a common characteristic among men, and as long as it is controlled it can be turned into an asset in bringing up obedient, respectful children. But if everyone watches you anxiously out of the corner of their eyes in the expectation that you will do something wrong, then slowly but surely, you begin to feel that you are that person they think you are, or rather, that your poisonous sister persuades them you are. This is not an isolated phenomenon; I have read that if you tell a child he is good then he will try and live up to that viewpoint, whereas if you convince him that he's bad then he will stop trying to be good, because he doesn't feel good. So the deterioration in my ability to control my behaviour is directly linked to Rana's evil influence.

Ahmed doesn't help either. What a foolish idealist that boy is. I don't know why I bother discussing anything with him; he doesn't listen. I try to paint the future for him, the uncertain future where we will be subjected to the whim of the uneducated masses, the dictators of our future government thanks to the efforts of Ahmed and his friends. Since religion is the opiate of the masses, what does he think will happen?

"The ranks of the rebels are swelling. Territory by territory, we are taking over the whole country!" he tells me proudly, convinced that this is proof I am on the wrong side.

"Who is swelling the ranks of the rebels?" I ask him.

"Defectors from the government's army, who are too disgusted by the government's actions to continue to fight for them."

"And?"

"Everyone! Everyone will eventually be on our side. The future is certain. It is only a matter of time before Kassam falls."

"Yes, many people are joining the rebels. Including Al-Qaeda-aligned jihadis and political Islamists stirred by the rhetoric of the Muslim Brotherhood. How could you forget them when they head the fighting? Just as they will head the country once they've ousted Kassam, and then we'll all live happily together in an extremist Islam state. We can cheer when some hungry pauper is dismembered for stealing a loaf of bread. Or perhaps I'll be flogged publicly for having a drink of arak."

"That's not going to happen," Ahmed mutters. But he doesn't know. None of us can know. We can only follow what is happening in other countries where the old governments have been overthrown. And it doesn't look good. I struggle to sleep at night, beset with overwhelming anxiety about the future of our country, about our money troubles. I gaze at Fatima's enticing profile as she sleeps and agonize futilely.

I could not live without Fatima. The only times I am really happy is when I am with her. I watch her move around the kitchen, or our bedroom, and marvel that the long dress she wears covers such beauty. Marvel that her beauty is mine. As she raises her arm to return the plates to their home on the shelf, I glimpse the swell of her breast, and revel in the fact that I am the only person who knows their contour and shape intimately, who has the right to bury his head between their soft roundness, to kiss and hold, as the brown nipples pucker and inflame. I love every inch of her; sometimes, at night, when she is lying next to me and I move my hand freely wherever it wants to go, I feel like weeping for my luck. My rough, working hand traverses the length of her body from her breasts over the pliant skin of her stomach to the hard bone and rough hair, and the lips of her private part, and the treasures within. I can snuggle any part of myself anywhere on that body. It is more important to have a loving wife than a stimulating job. I should not complain about my job — many would see it as an excellent one. Perhaps I've just been doing it for too long. A change would be good if it were only possible.

29/6/12

When I recall those thoughts now they seem almost prophetic. Two nights ago, I was coming home from the clinic at the usual hour. I could hear gunfire from the square and took a circuitous route home so as to stay as far away from the fighting as I could. As I passed through a dark alleyway, I almost stepped on a human hand. I peered down, and through the gloom, I saw a man lying on his side. He was looking at me.

"Can you hear me?" I asked.

"Help me," he whispered. "Please help me."

"Would you like me to take you to the hospital?" I looked towards the main street at the far end of the alley, wondering what the chances were of a taxi materializing if I stood there long enough.

"No," the man at my feet wheezed. "Not the hospital. They will kill me. And you too." He shook his head sadly. "You cannot help me. I will die here."

"Nonsense," I said briskly. "I'm a vet and I bet I could patch you up in two minutes if I could get you to my clinic. Where are you hurt?"

He gestured to his stomach. There was a spreading stain of blood on the shirt. I applied pressure to his wound while I checked him over for injuries and asked him to move his hands and feet to see whether there was any damage to his spinal cord. I took his pulse, then tore his shirt into strips and constructed a crude tourniquet, which could stem the bleeding during the transport to my clinic. There was no exit wound; I had never extracted a bullet before but how hard could it be? "Listen carefully. I am going to lift you up and carry you to the clinic on my back. This is going to hurt, but once we get there I will give you pain medication and you won't feel any pain at all when I extract the bullet. Do you understand?"

The man nodded, and I crouched down and tried to wrap his arms and legs around my neck, holding firmly with both hands. He groaned when I stood up, but I made sure his wound wasn't pressing against anything and practically glided all the way to the clinic, so he would suffer as little as possible from any jarring movement.

Once we got there, I laid him on the animals' operating table and told him that I was going to knock him out so he wouldn't feel any pain, and then extract the bullet and sew him up. He would be as good as new. He grasped my hands with tears in his eyes and thanked me until I felt quite embarrassed. Although I had studied the human body and its organs while at university, it would have soothed my nerves to research the exact layout of the muscular and digestive systems, where the bullet appeared to be lodged, but the Internet was down as usual. Despite my trepidation, the bullet was easy to locate and I thoroughly enjoyed the whole procedure, professionally transforming the gory mess of his stomach into a thin, clean, stitched line. There is so much similarity between animals and humans.

The problem now was where to put him. Wadi came in at eight every morning; I knew he wouldn't betray me to the authorities but the fewer people know about something the easier it is to keep it a secret. So I came in at seven-thirty the next morning to greet my patient who was, as expected, awake but woozy. I got an address from him and bundled him into a taxi, confident he'd be fine.

There is no contradiction whatsoever in my actions. I think the rebellion will lead to worse things, and in reply to those who tell me it needs to get worse before it gets better, I say that in that time it would have gotten better anyway, without all the bloodshed. Of this I am convinced. I am glad that other Arab states rose up and overthrew their governments — change would not have occurred without those pioneers, but we did not have to go the same route. It would have happened naturally.

But that has no bearing whatsoever on what happened the other night. There was a man in need, and I helped him. It is my duty as a human being, and doubly so as a doctor, to proffer aid when someone is in dire need. But if this is true, then how can I ignore the fact that many people are in need? Is it honourable behaviour on my part to withhold help that I am peculiarly suited to give, to people who are denied help elsewhere?

What am I considering? Taking my little black bag with me when I go home at night, in case I meet someone else in need? Or going to the source of the need and helping many? That would be dangerous. I would risk not only my own life, but that of my beloved Fatima and our children. I have no right to risk their lives. But if I save a thousand lives before I am found out, would that then be justified? Obviously, from an objective standpoint, a thousand lives are worth more than my family. It is outrageous that regular doctors are being thrown in prison and tortured just for fulfilling their duty as doctors. It is absolutely wrong, and I have a chance to right that wrong, just a little.

It is a hard decision. I will have to think on it over the weekend. But perhaps on Sunday after I have finished work, I will wend my way home along my regular route. And I will take my black bag.

4/1/13

So much has happened since I last jotted down some notes! Fatima is still angry with me because I punished the twins severely for desecrating a poster of Kassam in public. It hurt me to beat them, but there was no other way. They have no idea what might happen if the wrong people saw them do it. Not evil people, necessarily, just frightened. Trying to save their own skins. Age doesn't deflect punishment in this war. I did it to protect my boys, to ensure they don't do anything so foolish again. Better they fear their father than die a tortuous death.

Fatima spent several nights with them before I asked her to rejoin me. I did try and explain why the punishment had to be so severe, gently hinting that terrible things are happening that she knows nothing about. Her rigid body transmits contempt, as though she feels I'm the one who has no idea. Obviously, she doesn't know about my clandestine activities, but she must realize I keep up-to-date with everything that is going on, all the time. She has never felt contempt for me before, and I hope it is a misdirected maternal reaction rather than the result of Rana's slow poisoning.

Retaliation and counter-retaliation on a daily basis, now. The government has brought in the big guns, just as I had predicted. They have already dropped helicopter bombs and this new trend will no doubt escalate. If so, it will mark the end of normal life, even insofar as it is normal now. Perhaps I was destined to play a part in this war, albeit a minor one, because every time I went out with my little black bag in the beginning, someone in dire need begged for my assistance.

Then, one day during my wanderings last September — truly as though destiny guided my footsteps — I passed an abandoned building that had obviously participated in a violent drama that had shattered its windows and demolished part of the walls, even though it's in the same part of town as my clinic, quite removed from the centre of the fighting. My footsteps turned in that direction of their own volition.

That abandoned building contained a huge, well-lit space in the basement with two or three little rooms branching off the main space as well as a functioning bathroom. As soon as I saw it, my mind envisioned rows of cots lining the room along each side. It was uncanny, the perfect attributes of that space. A large, gaping hole in the wall let in light, but the hole faced the back of the building so that it couldn't be seen from the street side. I meandered through the rest of the building trying doors, some of which had been left open by their former occupants, others broken into. I explored apartment after apartment methodically and — this was so out of character for me — broke down three resisting doors. What treasures I found. Seven cots, which I lugged down to the basement apartment, starting the first row. I gathered numerous sheets, eating utensils, cups and glasses, soap, kettles. A strange energy pervaded my body and I practically ran to my clinic to gather medical supplies. Not enough, of course, but I could solve that problem when I came to it. I possessed a strange belief that everything would turn out fine. As it has, as it has!

That same night I went out with my little black bag as usual, but instead of bringing one patient back to the clinic and taking care of him, I left him in my new place of work (he wasn't at death's door) and exited immediately to bring another and another. As I trudged along, half-carrying my fourth patient, I met two men who were half-carrying another patient, and shouted at them to follow me. I was like a whirlwind, rushing from bed to bed, dispensing all the skill and medications at my disposal.

It must have been the very next day that I phoned Wadi and told him that I was taking a few weeks off, assuring him that he was experienced enough to hold the fort on my behalf. He was bemused, then pleased. Presumably, he still is pleased. If there are any problems, he can always contact me. I can't imagine how I was ever satisfied looking after animals.

The news spread like wildfire. Finished were my excursions with my little black bag: now, they come to me. More and more of them come, not just bearing patients but food, water, soap, and — oh joy — medical supplies. Within weeks I had started to make lists of the things I needed, handing them out to those mostly nameless men who are my allies, no matter what their background, political affinity, or level of religious fanaticism. I am grateful for everything they give me, and miraculously it seems that we always have more or less enough, and never lose a life through lack of supplies. I have never known such comradeship; it brings me great satisfaction. Of course, there are frustrating days with too much work and not enough hands, but these nameless, silent partners of mine offer their services as assistant and nurse, and suddenly I am teaching them how to clean a wound, how to sew it up. I teach them how to check breathing, staunch blood, measure pulses, check for bone injuries, so that when any given skirmish is over they can look after the patient until I can get to them. We concoct a stretcher so two men can carry the badly wounded patients relatively smoothly. I need more hands, always, but somehow, everyone is looked after well enough.

Rough politeness I expect, but the gratitude and deference of my co-workers and patients surprises and exhausts me. After all, they are risking their lives too, and can't expect to gain any credit from my pro-Kassam attitude, if worse comes to worst. In any case, my political affiliations are entirely irrelevant. I am helping mankind, and the more I help, the more the danger I am bringing to my unsuspecting family is justified. And the danger to myself.

I try to be kinder to Ahmed, who wears a shell-shocked expression half the time. Despite his strong belief that he is fighting for democracy, he's essentially a gentle soul like his sister, and this ongoing violence is hard on him. Sometimes, he looks at me as though he wonders whether I am coming around to his point of view, but I am not kinder to him because of that. Simply, I see all the shattered, bloodied young men crossing my threshold day after day, and I know one day it will be him.

The pity of it.

Strangely enough, I am no longer consumed by anxiety. My nights aren't disrupted with panic attacks. I sleep like a log. So I don't know why I lost my temper like that with Rana last month. I am exhausted, and her attitude towards Mazin has always bothered me. She focuses on him all the time in this intense, brooding way. She always has. Clearly, she is an intelligent woman and it's a shame she couldn't have had more children to use up her prodigious energy, but the situation being what it is she is completely obsessed in an unhealthy way with her only son. She can't leave the boy alone, and his strangeness is the result of that. Of course, he must learn to fight for himself — does she want him to be beaten up all his life? Still, there is no excuse for my violent loss of temper. I am obviously exhausting every reserve of energy with my new employment. I must be more aware of that, in the hopes that consciousness will enable me to master my temper at home.

There's no point dwelling on what will happen to my family if I am taken. If I don't help these men, then many of them will die. The choice is hardly mine to make; I have to do everything I can to save every precious life. Every morning, when I leave for work, regretting the necessity of lying to my open, gentle Fatima, I think it might be the last time I see her. Perhaps today, government forces will discover our basement hideaway in the wrong part of town, and drag the doctor to their sordid torture chambers. Or some poor bastard, splayed like a jellyfish as they beat his feet, will blurt out all the information he can find in his poor head, just to stop the pain. One day it will end, and every day I look into my wife's eyes and tell her goodbye. I try to invest that word with all the love in my heart, to apologize for the grief I will someday bring to her.

CHAPTER 11 **ZAYNAH**

ZAYNAH HUDDLED UNDER HER COVERS, pouring her heart into the pages of her journal. All the pain of the past few days. She held her head stiffly to the side, so that the tears leaking from her eyes would not smudge the ink.

I will look after him until we are both old and feeble, she wrote. *He will never be alone. Oh Allah, if I could only share his physical pain. I can see the suffering on his face, as I coax him to eat, insisting that he nourish himself, bite after bite. His eyes are deep with suffering.*

"What are you doing?" Mazin glided up to her bed silently.

Zaynah snapped her journal shut. "Go away, Mazin. I'm busy."

"You are always busy now that Ammo Ahmed has come home."

"Now that half of Khalo Ahmed has come home," she retorted, intending to chastise Mazin for the note of resentment in his voice. But Mazin, trying to look duly chastised, could not repress a snorted giggle at her words, and then to her horror they were both shaking in silent hysterics. Zaynah pinched herself viciously, and then smacked Mazin on his back.

"Be careful," he said, drawing himself up to his full height. "I know how to fight now." His face crumpled. "...Half of Ammo Ahmed."

"Shut up, it's not funny," she hissed, truly repentant now. "Can't you imagine what it must be like, to be such a wonderful, gifted man, reduced to a state of dependence and ... helplessness?"

Mazin wiped his tears with a serious expression. "Awful. I can't imagine. I really do feel sorry for him, but I still don't get why you can't hang out with me anymore. Ammo Ahmed sleeps half the time anyway."

"I am so miserable for him," Zaynah whispered through her hair. "He doesn't really want to live anymore. I can see it in his eyes. I sit there, focusing with all my might, holding his hand and imagining energy and joy flowing from my body to his. Trying to transmit the will to live. But sometimes I can feel his thoughts and feelings flowing into me, and suddenly I see his future, and it's so obvious why he doesn't care about life anymore that it feels stupid to keep willing him to want to live. As though I'm lying or something."

"Neat," Mazin said. "Did you think of doing that all by yourself? Transmitting thoughts like that? It's like telepathy. You're doing telepathy. That's so neat."

"Actually Ammé Rana gave me the idea. She told me to imagine energy and joy flowing from me to him. But I told you, it's not working."

"Have you tried hypnotism?"

Zaynah did not answer. Mazin could only see her hands beneath the sheaf of her hair, and the *drip drip drip* of her tears as they splashed onto them. He was overcome with a desperate desire to help his cousin and his uncle. "I know!" he said excitedly after a minute. "Let's show him the entry in your diary where it says what a hero is. Can you find it?"

Zaynah flipped back through her diary. "Here it is:

1. *Someone who fights for what he believes in.*
2. *Someone who protects his family from harm.*
3. *Someone who is noble.*
4. *Someone who helps others even when it puts them in danger.*"

"Yes!" said Mazin. "That's exactly what Ahmed did. You should show it to him. Tell him he's your definition of a hero. That'll cheer him up."

Doubtfully, Zaynah smiled. "Thank you, Mazin. I'll try it. Did you want something else?"

"Just to hang out."

"I'm busy."

She could see that Mazin was frantically raking through further persuasion tactics. She felt sorry for him, but she didn't have time for him right now. Every waking moment was spent tending to Ahmed, and after she had squeezed her chores in around her nursing duties it was time for bed. And bedtime was reserved for writing in her diary, so that she would never forget this terrible, terrible time of her life. So she could relate to disbelieving grandchildren the horrors of her time. Then, once a permanently tear-stained Fatima had kissed her good night, it was more essential than ever to do the rounds from door to closed door, to keep her finger on the family's pulse in this turbulent time of change. Ahmed had changed, of course, and he would never be the same. Fatima had changed; her once lineless face cast in an expression of dread. What would be the next, insupportable trial? How much more would they be expected to suffer in this dreadful war? Mohammed had changed most of all. She could not put her finger on it, nor had eavesdropping revealed the reason behind his change. He looked tired, but also more purposeful. Otherwise, there was no definable change. Perhaps she was imagining it, except she was positive that Ahmed talked to him in a completely different way. Not just feigned respect, but real. Why? Was it because he felt Mohammed had been proved right, finally? That his attitude about the war as an unnecessary waste of human life was correct? "No!" she wanted to scream at Ahmed. "You are right, you were right about everything. It's all worth it! It will all have been worth it in the end and the lines of people queuing to sign their ballots to elect a new leader will go down on their knees to thank you for it! And they will treat you with honour, and never forget."

She looked up. "Are you still there?" she asked Mazin, whose face was like a book, listing, contemplating, and rejecting an inventory of strategies to prolong his visit.

"You're a hero too, you know," said Mazin. "The bullies have stopped waiting for me after school. In fact, Sami even asked me for help in math the other day. I don't think you can beat up someone who has helped you in math, do you?"

"I don't care about what's going on with you right now, okay? I'm sorry, but my focus is on Ahmed, and you have to leave me alone and not demand attention all the time. Grow up and stop being so selfish. It's not all about you."

Mazin's face declared he was upset. "I wasn't thinking about me, I was thinking about you! I was trying to make you feel better by telling you that I think you're a hero. Not just because of what you did for me, but because of what you're doing for Ahmed. You're protecting your family from harm. He might die if it wasn't for you. You're a noble person, Zaynah."

She flushed with pleasure.

Encouraged, Mazin perched on the edge of her bed. "I have another idea that might help Ammo Ahmed. Do you have any money?"

"Some. My mother usually gives me a few coins on my birthday, but I've never spent it. Why do you ask?"

Mazin wriggled happily, pleased with his idea and Zaynah's interest. "Well, if I had been active in the fighting and then couldn't participate anymore, I'd feel bad too. Not because I couldn't fight anymore, because I wouldn't really like fighting. Can you imagine how awful it must be?" Mazin paused, frowning as he tried to imagine the horror.

"Go on," snapped Zaynah.

Mazin shot her a reproachful look. "I'd feel bad, because I couldn't *participate* anymore. I'd feel shut out from everything I'd been a part of."

"Your point?"

"So I was trying to think — how can an immobile man feel part of things? Well, if Ammo Ahmed gets better, eventually maybe he can reach out to other wounded people and maybe help them or something, but right now he still needs help himself. So, a radio!" Mazin pronounced triumphantly.

"A radio?"

"Yes! If he can listen to the radio he won't be so cut off anymore. He'll at least know what's going on. Besides, it'll give him something to do."

Zaynah chewed on her fingernail, trying to determine if this was a great idea or a stupid one. She tried to picture her beloved Khalo Ahmed in his little bedroom, gazing out the window onto the street, hour after hour, hopelessly. Occasionally, he would pick up a book, but he couldn't seem to concentrate. He did devour the paper every day, even though the state-controlled newspapers called the noble freedom fighters "terrorists." But his anger over that was better than apathy. Maybe the radio wasn't such a bad idea. Instead of finishing it in an hour, it could provide antidepressive rage-filled entertainment all day. "No way do we have enough money for a radio."

"Let's check out the store on our way home tomorrow and see how much they cost."

"Let's see how much we have."

"There's a second-hand store on Al Jalaa Road that sells that type of thing!"

"No way we'll have enough."

Mazin tugged her sleeve, bouncing on the bed with excitement. "We can ask the twins for any birthday money they've saved! We can frame it like it's a contribution to the war. They'll like that."

Zaynah beamed at Mazin, her desire for solitude forgotten. They both jumped to their feet and rushed to the twins' room together. Abdul and Ali were engaged in a ferocious tug of war over a piece of Lego.

"Is that all the two of you ever do?" Zaynah shouted at them. "Fight?"

"It's my piece of Lego," Abdul hissed, bending his brother's finger to breaking point.

"It is not," yelled Ali, whipping the abused finger from his brother's grasp and trying to poke him in the eye with it.

"It's a piece of Lego," snapped Zaynah with contempt. "One piece of lousy Lego."

"One piece of lousy Lego which is mine," shouted Abdul.

Zaynah glanced at Mazin for support, but he was hopping on one foot and giggling madly, enjoying the show.

"Right, give me the Lego *now*," Zaynah held out her hand, exactly as her mother would have done.

Both twins crashed to the ground as Ali managed to hook his leg around Abdul's knee and jerk; the surprise of the fall caused Abdul to relinquish his grip and for a split second Ali was the victor, holding the piece of Lego high in the air in triumph, before Abdul grabbed him by the neck and shoved him to the floor, pinning the triumphant hand under his knee and wresting the Lego piece from it.

"Give it to me," Zaynah barked, frightened to raise her voice too loud.

"I'll get it for you Zaynah," Mazin cried and leapt joyfully into the fray.

Zaynah regarded the three writhing bodies with disgust. *Boys, honestly!*

"In a minute, Abi will hear you and then you'll be sorry!" All three boys froze on the floor: Ali, prostrate but unbeaten, in the act of strangling his brother who was trying to dislodge a clinging Mazin from his back. Zaynah stepped forward and snatched the Lego piece from Abdul's reluctant grip. "Now listen and try to be sensible for two minutes. Mazin and I have something very important to ask you."

They boys arranged themselves in a row on the floor, eyes fixed on the Lego piece in Zaynah's hand. "Khalo Ahmed is very sad because of his legs, and we were trying to think about how to make him feel better. If he had more ways to occupy himself during the day it might help, so we've decided to try and buy him a radio. When he feels better, he'll be able to continue to contribute to the war effort, so by helping him we're also contributing to the war effort. If we all pool our money together, we might be able to do it."

Abdul reluctantly detached his gaze from the Lego and focused on his sister's face. "What money?"

"Doesn't our mother give you some money on your birthdays? And when our aunt came to visit last year, didn't she give you some money? And our grandparents?"

The twins scrunched up their faces.

"We spent Khalé Nadia's money…"

"…on sweets and toys."

"What, all of it?"

The twins disappeared under their beds and emerged a minute later, dusty but triumphant, and poured some coins into Zaynah's hands.

"That's it? One hundred liras? That's hardly anything! What are we supposed to do with that?"

"You can have it, Zaynah."

"All of it."

"We bought sweets and toys."

"We didn't know it would be needed for the war effort."

"If we get any more, we'll definitely give it straight to you…"

"…for the war effort."

Zaynah looked at them both, curling her hand around the money and the Lego piece. "Okay. Thanks, I guess. You greedy little pigs, wasting all your money on stupid things. Haven't you ever heard of saving?"

They looked at her blankly as she turned on her heel and left the room, Mazin hot on her heels. He continued onto his room and Zaynah felt relieved that she could finally be alone, but within minutes he was back. "Look, Zaynah, I've got almost one thousand liras," he said, pouring the contents of his money box onto her lap.

"I have almost seven hundred."

"Do you think it will be enough?"

"We'll find out tomorrow." Zaynah leaned forward and brushed the hair off Mazin's forehead. "Actually, I like to run home straight from school to look after Ahmed. Your mother is too busy, and my mother cries too much to do a good job. Can you check out radio prices for me?"

For her! Mazin nodded so hard his whole body shook.

"I have to be alone for a while now, Mazin. Okay?"

He kept nodding and beaming as he scampered back to his room.

Zaynah listened until she heard his door close, and within minutes she was crouched outside her parent's door, pressing her ear against it. Fatima was weeping. She had been weeping ever since Ahmed came home, and Zaynah wanted to shake her. She could tell Ammé Rana felt the same way about it, though there was only compassion and pity in her voice when she talked to Fatima. Zaynah wished she could block her mother from seeing Ahmed. Although Fatima dried her eyes before entering his room, her whole face was so despondent that she made everything worse. Mohammed had explained to them that Ahmed was in no danger for his life, after examining him upon his arrival. With his next breath, he had exhorted them to keep cheerful, or at least pretend to be, because the main danger for Ahmed now was depression and hopelessness. So Fatima tried, wiping her eyes and plastering a smile on her face that anyone could see was fake. Zaynah leapt to do everything herself, hoping that slowly Fatima would relax back into her regular routine and stay out of the sickroom, once she saw her brother was being taken care of so well.

Mohammed was soothing his wife behind the closed door. "I know, I know habibti."

"But why can't we leave, Mohammed," Fatima whispered in a tearful voice. "Everybody else is leaving."

Zaynah had to strain her ears to hear.

"Not everyone is leaving, Fatima. The vast majority are staying."

Zaynah could hear a trace of irritation in her father's voice. She knew in normal times he would have said, "Don't be so stupid," if anyone had made an untrue statement. She appreciated his efforts at gentleness. They were all making an effort.

It was all such an effort. For how long?

Fatima echoed her thoughts, as though she could hear her daughter through the wall. "For how long, Mohammed? How long am I supposed to agonize over my children every time they leave the house? And not only then! There have been house-to-house raids, Mohammed. At any point during the day I could hear a knock, and they'd come in and find my poor brother and they'd know…" Fatima's voice trailed off in repressed sobs. Zaynah knew she was pressing her mouth against the hem of her apron; probably rocking back and forth as well.

"I know it's very hard for you," said Mohammed, "and if I thought the family was in immediate danger I would consider the possibility of leaving or sending you away at least."

"What do you mean?"

"I would allow you to leave if I thought it was necessary to save your life, but this is my country and it is cowardly to flee when one's country is in peril."

"Our presence isn't helping our country."

"We are helping just through being reasonable people in the middle of chaos. Our simple presence weighs in on the power of good. We have a duty to stay, at least I do. I don't think I could forgive myself if I fled."

"How could we go without you?" said Fatima fearfully.

"You're not leaving yet, so there's no point in discussing it," Mohammed replied. "Meanwhile, try to keep your spirits up — we have a lot to be thankful for — and if anything happens to make you truly anxious, then phone my cell. You can phone any time you are frightened and I will come home immediately, okay, habibti?"

There was a shuffling and a creaking, as though someone was getting into bed. Then, Zaynah heard the muffled murmur that meant her mother was praying. Silently, she got to her feet and crept down the hallway towards Mazin's room. How would she feel if they went to another country? Would she feel like a coward, a traitor betraying her country, like her father? Or would she be caught up in the excitement of the novelty? She had never been in another country before.

Zaynah approached Mazin's door with trepidation. She knew it was getting late and she should be in bed, and she also knew that the consequences of being caught by Ammé Rana would be much worse than if her mother caught her. But listening to the progression of Rana's viewpoint since her big fight with Mohammed was like following a story, where every aspect of the main character's personality was examined from every perspective. First, she had declared that he was completely insane and they had to leave immediately. But then she had, through Hamid's arbitration ("Yes, his behaviour is reprehensible but we can't afford to move…. He's not hurting Mazin and it might be a good thing for him to learn to fight…. I think Mohammed regrets his violence and if you'd only face him I think he'd apologize….") begun to modify her views. He was still insane and his behaviour was both crazy and unpredictable, but the focus now was on how to live peaceably together. Was it better to lock oneself away or just play mute? Zaynah loved the way her aunt's mind worked; she strove towards the truth always, recognizing that her own perspective was not the whole truth. She indulged in fascinating, endless analyses of Mohammed's character and possible sources for his insanity, which included interesting tidbits about their childhood and parents. Illicit fascination grew, and Zaynah had made guilt-ridden, terrified forays into her aunt's bedroom, searching for her diary. Such a woman must keep a diary, Zaynah had no doubt. She regularly read Mazin's sporadic entries, and had skimmed through her mother's pile of exercise books as well, even though they were full of religious stuff and were rather hard to read. She had searched everywhere she could think of for Rana's diary — she was sure it contained all sorts of important revelations about life and would certainly shed light on Rana's relationship with her father as well — but without success. Stupid Mazin didn't even know whether his own mother kept a diary.

At least she could listen. She sensed that if Rana knew her motives for eavesdropping she would understand them completely. Zaynah sidled up to the door and pressed her ear against it.

"Please my love, stop teasing," moaned Hamid.

Rana's low laugh. "Is this teasing you? Is this called teasing?"

Zaynah froze outside the door.

Hamid groaned again. Then there was a huge thump as though bodies were thrashing in the bed. A muffled squeal from Rana. "That's not fair! You used your superior strength."

"Everything is fair in love and war."

"Ouch, let me up."

"Not a chance."

For a second, Zaynah wondered whether Hamid was hurting Rana, but another stifled laugh reassured her.

Sounds of kissing.

She should leave; this was dreadful of her.

"I want to be on top," said Rana. Scuffling. Giggles. The bed shuddered.

"Not a chance," repeated Hamid.

Zaynah was riveted to the door. She felt as if she couldn't move even if she wanted to. A strange yearning infused her body, and she hugged herself wickedly, holding her breath in order not to lose a sound.

"Well then, you have to do as I say or I won't let you in. Kiss me here."

A second of silence. Zaynah stopped breathing.

"Now there. Lick me ... here. Harder. Yes. Yes."

Zaynah's mouth hung open. Licking? She couldn't believe it. It was impossible to imagine her aunt and uncle licking each other. She wanted to dive into the privacy of her bed and lift up her nightdress and touch the places where she imagined and visualized and pictured and fancied.... Then Ammé Rana gave a groan, but it was not a groan of pain, and Zaynah was running, running along the hallway to her own bedroom, her body on fire with its insistence to be touched. She felt such gratitude that she shared the room only with Na'aman, when most of the girls in her school shared one room with all their siblings! But just as her foot touched the threshold of her sanctuary a weak voice called, "Water."

Zaynah stood still, breathing hard and with a strange heaviness in her body. But then the call came again and as soon as she heard a shuffling from her mother's room, she had raced into the kitchen for a glass of water and was holding it to Ahmed's lips before Fatima could open her door.

"I can hold it myself," said Ahmed petulantly. He sighed, and dropped his head back on the pillow. "Thank you."

Zaynah looked at his worn face with love. She wished she could smooth away his wearied look. "Can't you sleep?"

"No,"

"The pain?"

"Sometimes, even when Mohammed has given me something for the pain, I still feel it. And you know what's weird? I feel it in my legs, even though they're not there."

"Would it help if I gave you a massage?" Zaynah had never given a massage before, but she suddenly wanted to do it very much.

Ahmed threw her a peculiar look, and she felt agonizingly mortified. "It might help you sleep," she mumbled.

"My dreams are terrible."

"How can I help you? I want to help you so much."

"Who can help me? I am twenty-two years old, and my life is over."

"Don't say that!" Zaynah seized his hand, rubbed his palm frenetically. "You have lost your legs, but not your heart, or your mind. Who knows what else you might accomplish?"

"I can't accomplish anything in this war," Ahmed replied, pulling his hand from hers. "I don't even know what's going on! From being in the middle of everything, feeling that my finger was on the pulse of the action, I'm cut off from everything. I can't stand it."

Zaynah hugged herself as she thought of the radio. It was very hard not to tell him right away, but he might easily scoff at the idea in his present, negative state. No, it was better to put the actual radio right into his hands; she could not wait to see the look on his face.

"I didn't mean accomplishments in the war, I meant in your life. I bet you'll accomplish more than you would have if this terrible thing hadn't happened to you, because you have suffered so much, and can understand the suffering of others."

Ahmed snorted. "You sound like Rana."

"You see? I made you smile." Zaynah laughed, delighted.

Ahmed instantly stopped smiling. "It's meaningless words, to make me feel better. Who cares whether I understand the suffering of others. And I can tell you the suffering of others is the last thing on my mind right now. I can't help them. I'm useless, useless, useless." With each word, Ahmed struck the side of the bed in despair.

"You're not," Zaynah cried, grabbing his hand again. "You are the most wonderful person I know. You're a hero."

"Some hero."

"Do you know what the definition of hero is? It's my own definition, and I wrote it in my diary ages ago, long before you were hurt. A hero is someone who fights for what he believes in, and is noble, and helps others even when it puts him in danger. That's you, can't you see? You're a hero, and one day everyone will know it. And since you have the qualities of a hero, who knows what else you will do? Perhaps you'll have a role in the new government when this one falls!"

Ahmed pulled his hand from hers again. "Do you think I'll receive special attention just because I've been hurt? Thousands have been hurt."

"No, I think you'll receive special attention because you are a hero, and the others who were hurt aren't. It's not because you were fighting that you are a hero, it's just because you are. It's in your blood. So, when the war is over, your noble character and great brain will ensure you a place in the new government if you want it and go for it. But first you have to get well!"

Ahmed smiled, raising his hand to touch Zaynah gently on the cheek. Her cheek felt like it was on fire. "You say that because you love me, Zaynah. I'm not really a hero and you know it."

"You didn't really want to fight, did you? Yet you did. Like I said, you have what it takes, and I think great things are in store for you."

"My life is over, Zaynah. I can't walk. I'm dependent on others for everything. I can't even pee by myself. What kind of job can I do?"

Zaynah gestured at the pile of university books and binders in the corner of the room "Continue your studies, get your degree. We'll get you a wheelchair when you're a bit better and you'll get around just fine. Do you think every job requires feet? Maybe you'll have an office job, as a programmer. You like computers. Maybe you'll be leading the country. Do you think you can't do that from a sitting position?"

Ahmed took another sip of water. Zaynah watched his throat swallow with painful tenderness. "You're very good to me, Zaynah. It's a pity you couldn't have stopped at 'programmer' because I could almost imagine that possibility, but when you tell me I might be president in the next breath I realize you're just spouting anything to cheer me up."

"That's not true! You know there are lots of jobs you could do."

Ahmed began to rub his chest. "Even so, that's only half of life." His voice sank to a whisper. "I will never get married."

Zaynah gave him a passionate look. "I would marry you," she said.

Ahmed shifted uncomfortably in his bed, chafed at his stomach. "You're my niece."

A wave of heat tinted Zaynah's cheeks. "I'm just saying if we weren't related," she said, horribly embarrassed.

"I think I'll try and sleep now."

Zaynah leapt to her feet and stepped toward the door. She couldn't leave it like that; she must say something else. She wished she was already in her own bed, raking through every nuance of the conversation to see if she had been forward, or inappropriate, or insensitive. But she could not leave without another word. She would not be able to face him tomorrow. At the door she stopped. "Mazin, the twins, and I have got a surprise for you. It will make you happy."

Ahmed smiled at her. "Just by being yourself you make me happy. I am so lucky that you are looking after me."

Zaynah beamed, all shame forgotten, and skipped all the way to her bedroom.

Zaynah always felt a spark of pleasure when she saw Mazin strolling out the doors with the other children when school had finished. Although Mazin called her actions heroic, she knew he believed that the change would have happened anyway. He was forging a position for himself as academic head of the class, and many of the boys were approaching him for help with their studies. That, he believed, was the real source of the change. But Zaynah knew she had made a difference, initiating the shift between bullying and ignoring. Maybe his academic prowess had softened the ignoring into gruff acceptance of a sort, but she had started the ball rolling.

"I wonder if anything will happen today," she said to Mazin as soon as he had caught up with her. It was a question they had asked each other every day since the night of the bombs. The first day, walking home, they had been shocked by the number of damaged houses. Mazin had wanted to explore, but she had grabbed him by the hand and propelled him home, using dire threats to extract promises from the twins that they would not go near any bombed-out buildings that same evening. Who knew what was hiding behind those sad, drooping walls? She always enjoined the whole family to hurry home as fast as they could. Often, they could hear sporadic fire as they marched homewards, and fear churned with excitement as they rushed to reassure their anxious mother that all was well as soon as they could. Home was their sanctuary; the world had become menacing. There had been no overhead planes dropping packages of death since the night of the bombs, but the fighting continued and the sound of shells permeated their days and nights. The main thrust of the combat had moved to the outskirts of the town, where the rebels had apparently set up arms caches, kitchens, and sleeping quarters for their ever-growing army.

"I hope not," Mazin replied, marching proudly and throwing covert glances in both directions.

"Okay, stop looking around like that."

"Like what?"

"Weirdly. Can you see anybody else swivelling their heads right to left like some type of windshield wiper?"

Mazin doubled over with laughter.

"Nobody is doing that either," Zaynah snapped, irritated. "Focus, remember? Look around, and do what everybody else is doing. If nobody else is doing it, then probably you shouldn't be doing it either."

Mazin straightened up and gazed forward. Suddenly, his mouth dropped open. Zaynah, with her eyes still peeled to him, sighed. "Get with it, Mazin, that's another weird expression.

Now you look like Na'aman when my mother is feeding him."

Mazin grabbed her arm and pointed. "Something will happen today," he said.

Zaynah squinted in the sun, her steps faltering. There was a crowd of people right next to the house. They must have come for ... *Allah, please, keep him safe.* She hurried forward, tugging on Mazin's arm. "We've got to get home — they might be taking Ahmed!"

"It's not Ahmed," Mazin said quietly.

They moved closer, weaving through the people on the outskirts of the crowd, gradually worming their way to the front. They could see Fatima, peering out the window with a cell phone in her hand. Beside her stood the twins, with identical anxious expressions. They were all looking at the two sisters standing on the front steps of their home, holding each other's hands and gazing up into the face of the soldier. Two other soldiers reclined against the wall, facing the crowd with guns in hand in case anybody should try anything.

"They're doing house-to-house raids," Zaynah whispered to Mazin.

"What could they possibly want with Hessa and Hazar?"

"Shhh. Listen."

"I just told you, there are defectors hiding in this area," said the soldier.

The sisters looked at the soldier blankly. Perhaps they did not know what a "defector" was.

"We are doing house-to-house searches," the soldier continued.

The sisters gazed mutely.

"So I'm going into your house to conduct a search," he repeated, throwing a look of derision over his shoulder at his buddies. One of them peeled himself off the wall and followed this soldier into the darkened door. Hessa and Hazar continued to stand on the steps, holding tightly to each other's hands.

"It'll be all right," someone in the crowd called.

"Can't they see the sisters are simple?" someone asked.

The window to their home opened and Fatima's head appeared. "Zaynah, Mazin! Come in right now."

Zaynah looked over to her mother and nodded reluctantly, but before she could drag her feet away from the scene the soldiers burst out of the darkened door and each one grabbed a sister by the arm. A faint mewling sound came from their open mouths, but they did not move. Their hands remained entwined.

"There's a broken window at the back of the house. How did that happen?" asked the soldier who had queried them just moments before.

The sisters stood silent.

"You can take your time, but you must answer me. The broken window?"

Hazar opened her mouth. For a second, Zaynah thought she could not speak, but then her voice came in a whisper: "I don't know."

"You don't know?" queried the soldier skeptically. "You live in the house all the time, and the neighbours say you don't go out much. How could you not know?"

"The wind?" suggested Hessa tentatively.

"Now you're lying. We don't like it when people lie to us. Wind doesn't break windows."

Zaynah felt a presence behind her, and her elbow was taken in a strong grasp. "Come along, we need to get you inside," said Rana.

Mazin turned his face towards his mother, and Zaynah was astonished to see it bathed in tears. "We need to help them, O'mmy," he whispered.

Tears sprang to Rana's eyes and she hugged her son. "My loved one, my sweetheart, there is nothing we can do."

Dread clutched Zaynah's stomach. She turned her eyes back to the little scene on the doorstep. She had been held in the grip of petrified fascination a few moments before, not unlike what she felt listening outside Rana's and Hamid's door. But now she suddenly realized that the lives of the two gentle sisters who had lived beside her all her life, who had sneaked timidly out of their houses to press sweets into her hands, were in danger.

"Come on, tell us how the window got broken," the soldier yelled.

The crowd murmured in protest. "Keep back!" the second soldier called, aiming his gun at them.

"What do you want us to say?" whispered Hazar.

"The truth," thundered the soldiers, towering above them.

"It has been broken for a long time. Perhaps a child threw a ball?"

"Do you want us to take you down to headquarters, where they'll question you separately? Do you think we don't have ways and means to get the truth out of two old women like you?" As if to emphasize his point, the soldier reached forward and yanked their hands apart. Zaynah could see their little, wrinkled hands with their brown spots and large knuckles, hanging down at their sides. They trembled and trembled. Zaynah could hardly see through her tears.

"O'mmy, say I threw a ball," Mazin implored.

"And draw their attention to us? You're right, Mazin. It is the right thing to do. I should do it, to protect those innocent, kindly old ladies. All my instincts scream for me to help them," Rana's nose was an inch from Mazin's and tears tumbled from her eyes. "But first and foremost is my duty to protect you. And if I go up to those soldiers and demand they leave those women alone, then first they will laugh in my face, and then they will ask me where I live. I cannot help them, but I can try to protect you. So come into the house."

"No," sobbed Mazin, and tried to shake off his mother's hand.

"Why is it important?" whispered Hessa through quivering lips.

"Because I say it is important," said the soldier. He looked over the heads of the sisters at his companion. "Do you think they're too stupid to understand what we want?"

"Smack them and see," said the second soldier. "If they know something, they'll tell us then for sure. If they don't, no harm done. I don't really think we should take them..." and he motioned over his head towards where headquarters presumably were.

"Right," said the soldier in a booming voice. "Last chance to tell us how that window got broken, or we'll see if a good smack to the brain might loosen things up a bit. Often works with my radio, which is old and doddery just like you." He sniggered, and raised his hand in a threatening manner.

The murmuring of the crowd grew louder, and the soldier swung his gun to the left, where people were turning around and muttering. A tall man broke through their ranks. It took Zaynah a moment to register who it was. Then a smile broke through her tears: Abi! Abi was here! She felt sure that he would make everything all right, somehow.

"What seems to be the problem?" Mohammed asked, coming very close to the soldier with the raised hand.

"Stand back sir," the soldier snapped. "This isn't your business."

"Actually, I'm a doctor, so violence is my business by proxy." Mohammed stood proud and distinguished. "I have known these women all of my life. I have no idea what the problem is, but it couldn't possibly have anything to do with Hessa and Hazar."

"I said *back off*," shouted the soldier menacingly.

Mohammed turned to the crowd. "We all know Hessa and Hazar, don't we? Two little, non-threatening women. What could they possibly be accused of?" His eyes swept the crowd, registering Rana and the children with cold disapproval.

"There's a broken window in the back of the house," someone yelled.

"The sisters know nothing about it!" several people in the crowd called, and the volume of the murmurs grew.

"It's none of your business," the soldier spat out in Mohammed's direction. "But as it happens, this is a serious situation. We are looking for a government official who has defected to join the anti-government protesters."

"This is a logical place to search, since our town is directly en route from the capital to the border. Are you conducting house-to-house searches?"

"We are."

Mohammed turned around and gave one brief look to Rana. She leaned forward and hissed in Zaynah's ear. "I'd prefer you both to come with me, but I can't drag you away. Promise me you won't move and you won't say a word?"

Zaynah was gazing at her father with a look of adoration, her eyes shining. She drew her gaze away slowly and looked at Rana as if she was coming out of a dream. "I promise."

"And if Mazin does anything — if he tries to move or speak — promise you'll stop him, even if you have to clamp your hand over his mouth?"

Zaynah looked at Mazin dreamily; he too was absorbed in the little drama before him. There were still rivulets on his cheeks from the tears. "I promise."

Rana melted into the crowd.

"So if you don't mind stepping back and letting us do our job?" The soldier was still speaking to Mohammed.

"Your job is to search the houses, not bully little old women. Look at them. They're obviously as innocent as babies. Have you no shame?"

Hessa and Hazar gazed at Mohammed, like two chickadees debating whether to hop closer and take the bread. Two little hands crept towards one another, and clasped again with all their might.

"It's none of your business," screamed the soldier again. "Stand back or I'll shoot you."

To Zaynah's surprise, Mohammed stood back.

The soldier scanned the crowd through half-shut eyes, then

turned back to the women, speaking slowly as though to imbeciles.

"When glass breaks, it makes a loud noise that everybody in the house can hear. Agreed?"

The women stared at him.

"Nod your heads if you agree," the soldier said, with a hint of weariness in his voice.

They nodded.

"So you understand why I don't believe you, when you claim you have no idea how the glass got broken. Maybe you don't know how it broke, but you must have heard it break, right? So when did it break?" He waited for a minute. "Was it yesterday? This week?"

Silence.

"Was it a long time ago?"

Silence.

"Which was it, you stupid old bags? This week or a long time ago? Answer me!"

The sisters looked at each other, then back to the soldier. "We don't know."

"You're lying," yelled the soldier, and he raised his hand again.

Mohammed was by his side again, poised inches from his raised hand.

"I told you to get back!"

"They're not lying," said Mohammed calmly. "They're probably incapable of lying. The noises of entire houses blowing up and guns firing have been waking us up at night for weeks now, so why should they hear or remember one window breaking?" He turned to the crowd again. "Do you think you'd have noticed a mere window breaking, and recorded the date and time?"

"No," roared the crowd.

The soldier whipped around and pressed his gun into Mohammed's gut. "If you don't get the fuck out of my way I'm going to shoot you."

"You are a human being," said Mohammed. "Act like one."

The finger pressed against the trigger. "Are you going to leave or die?"

"I'm sorry, but I can't let you hurt two innocent old women for no reason other than savagery. You know they know nothing. If you hurt such innocent creatures, it will haunt you at night. Allah will despise you." Mohammed raised his voice. "If you do a despicable action, all these people are witnesses. Leave them alone, and Allah will bless you for it."

"We are witnesses," cried the crowd. "Let them go, let them go!" Then more and more voices joined in until the entire throng was chanting: "Let them go! Let them go!"

Zaynah and Mazin shouted along with the rest of them. "Let them go! Let them go!"

With a curse, the soldier swivelled on his heel, gesturing to the other soldiers to follow him. The crowd fell silent, watching them leave. Into the silence dropped a quavery, scratchy voice: "Thank you," it said. And when the eyes of the crowd turned forwards again, they saw two small hands engulfed in Mohammed's fingers. Then, as one man, they stampeded Mohammed, pumping his hand, slapping him on the back.

"You're a brave man, Mohammed. We're lucky to have you as a neighbour."

"Those cowardly bastards, bullying poor old women."

"Good man, Mohammed."

"Well done."

"Do you think I could have done it without you? They'd have shot me on the spot if we'd been alone. That was a joint effort," Mohammed boomed.

And the crowd heaved him up on their shoulders and began to chant again: "Together we're strong, there's nothing we can't do! Together we're strong, there's nothing we can't do!" and many of the crowd tried to touch Mohammed as he passed, as though touching him would impart courage.

Zaynah and Mazin leapt alongside the crowd like goats, laughing and chanting, and as they passed their home they glanced up at the window and saw Fatima beaming from ear to ear with a joy that Zaynah had not seen for months. Then the twins catapulted out the front door and vied with each other and the crowd to touch Mohammed too, which Zaynah thought was perfectly ridiculous, and the procession wound down the street and around the block. Lucky for the soldiers that they had disappeared because woe to any soldiers at that moment of gleeful victory! Then the crowd came back around and passed Mohammed's front door again, where he bellowed to be put down. The sisters were still standing with their hands clasped, and their lips moved in time with the chant too: "Together we're strong, there's nothing we can't do!"

That night they had supper late so that the whole family could celebrate together. Everyone crowded around the table; even Ahmed was carried down to his usual chair. Rana sat demurely at one end beside Hamid, her eyes downcast so nothing provocative could possibly escape them. She had produced a marvelous feast that spread from one end of the table to the other: salads and lentils, pita and hummus, steaming platters of cooked chicken and vegetables to spoon over mounds of rice, stuffed grape leaves and falafel. The fragrance of lemon and coriander intertwined with the stronger scents of onion and garlic, creating a dance of saliva on anticipatory tongues.

Everyone competed with one another to tell their version of the story, especially to Ahmed and Hamid who had missed it. Little embellishments crept in: the soldiers had threatened to rip the sisters' faces off and Mohammed had flung his arms out and challenged them to shoot him if they dared. "No, I never said that," interjected Mohammed, whose red face denoted that he was in a high good humour.

Zaynah looked from face to face and felt inordinately happy. This was her little family, and it was simply chockablock full of heroes. "Mazin wanted to jump in to protect them too," she announced at the first lull. "Ammé Rana had to hold him back with force."

"It would have been extremely foolish for you to have intervened," said Mohammed severely.

"But brave," said Zaynah. "Did everyone see how Abi sought Allah's help? See how clever he is? Even though he's not religious himself he knew that the name of Allah carries a lot of weight with many people."

Zaynah saw her O'mmy smile in Mohammed's direction, as though hoping he had realized how helpful Allah had been.

"Where did you go, O'mmy? When you asked Zaynah to look after me?" asked Mazin.

"I took Ahmed out the back door, in case they came into our house."

All heads swivelled in her direction in surprise that there was a new angle to this lucky day that they hadn't known about.

"How did you manage that?" asked Hamid, smiling at his wife.

Rana flushed slightly and glanced towards Ahmed. But Ahmed, energized by the exciting day, thumped his back. "Piggyback!"

Everyone stared at them in amazement. "But how did she get you on her back?" asked Hamid.

Ahmed chuckled. "Rana can do anything she wants to do. She hauled me on her back like I was a sack of potatoes and traipsed down the stairs and out the back door like we were going for a pleasant stroll. The chickens were surprised, I can tell you."

Hoots and cheers erupted in the kitchen, while Hamid looked at his wife in admiration.

"I can always rely on you in an emergency, Rana," Mohammed said quietly when the noise had died down.

"Thank you," she said simply.

"So, Mohammed," Ahmed continued. "Have you changed your mind about the war? Now you've seen with your own eyes the brutality and savagery of the other side?"

"My views haven't changed one iota. You're either naïve or stupid if you believe your side is less savage than the government's army. I am against violence, Ahmed, and there would have been far less violence if you revolutionaries had stuck to your peaceful demonstrations instead of taking up arms."

Zaynah looked at Ahmed protectively. She wished her father wouldn't use such a contemptuous tone with him when he was so frail. She noted with surprise that Ahmed wasn't staring down at his plate red-faced like he used to do in the past when Mohammed argued with him. Instead, he was looking at Mohammed and nodding, as though he was really trying to understand what he meant. His next words surprised her even more.

"How come you risked your life for those two little women? Thank Allah it had a happy ending, but it could have been otherwise. Did it occur to you that many people would suffer greatly if you were to die?"

Zaynah wondered at Ahmed's strange look as he said this, as though he was communicating something of special importance.

Mohammed lay down his knife and fork. "I'll tell you why. I read this provocative poem once and it made a deep impression on me. It is attributed to a German man called Martin Niemöller who was a pastor living in Germany during the Second World War. I shall quote it to you:

First they came for the Jews
and I did not speak out
because I was not a Jew.
Then they came for the Communists
and I did not speak out
because I was not a Communist.
Then they came for the Trade Unionists
and I did not speak out
because I was not a Trade Unionist.

Then they came for me
and there was no one left
to speak out for me.

In the middle of the night, the sound of screaming jerked Zaynah from her slumber. She sat bolt upright, listening. It was Mazin. He must have had a nightmare. She lay back and closed her eyes, and immediately her own dream came back to her. It had been long and convoluted, with different people appearing and disappearing at random. Ahmed was there, and she was trying to help him, but there was something nasty sitting on her shoulder biting at her every time she tried. She desperately wanted to rid herself of this Thing that was grotesquely ugly and discharged some burning snotlike substance onto her neck. Zaynah felt sweat on her forehead and threw back her covers, then drew them back again nervously, tucking them around her neck for protection.

Her dream-self began to run around, scraping itself against walls and banging into door jambs in an effort to dislodge this wicked creature. Ahmed was crying now, reaching out to her and begging for help. She could not help him. The Thing was burning her neck and she had to get away. She tried to run, to fly, but her legs were weighted down. Zaynah's eyes flew open and scanned the dark corners of the room till they rested gratefully on Na'aman's sleeping form. How strange that she had had a horrible dream, just like Mazin.

A few days later, Mazin burst into her room and made a flying leap onto her bed, bouncing her out of her cocoon of blankets.

"Don't do that! You totally mussed up my covers."

"Sorry. I didn't want to touch the floor."

"What?"

"There might be something under your bed waiting to grab my foot. Don't look at me like that. I know there isn't in my logical mind, but my heart doesn't agree, and it's very good at winning arguments."

"What are you, four years old?"

"And I don't want to go to sleep either."

Zaynah put down her book wearily. "Why not?"

"I'm afraid to dream."

Then Zaynah remembered her own dream. She sat up and looked at Mazin. "I heard you wake up a few nights ago."

"I wake up every night. I don't yell anymore because Khalo Mohammed told me if I woke him up like that again he'd put me outside with the chickens. It's like, even in the middle of my bad dream when I'm being tortured and want to yell, I remember that I can't."

"The chickens wouldn't be able to comfort you like Ammé Rana."

Mazin crossed his arms. "It isn't funny."

"What do you dream?"

"I always dream the same thing, that they're hurting me. Last night I was walking down a long corridor and at the end there was a door. I knew that something terrible was going to happen behind that door, so I tried to turn around. Then I realized there were two soldiers behind me, and they were carrying whips and tires and ropes, and then I knew that I couldn't get away...." Mazin began talking in a rush, as if to get the words over with. "I still tried. I sprinted down the corridor looking for other doors that I could go through and there was one and it was locked and suddenly there was a key in my hand — you know how dreams are — and I was fumbling with the key trying to get it in the lock before the soldiers got to me, but I couldn't and I was so scared to go through that door but they pushed me in and tied me up and began to hurt me. They grabbed my hands and started to ... pull out my fingernails." Mazin hid his eyes behind his hand. "I don't want to talk about it anymore."

Zaynah slithered over to him and pushed his hair off his forehead. "It's just a bad dream. You won't have one tonight."

"I will! I have them every night. I'm so scared, Zaynah. You saw what happened to Ahmed."

"He was fighting. That's not going to happen to you."

Mazin stretched his feet out, then drew them back and covered them with a blanket. "Look what happened to Hessa and Hazar. Nobody is safe in this war. Anything can happen to any one of us. There is no logic or reason behind it. You know that children have been captured and tortured. Who's to say it won't happen to us? I hate this war! I hate it!"

"I hate it too," Zaynah whispered. "I'm so frightened that I'll die. The thought of death terrifies me. Even though I know that I've never hurt anybody, and I've tried to be a good person, I worry about whether Allah will judge me for not being religious, even though it's not my fault! When we are judged for our deeds, maybe we'll go to hell because our deeds didn't include enough praying! Do you think about Allah? I think all the time, and I pray in my mind. Just not physically."

"You will go right to heaven, Zaynah. If Allah is just, there is no question about that. So will I. I'm not frightened about going to hell. I'm frightened of death. What if it's nothing? What if there's no heaven or hell, and we just turn to dust?" Mazin began to weep. "All that is me, all my complicated thoughts and feelings, reduced to nothing. I don't want to die, Zaynah. I don't want to die."

"We won't," Zaynah hugged him, tears seeping out of her own eyes. "We're not going to die."

"How can you say that when so many people are dying? We probably will if this war continues."

"Let's pray to Allah to end the war," Zaynah said suddenly. "Come on!"

"Are you crazy? Probably the whole country is praying for that. It's not going to help."

Zaynah stood up and pulled Mazin by the arm. "Let's get the twins to join us. That'll make it stronger. Come on, Mazin! It can't hurt, and it might help. Pray for your bad dreams to stop, and believe that they will if you pray hard enough. Come on, Mazin. I have to do something!"

"Stop pulling me," shouted Mazin in sudden terror. He stood up on the bed and made a flying leap, landing near the door and diving into the corridor as though all the monsters under the bed were stalking him.

The twins were already in their beds with the lights out. Zaynah shook them roughly. "Wake up! We're going to pray to Allah."

"Abi doesn't allow it," Abdul said sleepily.

"Of course he *allows* it, stupid. He just doesn't want us doing it five times a day. But this is a special prayer, anyway. To end the war."

Both the twins sat up in bed. "How will that end the war?"

"Do you think Allah isn't listening?" snapped Zaynah. "Every moment of the day He's listening, and if we add our prayers to the millions of other people praying for the same thing then it might work."

"I don't think it'll work and..."

"...it's a hare-brained idea."

"I'll hare-brain you!" cried Zaynah in a passion. "We need all the power we can get, and together we're stronger. Don't you remember chanting that? We're going to join hands and pray, from the heart. All of us."

"I can't believe you think..."

"...this is going to work."

"You don't have to pray for the end of the war," said Mazin. "You can pray for whatever you like. I'm going to pray for my nightmares to stop."

Abdul and Ali glanced at each other. "That's weird, we've been having nightmares too."

"So pray for that to stop. Or make it general. Pray for all bad things to stop."

"Can't hurt," said Abdul uncertainly.

"Right," declared Zaynah. "Everybody make a circle and hold hands. I'll say a few words, and then each of us can add a private prayer in our heads. I really think we should all pray for Allah to stop the war to make it as powerful as possible. If the war ends, your bad dreams will end too so you'll get that prayer anyway."

The twins looked at her inscrutably. "Aren't we going to pray in the right position and pointing towards Mecca?"

"This isn't a regular prayer, stupid. This is a special prayer that we're going to hold hands for to lend it power. Anyway, I wouldn't press my forehead anywhere on your filthy floor. Now come on! We don't have much time before O'mmy checks on me."

The four children formed a circle, their hands joined. There was a moment of silence. Zaynah began to speak in a clear, soft voice. "Allah, we thank you for the many blessings you have given us. We thank you for the health of every member of this family, and for the fact that we have enough to eat, and a beautiful house to live in, and wonderful chickens. We thank you that we do well in school, and for stopping the bullying that some of us suffered from. You have given us so much, Allah, that it seems wicked to ask for more, but we are not asking only for ourselves. We are asking for the whole country, for the whole world. Please make this war end. Everybody is suffering terribly from it, and we are too frightened to go to sleep because of our nightmares. Please stop the war, Allah. Please make the two sides come to an understanding and grow to love each other, as all men should. And women. I am sorry for such a big request. Thank you for listening to us, Allah."

CHAPTER 12 **RANA**

ANA LOVED THAT HALF HOUR in the early morning when the children sat around the table eating breakfast. Mohammed had already left for work and Ahmed continued to eat breakfast in his room, although he came down for supper if he was feeling up to it. With Fatima still cuddling Na'aman in bed, Rana pretended that this was her family — this large brood of wonderful children. She slid her gaze from child to child, all so handsome and innocent, making little tents out of their pitas and scooping salad and scrambled egg into the opening. She tried not to let her eyes linger on Mazin too long, even though the contours of his face were so fascinating to her, and it was such a pleasure to watch him cram his mouth with food with such intense enjoyment, like any healthy, normal, almost twelve-year-old boy, which of course he was.

The twins stood in unison, wiping their mouths with the back of their hands in sync and picking up their schoolbags on the way out the door. "Goodbye, Ammé Rana."

Mazin looked up, saw her eyes on him before she could snatch them away, and smiled as he got up and shouldered his schoolbag. "Do you know, O'mmy, I help my friends Naïf and Sami with their work now, so I am not bullied anymore."

"That is wonderful. I am so happy."

"See," Mazin added as he shot out the door, "there is a way to get along in the world without violence."

Rana smiled at Zaynah good-naturedly. "I don't remember exactly what I said, but I certainly didn't mean that violence was the only way to get along."

"Course you didn't. You were probably trying to get him to be less of a wimp and he just misunderstood. He misunderstands things all the time. Bye, Ammé Rana. Don't forget to look after Khalo Ahmed until I get back!"

Rana smiled to herself as she poured out a cup of coffee and put it on a tray, along with a plate of scrambled eggs, pita, and salad. She was about to carry it up to Ahmed's room when there was a knock on the door. She froze, as she always did these days at any unexpected event. Apart from the constant fear of potential army brutality, there were so many refugees straggling through the town on their way to the border. She used to think that fate had placed her in a town near the border as a sign that she should travel. But now it was a disadvantage as dispossessed and sometimes desperate people marched down the main street past her house, hoping that once they crossed that arbitrary borderline all their troubles would magically disappear.

Rana set the tray down carefully and crept to the door to peer out the peephole. A young man stood on the doorstep dressed in an army vest, but instead of a gun he was carrying a basket of fruit. The plumpness of the banana on top erased the last vestiges of fear, and Rana opened the door. "Yes?"

"Is this the house of Mohammed Al-Fakhoury?"

Some of the fear returned. "Yes."

The man proffered his basket of fruit. "I would like to leave this for him as a gift, to thank him. May Allah bless and reward him." The man turned and walked swiftly away, and did not answer when Rana called after him, "Who are you?"

Well, she thought. *Whoever you are, fruit is scarce these days and we appreciate it very much.*

She was adding an orange to Ahmed's tray when she heard a soft cough behind her. Realizing she had neglected to close the door she whirled around, and then gave a cry of gladness.

Moussa stood framed in the doorway, smiling sheepishly.

"How wonderful to see you, come in, come in! We weren't sure whether something had happened to you! Ahmed will be so happy!"

Moussa stepped inside, shutting the door behind him.

"I'm just going to give Ahmed his breakfast and then I'll make you some coffee. Actually, why don't you bring Ahmed his tray? He'll be so delighted!"

Moussa shuffled from foot to foot. "I'd prefer to go up with you. I'll wait a few minutes, and then I'll surprise him."

Rana carried the tray up to Ahmed's room and knocked softly, in case he was still asleep.

"Come in," he called, flinging the covers off his head as she entered and revealing the radio that had spent its life plastered to his ear since its entry into the house.

"I hope you can't get cancer from radio waves," Rana said as she set the tray down on the bedside table. "Why do you listen to it under the covers anyway? Let me help you sit up."

"I don't care if I get cancer. I listen to it under the covers so as not to disturb the rest of the household, and I can sit up by myself very well, thank you."

"Uh-oh, are we grouchy today?" she asked, fluffing up the pillow behind his back and waiting with bated breath for Moussa's dramatic entrance.

"Thank you, Rana, that will be all," said Ahmed as though she were serving him, then she saw his disgruntled expression go rigid with shock. She backed away from the bed as Moussa approached, a smile stretching his face from ear to ear. Bizarrely, he leaned forward and patted Ahmed on the head, and Rana realized he was nervous about touching him, not knowing where the healthy parts ended and the painful parts began. But Ahmed stretched up his hands and grabbed him around the neck, pulling him down in a bear hug. "I can't believe it — Moussa — I thought you were dead. How come you're not dead?"

Moussa, hugging and laughing and weeping all at the same time, managed to gasp, "I thought *you* were dead!"

Rana backed towards the door. She knew she should leave them alone, but it was so glorious to see Ahmed grinning like that.

"I never found you in that room — that room in the abandoned house, except it wasn't abandoned," he gabbled. "The last time I saw you, we were standing on either side of the door to the room waiting for the soldiers to come through, do you remember? They came shooting right, left, and everywhere and then the bomb ripped off the side of the building and..." Ahmed began to sweat as he remembered the day. "I turned over every body, every single one. You weren't there."

"You should have counted them, my friend," Moussa laughed, extricating himself from Ahmed's grip and sitting on the side of the bed. "The blast literally blew me out the door and into the landing. I must have smashed my head because it was lights out until I woke up with a splitting headache. The first thing I did was look for you, but there was a ton of debris blocking the door of the room. I dug it all out and forced the door open. You weren't there." Moussa shuddered. "It's weird, but I also went from face to face, looking."

"Was there anyone alive? I gave water to one of the soldiers."

"I don't know. I just looked. I didn't wake them up for a chat."

Ahmed reached for his coffee, then realized his friend didn't have any. He glanced towards Rana.

"I'm going downstairs to make you a nice breakfast, Moussa," she said. "But I just want to ask one thing. When you didn't find Ahmed in the room, why didn't you come to inquire here?"

"I went to the university and asked students and professors if they'd seen him. I went to all the places where we hang out. I knew he was either dead or badly hurt, and if he was hurt, he'd only be alive if he'd managed to find a field hospital. And if he'd had the luck to find one, you probably wouldn't know anything about it, for safety's sake. There were so many ifs,"

Moussa said, turning back to Ahmed. "You have to explain some of those ifs to me, my friend."

Rana slipped down the stairs and entered the kitchen, bustling happily about to make Moussa's breakfast. When Fatima came in with Na'aman hanging off her back, Rana imparted the news.

Fatima grasped Rana's hand. "I'm so happy. That is wonderful news! It will surely be the end of Ahmed's depression. Let me take up Moussa's breakfast so I can see them together."

It was the first time in many days that Fatima had marched to Ahmed's bedroom with enthusiasm. Rana stretched out her hand to Na'aman. "Shall we go and feed the chickens?" Na'aman nodded eagerly; chicken feeding was one of his favourite activities.

As soon as they opened the door to the coop, the chickens rushed out at them with their familiar flurry of clucking desperation. Na'aman held out his hand gingerly, wary of Henny Penny's nasty habit of swiping all the feed from his palm with the sharp side of her beak. He ran to the other end of the yard, strewing chicken feed behind him and giggling madly as the hens gave chase. Rana wended her way between hens to her garden, bending to examine her vegetables and pull out some weeds.

"Tomato, Ammé Rana?"

"Certainly," Rana answered, stripping a tomato from the vine and cleaning it with a little bit of spit. "You can give the green bit to the chickens." Rana lifted her head and looked at her chickens fondly. Some were scrabbling in the dust for the remaining feed. Others had plopped down for a dust bath in the hot sun, cognizant, she felt, of the limited stint of enjoyable outside time. Henny Penny was lording over the tomato stem, while a pretty speckled hen watched her closely, in case a morsel should fall. Henny Penny swallowed the stem whole and eyed the other hen balefully. Rana hoped she wouldn't peck her.

With an odd little squawk, Henny Penny suddenly leapt onto the back of the other hen, grasping her head feathers in her beak and kneading with her chicken feet, wings spread on either side of the astonished speckled hen in an attempt to keep her balance.

"Hens love," said Na'aman, tomato juice trickling down his chin.

Rana straightened and looked at the chickens in amazement. They were mimicking the actions of mating.

Na'aman looked up at her. "Hens love?" he inquired.

"Yes Na'aman. Two hens love each other."

She watched Henny Penny for a few more minutes. There was a small smile on her face. Here, in the most basic of beasts, in the natural world where unnatural behaviour was impossible, a female hen was trying to mate with another female.

She held out her hand to Na'aman and walked with him into the kitchen, settling him on the table with a puzzle and some books. "Don't fall off," she warned him.

Fuelled by a rush of energy, she lifted the chairs onto the table, then filled a bucket with water and cleaning liquid at the same time. Grabbing the broom, she began to sweep the floor. If Hamid's theory that most negative human behaviour stems from basic emotions like fear or anger, could it be that the strong reaction human beings had towards different sexual orientations was based in fear? Fear of the different, fear of the "other"? If animals exhibited sexual behaviour towards other animals of the same gender, how could that be called unnatural? Rana bent to sweep up the crumbs under the table. "Hungry," Na'aman murmured, dropping a puzzle piece on her head.

Absent-mindedly, Rana handed him a bit of pita. *So if I feel revulsion at the idea of homosexuality, is that because I've been conditioned by society, whose main motivation is fear? Or is it in fact a natural revulsion that only human beings feel, because we have minds and we can make choices? Does the homosexual act truly become disgusting when it is the result of a conscious decision rather than some basic, primal instinct, as it is with a chicken?* she reflected. *Yes. If you know that society condemns a specific act — even if you don't agree with the reasons behind that condemnation — you are consciously inviting condemnation by your actions, which are therefore subject to a whole different set of judgments. Well obviously, the acts of a chicken aren't judgeable.*

"Still hungry," mentioned Na'aman.

Rana peeled an orange for him from the basket of fruit. He fell on it with cries of delight. "Fank you, Ammé Rana, fank you!"

She grabbed the mop and plunged it into the pail of water and soap, wringing it out with both hands and thrusting it vigorously into the corners of the kitchen. *So if society's re-action to homosexuality is based in fear, does that mean that intelligent, thinking people like myself should work against the natural revulsion that has been planted in me by society, deeply ingrained though it is? Or does a man with the same inclinations as the chicken have a responsibility to curb those inclinations as anti-societal and unacceptable, given how deeply ingrained that particular prejudice is, wound as it is through religion and culture. Allah destroyed Sodom and Gomorrah because of their sexual practices, saying through Lot: "What! Do you commit an indecency which anyone in the world has not done before you? Homosexuality is illegal."*

Yes, a man with those inclinations should curb them, just as a man with an inclination to make love to another woman who is not his wife must curb his inclinations. It is futile to ponder the reason behind every societal norm; there would be no end to it. For instance, why should societal structures be based on the institution of marriage? Why are men and women not completely equal? Why can American women wear pants but American men cannot wear skirts? Why, why, why? Perhaps all societal norms are based on arbitrary rules that in turn are based on one of our primary feelings rather than logic.

"Knock on door," announced Na'aman. "Down please!"

Rana froze, then heard Fatima's steps, and her lilting voice. Nothing to fear in her tone. She threw a cloth on the floor and stood on it to shuffle over to Na'aman, so she wouldn't mark the wet, gleaming floor. She took the little boy in her arms and hobbled towards the door to set him in the hallway. She peered at the door. Fatima was holding a carton of baklava.

Rana shuffled back into the kitchen and began lifting the chairs onto the floor, careful not to disturb the little pile of crumbs caused by Na'aman's pita. *So one cannot ignore the rules. Even if those rules are entangled in baseless fear, human beings need to live by rules. These codes of behaviour are the only things that differentiate us from animals. Rules force men to behave civilly.* Rana smiled grimly as she thought of the war. *Exactly so. War proves that men are basically uncivil animals. Rules and religion enforce civilized behaviour. That's why they exist. So one must respect them. Still* — and she smiled again — *it is quite a different thing to conform to a rule in order to live peaceably amongst one's fellow men, than to be unnatural. Quite different.*

Fatima stood in the kitchen doorway bearing the box of baklava. "The strangest thing just happened," she said. "These are for Mohammed."

"That's the second gift today," replied Rana. "I must say they're going a bit overboard. Picking him up and carrying him around on their shoulders was quite sufficient. Stop!" she yelled as Na'aman began to scoot his dinky car across the floor. "You can zoom your cars down the corridor."

Na'aman looked at her for a second and then was seized with one of the powerful temper tantrums that seemed to threaten him frequently these days. "No!" he shouted, vying successfully with Rana for volume and letting his little dinky car fly. Rana shuffled over to him and picked him up. "Do you want to go and sit on your bed by yourself until you calm down, or do you want to play with your dinky car in the hallway?"

Na'aman thrashed and kicked and turned purple in the face.

"Let me take him," murmured Fatima. But before she could open her arms there was another knock on the door, and Na'aman's face transformed from ugly gargoyle to pink cherub in an instant. "Door?" he said in questioning wonder to his aunt.

Rana wrested the door open and stared at the proffered pail of goat's milk. "I know," she began sweetly, "that we are desperate for heroes in this war, and what Mohammed did for Hazar and Hessa reminded us what we can accomplish if we stand together against atrocity. But bringing gifts, while so very kind of you, is really unnecessary, even a little bit extravagant."

"Hazar and Hessa?" asked the man, snapping his eyes in both directions down the street.

"Are you in trouble by any chance?" asked Fatima, who had materialized beside Rana.

"No, but the last thing I want to do is draw attention to this house in any way. If I see any soldiers approaching I'll bolt. Please take this. Tell Mohammed that I will never forget him and will pray for him every night."

"That's absurd," said Rana, grabbing the man's sleeve. "Are you saying you won't forget him because of Hazar and Hessa?"

The man glared at his sleeve, astounded by her audacity. "I must go. The last thing you need is for anybody to see me here. I have no idea what you are talking about."

He turned and marched down the street, but Rana marched determinedly behind him. "What do you mean? You must explain to me! Don't you know Hazar and Hessa?"

The soldier whirled to face her, gazing down the street with a haunted expression. "If Hazar and Hessa are the old women connected to the event yesterday, then yes, I did hear about it. That's why I came. Now everybody knows that Mohammed is a hero and we can come openly and thank him." He started to edge away. "I must go. It is dangerous to be seen here."

"Wait! Has he done something else heroic?"

The man began to run. Rana chased after him, oblivious to the potential eyes of neighbours. "What are you thanking him for?"

"This!" he yelled over his shoulder, waving his hand in the air as he executed a ninety-degree turn into an alleyway. Rana ran as fast as she could, but the twenty-year-old man ran faster and disappeared into the hodgepodge of lanes between the buildings.

Rana stomped back to the house. "This is so weird," she called exuberantly. "When the next person shows up bearing a gift we'll have to work together. You engage him in conversation while I nip around behind him and block him so he can't run away."

Fatima looked at her doubtfully, but Na'aman shouted, "Yes!"

"Let's go into the kitchen and have some tea," said Rana. Laughter drifted towards them from Ahmed's room, filling her with indescribable happiness. Turning, she saw the same look on Fatima's face.

She took her sister-in-law's arm and propelled her towards Ahmed's room. "Let's look in on them and ask Moussa if he needs a refill. Let's contemplate Ahmed's face to remind ourselves how it looks when he's happy."

The room was wreathed in smoke. Moussa was using Ahmed's water glass as his ashtray. Ahmed was leaning forward in his bed, his whole face animated. "Do you know what Moussa has been telling me? The rebels have been fighting with the government forces in major cities all over the country. And despite their warplanes and bombs, we're taking over! City after city, region after region. More and more soldiers are defecting from the government ranks and joining us civilians to bring down our tyrannical government. We're winning the war, Rana! I can't believe it, but we're actually winning!" Ahmed buried his face in his hands, overcome with emotion.

"Is it true?" Rana asked Moussa.

"Of course it's true," he answered, lighting another cigarette and tapping the packet against Ahmed's bowed head to see if he wanted one. "Do you think I'm making it up to make Ahmed feel better? It's just a matter of time before we bring down the government. But that doesn't mean we can become careless. On the contrary, we have to be extra careful now. A threatened dog is a dangerous dog. It could get nasty, but I'd say the end is in sight. If we can survive the next few weeks, we're home free. Peace."

Rana reached out a hand to grasp Fatima's. "Would you like some more tea?" she asked weakly.

Moussa shook his head in thanks and the sisters stumbled out of the bedroom and down the hallway to the kitchen, little Na'aman trailing after. They both hesitated at the kitchen door.

"We can go in now, the floor is dry." Rana plugged in the kettle to make some tea. "What a crazy day this is turning out to be. One thing after another."

"Didn't you know?"

"About the success of the rebels? I guess my main source of information was Ahmed before he got hurt, and since the government controls all the media, I don't bother listening to the news or reading the papers. I'm not really a very informed person, come to think of it. How did you know?"

"Mohammed talks of it. He doesn't think like Moussa at all. He says it'll be just as bad when and if the rebels take over, and the lives of the average citizen will be just as awful." Fatima cleared her throat. "He says that extreme, religious Muslims will probably take over the country, and people like him will be in even more danger."

"Oh, he shouldn't worry. Everybody seems to love my little brother these days. Do you have more information than me about that, perhaps?"

Fatima shook her head. "I have no idea what's going on."

"That guy just waved at me when I asked him what he wanted to thank Mohammed for. I have no idea what's happening. But it feels like a good mystery, doesn't it?"

"Perhaps he helped him in some way."

"Mohammed?" Rana snorted, stirring mint leaves and sugar into the tea. "When has he ever helped anybody?"

"He helped Hazar and Hessa yesterday," Fatima replied quietly.

"That's true. Do you think he goes around like some type of Good Samaritan, helping little old women everywhere?" Rana gave a little spurt of laughter. "At least we can have baklava with our tea."

Fatima eyed her as she wolfed down the pastry and licked the honey off her fingers. Na'aman stood at Rana's knee, ogling her every move. "Perhaps he does. Perhaps there are a lot of things about Mohammed that we don't know."

Rana stared at her, then grinned. "I'm sorry Fatima, but Mohammed is *definitely* not a hero. He's insane. Hmmm. Perhaps insane people are capable of heroic actions in their few unparanoid moments."

Fatima felt a surge of irritation and sought to change the subject. "I noticed the scrambled eggs this morning," she said.

"What?"

"Scrambled eggs instead of boiled eggs. I hope it's because you're feeling better."

Rana sat up straight in her chair and considered. "I am feeling better," she said. "Much better. My strength has returned and I feel strangely peaceful. At least for today. Thank you for drawing my attention to it. It amazes me how obsessed I am with every emotion when I'm feeling bad, and how I just take it for granted and ignore my emotions when I'm okay. I should feel gratitude that I feel better."

"So you are completely over that horrible incident between you and Mohammed?"

Rana took another pastry and dipped it in her tea, then took pity on Na'aman, who had begun to drool a little. She handed him her least favourite kind of baklava, rendering him mute with gratitude.

"Living with my brother is a constant learning curve, and I don't think I'll ever feel relaxed or happy around him. He's a really screwed-up individual, and I pray that we won't live with him forever. Nevertheless, at this moment, focusing on living in this moment as I always strive to do, things aren't too bad between us. He's working more hours than ever — you've got to be grateful to the war for blowing off all those little puppy paws — and he is quieter when he's here."

Moussa stuck his head around the door. "I'm going now. There's someone at your door, by the way."

"Not again," moaned Rana in high delight, and skipped to open it, passing Moussa the box of baklava en route.

"Wait," cried Na'aman in some anxiety. "O'mmy go talk, Ammé Rana block."

Rana looked at him in some admiration that he had grasped the essence of her plan and even had the sense to remind her of it. She slipped neatly around the proffered eggs and took up her station on the other side of the new gentleman caller. "We have enough of those already," she muttered ungraciously at the eggs.

"That is so kind of you," smiled Fatima, with Na'aman nodding encouragingly at her side. "Do you mind if I ask why you are thanking my husband?"

"He saved my life," said the young man, who was dressed in an army vest like the first visitor.

"How did he do that?"

The man gave her a puzzled look, then glanced down the street to see if anybody was coming. He looked surprised to see Rana standing guard. "He stopped me from bleeding internally. I must go. It would not be good to be seen here."

Rana blocked his path. "Where did he help you? How did you meet him? There have been a stream of people like you coming to thank him all day. Are we to understand that he saved all their lives?"

"Yes," answered the man simply.

"But why today? Why are you all showing up to show your gratitude today?"

"Everyone knows he is a hero now," the man replied. ""Nobody has to know it's because he saved my life. Now it is safe to come out in the open and thank him as he deserves."

"He's still pro-government," insisted Rana. "He's not on your side, you know."

"I don't think Mohammed is on anybody's side. He is above sides," the man said gravely, and turned back to Fatima. "Your husband has saved hundreds of lives. He is the bravest man I have ever met. I know he is doing something very dangerous, but you should know that if anything happens to him we will take care of you."

"We?" queried Rana.

"Me and a thousand other men who would not be living today if it weren't for him."

The man slipped past Rana, who gaped after him in complete shock.

It went on like that all month. Rana stood by Fatima as the men came and slipped away, watching her face growing more and more incandescent as time went on. "Rana, can you believe how much good Mohammed has done? Allah be praised. My husband has done more good than anyone I know. He is a hero, Rana. A hero! My husband!"

After school, the children would take turns racing each other to the door, jostling in their excitement to see what the next present would be. Rana noted how they all, including Mazin, laughed infectiously, delighted at the joy of the gifts, accepting without question that the man they feared and avoided was a hero. "What did he fix for you?" Mazin would ask each nervous debtor. Zaynah was making a list: "That's sixty legs, two hundred and twenty eyes, eighty arms, ninety-two chest wounds."

Rana smiled and smiled, trying to figure out why all this was so irritating. Shouldn't she be proud of her brother? Glad that he was doing some good in the world, contributing to mankind? "Do I want him to be a one-dimensional evil loony?" she asked Hamid at night as they lay side by side in their bed, the only time she felt she could be absolutely honest.

"Could you be jealous?" Hamid asked, stroking her hair in compensation for suggesting such a thing.

Rana raised her head. "Could I be so shallow?" she asked, searching her soul to discover the reasoning behind her irritation.

Hamid did not answer. Rana sat up suddenly, and he watched her breasts shift under her nightgown.

"I suppose, if I'm being really honest, which I can only be with you, by the way, part of my irritation lies in the feeling that I've lost my best friend. I can't talk about anything with Fatima these days. Her only subject of conversation, and I mean her only subject, is what a wondrous and phenomenal husband she has. It drives me nuts. I bet if we had another fight and he plowed me to the other side of the room she'd take his side."

Hamid laughed and moved his hands to the swell of her breasts, but Rana shoved his hand aside. "I can't think about that right now. I feel ... uncomfortable ... and I have to find out why. At least if I discover I'm a vain and shallow human being, I'll know why it makes me so mad to see that line of silly men idolizing my insane brother."

Hamid sighed and turned on his side. "You're impossible to please. Everything is great between you and Mohammed now and you're still unhappy."

Rana rubbed his back in contrition. "I'm sorry. Why are human beings so complicated? I just feel, you know. I'm the person who works on my faults all the time, tries to become a better person, strives towards self-understanding and growth. I could have helped other people in this war if I'd been given a chance."

Hamid turned back to her and took her face between his hands. "Of course you could. You have exactly the same capac-

ity for greatness as Mohammed does, without the psychosis."
Rana stifled a laugh, but Hamid kept speaking. "You keep this
house going. Every single person in this house depends on you,
including Mohammed. You are my life and my love. Please,"
he said, pressing his fingers into the lines around her eyes.
"Please be satisfied with that. Please see that the happiness of
your nine dependents is as important as Mohammed's ability
to stitch wounds. Please make that enough for you, and be
satisfied and fulfilled."

Rana took her husband in her arms. "It should be enough,"
she whispered. "I will meditate and mature until I am wise
enough to know it is enough."

The next day Rana began the process of self-improvement.
She meditated for an hour after breakfast, shutting herself in
her bedroom and leaving Fatima to deal with the dribs and
drabs of grateful young men. She struggled vainly to focus on
her breathing: on her in-breath she thought, *I am a wonderful
person*, and on the outbreath she thought, *I am so grateful
for everything I have.* She listed all the many things she was
grateful for and felt gratitude fill her chest. "Thank you, thank
you," she murmured; words that were inextricably linked to
gratitude, even though she couldn't say whom she was thanking. Afterwards, she felt better. *I must do this every day*, she
thought. *It makes me aware of how lucky I am. Focuses on the
good things and makes the rest seem trivial, which indeed it is.*

She made her way to the kitchen to fetch some chicken
feed and found Na'aman under the table wearing a mournful
expression.

"Everything okay?" she asked.

"No breakfast," Na'aman mourned. "O'mmy at door." He
gazed up at his aunt hopefully. "Bad men at door," he said.

"Bloody annoying," Rana said in an amused voice, thinking
Hamid's estimation of her micro-Atlas abilities were bang on,
as she spooned some salad into a bowl. How would this house

keep going if she weren't there? "Why don't you eat this outside with me while I feed the chickens?"

"Yes," enthused Na'aman, standing unsteadily on his feet and holding his hand out to Rana.

"But you mustn't let the chickens have any because they love salad."

"No," Na'aman answered firmly.

They discovered Ahmed sitting in the sun with his radio on his knees, watching the chickens that he had released from their coop. Mohammed had brought home a rather battered wheelchair and Ahmed had abandoned his room and, most of the time, his depression along with it. Moussa's regular visits and detailed reports of every battle and every outcome also contributed to the improvement in Ahmed's humour. There were still bad days, when he pulled the covers off his legs and stared at his stumps in despair, but there were more and more good days, in-between.

"Do you want to feed the chickens?" Rana joked at him. "The more the merrier."

"No me!" insisted Na'aman.

"I like the chickens," said Ahmed.

Rana handed a plastic container of chicken feed to Na'aman. "They are rather nice, and they teach me a lot."

Ahmed snorted. "What do they teach you?"

Rana settled down beside him, on the chair Mohammed had made for her. "You'd be surprised. They teach me about societal interactions."

Na'aman turned his back on Henny Penny in order to give the other hens some feed. She stalked between his legs truculently and gave a flying leap at the plastic container. Na'aman sprang backwards in shock, unable to soften his fall with his hands because they both clutched vessels of food. Chicken feed scattered everywhere and Henny Penny, triumphant, pecked furiously at feed and the other hens. Na'aman turned a stoical face towards them. "I'm okay," he said.

"Good boy," Ahmed encouraged. "I suppose you're right, Rana. Henny Penny is the boss and she pecks at everyone until they succumb. I guess that is kind of what we're doing here."

"Exactly."

Ahmed tapped the radio on his lap. "This has been deeply appreciated, almost as much as Moussa's resurrection."

Rana, always restless, lurched to her feet and went to inspect her garden. "I thought it was so sweet that the children pooled all their money together to buy you that. Stops me from despairing of my fellow men."

"It was quite incredible," Ahmed said softly. "I told Zaynah what a difference the radio has made. She said it had been Mazin's idea, but I don't believe it."

"Why shouldn't it have been Mazin's idea?" Rana snapped.

Ahmed shrugged uncomfortably. "Zaynah is ... excessively fond of me."

Rana laughed. "She has a young girl's crush."

"You make it sound as if it were nothing. It could be very unhealthy."

"Nonsense! All young girls have crushes like that. It's got nothing to do with actual suitability. I probably fancied Mohammed at that age."

"Really?"

"No."

Ahmed fiddled with the dials on the radio. "So you think there's nothing to worry about?"

"Don't be ridiculous."

Ahmed smiled. Despite Rana's Mohammed-like tone of contempt, the seed of anxiety in his heart was stilled.

Na'aman's delightful laughter swept over them. Still lying prone on the ground, he had scattered feed on his chest and two brave hens had stepped gingerly from arm to chest and were pecking away. "It tickles. It tickles."

Rana bent over him and poked him in his armpit. Na'aman shrieked with laughter and within minutes was choking. Rana pulled him to a sitting position and thumped him on the back. The displaced hens took a dim view of this and waddled off in a disgruntled fashion. "Breathe," Rana ordered. Na'aman sucked in a shaky breath and grinned at his aunt.

Rana then abandoned him and bent over her vegetables again. "Do you have any updates on the war?"

Ahmed rolled a cigarette between his fingers. "Moussa has spoken the truth. The rebels are definitely taking over the country, town by town. In the beginning, it was hard for me to wrap my head around the headway the rebels have made. It feels like a complete turnaround from when I was involved. In such a short time, relatively."

"Fatima tells me that Mohammed is frightened by the real possibility that we'll turn into an extremist Islamic state if Kassam leaves."

"Mohammed doesn't talk to me about politics anymore," replied Ahmed, with some bitterness in his voice.

"That should be a relief," responded Rana, holding one side of her apron pocket out and piling herbs into it.

"We would probably agree now. He loves it when the United States is at fault, and if we become an extremist Muslim state it will be entirely their fault."

Rana straightened, rubbing the ache in the small of her back. "How so?"

"If they'd supplied mainstream rebels like us with arms, we'd never have turned to the Islamists. But they dillied and dallied and now they'll have another implacable enemy in the Middle East." Ahmed took a long drag from his cigarette. "So much for the hopes of civil democracy."

Rana looked at him in surprise. "Aren't you pleased that the rebels are winning?"

Ahmed threw his half-smoked cigarette on the ground. Rana stamped on it, then picked it up and maneuvered it into her apron pocket, behind the pile of vegetables and herbs.

"Yes, of course I am. And in my heart I don't really believe we'll be an Islamist state — we only need them now because they have so many arms. Who knows what will happen?" Ahmed sighed. "I don't know why I feel so angry."

Rana carefully turned her eyes on Na'aman, who had managed to corner a chicken and was cradling it on his knee, holding it by the legs like Rana had shown him to do. He was whispering to the chicken, who clucked in response. They were deep in conversation.

"Mohammed must have known that the tide had turned and the rebels were taking over more and more strategic regions. He knew that defectors from the army were swelling our ranks and justifying our struggle. Why didn't he tell me?"

"I don't know," said Rana.

"He could have done me the kindness of keeping me informed. He knew how depressed I was. Most days I couldn't care less whether I died, you know." Ahmed sighed, his hand hovering over his stomach as though it were itching to chafe. "Of course, I had lost my legs, but the source of my depression lay in the feeling that I would be useless forever: a drain on my family, a drain on society. This feeling of uselessness was exacerbated by the fact that I was cut off from everything, even information. But Moussa and the radio have made all the difference because now I know what's going on. Only why didn't Mohammed tell me? Why didn't he help me?"

"I don't think he understands what causes unhappiness in others," said Rana. "I think he helped you in the only way he knew. By patching you up physically. "

They looked at each other in silence.

"Dinner?" Na'aman asked hopefully.

One night as the family sat around the table eating, Rana realized that it was true: Mohammed rarely talked politics at the dinner table anymore. He was always tired and ate quickly, centering his attention on his children during this one hour he saw them. There had only been one exception — the night

Ahmed had told them in a tremulous voice about the chemical attacks. They had all stared at him, shocked and silent.

"This can't be true," Mohammed had whispered.

"I wish it wasn't true. The whole world is up in arms about it. Perhaps they will help us at last."

"How many dead?"

"I don't know." Ahmed had leant back in his seat and chafed his stomach.

"How could Kassam attack his own people that way? How could this happen?"

Ahmed had not been able to resist. "Surely he's lost all his supporters now. The reasonable ones, in any case. He's obviously insane."

"He wasn't insane when you protesters started this whole thing," Mohammed had snapped, somewhat unreasonably. "He has changed, can't you see that? This is the depraved, inhuman act of a madman. Perhaps the fear of losing power has contaminated his mind. Or perhaps it was the rebels who used chemical weapons. What proof do you have that Kassam did it?"

"It's just ... common knowledge," Ahmed had stammered.

"Common knowledge amongst your protester friends perhaps. Nonsense. I don't believe it."

"But every cloud has a silver lining," Ahmed had said after a moment of silence. "The Americans believe it. Surely the world will help us now."

Mohammed had speared a meatball and raised it slowly to his mouth. "Don't count on it. They'll hum and haw about the use of chemical weapons, certainly, but the West will support whatever side suits them."

Rana had watched him chew his meatball with an expression close to disgust.

"Why would the West ever support an Enemy of Democracy like Kassam?" Ahmed had asked. "An oppressor; a monster who uses chemical weapons — who they believe has used chemical weapons — against his own people? It's impossible."

The twins had begun to nudge each other's feet under the table, jockeying for the best position — which naturally had to be exactly the same spot.

"Nothing is impossible," Mohammed had answered. "What if a new extremist force rises up, like Al Qaeda? A big, powerful force which begins to take over the region. A blood-thirsty, cruel force that commits atrocities against our Moslem brothers, and even against the Americans, whenever they can. All in the name of Islam. And more people join them, just like you joined the protesters. The extremist force grows, and occupies more lands and regions. Kassam, of course, would fight them. And then what do you think the Americans would do?"

Na'aman couldn't have cared less what the Americans might do, and began to bang his spoon on the table. Fatima, intent on the conversation, had pushed a bowl of humus in front of him absent-mindedly. Na'aman had gurgled in delight and plunged his fat little fists into the thick texture. The twins, also rather ambivalent about the Americans, had intensified their foot war. It was imperative for both to conquer the area between their chairs.

"That's not going to happen," Ahmed had said urgently. "I know you don't like the fact that there are extreme religious factions helping our cause but what you're projecting is impossible." Ahmed had leaned forward and speared his own meatball with determination. "It's such a radical, negative prediction of our country's future ... it won't happen. How could a murderous group like you describe attract followers?"

Rana had tensed in expectation of Mohammed's rage. Ali's foot had ousted Abdul's from the disputed territory.

But Mohammed hadn't spewed forth a contemptuous rebuke. Instead, he had leaned forward tiredly and rested his forehead in his hands. "Anything is possible. Chemical weapons; whoever is responsible, it's too unbearable to believe."

"What are chemical weapons?" Abdul had asked, sulkily rejoining the conversation.

Mohammed had raised his head abruptly. "We shouldn't be talking about such things in front of the children," he had barked at Ahmed. "I'll thank you not to discuss politics at the dinner table ever again."

There had been a brief silence while Mohammed kneaded his forehead until it was red. Then he'd caught sight of Na'aman's humus-bedecked face. "What are you doing, Fatima?" he had shouted. "Get that child cleaned up immediately — what a waste of food! Do you think we're made of money?" Shutters had slammed down on the interest and focus radiating from every face. The boys had frozen in consternation. Zaynah had sprung to her feet and begun clearing the table. Fatima had borne the squalling Na'aman away. After a moment, Rana had risen to her feet and begun to help Zaynah, banging the dishes with unnecessary force.

Rana had refused to find out any more about it. It was as if the news was so shocking that her mind closed down against it. She had one contradictory argument with Hamid where she veered between denial that such a thing could have happened in their beloved country, to insisting that she travel to the affected areas and offer her help as a nurse. Hamid had gently nixed that idea, to her secret relief, on the basis that the entire family needed her so much it could not survive without her. She had bouts of guilt for not suffering more herself when so many lives had been decimated. She felt the old, familiar tendrils of depression wind around her heart, so she meditated furiously.

Politics were not discussed again at the table. Dialogue contracted into a litany of numbers: how many had called, how many presents they had brought, how many ailments Mohammed had cured. *While Fatima looks on blissfully and vacuously*, Rana thought maliciously. More frequently as the days went by, Ahmed declined to join them in the evenings, pleading headaches. Each conversation was indistinguishable from the previous day, and the day before that.

"Are those numbers really true?" Mohammed asked his wife.

The first sign of vanity? Rana wondered. Mohammed's only reaction to his family's knowledge of his secret life was to ignore it. He never answered questions and grew irritable when pressed. When the number of callers was discussed during dinnertime, he looked faintly bemused and rather bored. It would be interesting if, underneath his exterior of indifference, he was puffing up like a turkey.

"Yes, of course the numbers are true," answered Fatima. "Every day they come, calling upon Allah to bless you." As if to confirm her words, there was a knock on the door.

"Sit down!" Mohammed shouted at the children. "How dare they come during the evening? Do they think they can march into the privacy of my home whenever they feel like it?"

The knocking became more insistent and Rana slipped out of the kitchen, praying he would shut up before she got to the door.

She opened the door a crack, suppressing the desire to say, "Not today, thank you." The usual proffered gift, this time a basket of varied breads. The usual blessings showered on Mohammed's head, even as he bellowed, "Can't they bloody leave me alone? Isn't it enough that I give them my days? How am I supposed to replenish my energies if they come barging into my home every minute of the day?"

Rana and the young soldier looked at each other, their smiles frozen. She stood mortified at the door. "May Allah bless the bravest of men," the soldier whispered and turned to go.

Rana stumped into the kitchen and threw the basket of bread on the table. "The kind benefactor who gave us this bread heard every word, you'll be glad to know."

"Good," said Mohammed. "Maybe they'll stop coming."

Rana sat down at her place and continued to spoon vegetable soup into her mouth. The faces of the children looked stricken.

That is still the effect he has on us all, she reflected, *and it will never change. A bully, inside and out.*

At the other end of the table Zaynah cleared her throat. "I got an A in my math test today, Abi."

Mohammed grunted, discontent sitting heavy on his face. Rana saw the apprehensive glances Mazin slid in his direction, and hated her brother. Hated anybody who would transform the look of joy on a child's face into a look of terror, without a moment's thought, without even enough awareness to be conscious of it. Nobody had the right to destroy happiness, especially the fragile happiness of children — their children — who were forced to witness horror every day in this war zone. Their children needed and craved every second of happiness they could possibly give. What benefit the ability to repair physically when one simultaneously destroyed mentally? What type of hero was that?

A strangled yell came from the hallway. Zaynah and Rana leapt to their feet simultaneously, while Fatima gawked at Mohammed wide-eyed. Rushing to the door, Rana saw Ahmed careening along the corridor in his wheelchair with one hand while his other hand waved the radio in the air.

"The rebels have taken the capital," he shouted. "The tyrant has fled!"

CHAPTER 13 **FATIMA**

A S SOON AS DINNER WAS OVER, Rana sent the children to their rooms. "We did it!" shouted the twins as they hurtled past Zaynah's door on their way to their bedroom. "It worked. Allah heard us, Zaynah. It worked!" Fatima bustled along behind them, determined to stop the noise before the wrath of Mohammed fell on their heads.

"Be quiet," Zaynah shouted after the twins as Fatima passed her doorway.

The twins toppled into their bedroom in a state of high excitement without acknowledging their mother, shutting the door behind them. Fatima felt annoyed, as though they were shutting the door in her face. "You get ready for bed now," she called after them. "I'll be there in two minutes to kiss you good night."

She hesitated before going back to Zaynah's room. She could hear Mazin's voice, which didn't surprise her. "We did do it, Zaynah."

"Will you shut up?" Zaynah said fiercely. "My mother might hear you."

There was a silence. Then: "My favourite is the one of Abdul laughing — or is it Ali? I can't tell them apart as babies. His whole face is one big laugh."

Fatima knew that Mazin was looking at the photos that plastered Zaynah's wall. She even knew which photo he was referring to; it was one of her favourites as well. Rana had been swishing Mazin back and forth in the air like an airplane, and Ali had been watching them with his whole mouth stretched open in a laugh so huge his eyes could barely see around it.

"I like this one as well," Mazin said. Fatima repressed the urge to push the door open a crack and peek through, to know which photo he was looking at. Fatima often stopped to look at them herself. Each one held a memory. She could remember the circumstances of each and every photo, even the two framed professional photos of her entire family, taken when she was about five years old. She remembered the day, an auspicious day, when the photographer had come to the house to take their picture. They had all been dressed in their best clothes, and she had stood like an angel while her mother brushed and braided her hair. She had felt primly self-righteous when Nadia began to squirm in protest at the heavy-handed dealing with the knots in her hair. Possibly she had made horrible faces at her sister, to ramp up her squirming.

The photographer had lined them up outside their front door, the adults behind and the children in front. They had all stared at him unsmilingly, without moving, caught for eternity in their stern finery. Once, Fatima had admonished Zaynah for "appropriating" the photos, mostly without asking. "But O'mmy, they're just stuck in a drawer. At least this way we can look at them." Fatima's intention had been to arrange all the photos into neat little piles, organized by date, and then insert them into photo albums complete with captions. But somehow, there had never been the time or the energy for such a complicated project. Another time, she had tried to rouse Rana's interest in the plan, knowing Rana's energy would have transformed the messy mounds of photos in the drawer into neat stacks of chronological albums within a week, but Rana didn't seem to care about photos and never stopped to look at the collage on Zaynah's bedroom wall. So the photos remained entombed in their drawer, except those that Zaynah fancied.

"Your expression is so funny," said Mazin, and then Fatima knew which photo he was looking at. Zaynah on her tenth birthday, proudly sporting a crown of flowers and holding up a silver coin, her attention diverted from the camera for a minute by some irritating antic of the twins, a glowering grimace contorting the face underneath the angelic crown. Fatima was amused to see that one on her wall, when several perfect photos had been taken immediately after the grimace. She questioned Zaynah about it, but the girl had only shrugged irritably. "Why do you think she chose that one?" she had asked Rana.

"It's obvious, isn't it?" Rana had answered. "All the photos are chosen for their amusing properties, haven't you noticed?"

"What's funny about the photo of my family? A professional photographer took that."

"Something must have struck Zaynah as amusing. Perhaps the identical solemnity on all the faces, young and old."

Fatima hadn't noticed, and had spent a long time examining each photo in turn after that, during the day when Zaynah was at school. It was true. Each photo had a story to tell. Instead of choosing from the many smiling bride-and-groom photos, Zaynah's wall exhibited Mohammed's frowning face behind his raised hand as he moved to block the camera: "That's enough photos for one day," Fatima clearly remembered him saying. "I'll go mad if you stick that thing in my face one more time."

Beside him, the mouth of his pretty little bride formed a comic little "O" as she gazed up at her new husband in surprise. She hadn't had a clue what she was getting into.

There was one of a tiny Mazin hugging the leg of his adored cousin, as she tried to march out of the room, dragging him with her. There was another of the two of them embracing passionately, while the twins pulled frantically on the backs of their shirts, faces streaming with tears as they clamoured for attention.

"Let's go to the twins' room," Fatima heard Mazin say, and prepared to back away from the door.

246 CHARLOTTE R. MENDEL

"Why?"

"We need to thank Allah for listening to our prayers. We should do it together with the twins, since it was all of us together that succeeded."

Fatima bent closer to the door. *What on earth are they talking about?*

"I wish you'd be quiet," Zaynah replied.

"Why? Your mother can't hear us anymore."

"All right," said Zaynah, still in an aggrieved voice, as though she had much better things to do. "But not until our mother has kissed us all good night."

Fatima withdrew from Zaynah's door with furtive guilt, overcome with a feeling of irrepressible curiosity. She kissed the twins perfunctorily, reflecting that if she wanted she could wheedle the truth out of them fairly easily. She debated with herself as she parried their arguments for more TV time, watching their repressed excitement as they looked at her coyly. It would be better to find out the truth honestly from them rather than listening at doors. Eavesdroppers never heard anything positive, and she so wanted this to be positive. Her children, praying to Allah! Her own quiet, unobtrusive influence forging the path of future spirituality within the family? Fatima felt choked with excitement. She had to know what Mazin had been referring to. But how to obtain the information?

In the end, it was her own suspicions about Zaynah's ongoing habit of listening at doors that convinced her to choose the path of twin-wheedling — she would hate for her daughter to think it was reasonable behaviour because her mother indulged in it.

The twins were delightfully astounded when their mother chose to sit down on Abdul's bed after her perfunctory kisses and short negatives to their TV-related pleas.

"Now what did you do that Zaynah doesn't want you to tell me?" she asked without preamble, tousling their dark curls affectionately.

"Zaynah will…"

"…kill us."

"Of course she won't," said Fatima, switching her hand to the other head. "If it's something bad, then you should tell me because a mother needs to know. If you've done something bad, then maybe I can help you not to do it again. On the other hand, if it's something good, then why can't you tell me? I like to hear good things."

There was a short silence while the twins gazed at each other in longing, seized between an intense desire to tell and fear of breaking their promise to Zaynah.

"What did you pray to Allah about?" Fatima prompted gently. The twins looked at each other in relief — O'mmy already knew! In unison, they opened their mouths.

"We are the ones…"

"…who stopped the war."

"We prayed…."

"All of us…."

"And it worked."

Fatima smiled with great love upon her twins. "All of you prayed together? All you children? You prayed and asked Allah to stop the war?"

Two dishevelled heads nodded vigorously.

Fatima fell onto her knees on the narrow strip of floor between the beds, wrapping an arm around each of the twins and pulling them down with her, hugging them. "You are my wonderful children. Only Allah knows how much I love you." She laughed with pleasure. "Your prayers stopped the war!"

The twins beamed with delight, burrowing against their mother like little animals.

"Do you understand the power of Allah? He can do anything, and He is listening to you. That doesn't mean that you will always get what you pray for, but Allah is always listening, and knows when your requests emerge from pure hearts."

Fatima glanced up and saw Zaynah and Mazin standing in

the doorway. She raised her voice slightly. "When life seems unbearable, Allah will help you. I have not taught you too much about religion, but I am so very happy that despite this, my children, my brilliant children, know where to turn when they are in trouble. Only Allah can truly help us."

Whether the twins were listening or not it was hard to say; certainly, they hadn't registered Zaynah's presence. A paroxysm of passionate ardour overcame them suddenly and they threw their arms around their mother from either side, kissing her neck, trying to wind their overlong limbs around her.

"All right, that's enough," said Fatima gently, trying to peel their arms away. She looked up towards the door again. Zaynah had disappeared. She extricated herself from the twins and stood abruptly, admonishing them to be in bed with the lights out within two minutes.

"We need..."

"...a kiss good night."

She bent over, peremptorily pecking their cheeks and ignoring their outstretched, yearning arms.

"Would you like us to do Salaah?" whispered Ali.

Fatima had a sudden vision of Mohammed catching his boys in prayer. "I think if you want to pray to Allah, you can do it just as well in your heads. Allah hears you just the same," she said.

"But why doesn't Abi want us to pray?" Abdul chimed in.

There was no way she was going to try and answer that. Not at this time of night. Not ever. "People pray in different ways," she said evasively. "For now, it is enough to pray in your heads."

The twins nodded in unison, struggling to keep their eyes open on this exciting end-of-war day as their mother passed out of the room.

Fatima hesitated for a minute before Zaynah's door, but she could not hear Mazin's voice. She opened the door and slipped inside, casting a glance towards the photos on the wall. She bent over to kiss her daughter. "You must not be angry at your brothers. I knew something was going on and I forced them to tell me." Fatima waited for a moment, but Zaynah did not answer. "I am so very glad that you turned to Allah in your need, and I know that Allah heard your prayers."

"There are a lot of bad things happening right now all over the world, O'mmy, and many poor people who are praying for their suffering to stop. Usually, Allah doesn't help them."

Fatima smoothed the hair off her daughter's face. "Human beings cause the suffering. It is written in the Koran: 'Whoever does the smallest good deed shall experience the result of it, and whoever does the slightest evil deed shall experience the result of it.' It is also written: 'If Allah so willed, He could make you all one people: but He leaves straying whom He pleases, and He guides whom He pleases: but ye shall certainly be called to account for all your actions.' That means Allah gave us free will, and it is like a test for us. We must all try to be as good as we can. However, there are many who call themselves Muslims and do harm. Allah sees all, but He will not interfere in the free will He chose to give us."

"Then why did he help us?" Zaynah insisted.

"Perhaps the war was going in that direction anyway. Perhaps your prayers just hastened the end a little. Perhaps the innocence and purity of your selfless prayer moved him."

Fatima could see her daughter's mind absorbing her words, turning them over. She nodded at her mother, and Fatima bent to kiss her again before making her way to the kitchen to retrieve Na'aman from his aunt's loving but wearied care.

Fatima climbed the stairs slowly, savouring her exhaustion. Mohammed had looked so tired during dinner. It was not an easy task, being a hero. Her husband, a hero! Every time she opened the door and saw a new face filled with gratitude and awe at the sacrifices her husband had made for them, her heart swelled with love. To think she had once fretted over her husband's attitude towards religion! Allah had shown her that true religious meaning lay in acts that came directly from the soul, not in the physical day-to-day customs. Allah, in His wisdom, had seen that her husband was a great man, a noble human being, despite his tormented mind and subsequent rejection of those important traditions and customs. All heroes were complicated men. All brilliant people were a little larger than life. She was not worthy of such a husband.

She was so proud.

Slowly, she mounted the steps. She no longer wished for him to be sleeping when she entered the room. She wanted to give him five minutes of pleasurable relaxation at the end of his heroic day. He was exhausted and tense, she could feel it. Of course he was, rushing from calamity to calamity, saving lives. There wasn't a second during the day when he could sit back and take it easy. What must it be like to have thousands of people dependent on you for their very lives? Incredible, but stressful. Nobody ever thought about Mohammed. Nobody catered to his needs, except her. She alone in all the world had the power to relax him, to give him five minutes of pleasure at the end of a gruelling day. She wanted to do her part.

Mohammed was not sleeping. He was lying comatose in bed, but she could tell by the way he breathed that he was awake. Waiting for her. Too tired even to read. Fatima plunged through the evening prayer as quickly as she could and slipped into bed beside her husband, turning to him, lifting her hand to his brow and smoothing the deepening lines. He did not open his eyes, but neither did he shift away in irritation, so she continued to knead and smooth. It was so unlike him to be absolutely quiet. He must be utterly exhausted.

"Are you all right?" she whispered.

He nodded, then turned to her and gazed at her face for a few moments. She looked back, adoring him, worshipping him. He slipped his hand under her nightgown and stroked her. She felt honoured that he loved her body so much, that it gave him so much pleasure. He slipped lower, still looking into her eyes, and she wanted to open her legs, to pull him to her. She did not care if it would seem immodest, or unwomanly, or even whether he would like it or not. She wanted him to know she loved him. It was important. All day long, he endured one-dimensional, unequal relationships with those around him. In the evening, he frequently came back to strife or subdued negativity. She, Fatima, was the only person who loved him truly. She was part of him, as he was part of her. She wanted him to know how much she loved him. How proud she felt.

She could not do it while he was looking into her eyes like that. She could not stop the feeling of embarrassment, even when she was so sure that it was the right thing to do. She closed her eyes and turned her head to one side.

Mohammed shifted on top of her, running his hands along her body. Eyes tight shut, she lifted her own hands and crept around his torso, starting at the small of the back and travelling upwards, pressing and releasing, stroking and massaging. She arched her back towards him, thrusting her cotton-covered breasts against him. Then he was pulling at her nightgown, pulling it over her head. She sat up to accommodate him, feeling her whole body flush, keeping her eyes sealed and banishing the instinct to cover herself. He touched her breasts lightly and again she arched towards him, face averted, almost rigid with discomfiture.

He kissed her breasts and she allowed her breathing to quicken audibly, trying to communicate to him how much she loved him, how she yearned to give her body to him.

"Fatima," he murmured in surprise, but she could tell by his tone that he was pleased. That was all she needed. She stroked her hands up his back and buried her hands in his hair. "I am yours," she whispered, lifting her head to his ear so her burning face would be concealed.

He slipped his hands under her buttocks and lifted her up a little as he entered. She wanted to groan, but she couldn't quite manage it. She tried to focus on the feeling of her husband pushing in and out. She focused with all her energy, her embarrassment forgotten. She placed her hands on his buttocks, for the first time in his life, and pulled the flesh to slow him down. He hesitated. She could feel him staring down at her, but she kept her eyes tight shut. She pushed his buttocks firmly, then pulled them, push and pull, and he slowed, and tried to respond, entering and exiting according to her hand commands. And she felt a rising heat inside, and she pushed and pulled more aggressively, eyes screwed shut, focusing, concentrating. His movement stopped and she grimaced with irritation, pinching his buttock and pushing it. "Shall I come?" he whispered.

She could not look at him. She shook her head once, so slightly she was scared he would not see. He pushed in slower, and she wanted it faster, so she pushed and pulled the solid skin of his buttocks.

Suddenly, he withdrew altogether and her eyes flew open. "Just a moment," he said. Love coursed through her as she realized he was trying to control himself, for her sake, for her pleasure. She waited, impatient, and in a minute or two he slid into her wet vagina again, and again she directed him with shut eyes and averted face. The heat built inside her, and she wanted it more and harder. And then there was a powerful, immense sensation as her vagina pulsated in a series of spasms and it was astounding, it was so unbelievable, that she was almost frightened. Despite herself, her mouth opened in complete astonishment and she cried out, and Mohammed dropped his lips to hers and kissed her.

Afterwards, they did not speak. He hugged her body to his and placed his head right next to hers, noses almost touching. Fatima knew she couldn't sleep like this, but she lay absolutely still, soft and compliant in his arms until his breathing changed.

Then she dared to open one eye a slit and risk a glance at his sleeping face.

He was smiling.

Fatima sat in front of the mirror and watched the bristles of the brush travel through her long, dark hair. From root to end she brushed, slowly and sensuously. Na'aman had been intrigued as well, reaching out grubby little hands to catch the falling black tresses, and indulgently, she had let him catch them and squish them between his fingers, bringing them to his nose and inevitably, to his mouth.

"No, Na'aman," she said, pulling the sticky strands towards her and brushing out his saliva. He stretched his arms and grabbed a mass of it, giggling as it cascaded through his fingers. Fatima tickled him until he desisted and led him to the twins' room to "borrow" their Lego. They had built a truck, which she reluctantly withheld from Na'aman's destructive fingers, but there were lots of loose pieces which she spread on the floor for him, crouching down to show him how to stick them together. "Make a tower," she said.

She could hear Rana downstairs directing the children's homework as she began preparations for dinner. She knew Mazin and Zaynah would vie with one another over the neatest homework, the easiest comprehension, the fastest completion. The twins, whose natural interest in schoolwork might not have triumphed over the lure of more physical adventures, were swept into competitive mode and raced to complete their homework first. How lucky she was, to have a studious girl born first. First children were destined to be the trailblazers, their habits and inclinations trickling down to their younger siblings. And to have a studious, older male cousin thrown into the mix! Fatima threw a smile over her shoulder at Na'aman, fitting one piece of Lego into another with great concentration. "Well done," she applauded him, remembering too late her own advice to Rana to give attention only when it was demanded.

Two minutes later, Na'aman held up two more pieces. "Watch me build it, O'mmy."

Fatima sighed. Her own fault. She smiled and nodded and brushed.

"Have you finished?" she heard Rana's voice. "Because don't think you're leaving that mess on the table."

"That's Abdul's mess."

"Is not."

"Is too."

"Is not."

Fatima knew this could go on for quite some time, and lowered her brush the better to listen to Rana's inevitable outburst. "I don't care whose mess it is, I want those papers off the table in three seconds flat. *One.*"

"Look, O'mmy," said Na'aman. Fatima began to twist her hair into its familiar bun. She could hear Mazin and Zaynah chortling together.

"Right, chores," said Rana. "Zaynah, wash the dishes. Twins clean your room. It's disgusting. Mazin, feed the chickens and bring me some stuff to make a salad."

There was a short silence. The twins appeared in the doorway of the room and smiled at their mother and Na'aman.

Then: "You made the mess in our room," Abdul accused.

"Did not."

"So it's my mess? Those dinkies are my dinkies, and the books are my books? Great! I'll take them to my side of the room then."

"Is not!" screamed Ali, and flung himself on the disputed items.

"Just clean it up, boys," Fatima sighed. They looked at her tired face and silently began to clear up the respective halves of their room.

In a minute she would go and help Rana with the dinner.

A groan of pure vexation erupted behind her, and Fatima turned just in time to see Na'aman pounding two pieces together in a useless attempt to get them to fit before he threw them across the room in frustration. Fatima scurried to retrieve them. She wished they had bigger Lego pieces to fit smaller hands. "Here, O'mmy will help you," she said, restraining him just in time before he smashed his whole tower to pieces. "That's a great tower. Do you want this piece on top?"

Mollified, Na'aman nodded, watching her closely as she attached another piece to the pinnacle. She could see it was getting taller and more difficult to keep adding pieces. "This is a big tower. I think it is big enough."

"No," said Na'aman, grabbing another piece.

She sighed. His persistence so often ended in absolute rage. "I am going to lie on the bed in your room and read a story. You can stay here if you like, but if you come I will cuddle you while I read."

Fatima lay on Na'aman's small bed and began reading a Greek story called, "The Wooden Horse." Soon Na'aman marched after her and stood in the middle of the floor, Lego still clutched in his hands, staring at her obstinately with arms crossed. She knew the story was one of Na'aman's favourites, and she read with expression, lending different voices to different characters and trying to stay consistent. She didn't lift her eyes up when she felt a little body snuggle up to her, and a little hand reach out to touch the picture. *I am happy*, she thought to herself with surprise.

Rana had told her people never knew when they were happy during their happy times, only in retrospect when it was too late. She said that part of her new meditation process was the counting of blessings, when she focused on the many wonderful things in her life that she was thankful for. "It really helps me," she had told Fatima. "I'm such a negative person that I'm always focusing on the bad things that happen. If I have ten great conversations in a day and one unpleasant one, I'll focus on the unpleasant and brood on it. Now that I'm meditating, I am consciously focusing on the positive, and I really think it's making me a happier person."

Fatima thought Rana looked happier too. She was no longer fighting with Mohammed, nor did she seem worried about Mazin. What was there to be worried about? He was a great kid. Her voice recited the familiar lines smoothly as she began to think of all the things that made her happy. Her children, first and foremost and always. Mohammed. Rana. Ahmed. The fact that Ahmed had travelled to Moussa's house by himself yesterday, pushing his rickety wheelchair along the pavement with his increasingly muscular arms. He had come back in a great humour. It was only a matter of time before he would start to think about finishing his studies, about a future career. Possibly, his legs would limit his opportunities, but it was just as possible that people would want to hire a wounded soldier more than someone who had never fought. She was thankful for her lovely house and the lovely meals they ate every day, despite the war. She was so very, very thankful that the dictator had fled and the war was over, safe in the knowledge that with two war heroes in the house they would be all right no matter who took over the helm. Why, healed soldiers still came by every day, proffering gifts and swearing to look after them if anything should ever happen to Mohammed. They were surrounded by gratitude and love, immersed in it. She was so thankful.

Fatima finished the story and rolled on her side, walking her fingers up Na'aman's belly as he waited with bated breath, scrutinizing every finger-step, until she got to his armpit and burrowed in. He screamed with laughter. Then again and again. She could do this a million times and each time he would watch her finger with mesmerized anticipation, almost hiccupping in excitement. Once, he broke into hysterical giggles before she reached his armpit. She stopped, and he realized his mistake and caught his breath in a big gulp and held it, his eyes round and elated, waiting.

There was a sound of running feet along the corridor. Abdul and Ali pushed the door open and rushed in, falling on the bed beside them. Fatima reached out to include them in her tickles, but they leapt immediately to their feet. "Come, O'mmy, come...."

"They've caught him!"

"Right in our street!"

"Right outside!"

"Come," they shouted desperately, pulling at both her hands.

"Caught who?" she asked, bewildered.

"Kassam," they shrieked, pulling urgently on her arms, terrified they were missing the action, desperate for their mother to see it too.

Fatima allowed herself to be drawn upwards. "Kassam in *our* street? How can this be?"

Na'aman was by now pulling at her skirt, helping to maneuver her out of the bottleneck at the door. "Come, O'mmy," he commanded, certain that he was missing something important.

And she tripped after them, certain that they were mistaken, humouring them, but when she got to the window Rana turned around and her face was grey. "Send the children away," she said. "They shouldn't see this."

Fatima edged up to the window and looked out fearfully, flanked by the twins. At first, there just seemed to be a mass of people, shouting and gesticulating, not unlike the numerous protests over the past few years. She turned inquiringly to Rana who grasped the windowsill with whitened knuckles. "Don't you see?" she asked, and then suddenly shouted at the twins. "Go to your rooms!"

"O'mmy...." they begged, and Fatima still peered out the window, trying to see what was going on. There was a man on the ground. The mob was pulling him this way and that. Cries of "Allahu Akbar" seeped through the window. The man's face was bloodied. People were striking him in the face, pushing him, screaming. Even through the blood, Fatima could see that this man resembled Kassam. Nausea clutched her stomach.

She clapped her hands over her sons' eyes. "Go," she cried to the twins, almost crying. "Go to your room."

"There is a window in their room," Rana said quietly. "Send them out to the courtyard, to Mazin. Zaynah is there too."

"Up," demanded Na'aman.

"No!" Fatima snapped at him as the twins began to retreat before her fluttering hands.

"Why can't we watch, O'mmy? Kassam was a bad man. We are happy they are killing him."

"It's how they are killing him," Rana said. "No man should die like that. No child should watch it. Go. Go!"

The women turned back, their eyes drawn to the horrific scene down the road. Kassam toppled over and they heaved him upright, smacking him in the face. Fatima put her hand over her eyes and turned away. She did not want to watch it either.

"They are animals," Rana said. "Some of our neighbours are down there. Normal people, transformed into animals in a mob."

"Doesn't he deserve it?" asked Fatima, staring at her hands. "The blood of thousands is on his hands."

"So, let him be tried in a court of law, not tortured and humiliated by a bunch of animals." Rana closed her eyes briefly. "Many governments justify torture under certain circumstances, but I think the act of torture destroys the man who is doing it...." Rana's words were cut off as Fatima grasped her wrist, digging her nails into her arm painfully. The two women peered out the window again, reaching for each other's hands, clasping on for dear life, not wanting to believe what their eyes were showing them.

Mohammed was forcing his way through the crowd toward the centre, using his height and strength to thrust people out of the way. Within minutes, he had cut a path to the first ring of people surrounding the dictator. "Listen to me!" he shouted impressively.

Rana leaned forward and opened the window, the better to hear.

"This isn't the way!" Mohammed called, looking from one to the other of the perpetrators in the front row. "I know you are filled with hate for the crimes this man has committed, but don't we want to create a civilized country from the ashes of this war? This is not an act of civilization! This man must go to trial."

Rana turned from the window and ran for the door, snatching Fatima's burqa on the way.

"Where are you going?"

"To help him. To protect him."

"Rana, no! We can't go out there."

"You stay here and make sure the children don't come out of the courtyard."

"If you go, I am going too," said Fatima with great force, and she picked up a burqa too.

Rana ran to her and took her hands. "You mustn't go out there. A mob like this is dangerous and unpredictable."

"You mustn't go out there either."

"To help my brother."

"And my husband. But how can we help him? He is a hero, many people in that mob know him. Perhaps his logic will prevail." There was a pause, then Fatima whispered, "What can we do to help him?"

Rana looked at her, brow furrowed. Then she bent her head. "Nothing. There is nothing we can do." In one stride, they were back at the window, gazing fearfully out.

"Get out of the way," the mob was shouting.

"I will not get out of the way. I am a doctor, and this man needs my help!" Mohammed roared, elbowing aside one of the men holding Kassam and kneeling beside the former dictator.

Instantly, hands seized him. "You are a traitor," they bawled. "Anyone who tries to save this wicked dictator is a traitor."

"I am a healer," said Mohammed, and he pointed at one of the men. "Did I not heal you?"

"Traitor!" they screamed. "Traitor!"

Then Fatima saw among the faces some of those same soldiers who had come to their house. Those same mouths that had poured forth gratitude and called her husband a hero were now screwed up in hatred, yelling, "Traitor, traitor."

She wrenched the window open. "Mohammed! Come home," she screamed above the din, and Rana added her voice to hers and together they screamed with all their force, "Mohammed, come home!" And miraculously he heard them, and turned towards them, and raised his hand.

"Come home," they cried.

"They want to torture and kill this man in violence," he called to them, his powerful voice cutting through the rising chant of the mob. Even so, they could barely hear him.

"There is nothing you can do!"

Mohammed looked at them for a moment, and it seemed to Fatima that his face was full of sadness. Even the taunts of the crowd stilled, as though awaiting his answer.

"This is what I do," he said. "I heal. I speak out against wrongdoing. What these men want to do is wrong."

"Traitor, traitor, traitor," chanted the crowd. Fatima could barely hear his next words, though he looked at her directly. "If I do not speak out, who will speak for me?" and Mohammed turned to the supine dictator, and bent over him with his black doctor's bag, and the men tried to pull him away, and he implored them, and they could no longer hear what he said, but knew he was begging them to behave like human beings, to let the man stand trial and take his punishment in a civilized way, and he continued to speak, his mouth still moved, but they were no longer listening, and now they were pulling him back and forth, chanting, "Traitor, traitor."

Fatima closed her eyes. Tears seeped through her tightly shut lids. The horror of it. She felt Rana's hand on her arm, and then she was enveloped in a tight embrace. "Don't look," whispered Rana. "Don't look."

Their focus on the din swarming in from the open window

foiled the sound of rattling wheels and Ahmed was in the room and careening towards the window before the women registered his approach. He grasped the windowsill and heaved himself up so he could see out the window, his whole body elevated in mid-air, muscles and sinews rippling under his skin.

Admiration for her brother's strong, male torso rose unbidden to Fatima's mind.

Ahmed's arms relaxed and he dropped back into his chair. "I am going out there."

"You mustn't," cried Fatima, crouching beside her brother's chair and wrapping her arms around him. "It's futile. There's nothing you can do."

"I want to see it," Ahmed hissed, his face contorted. "I want to revel in his suffering and humiliation. Every second of pain they inflict on him will brand joy on my heart."

"You want to join that vermin?" snarled Rana.

"Vermin?" hissed Ahmed. "Are you crazy? Who are you calling vermin? Kassam is the vermin! Vengeance! Vengeance!"

"Go ahead. Mohammed is out there trying to convince the mob to let him be so he can stand fair trial. Maybe you can get in a kick there too — vengeance for years of suffering under his alpha male rule."

"What? What did you say?"

"Oh, didn't you see him out there? Maybe he's already dead. Maybe they've already killed him, because they're vermin, vermin, vermin!" Rana's voice rose in a scream.

Ahmed's hand shot out and wrapped itself around her upper arm, squeezing her into silence. His voice, when he spoke, was quiet. "I lost my legs because of Kassam. I will never marry because of Kassam. This is my vengeance for my ruined life. He is the lucky one, because within half an hour it will all be over for him. But my pain will go on forever. The fact that Mohammed is out there too doesn't change anything. He is propelled by his purpose, and I am propelled by mine."

Fatima felt tears start to her eyes. She turned away and saw all the children in a huddle, framed by the doorway of the kitchen, staring at them with terrified eyes. She wanted to embrace them and tell them everything was going to be all right, but Rana was already yelling at them to get out to the courtyard double-quick or she would give them a beating they would never forget.

"They can hear everything in the courtyard," Fatima protested.

"They'll hear a mob screaming," retorted Rana. "They've heard that before."

Ahmed thrust himself towards the door.

"You're going? Even though you know your brother is out there trying to stop them?"

Ahmed turned to Rana with an anguished face. "I must be there. I must see what happens. Let me go."

The two women watched him leave, then moved instinctively back into their embrace, holding each other tightly.

They stood like that for a long time with their arms entwined. They did not move, even when the shots rang out.

After a few moments, Fatima whispered into Rana's hair. "Have they killed him?"

"I don't know. I expect so. That is what animals do."

Fatima wondered why she felt numb. Was this pain or indifference?

They both started tensely when the kitchen door creaked open and Zaynah's head appeared. "Can we come in?" she asked tentatively, ready to approach or run for cover, according to the look on Rana's face. "Is it over?"

Fatima glanced fearfully out the window. The crowd was lurching down the road behind a pick-up truck in the middle of the street. There were two bodies inside the pick-up truck, but it was impossible to identify them. Was it her husband? All her instincts screamed that it was.

She nodded at Zaynah. "For now."

Zaynah stepped a little further into the room. The frightened faces of the twins appeared in the space she had vacated.

"Abi doesn't want to kill the murderous dictator who has killed and tortured millions?"

"He wants him to have a fair trial," explained Rana. "He wants the courts to sentence him to death, rather than a vicious mob."

"But why...?" began Zaynah.

Fatima saw the frown gather between Rana's eyes and said quickly, "We will talk later, Zaynah, and explain everything. Right now we need a quiet time. Can you take the kids up to your room? Take some biscuits with you; you can eat them in your room as a special treat. Read them a story. Please."

Zaynah looked at her mother and at Rana. Then she nodded and marched towards the door, gathering the twins en route and snapping orders about what to bring from the kitchen.

The women looked at each other, their faces frozen with shock. Rana smoothed Fatima's hair away from her face. "It will be all right. It will be all right," she said, again and again.

"How, how will it be all right?" asked Fatima. It was hard to move her lips, to form words. She wished, for a moment, that she could die, too. But of course she couldn't; there were the children to consider. Her beloved children.

"It will be all right. We will survive. We are survivors." Rana placed her hands gently on either side of Fatima's face. "I am with you. I will look after you. Always."

Tears sprang to Fatima's eyes. She wanted to howl and rend her hair to lessen this horrible pain in her heart. "You're not ever going to be a hero?" she demanded.

"God forbid." Rana tried to smile. She stroked Fatima's cheeks and whispered again: "I will never leave you."

CHAPTER 14 RANA

FOR MONTHS, RANA FELT ANXIOUS every time she went to the souq, terrified that the same people who had branded her brother a traitor and murdered him in the street would point fingers, mutter against her. At first, she kept her head down and avoided eye contact, her ears on high alert. Then, she began to raise her head and stare people directly in the face as she made her purchases and strode down the aisles. Nobody behaved any differently towards her; she couldn't detect the slightest deviation from their usual greetings. Gradually, she began to relax. Human beings were strange creatures, utterly unpredictable in everything except their short memories. The next political event occupied their minds, as potential leaders jockeyed for position in anticipation of an election while the army imposed order, arm-in-arm with the rebels. It seemed like everything that had happened up to that point was history, and not part of current events at all. Out of date. Not of interest. *And thank Allah for that*, thought Rana, happily fingering both fish and fruit with equal contempt as she had always done.

There were even occasional presents left on the doorstep — not as many as before, but at least one a week. The givers no longer knocked, but left their silent offerings on the doorstep and crept away. Rana was desperate to catch one of them in the act, so she could kick the eggs in his face, spill the milk over his head. "Where were you?" she dreamed of screaming

at them, "When the man who saved your life was murdered?"
Miserable cowards.

Still, she had a lot to be thankful for. In her daily meditation
sessions on the little chair that Mohammed had built for her
outside the chicken coop, she listed her blessings one by one.
First and foremost, Mazin seemed happier at school. Zaynah
had mentioned that the bullying had stopped, although it was
hard to get more details than that. Equally deserving of thanks
was the fact that Ahmed was working. Moussa had recruited
him in the drive to get Muhammed Deeb elected as the most
moderate candidate in the region. Ahmed sat all day at a desk
where legs weren't needed, answering phones, stuffing enve-
lopes, and feeling once more in the thick of things. The money
was welcome as well.

Rana staggered up their front steps and pushed the door
open with her foot. They rarely locked it anymore, once they
realized nobody was going to link them to the "traitor's" fall
and murder them for good measure. Na'aman rushed out of
the kitchen joyfully to greet his aunt. Fatima followed him
slowly, and Rana scanned her face. She was pale and tired all
the time these days.

"I've bought some fresh pita and hummus from the souq.
With a nice salad, it'll be a perfect lunch."

Fatima nodded and silently took one of the bags.

"I'll make lunch!" Na'aman exclaimed excitedly.

Fatima's cell phone tinkled from the direction of the kitchen
and both women moved towards it. "I'll get it, Fatima," Rana
instructed peremptorily and picked it up. As she listened, her
face became grave. She nodded once or twice, conscious of
Fatima's worried eyes boring into her face. "I quite understand.
Please take whatever steps you think are necessary, and we
will reinforce the message here at home also." She clicked the
phone off and bent down automatically to provide Na'aman
with some plastic cups to stack. "That was the school. The
twins have been misbehaving again."

Fatima sank into a chair and hid her face in her hands.

Rana kissed the top of her head. "I know it's upsetting, and at some level it's understandable. It's only been a few months since they lost their father. But the teacher says they're skipping school and causing fights with their classmates. Then, when they do attend, they just sit there sullenly and don't do any work."

"They're scared and unhappy," whispered Fatima.

"I know they are, and I will certainly tell them that I understand that before I discipline them."

Fatima raised her face slowly. "What?"

Rana busied herself making tea. "You must see that the twins have to be disciplined, Fatima. I know they're unhappy. So, it's making them happier to screw up at school and beat people up? Of course not. In the long run, curtailing this behaviour will help them...."

"What are you suggesting?"

Rana hesitated as she poured tea into two ceramic mugs. "I'll just talk to them, Fatima. But I'll let them know that if they do these things again they'll be beaten." She placed the mug before Fatima on the table, avoiding her eyes. "The bottom line is that this behaviour is absolutely unacceptable and it has to stop. I'll give them every chance to stop. I'll give them a warning. But if the warning doesn't stop them, then stringent messages are necessary."

Fatima's white, accusing face shone at her. "They are unhappy," she hissed through clenched teeth. "You may never, *ever* hit my children."

Rana sat down close beside her. She covered Fatima's hand with her own, but Fatima pulled her hand away, curling it around the heat of the mug. "Fatima, you must agree that this behaviour has to stop. We've spent our whole lives instilling the vital importance of education into our children. Studying as hard as they can is their only option. Period. No exceptions. If they're sad, studying might help. Failing certainly won't."

Rana took a sip of tea, looking at Fatima's downcast face. "Education is the most important thing. Do you agree with that?"

Fatima gave a single nod.

"So, do you have any ideas how to lead the twins back to their desks, other than through punishment?"

"You are not hitting my children," Fatima repeated through tight lips.

"What should I do then?"

"You are not hitting my children," Fatima screamed suddenly and violently, leaping to her feet and dashing out of the room. Rana jerked in alarm; it was so uncharacteristic of her. Na'aman burst into tears. Rana gathered him up, feeling close to tears herself. "I didn't ask for this responsibility," she yelled, so Fatima might hear. "I don't want to beat your stupid children. It's not like you can take care of anything yourself though, is it?"

The continued silence enraged her. "Do you think it's helpful to blame me? *You* think of a solution! *You* solve it!"

Na'aman redoubled his cries and Rana, feeling miserable and guilty, kissed his wet cheeks. "It's okay, your O'mmy and I have little fights sometimes. Everybody does, don't they?" Na'aman looked at her solemnly, hiccupping back his sobs. "People are silly, really."

"Why you beat Ali and Abdul?" Na'aman queried, his chin wobbling dangerously.

She felt a twinge of surprise at the extent of this small child's understanding. "I don't want to beat them. They must do well at school, and they are skipping classes and not doing their work. Don't you think they should be punished if they don't do their work?"

Na'man shook his head, staring hard at his aunt's face.

"You're not allowed to eat sweets without permission, are you? What should I do if I catch you stuffing sweets without asking?"

Na'aman remembered plenty of occasions rather like that. "Hit my hand."

Rana nodded. "Perhaps."

"Or my bottom," continued Na'aman, casting his mind over the pond of remembered corporal punishment.

"Exactly," said Rana.

"Or my leg," continued Na'aman.

"So you get the point. When you or the twins do something bad, a good smack helps you to remember not to do it again."

"Or my face."

It was amazing how children went on and on about things. They really were exceptionally boring. "Not your face. You've never been hit in the face."

"Yes I was," insisted Na'aman, and launched into a very detailed account of an incident with a rude word, even as he was deposited roughly on the floor again beside his growing stack of cups. "...Then Abi hit me on my mouf and made blood come."

Rana banged around the kitchen, preparing the salad. "He didn't mean to make you bleed." How angry she had felt at Mohammed at the time. All the time! He had just meant to chastise Na'aman for using a naughty word, and was probably as shocked as anyone when blood trickled out. For the first time, Rana realized how difficult it was to look after a large family, to make the right decisions in order to lead them in the right direction. How annoying it was when those who were too weak and stupid to lead themselves criticized. She froze, cucumber in mid-air. She wasn't becoming her brother, was she?

Rana swept out of the room, scooping Na'aman up en route, kicking and squealing as his eight-cup tower receded over his aunt's shoulder. Fatima was lying face down in the bed. Immediately, Rana's anger subsided and she curled up behind her sister and hugged her. "Fatima, I know you are unhappy. I know you mourn Mohammed all the time. I wouldn't do anything to hurt you for the world."

"So don't threaten my sons," murmured Fatima into the pillow.

Rana repressed another surge of irritation and struggled to speak in a gentle voice. "I'm trying to think how to solve the problem, Fatima, and it upsets me when you insinuate that I'm trying to harm my nephews. Do you understand? We have to solve this problem."

Rana sat upright on the bed and spoke in a schoolmarmish voice. "Any ideas?"

After a moment's silence, Rana raised her arm in the air and waved it at herself, the imaginary teacher. Na'aman, who was laboriously climbing onto the bed, tried unsuccessfully to lift an arm to wave back.

"I've got an idea!" Rana answered herself enthusiastically. "Let's warn them about the seriousness of their behaviour and explain the consequences if they continue."

"What consequences?" asked Rana in the schoolmarm's voice.

"A beating. Hopefully, fear of a beating will be enough, but if not, then a beating."

"Rather violent and upsetting," admonished the schoolmarm. "Any other ideas? Hmmm?" Rana prodded Fatima. "We'd welcome any other ideas."

Na'aman began to worm his way determinedly between the two women. Relief filled Rana's heart at the sound of Fatima's giggle.

Fatima shifted to make way for Na'aman and tickled him as he fell on his back, chuckling madly and gazing from one face to the other in delight.

Rana waited patiently.

Fatima lifted up her tired eyes and regarded her. "We could try a reward system."

"I'm listening."

"We could promise them something they really want if they do well at school."

Rana thought for a moment. "Okay. If it works, great. If not ... can we agree now that if the offer of a reward doesn't work then we'll try a beating? So we don't have to have this conversation again?"

"No," said Fatima. "I'll think of something else if this doesn't work."

Rana sighed and got off the bed. "I'm glad you have ideas Fatima, and I hope they work. But if they don't work, and we've exhausted every possibility, then we'll have to beat them. Working hard for a good education is critical; slacking off is not an option.

Fatima bent her head and tickled Na'aman.

Perhaps there was less work at the bank, or the uncertainties of the future political situation had impacted hours, but Hamid was always home for dinner these days. Rana would bring him a pre-dinner cup of tea in the bedroom and watch while he changed into sweatpants and sipped his tea, telling her about his day. It always felt like a stolen luxury, this extra time while the food simmered gently and Mazin rushed to finish homework and chores before the meal. Rana stretched across the bed and told Hamid the entire conversation that she had had with Fatima.

"That whole family would unravel if I wasn't holding the reins. The twins are running wild, and Fatima just sits around looking tragic all the time."

"Habibti, they're all in a state of depression. They've suffered a terrible tragedy."

Rana kicked the bedpost irritably. "It's been months. How long does it take to get over the death of a father? A year? Two? Ever?"

"Really, Rana. Could you be less empathetic?"

"I don't say things like that to them, do I? I've spent months catering to Fatima's needs, treating her like an invalid, buying treats for the twins to cheer them up. Now I have to be the bad guy because they're behaving terribly, and I'm forced to play disciplinarian."

Hamid put a hand on her head. "You have been a rock; everybody knows that. Don't ruin it now by losing your patience. There's no question that the twins' behaviour at school stems from the death of their father. Perhaps we should talk about Mohammed more with them. Maybe talking about him will make them feel better. Maybe they can shed some light on why they're acting this way. Have you asked them?"

"Well, obviously. They *ummed* and *ahhed* and scratched and said they'd try to do better."

"You extracted a promise that they wouldn't miss any more classes, right?"

"Yes. Then the teacher phones with more complaints today. It's becoming a daily occurrence."

"About missing classes?"

"Fighting. Not doing the work even when they're there. Even being insolent to the teachers. It's socially unacceptable behaviour and it cannot be tolerated."

"Try talking about Mohammed," Hamid repeated, inspecting his teeth in the mirror. "Slip in something about the high expectations he had of their behaviour."

"I don't know why Fatima can't do that sort of thing, at least," Rana replied, with a note of irritation in her voice. She looked up to see Hamid's eyes fixed on her in the mirror.

"The children are the reason Fatima is alive," he enunciated slowly. "Their need of her provides the nourishment that binds her to the will to live. You might remember that."

Rana bowed her head in embarrassment. "I promise to speak to them about Mohammed."

Mazin came bursting through the door, grinning with joy at the sight of his father. "What are we playing tonight, Abi?"

"Bridge!" announced Hamid, turning to hug his son. "There's no time now before dinner. We'll play afterwards."

"I'll just shuffle the deck in preparation," said Mazin excitedly.

Rana lay back on the bed, watching father and son bending over the cards on the table. *How lucky Mazin is to play games with his father every night*, she thought. *The twins will never play with their father again. Humph, I'm sure Mohammed never played with them anyway.* But she remembered how he used to tickle and roughhouse with them. She could not give that back to them, but maybe interaction with a father-like figure would do them good. She glanced at Hamid. Probably any adult male relative would do.

"Dinner!" she called out suddenly, causing both of them to jump.

These days, the whole family sat down to eat together every night. Rana never failed to notice how freely Mazin chatted, turning his head from side to side while enormous amounts of food disappeared from his plate. It was unbelievable the amount growing boys ate. Her eyes darted to the twins. Thank goodness their appetites had not diminished with their depression. Only the desire for schoolwork. She pursed her lips and remembered her promise to Hamid.

As soon as there was a lull in the recounting of days, she beamed across at the twins and said, "I was thinking about Mohammed today."

They looked up at her warily.

"I was thinking that he would be glad that we're all sitting here together, well-fed and united, remembering him and missing him but still living our lives the best we can."

Rana intended to segue into what "living one's life the best one can" meant in terms of the twins at school, but Zaynah suddenly burst in with a nighttime story Mohammed used to tell his children when they were in bed. "Do you remember that story?" she asked the twins.

They nodded their heads vigorously. "He used to measure our muscles," said Abdul.

"Mine were biggest," said Ali.

"Not true!"

Zaynah interrupted with another story, this time about how her father always used to bring her sweets when she was ill.

"Us too!"

"I remember that!"

Rana sat back and smiled as she watched the animated faces of her niece and nephews. Even Fatima was glowing with pleasure at the conversation. Hamid was right, as always. She caught his eye and gave him a wink.

"He was the best father anyone could ever have," announced Zaynah.

Rana felt a twinge of annoyance.

"He was a hero!" crowed the twins together.

"Yes," said Zaynah excitedly. "I noticed signs of heroism in him long before we discovered how he sacrificed his life to save others," and she launched into anecdote after anecdote describing his goodness, his selflessness, his nobility, while the twins added their "I remembers" to this description of an apparently faultless human being. When there was a pause in the conversation, Fatima chimed in with a list including everything from kindnesses to intellectual superiorities, and then Ahmed took up the slack by proclaiming him a leader of men and the human who had taught him more than anyone else in the world. Rana sat there getting redder and redder in the face.

This is absurd, she thought. *Surely, it would be more helpful to their healing process to speak the truth?*

"They should put up a statue of him, as one of the true heroes of this war and this country," Zaynah pronounced, turning to her mother. "How would you sum up the exact nature of his heroism, O'mmy, if you had to explain it in a single sentence?"

Fatima smiled. "I would say he was true to his values, always."

"He was..."

"...a hero!" shouted the twins gleefully.

Then both their faces fell simultaneously.

The link between twins is really bizarre, thought Rana, watching them. She hoped their downcast expressions might portend more realistic memories.

"How could he be true to his values in that situation..."

"...with such a fiend?"

Fatima looked at them. "Is that what your friends at school are saying? You tell them values aren't something one can turn off when they aren't convenient. Certainly there was nobody calling him a hero in that crowd of cowards who murdered him." Fatima leaned across the table. "But those same people carried him on their shoulders when he saved our neighbours, didn't they? There were lines of people at the door calling him a saint. Do you remember? Then they changed, without even knowing what they were doing, because they have no values to stick to. They are like animals, running with the herd without thinking. Fickle fools, not heroes like your father."

The twins brightened, and shouted once again: "He was..."

"...a hero!"

Rana couldn't stand it anymore. "Do you remember the time he beat you?" she asked the twins. "Do you remember our fight with him, Mazin?"

Fatima gave her such a reproachful look that she shoved herself away from the table.

"Let's play a game," Rana said desperately. "Who would like to learn bridge?"

Later that evening, when everyone was in their rooms, hopefully asleep, Rana made her usual circuit around the house, checking doors and rattling windows. She felt more exhausted than usual even though the evening had been a success, once everyone had got into the game. She had explained her idea about having game nights a few evenings a week "because our family makeup is a little different now and this is a good way to adjust to it."

When startled voices asked what that meant, she said that there were fewer fathers around so Hamid could do double-duty, and Ahmed was expected to step in and take over a few more fatherly functions for his nephews and niece as well. "Especially for your nephews," she had smiled at him, making it clear that attendance was mandatory for him on game nights. Everybody seemed so stupefied by her resolve that no argument was raised. They seemed to enjoy the game though, and the twins picked it up immediately and made a formidable team.

Rana felt exonerated for her earlier wickedness. Fatima had smiled at her across the fan of her cards.

She massaged her back as she moved towards her room. She was so tired. A noise behind Zaynah's door made her pause, and she approached with her ear. Mazin and Zaynah were talking in low voices … and the twins were in there too. Was there not a single second of the day — even late at night — when she could relax from human interaction, sure everyone was safe and tucked inside their rooms? Nanoseconds before she erupted like a volcano, she heard Mazin pronounce the name of his teacher. "I talked to Mr. Adad about you."

"No point," said a listless, indistinguishable twin.

"Sure there is. Don't be stupid," snapped Zaynah. "If the teachers know you're being beaten up every day, you think they won't do something about it?"

Rana felt her chest tighten. She pressed her ear against the door.

"They didn't help Mazin," retorted a twin.

"Mazin didn't tell them."

"We don't want to tell them either," said both twins together.

"It's not the same," insisted Zaynah. "Mazin was bullied because he's weird, and what can the teachers do about that? But if they knew that the kids were calling your father a 'traitor,' they'd do something."

"Are they saying it to you too?" Mazin asked Zaynah.

"No. All my friends agree that he's a hero. I've explained it to them."

Rana smiled outside the door.

"What is the matter with you, Mazin? You're not going to

blubber, are you? I should think the twins have more reason to blubber than you do."

"I'm not blubbering," came Mazin's furious voice. "I just can't understand why I'm not bullied anymore when Abdul and Abi are suffering so terribly. And they're not weird or anything. It doesn't seem fair."

"We're not suffering. They're the ones who're..."

"...suffering. We win every fight. You should join us and get some practice in winning."

"I can't help you that way," Mazin said in a low voice. "But I will continue to badger the teachers. I don't understand why they can't help."

"It's mostly off school property," said a twin.

"Not their jurisdiction," said another.

"Go away already," came Zaynah's voice. "I want to read a bit before I go to sleep, and Ammé Rana will kill you if she discovers you're out of bed."

"Oh no, look at the time," came Mazin's terrified voice.

Rana pushed herself away from the door and dashed to her own room, where Hamid snored loudly on the bed. When the door opened stealthily, she turned to face her son with raised eyebrows.

"Sorry, O'mmy. I was talking to Zaynah and I lost track of time."

She felt too subdued to question him about what she had overheard although she longed to know more about it. She nodded and slipped under the covers of the bed, waiting rigidly for what seemed like hours until Mazin's breathing told her he was asleep. Then she rolled over onto her side and began to cry. Quietly at first, then louder and louder, her scrunched-up eyes peering in disbelief at Hamid's snuffling, indifferent nostrils. Finally, she poked him.

"What's the matter?" he asked in alarm.

"I am turning into Mohammed."

Hamid turned to look at her blearily. "Why do you say that?"

"I was all set to beat the twins for their performance at school when they're already being beaten on a daily basis." Rana related to him what she had overheard. When she had finished, she broke down entirely, weeping into his shoulder and forcing out words between her sobs. "It's like a nightmare, the idea I'm like him."

"You're not like him."

"You've told me many times that I am. And now I see it. I'm so wrapped up in my own perspective that I hurt the last people who should be hurt. Those poor little fatherless boys."

Hamid patted her, his eyelids drooping with fatigue. "You didn't know they were being bullied. The teacher insinuated that they were starting the fights. For the information you had, your thought processes were entirely correct." He yawned hugely.

"I hope I'm not boring you," she snapped.

Hamid smiled and pulled her head into his armpit. "Stop crying, habibti. You are nothing like Mohammed."

"You said I was!"

"Okay, you are very similar to Mohammed."

Rana pulled away from him violently. "My desperate misery amuses you?"

"No, I'm being serious. You are similar to Mohammed, but there is one important difference."

Rana raised her hand, her tear-streaked face full of fury. "If you start talking about sex I'm going to kill you," she said.

"Listen," Hamid looked at her calmly. "You're often immersed in your own perspective, but aren't we all? You can also be impetuous and hotheaded, domineering and intimidating, just like him." Hamid gestured her to wait, as her face grew purple with anger. "But there is one vital difference, which makes all the difference."

"What?" demanded Rana.

"You seek the opinion of others."

"So what?"

"So you married a sensible spouse, who can always lead

you in the right direction. Even when you are convinced that you are one hundred percent right, which is usually the case, just like Mohammed, you always check in with me before pursuing a course of action. For example today, when you came to me, you were berating Fatima for her weakness and seeing yourself as a martyr, forced to discipline against your will and criticized for it to boot, sure that a beating was the only thing that would really work. Then you talked with me and immediately changed your mind."

"I changed it when I realized that they were suffering so horribly at school."

"Your mind veered from anger to compassion. Then you went downstairs and implemented a wonderful new tradition, which will give your nephews infinite pleasure. Not only that, you have presented them with new father figures to look up to, and compete with, for years to come. You are brilliant." Hamid kissed the top of her head.

Rana began to smile. She lowered her head into the cave of his armpit. "I am brilliant, aren't I?"

"Actually, I think you're probably insane, just like Mohammed. The difference is, you know it, so you seek the advice of others.'

"Even so, that difference transforms me from mad to brilliant."

"Thanks to your dear husband. You'd better stick with me, kid. I'm the only thing between you and the loony bin. Ouch!"

Rana spat out the armpit hairs she had pulled out with her teeth.

Rana sat on the chair Mohammed had made for her, which was propped under the shade of the house. Even so, she could feel sweat dampening her armpits. The heat was unbearable in the summer, and it was only getting worse. She could hear the children banging around inside the house. She would have to lock them into some type of work schedule, otherwise they'd all go wild during the long summer holiday, especially the twins. Too much freedom was a bad thing for children. *You're supposed to be meditating*, Rana told herself sternly. *Focus on your breath and stop thinking. Your head is like a broken tape recorder, useless thoughts going round and round, ceaselessly.* Rana counted to ten, slowly, relaxing the muscles in her neck as she breathed out, trying to ignore the squawks of the chickens. *Henny Penny obviously has some poor devil in a stranglehold. Bloody chickens. Stop it! Focus on the positive.* Another deep breath. *Thank you*, she thought. *I love my son so much; I love my husband, I love my sister and her children. I love my chickens and my garden. I am so lucky to have all these things. I am so grateful.*

She was convinced that focusing on her blessings every day made her a happier person, simply because it stopped the (mostly negative) broken tape recorder and forced her to be aware of her blessings. Really, she was so lucky.

She began the count to ten again,

A small cough ruined her concentration. Instantly, her whole mind was focused on the fact that there was someone behind her; relaxation and luckiness forgotten. *This is my time, wrenched from a day spent catering to others. Whoever you are, bugger off.* Rana kept her eyes closed, but the soft sound of breathing didn't retreat.

Rana's eyes and mouth flew open at the same time, prepared to bellow at the intruder. Fatima was smiling down at her, twisting a strand of worry beads in both hands. "Don't get up. I just came to see where you were."

Rana jumped to her feet. "Sit down. You look tired."

Fatima bent to stroke the chair before she sat. "It's beautifully made," she said. "Mohammed made it for you, didn't he?"

"Yes." Rana gave a short laugh. "I remember exactly what he said when he gave it to me: 'Since you spend so many hours out there anyway.'"

"It was such a lovely thing to do," murmured Fatima.

"Mm-hmm."

"Was he a hero?" Fatima asked tentatively.

Rana took her hand. "Yes," she said with emphasis. "He was."

"I am so proud of him," Fatima whispered through dry lips. She stood up, her worry beads clasped in her hands.

"He might have been a hero," Rana paused to push a strand of sweat-soaked hair out of Fatima's eyes. "But he was a bugger to live with."

And the two women clutched each other and sank to the ground, crying and laughing together.

ACKNOWLEDGEMENTS

I would like to thank first and foremost my dear mother Margherita Mendel and sisters Tessa and Anna for their excellent feedback and help as I wracked their brains for ideas and direction. Thank you Lindsay Brown for your brilliant editing and consistent support. Thanks to Luciana Ricciutelli, Editor-in-Chief at Inanna Publications, for publishing this book. I also appreciate the work that has gone into promoting *A Hero*, and thank Renee Knapp and Wendy Phillips for their excellent work. I would also like to thank my writing group for their thorough reading and patient advice as we leap from book to book without ever finishing one — thank you Gwen Davies, Joseph Szostak and Nick Sumner!

I am often amazed by the support of my readers — especially my family, friends, neighbours, teachers at my kids' schools — many of whom have gone out of their way to promote my book through word of mouth. Thank you for enjoying my writing.

I appreciate the input of my Halegonian Syrian editor, who wishes to remain anonymous. Last but not least, thanks to my husband Eli Elias, my anti-muse.

Charlotte R. Mendel was born in Canada, but has lived in many different countries. Her first novel, *Turn Us Again,* won the H. R. Percy Novel Prize, the Beacon Award for Social Justice, and the Atlantic Book Award for First Novel. She currently lives in Nova Scotia with one husband, two children, two cats, three goats, eleven chickens, and thousands of bees.